Red ZONE

LISA SUZANNE

Also by Lisa Suzanne

Grayson & Ava

Spencer & Grace

Asher & Desi

Tanner & Cassie

Miller & Sophie

FIND MORE AT
AUTHORLISASUZANNE.COM/BOOKS

Dedication

For the 3 they're always for.
♡

CHAPTER 1
Everleigh Bradley

Thirty-Two to One

Vegas?

Vegas?

I blow out a breath. "I've never had much of an interest in transferring out of this office, sir," I say to my boss. I fold my arms over my chest.

I have thirty-two clients here in Chicago. Some I speak to weekly, others daily, and a few micromanagers get me on the line multiple times a day.

But in Vegas, I lay claim to exactly zero.

And now my boss is offering me one. *One.*

"Give it some thought before you bow out, Everleigh," Mr. Langford tells me. He leans back on the edge of his desk.

"How do I go from thirty-two clients to *one* and believe it's a promotion?" I counter.

"I told you it's unconventional. This is a complete rebrand, and we'll need you by this client's side at all times."

"Who is it?" I demand.

"It's confidential."

"Then it's a no, Stuart. I'm not moving across the country to work with a client and giving up everything I have here when I don't even know who it is."

He sighs. "It's confidential because it's high-profile. What's your end goal?"

We've been over this a thousand times. "To open my own branding firm working with my own high-profile clients instead of working for someone else."

"I know, Everleigh. And this is the step that could open that door for you. Trust me on this."

"Do you know who it is?" I ask.

He presses his lips together and shakes his head. "All I know is that it's in Vegas. I could make a guess, but I won't. Don't you have a brother there?"

The fact is that yes, I do have family there. But I have family here in Chicago, too. And friends, including my best friend. My entire life is here.

"Don't try to sell me with family," I say. I want to hiss it at him, but I'm trying to maintain that professional level of respect you're supposed to have for your boss—which I *do* have. I've always had it.

I just don't know what to do. I love my job, and I worry that changing things could be a huge mistake. I'll lose all of my clients, but if I open my own firm someday down the road, I can't take them with me anyway.

"If you agree to this, I'll remove your non-compete, so after the terms of the agreement are met, you're free to start your own firm," he offers as if he just read my mind. "If things go well, you can take this high-profile client with you."

"Why would you do that?" I narrow my eyes at him as I try to get to the bottom of his motivation.

He shrugs. "They asked for my best strategist, and that's you. We'll get the credit for the first year, and from what I've heard, this client needs a lot of work. I know you're going to leave Langford eventually, so I guess I'm just doing my part to set you up for success."

"That's really kind of you."

He holds up a hand. "Before you go getting all mushy on me, let me be the first to admit that they're offering five hundred grand to take on this client. They're paying up front, and we plan to take forty percent of that. You'll get the rest plus moving expenses."

Money isn't really an issue for me since I hail from Thomas Bradley, the man who started the very successful Bradley Group development and construction company, but it's still quite an attractive offer. I'm currently making a third of what he wants to give me, while it feels an awful lot like he's cutting my workload.

It makes me wonder if there's more to it, but we've worked together for the last decade. I believe him when he says that I'm the best brand strategist he has and that's why he's offering this position to me.

"Can I have the night to think about it?" I ask.

He nods. "Absolutely. But I'll need your answer first thing in the morning. If it's a no, I have to figure out my next plan."

"Understood," I say, and I tap my fingers on my bicep where they're resting with my arms still crossed over my chest. I try one more time. "You can't give me any hints at all about who this client is?"

He presses his lips together. "If I had specific details, I'd give them to you."

"What if it's an athlete?" I ask, and I wrinkle my nose. Four of my five brothers play in the NFL, and the other one is a pro baseball player. I'd really prefer *not* to work with athletes, as Stuart well knows after all our years together.

But he's insisted the entire time that we've worked together that athletes not only make great clients, but I'd be a built-in expert because of my brothers.

"Then what if it is? Could still be a pretty interesting stepping stone, don't you think?" Silence passes between us, and his phone starts to ring. "I better take this. It's my wife. Let me know first thing tomorrow, okay?"

I nod, and the first person I call when I slide into my Audi is my brother.

Not the one in Vegas.

I've always been closest to Ford, and I think it's because my two older brothers, Madden and Dex, were close on their own. I was just the annoying little sister who came along and picked up NERF guns only to accidentally shoot my older brothers in the balls.

Yeah…"accidentally." It's not my fault I always had good aim.

Aside from that, Madden is four years older than me and tends to go off and do his own thing. Dex has always had a bit of a delinquent edge to him, though he seems to be straightening out. I think I've always just been the rather prim and proper, somewhat wholesome younger sister who cared about her studies and her family above everything else.

And Ford is a lot like me. He's more of a traditionalist. A pragmatist. He's two and a half years younger than me, and I got to pretend he was my baby when I was a toddler and he came along. I guess in a lot of ways, I've always been a bit of a caretaker when it comes to my siblings. My entire family, really.

And that's why I'm not sure I want to leave Chicago.

My family is scattered all over the US, but this is our home base.

And when Stuart brought up the fact that I have a brother in Vegas, he meant Dex. He's been all over the news lately with his new wife and baby, and the truth is that when I got to hold my nephew at the funeral of one of the high school football coaches a few weeks ago, I had this tug on my heartstrings that one of my brothers has a baby that I won't get to watch grow up.

But Stuart forgot that I have another brother in Vegas, too—Archer. People always seem to forget Archer, but not me. It's that whole caretaker thing I have going on. He's the only baseball player in a family of football stars, the lone wolf, the one who I text once a week but rarely get a response from.

I text him the same thing every week.

Me: *Thinking about you, little bro.*

Sometimes he thanks me, sometimes he simply thumbs-ups my text, sometimes he ignores me…but sometimes, on very rare occasions, he actually writes back.

I wouldn't mind being a little closer to him, either.

"Hey, Ev," Ford answers. "What's wrong?"

I laugh. "Nothing."

"Then why are you calling? You never call."

"I know, and I'm sorry. But I have something I need to talk out. Is now a good time?" I pull out of my spot. I could've called Penny, my best friend who I also work with. But I'm not ready for her to know that I got this offer. I'm not ready to tell her that maybe we won't get to see each other every day anymore.

"I'm just finishing dinner," he says. "Go for it."

I sigh. "My boss offered me a job in Vegas. It's one client and triple the money."

"What's the catch?" he asks.

"I have to move to Vegas."

"Do it. Have you been there? Fuckin' paradise," he says.

"Yes, of course I've been there. But to *move* there? And for a single client when I have to drop all of my others?" I ask.

"Sounds like a goddamn vacation, to be honest. How many clients do you have?"

"Thirty-two."

"And you'll have *one* in Vegas for triple the money?" he asks.

"Yeah, but I have no clue who this client is. Just that he's high profile and this is a nontraditional job. It could be me shadowing some stuck-up asshole day in and day out."

"So…basically working with yourself?" he jabs, and I laugh.

"Shut up."

"I'm kidding. It could be anyone. What if it's one of the Hemsworth brothers and you have to spin a tale about his divorce so he can marry you?"

"You know better than to tempt me with the Hemsworths," I say.

"Have you done a pro-con list yet?"

"Can I verbalize it?"

"Of course," he says.

I tick them off, organizing them as I talk. "Cons are having to give up my client list, not knowing who I'm working with, and moving across the country. Pros are that I have family in the area, I'd cut from thirty-two to one, and my boss said he'd delete the non-compete from my contract so I could take this client with me and open my own firm when our contract terms expire."

"Dude. Take the fucking job. You can't spell it out more than that."

"What if it's an athlete?" It's the same question I posed to my boss.

"We're not so bad, you know."

"Yeah, yeah, yeah. I've just been around a lot of you my entire life, and my job provides an excellent escape," I say.

"Listen, plenty of athletes need someone like you in their corner," he points out. "And if you really and truly want to branch off on your own, this might be your chance. At least get out to Vegas and give it a real chance."

He's right. I know he is. There's never a good time to jump ship when I have as many clients as I do, but this contract will have a start and end date stamped on it, and that end date will be the key to my entire future.

If that's what I really and truly want.

It is. It's always been what I want for as far back as I can remember. I first learned what a brand strategist was when my mother wanted to project a certain image to the media. I was in first grade when Paola came into our house, shooed my siblings and myself out of the room, and got down to work.

I loved Paola's gorgeous, designer business suits and dresses, and I knew that someday I'd step in the same kinds of Louboutins she did.

And now I do, except I'm still working for someone else.

I guess this means I have my answer.

CHAPTER 2

MAVERICK JENNINGS

Cocktail Straw

I toss my cards on the table and pick up the cocktail straw from my glass of scotch, clenching it down between my teeth. I frequent this casino in particular since they carry Lagavulin 16, my preferred single-malt elixir, though the crowds of people aren't to my tastes. It's why I find myself in the high-stakes room playing three-card poker on a Thursday night.

I have practice tomorrow. I'll be starting for my new team.

I don't want to be here.

I guess I don't want to be here anymore than I wanted to be in Dallas, but the difference is that here, the giant star tattoo on my shoulder feels traitorous.

But I don't care where I play. I just want to play

Getting traded in my tenth season is a punch to the gut. I haven't bonded with anyone here because I don't really want to. I didn't bond with anyone in Dallas, either. Every time I tried, they'd leave anyway. Just like everyone.

So I stopped trying.

And that's who I've become. The guy who hates everything and everyone except for my sport. My bad attitude is what got me sent here, though some would argue Vegas is likely the exact wrong place for someone like me to be.

Yet here I am.

I guess the Aces think they can fix me. Coach Nash can set me on the straight and narrow.

Good fucking luck.

People have tried, but not a single one has been successful.

I'm fine the way I am. It's far easier not letting anyone in since every time I have, I've only ended up hurt.

My phone rings, and I click off the call without answering. It's my agent. The voicemail will be there when I'm done playing poker. I can't pick up a call at the table anyway.

I should get up. I should take it as my signal that it's time to go. I should stop throwing money right into the pockets of whoever owns this godforsaken place and get a good night's sleep ahead of tomorrow's practice.

I don't.

Instead, I just keep drinking. Just keep playing. Just keep losing. Just keep chewing on that tiny little cocktail straw until I feel the sharp edges digging into my gums to remind me that I'm alive. It's the same reason I keep going back for more ink. The needle injecting ink into my skin is fucking addictive, a reminder that I may have numbed the inside, but the outside can still feel everything.

Maybe it's why I'm addicted to football, too. I live for feeling the pain because pain's a hell of a lot better than the hollow feeling of being numb.

Every time the cocktail straw digs into my gums, I'm reminded of *her.*

I don't want to think about her. I *never* want to think about her. When I do, sometimes a piercing ache slips through, and that pain is far worse than some temporary needle driving against my skin.

I raise my bet to give myself something else to focus on.

It's a distraction technique. Raise the stakes somewhere else to combat the memory.

She's the reason I choose to be numb.

A woman wearing a red slip dress with a black jacket over it sweeps past me, the scent of her perfume following behind her. It's intoxicating, and my eyes flick to her ass and trail down to her tall, black heels with red on the bottom.

Could I see those heels wrapped around me as I pump into her? Abso-fucking-lutely.

Is it going to happen? Not tonight.

I've learned my lesson when it comes to women.

The occasional one-night stand is about all I can stomach these days, but I'm at a point in my life where even those are fewer and further between than they used to be. People know me—or they think they do, anyway. They know who I am, and it's inevitably the same story.

The woman runs to social media to brag about her night with a future football Hall of Famer. It never has anything to do with wanting me for anything other than bragging rights.

I'm sick of it.

I've gone the nondisclosure agreement route, and the woman was offended—not because I asked her to sign one, but because she couldn't brag about our night.

So I've written women off at this point.

It's easier this way.

I'm not getting married again, and if someone did happen to come along who wanted me for more than bragging rights, isn't marriage what she'd want in the end anyway?

It's off the table.

And speaking of tables, I'm losing my ass at this one. I pull the straw from the clutches of my teeth and toss it into my empty cup, and I cash in.

I head to the bar for one more drink before I head home, and I sit on a stool while I wait for the bartender to bring my scotch over.

And that's when the woman in the red dress slips onto the stool beside me.

I glance over at her, and my breath catches in my throat.

She's breathtakingly pretty. Big, brown eyes that have this sort of edge in the way she's looking at me like she wants to fuck me. Smooth, creamy skin with a sun-kissed glow. Plump, red lips that match her dress, ones that allow my rather vivid imagination to run away for a few seconds. Long, dark hair that tumbles to the middle of her back in waves.

That same scent that followed her as she passed by me earlier swirls back to my nose here, giving me a hit of something unexpected.

So she's attractive. Sexy as fuck. Gorgeous in red.

None of it matters.

I return my gaze to the bottles of alcohol stacked behind the bar.

"You're Maverick Jennings," she says matter-of-factly.

I grimace a little. "So says my jersey." Not that I haven't thought about changing that name considering where it came from.

"Jennings one," she says, naming my number. "New to the Vegas Aces. You settling in okay here?"

"Fine," I mutter.

She leans in a little. "I'm new to town, too. Trying to get my bearings."

"Yeah, well, good luck," I say, and I hope that's the end of the conversation.

I war with myself over looking over at her again. One more glance, and it'll all be over. I'll go with her to her hotel room, or her condo, or wherever, and I'll stay until we're both satisfied. And then I'll leave.

I don't look over at her.

I should call my agent back.

"Thanks," she says, her tone telling me she's not getting up anytime soon.

The bartender drops my drink in front of me, and I immediately pick it up and take a sip. I should've just left. Instead, I'm stuck here trying to figure out the best way to let this gorgeous woman down. I tried being standoffish, bordering on the rude side, and she's not taking the hint.

"So how'd you really feel about getting traded from Dallas?" she asks.

It's a question I've been asked a hundred different ways in the last few months, and the truth is that I'm tired of answering it.

It sucked, but I don't care where I land as long as I get to play.

Football is where I turned when I lost everything. It's all that matters. I'm still young at just thirty-two, and it's not unusual for quarterbacks to play well into their forties. I have a long career ahead of me, and I'm not worried about what comes next.

I don't answer her question. I don't even know her name, but what I do know is that she's not entitled to anything from me.

Instead, I leave some cash on the counter, grab my cocktail straw, abandon my drink, and head home.

CHAPTER 3

MAVERICK JENNINGS

Non-Displaced Fracture

It's the Friday before our first game of the season.

My first game as the starting quarterback for the Vegas Aces.

I'm up before the sun as usual, but today it's with an extra purpose. I have something to do before practice this morning.

I had one request of my agent when I was shipped off to a new town, and that was to find me a place like the one in Dallas. That's why my agent called last night—to remind me about my commitment this morning. As if I could forget the one bright spot in my week.

I pull up to Sunny Acres Animal Shelter at five thirty. I find early morning the best time of day to volunteer here, mainly because it's not full of other volunteers yet, so I can do my own thing.

Someone once told me that petting a dog can genuinely make you happier.

I looked into it. Studies show that petting a dog can lower stress and blood pressure. It can trigger the release of serotonin and reduce anxiety. Still, ever a disbeliever until I see it for myself, I walked into an animal shelter in Dallas one day to test the theory.

It worked.

They roped me into coming back the next week, and the next, and soon I was a regular volunteer.

Maybe it's because I'm thinking about the animal for the few moments I'm with it rather than about my own history, or maybe there's something in their fur. Maybe it's because I'm volunteering my time to help another living being. Whatever the case, things don't quite feel as heavy when I'm at the shelter.

My tasks are simple. Because I'm a big guy, I usually get the big dogs. I spend an hour of my time taking a few dogs on walks or playing with them in the yard. It's a simple connection to another living thing for an hour a week when my schedule allows.

I've been volunteering here weekly since I moved to Vegas, and this week, a litter of Golden Retriever puppies showed up.

They're fucking adorable. Fluffy and soft, with fur that leans more white than golden except for their ears, which are softer and darker.

I stand in a small room with three of them. Two are fighting over a toy while a third attempts to chew my shoelaces.

I'm tempted to take one home. Maybe not the one making a chew toy of my shoe. Or, hell, maybe I should just take all three.

I can't. It wouldn't be fair to the dogs. I'm in and out too much. I travel a lot. And I like my solitude, anyway.

I pick up the one on shoe duty, and I hold it close to my face. "What are you doing to my shoe?"

The pup responds by licking my nose.

I set it down before I actually do end up taking it home, and when my hour is up, I leave with more reluctance than usual and head straight for the Complex, the nickname given to the Aces' practice facility.

Friday practices are a bit lighter ahead of game day, and I'm rotating with the other quarterbacks on each play. We wear red jerseys as a reminder that nobody's supposed to hit us since we're not padded, and I'm watching Dex Bradley as he attempts to make a go at Brandon Fletcher, our second backup after Miles Hudson, who's been struggling with lingering complications from an ACL tear a couple years ago.

That makes me QB1.

I'm up for the challenge, but part of being a starter is having a bond with your teammates. I need to know these men as well as I know myself—as a player, at any rate—so I can trust my instincts when it comes to launching the ball to them. I've started to get to know them on the field, but as for off…we're just not there yet.

I've declined the invitations, and there have been plenty.

I'm not sure *why* I've declined other than the fact that I still feel betrayed by this trade. The Aces took me because they think they can fix me, but some breaks are beyond repair.

I watch as Dex and Asher Nash, the tight end responsible for blocking Dex from getting to the quarterback, share some words, and Dex looks pissed. I'm sure I can find a way to use that to my advantage.

I rotate in after the play Brandon led, and I call the play. I spot my open receiver downfield, and I'm about to launch the ball to him when I catch the shadow of Dex out of the corner of my eye.

I don't have enough time to react, though. I'm not supposed to be taking hits during practice, so I'm not properly braced or protected. I try to back out of the way, but Dex's shoulder plows directly into my ribs.

I hear a snap.

Fuck.

Fuck!

Snaps are never good, especially not when the fresh, hot sting of pain follows.

Something's broken, maybe. How long will this take me out? A few weeks? Months? An entire season? I watch it all swirl down the drain because of one asshole who wasn't following directions. All this plows into my mind before I even hit the ground. When I do, I let out a grunt as I hiss and gasp for air.

"Fuck!" I yell. I clutch at my ribs as I hear Asher start yelling at Dex, but it's just loud voices to me as that old friend called pain shows up with a blindingly white-hot greeting.

I try to get up, but I hiss at the pain as it takes over.

Coach Lincoln Nash shows up a second later. "Ribs?" he asks.

I nod and wheeze as I try to take a breath, but I can't take a deep enough one. It's too goddamn painful.

"Fuck," he mutters.

Trainers surround me as I curse Dex and his entire family. Fuck that dude.

"Can you breathe?" someone asks, and I nod.

It hurts, but I can do it.

They pull my jersey up, which hurts like all fuck, and they assess the damage. Someone brings an ice pack over, and they take my vitals.

They help me to my feet, and I'm hunched over as I try to walk toward the medical exam room. They offer me a wheelchair, and I decline.

I don't know a single one of their names.

It hurts to walk. It hurts to breathe, so I take shallow breaths as I grit my teeth together. But where there's pain, there's life.

They take me back to the exam room, where they run X-rays.

Fifteen minutes later, the team doctor walks into the room with Coach Nash.

"Non-displaced fracture, left side," the doctor says. "I want you to do a CT scan just to rule out any other possible damage, but we're looking at no contact for four to six weeks before I can clear you. I can get you started on pain management right away."

"Four to six weeks?" I wheeze, the most words I've put together since it happened.

I can play through the pain.

"We'll start you on Toradol," he says. "If you need something stronger, let me know."

"I'll be fine," I hiss.

"Do you have someone who can stay with you?" Coach asks.

My mother is the only person in the world who comes to mind, but that's not an option. I shake my head. "I'm fine."

"The hell you are," he fires back. "Adrian will be traveling with us to New York," he says, naming our team trainer as if to say he's out since he won't be around.

"I don't need a babysitter," I grit out.

I move to get off this goddamn table, but I realize…I can't move without an exorbitant amount of pain.

Maybe I *do* need a babysitter.

I'd just never fucking ask for one.

I never ask anyone for anything.

So I lie back, staring at the ceiling as I try to come to terms with my fate.

"Look, Mav," Coach says. "You're our number one. This is a minor setback. You'll be back in a few weeks—"

"Four to six," the doctor interrupts.

"Right," Coach says, glaring at the doctor, and I get the feeling he'd let me come back sooner if I'm ready for it. I fucking will be. "Four to six weeks," he continues. "So in the meantime, I need you to take the best possible care of yourself that you can, and if that means a babysitter, that means a fucking babysitter."

"I can help," one of the trainers who's still in the room pipes in.

"Robbie, thank you," Coach says. He glances at me. "Do you have a spare room or a couch Robbie can crash on while he makes sure you're not doing anything stupid?"

I fight the urge to roll my eyes and wheeze instead. "Yeah."

So I guess that settles that.

The first three days are the worst, and I'm actually glad I have Robbie around. I spend most of my time trying to simply get comfortable, which feels like an impossible task. The other part of my day, I'm icing my injury.

I watch the games all day Sunday, so at least there's that. I wish I could do it with a beer or a nice glass of scotch, but that's out for now.

By the end of the next week, I feel a marked improvement. Good enough to get around on my own, which means Robbie can now leave me the fuck alone.

Deep breathing is still pretty painful, but at least I can take a breath. And by the end of the second week, I feel more improvement. Coughing hurts, as does twisting, and I assume laughing would if that's something I ever really did.

I feel good enough for a night out. I'm getting cabin fever being stuck in this condo. It's got a great view of the Strip, sure, but I'm used to movement. I'm used to traveling—every other week in season, and wherever the fuck I want to go in the offseason. Instead, I've been stuck in my own home waiting to feel good enough to be able to move around on my own.

I head to one of the casinos that carries my scotch on a Friday night, and I've barely taken my first sip when someone slides onto the empty seat beside me.

"Maverick Jennings," a male voice says, and when I look up, I see Ben Olson, a former tight end who retired a few years ago. We never played on the same team, but we did attend a few charity events together back in my younger years, and he was always the life of the party. Everyone's seen the viral videos of him smashing beer cans on his head at this point, right?

"Ben," I say with a nod of my head.

"How are the ribs?"

"Could use more barbecue sauce," I quip dryly, and he laughs like it's the funniest goddamn thing he's ever heard.

"You still hopped up on meds?" he asks, nodding toward my glass, and I shake my head.

"Just needed to get the fuck out of my place for a bit. And to answer your question, I still feel it, but I'm improving every day."

"Get this man another drink!" he yells to the waitress who walks by at that moment.

He gets himself a drink, too, and a couple hours later, I've lost track of how much money I've spent at this table, and both Ben and I are drunk.

For the record, I'm still not laughing. But this feels strangely...*good.* Like I needed this. I don't have any friends here in Vegas, though it feels like maybe I can count Ben among them now. He's been around here and there for practice, though we haven't interacted much. He's good friends with the team owner, and he consults with the coaches since he's still local and was a huge asset to the team when he played.

It feels like I have someone to call to get drunk with while I'm losing too much money playing cards.

"There's a new VIP lounge down the road, and they have your scotch," he says. "It's the same scotch I've been drinking lately. Want to check it out?"

"Wait. When did you switch from beer cans to scotch?" I ask.

"Fatherhood really fucks with the balance of pretty much everything," he says with a laugh. "But I wouldn't have it any other way. Come on, let's go."

We're walking toward the doors when a group of women start screaming after one of them yells, "Oh my God! Maverick Jennings and Ben Olson!"

We're recognized. It's not unusual to be recognized, but I have a baseball cap pulled low over my eyes and sleeves covering my rather distinctive tattoos. Usually that's enough to do the trick—or to at least have someone look at me and *wonder* if it's really Maverick Jennings rather than immediately *know* it's Maverick Jennings.

But since I'm out with Ben, a celebrity in this town, these ladies must've put two and two together.

"You single?" Ben asks me, and I nod before I realize what I'm really answering. "Ladies, I'm so sorry, but I'm very much in love with my wife. My man Mav here, though, he's single."

I wince, and it's partly from one of the women who rushes toward me and partly from his words.

"Fuck," I hiss. "Sorry, I'm recovering from a rib injury."

"Oh, God, I'm so sorry!" the woman who just ran into me says. She seems a little drunk, too. "What happened?"

"Fuckin' Dex Bradley plowed into me during practice and broke a rib. Everyone knows you don't hit a red jersey during practice," I mutter. This *might* be the attitude Dallas was talking about when they gave me the boot. "But Dex didn't give a fuck. He plowed into me shoulder-first and took me out for four to six weeks because he was pissed his wife left him. Fuck that asshole, man." I shake my head in disgust.

And that's the viral video Coach Nash shows me the next morning after calling me into his office *far* too early when I'm hungover as fuck.

"What the fuck were you thinking?" he yells at me. Before I can answer that I was too drunk to be forming actual thoughts, he plows forward. "You *never* share personal information about a teammate. You know that."

"I apologize," I say flatly.

"You stirred up drama for Dex and made people think I don't have a handle on my own fucking team. That's going to take more than an apology, Jennings."

Ooh, he must mean business if he's using my *last* name.

"I knew I should've trusted my instincts with you," he mutters. "But Jack told me to hold tight."

I'm not sure what that's supposed to mean or why he's bringing Jack into this, but I just want to know how to fix this so we can move on. I want to head back home, crawl back into bed, and sleep off this headache.

"What'll it take?" I ask.

"More like *who*."

I narrow my eyes at him. "Who?"

"It's not a babysitter. Let me make that clear."

"Who?" I repeat, a little louder this time as my chest tightens at his words.

"We hired the top marketing firm in the country to help you rebrand your image. They've sent out their best rep to work one-on-one with you day in and day out."

"The fuck they are!" I thunder, lifting to a stand, and *fuck*, it still hurts. Jesus Christ.

I sit back down as I grimace.

"It's not negotiable, Mav. You knew coming in here that we were going to do things my way, and this is what I've decided. It was actually Jack Dalton who suggested it," he says, naming the team owner. "He did something similar when he came to the Aces."

Jack Dalton is one of my role models. His passer rating still holds as one of the best of all time, and watching his footwork while he scrambled his way out of a tough situation is still impressive to this day.

To be completely honest, Jack Dalton may be the one reason I didn't fight kicking and screaming to come to the Aces.

"Then have him come in here and tell me that," I mutter.

"We were going to get started after the game in New York, but we decided to hold off until you were feeling better. After last night's fiasco, we've decided it's time. Let's head up to his office instead so he can personally introduce you to the strategist."

My jaw slackens. "He's already here?"

"*She*. And yes, she's already here. She's been settling into Vegas, and after last night's viral drunken rant, this feels like the most opportune time to introduce the two of you."

"Are you fucking with me right now?"

He presses his lips together and shakes his head, and then I have no choice but to follow him up to Jack Dalton's office.

CHAPTER 4

Everleigh Bradley

Unprepared

I twist my hands a little nervously in my lap, and I send a text to the group chat I have with my siblings.

Me: *Checking in on all of you. Vegas has been pretty quiet so far, but I'm about to meet my client. Any guesses where I'm sitting right now?*

The *one* thing I said was that I didn't want to work with an athlete, and guess where I am?

That's right. Sitting outside of Jack Dalton's office. He just so happens to be a former quarterback for the Vegas Aces and the owner of the team my brother plays for.

When Jack's assistant, Lily, first called me early this morning, I wondered if it was Dex they wanted me to rebrand, but he's recently turned himself around all on his own when he found out he was a father and became a husband in the span of a few weeks.

I left Chicago behind for Vegas two weeks ago, and I've spent a little time with Dex and a lot of time with my new sister-in-law, who happens to be my youngest sister's best friend.

Yeah…it gets interesting with six siblings, that's for sure.

Saying goodbye to my parents wasn't that hard since I moved out of their mansion years ago for my own place and we're not all that close, but saying goodbye to Ivy and Liam, my youngest siblings who still reside in Chicago, was a little harder. I'll just have to work to make sure I stay in touch with everybody…hence the text I just sent.

I'm still not sure who I'm going to be working with. I didn't even get a location until Lily called me. I was told the client was postponing my start date, and for a while, I was a little nervous that they were going to send me right back home.

They didn't.

So I've spent the last couple weeks slowly making my transition to Vegas, knowing full well that I need to be on call at any given moment.

I've also been lamenting about my situation with Penny. Daily. Sometimes multiple times daily.

She's still back home, still working at the same place, and she's told me a million times that it's not the same without me.

And all I've done is whine about everything I gave up to be here. It feels like I'm out of work even though it's more of a temporary paid hiatus, so I'm living vicariously through her.

I've been living out of a hotel as I look at places, not sure whether this is going to be a temporary or more permanent situation, and Ainsley—Dex's wife—called me on Friday to let me know one of the tenants had a moving truck parked on the street in front of the building.

I checked it out. The space is gorgeous. It has a view of the Strip, and while Dex has the penthouse, it's a few floors down from his place and doesn't take up an entire floor the way his place does. This one only takes up half of the floor since there are a total of two condos on this floor.

I took Penny on a tour via FaceTime, and she gave it the stamp of approval. It has a guest room, so she can come visit me at any time, and we're already making plans for when we can make that a reality.

I signed the contract on Friday for one year, and workers from the tower spent the weekend putting up a fresh coat of paint and cleaning the place so I can move in this week.

In fact, after my meeting here, I'm heading in that direction to pick up the keys to my new place.

Yep, that's right. A new client and a new condo all in the span of a few hours. Life in Vegas is about to get exciting.

"Mr. Dalton is ready for you," Lily says, and I thank her as I stand and walk into his office. I feel my phone buzz in my purse—probably a reply from one of my siblings.

It continues to buzz throughout the meeting. I'll have to check it later.

Jack Dalton sits behind his desk, an imposing figure in a business suit who used to be an imposing figure in a football uniform. He exudes power, and he's actually quite sexy with his shadow of a beard and piercing blue eyes. He pushes to a stand when I walk in.

"Good morning, Ms. Bradley," he says with a nod of his head. He reaches his hand out to shake mine.

"Good morning, Mr. Dalton," I say, and he sits when I take a seat across the desk from him.

"Stuart Langford and I go a long way back," he muses, offering a smile as he names my boss.

"How do you two know each other?" I ask.

"We attended the same high school. I'm originally from Michigan, as is he. He moved to Chicago after college, but we stayed in touch."

"He's a great boss," I say. "I've enjoyed working with him the last decade."

"He's a good guy, too. A good friend. I knew I could trust that he'd send me the best of the best, and I suppose that's how you ended up here."

"So what, exactly, am I doing here?" I ask. I'm still not sure if I'll be working with an individual player, the marketing department for the team, Jack himself, or some other option I haven't even thought of.

"We recently acquired a player whose image and attitude both need some serious work."

Oh, shit.

There's really only one person it could realistically be. I have a feeling I already know, and I'm dreading his next words as I think back to the night I got to town, went to a casino, and happened to run into one of my brother's teammates.

He was a complete and total asshole.

He had no idea who I was. I was trying to be nice. He walked away without answering my question.

It's him, isn't it?

So he's hotter than the surface of the sun. He's also more abrasive than sandpaper.

"I do my research on the people we hire," Jack continues, "and I've learned that your brother is Dex. Is that correct?"

I nod.

"Then I assume you've seen the viral rant about him from last night?"

My brows pinch together. I should know this, right? I should be aware of what's going on with my brother and with the team I'm about to start working with.

But my phone woke me up with its ringing when Lily called at six this morning, and I jumped in the shower and darted over here. I haven't had a chance to check socials to see who ranted about what last night.

I shake my head. I feel small as I do it, as if it's my fault I'm not prepared this morning. That's not really true. I didn't know I'd be working here or when I'd start, but there's nothing I hate more than walking into something unprepared.

Jack lets it go. "Dex took a dirty hit on Maverick Jennings at practice a couple weeks ago and fractured a rib. Maverick took it upon himself to let the world know what he thought about that when he went out last night. While your brother was dealt with separately by this organization, it's these types of outbursts we're trying to mitigate."

"So I'll be working with Maverick Jennings?" I ask, my hunch absolutely correct.

He nods. "Yes. We'll need you on top of him twenty-four seven. You'll be his agent, his publicist, and his strategist all rolled into one person, with, of course, a budget to work within should you need to hire additional help. Stuart told me you gave up thirty-some-odd clients for this one, but this is a *big* one. It's going to be a tough job. Are you up for the task?"

The truth is that *no*, I'm absolutely *not* up for babysitting Maverick Jennings. He's a total jerk, and he couldn't get away fast enough from me that night.

I'm about to open my mouth to tell Jack that I'd like to opt out and head back to Chicago when there's a knock at the door.

"Come in!" Jack yells.

"Sir, Coach Nash and Mr. Jennings are here."

Jack glances at me, and it's the kind of look that tells me he knows I'm up for the challenge.

I'm not so sure…but as the sexy football star walks in with a sour look on his face that turns into recognition when his eyes land on me, I'm not about to say no.

CHAPTER 5

MAVERICK JENNINGS

She Hit on Me

"Oh hell no. Hell motherfucking no," I say. I realize I sound like a petulant child, but Jack hired a babysitter for me, and it's the chick who tried to hit on me the other night?

Absolutely the fuck not.

She's wearing black pants and that same black jacket today over a red shirt. She likes red, I guess. Her lips are still as plump and red as they were at the casino, and she has those same black heels on.

Fuck my life.

"Sit," Jack commands, and I do. He's my boss. If I don't bend to his will, I'm as good as benched. "Maverick, meet Everleigh. Everleigh, Mav." He makes the introductions, and she reaches out a hand to shake mine as if she's some professional who wasn't ready to drop her fucking panties for me the other night.

"Nice to meet you," she says, and I ignore her outstretched hand.

"What's this about?" I demand from Jack. Lincoln grabs a chair from the circular table in the corner where I signed my paperwork when I was traded to this team and pulls it over so he's sitting next to me.

Jack studies me for a few beats. He steeples his hands in front of his mouth, leaning forward a bit, and then he leans back in his chair. "When I was first traded to the Vegas Aces from Denver, I didn't want to be here. It was the one place in the world I didn't want to be. Calvin Bennett owned the team at that time, and I'd gotten his daughter pregnant. I knew the main reason he wanted me here, aside from my skillset, was so he could push me closer to his daughter. And so he hired me a babysitter when I got to town. I'll be honest. I hated the very idea of it. He called it a behavioral coach, but I knew it for what it was. A way for him to keep his thumb on me. He threatened me with bench time if I didn't do things his way. I hated his very guts for the way he treated me."

"And now you're doing the same thing to me?" I guess. Why the speech telling me how much he hated it if he's going to do the same thing to me?

He huffs out a chuckle. "Not exactly. I'm not siccing a babysitter on you to keep you under my thumb. I'm helping you rebrand because the Vegas Aces are in desperate need of a strong leader. Hudson, Fletcher…they're great guys, but we need *you*. As the starting quarterback, there's a hell of a lot that rests on your shoulders. You haven't bonded with your teammates. You haven't bothered getting to know anyone in this town. You've spent the last two weeks holed up in your condo, treating Robbie like shit while he was there and exiting once to go on a tirade about a teammate."

"Dex had it coming after what he did to me," I hiss.

He raises his hand. "And he's gotten his own punishment for his part. That's not what this is about. What I need from you is a change. I need you to rethink your brand, the image you're projecting to the world. The legacy you want to leave behind. Because right now, people see Maverick Jennings and they think, wow, his stats are great, but what kind of mark is he leaving behind? Numbers are important, and right now, to you at least, they might be everything. But there's life beyond this game, too. And once you're unable to continue playing, what will that life consist of?"

"So you're doing all this to set me up for retirement?" I ask bluntly.

Jack sighs and shakes his head. "No, Mav. I'm doing this for you. For your teammates. For you to get involved in this community. For you to figure out what your core message is and what campaigns we need to execute to help deliver that message. And that's what Everleigh is here for. She'll essentially be your shadow for the next year, assisting with engagements, speaking on your behalf for press releases, creating a social media strategy, connecting with your agent on partnerships and collaborations, that sort of thing."

"I have a publicist who does that already," I protest.

"Consider a pay reduction for that person, then, because they're not doing a great job," Jack mutters.

"Look, Mav," Lincoln says, stepping in. "One of the most important tenets of our team is character. Accountability, discipline, preparation. Ranting about your teammate doesn't fit into that. Volunteering in the community? That does. Attending charity events? Yes, absolutely. Is it okay to get into a little trouble every now and then? I wouldn't condone it, but it happens. Is it okay to act the way you have been? Not in the least. If you decide you don't want to cooperate, we'll have no choice but suspension."

I sit back in my chair. Suddenly, my ribs feel like they're aching. My head is throbbing.

I don't want any part of any of this, but one thing Jack said keeps pulsing in my brain.

There's life beyond the game.

I've never considered that. I've spent my entire life putting my all into football. In the back of my mind, I know that this career is fleeting. It's finite. It has an end date stamped upon it even if I don't know what that end date is just yet.

And what mark am I leaving?

I have a terrible reputation.

But I like it that way. It lets me do my fucking job. It encourages people to leave me alone.

I wasn't always like this, but I am now.

The last thing I need is some gorgeous woman following me around.

"On that note," Jack says, "I'll have Lily ask you each a few questions and draft a schedule. I'll need you working together on a daily basis starting today so Everleigh can get to know you and start drafting out the brand rebuild."

I press my lips together. It feels like everything is spinning out of my control.

"She hit on me the other night," I say, tossing a thumb in her direction.

She gasps as her jaw drops. "I did no such thing!"

"Have you two met before?" Jack asks.

She nods. "Yes, we were at the same casino the other night, and I thought it was him, so I said hello."

"She shot her shot," I say, my lips curling. "But I walked away."

Her face flushes, and Jesus, she's pretty.

"He's fabricating a story so he can get out of this," she says, pursing her lips at me. She looks back at Jack. "We talked for all of thirty seconds, and I must have left an impression if he recognized me since it was a quick chat. He got up and walked away when I asked him how he felt about being in Vegas."

Lincoln's brows rise. "Sounds to me like it was innocent enough."

"Like she was just checking in on a brother's teammate," Jack agrees.

"Wait a minute," I say, holding up a hand. "Hold the fucking phone here. A brother's teammate?" I repeat. I turn toward the girl. "Who's your brother?"

She squares her shoulders at me and tips her chin up, and goddamn, it's a sexy power move. "Dex Bradley."

I leap up from my chair, and I immediately grab for my ribs. That was a fucking dumb move.

But so is hiring my enemy's sister to babysit me.

"No fucking way," I say to Jack, shaking my head and wincing.

"Sit down," Jack barks. "You're not in a position to negotiate. You will do as she says, or you will sit on the bench." He shakes his head as his eyes dart to the window before he glances at Lincoln. "Goddamn. I always said I'd never be like him, and look at me quoting him." He's muttering as he lifts a shoulder. "Calvin has gotten better since I took over fifty-one percent of the team, I guess. Being a grandfather has softened him." He's talking to Lincoln, not me, and meanwhile, I'm seething that he's forcing this on me.

Lincoln chuckles.

"Ms. Bradley, are you ready to get started?" Jack asks Dex's sister.

She nods and taps her tablet. "Yes. I have several questions for Mr. Jennings so we can start an action plan."

"Great," Jack says. "I'll have Lily set you up in a conference room, and she'll be in to work with your schedules."

I let out a frustrated sigh, but as he said, I'm not in a position to negotiate.

CHAPTER 6

Everleigh Bradley

A Divisive Asshole

My hands are shaking as we follow Lily to one of the conference rooms.

Is he freaking serious? Maverick has a hell of a lot of nerve telling Jack Dalton that I hit on him the other night. That's *not* what I was doing.

I was being nice. Trying to welcome someone new to the town where I'm new, too. My brother's teammate.

My brother's enemy. *My* enemy.

At least that's the way he's playing it. We're not off to a good start here, and I clench and unclench my fists as I follow behind him. I need to be the adult here. It's why I was hired.

He's just not going to make it easy.

But Stuart didn't recommend me—and Jack didn't hire me—to take on an easy position.

Lily stops at a conference room and opens the door to let us in. "I'll give you two the room for the next half hour or so, and then I'll be back to work out scheduling details."

"Thank you, Lily," I say, and she closes the door behind me as she leaves.

Maverick doesn't say a word as he slips into a chair with a sulking expression on his face, and I suck in a deep breath.

I don't sit.

I'm more comfortable standing. He's making everything uncomfortable as it is, so I assert what little control I have here by standing.

"I'd like to start by assessing your current reputation. An audit, if you will," I say.

He huffs something out without responding, and I pull open my tablet. I open a browser and type his name into a search bar, and I scan the results.

"Maverick Jennings, football quarterback," I murmur, reading from the results page. There's a host of photos of him: two from the field, one off, and a team headshot where I'm forced to ignore the fact that he looks sexy as hell.

Across the top shows his birth date and age along with his current position, team, and number. We're the same age.

The next row has an article published six hours ago along with a *see also* section naming the Cowboys, the Aces, and Lincoln Nash.

Underneath that are recent posts about Maverick on social media, an overview of who he is, and the top recent stories about him.

I flash my screen at him. "This is the section we need to focus on." I point to the top recent stories. "These headlines are all about your viral rant about Dex last night. We want positive headlines here, not ones casting you in a negative light." I point to the article published six hours ago. "Jennings Causing Division at Aces," I read. I raise a brow.

"I know what the fucking headlines say," he hisses.

"Do you understand that this is your brand?" I ask, shaking my tablet screen at him. "This is the image you're projecting. That you're a divisive asshole who will sell out a teammate for a headline."

I nearly slap a hand over my mouth after the words are out. To be perfectly honest, I'm shocked I called him an asshole to his face.

But we have to know what's broken before we can start to repair it, and right now, we're assessing. I scroll down and read some older headlines aloud, and when I'm done, I say, "Not a single one of these paints you in a positive light. What about charity work? Appearances? Family, friends, acquaintances that can vouch as character witnesses?"

He remains silent.

I sigh, and then I give it to him straight. "If you want to play, I need your cooperation. Don't for a second underestimate me. I'm being paid by the Aces, not by you, so my loyalty is to them."

He raises a brow. "Do you even want this job?"

"Less now that I know it's you I'm working with." It's another bold statement I shouldn't be making, but it helps to even the playing field a little.

"Feeling's mutual. I wouldn't have liked anyone in this position, but even less that it's someone related to the asshole who took me out for the first six weeks of the season. And, you know, the girl who hit on me a couple weeks ago." He reaches up with his right hand to brush off his left shoulder in a show of complete and utter egotism.

"Do you really think that's what I was doing?" I ask. "Do you think every woman who talks to you is hitting on you?" I emphasize the word *woman* since he called me a *girl* a second ago. Before he can answer, I plow forward. "Because I wasn't. I was being nice to the new guy in a new city. That's all."

"Yeah, you mentioned that. I still don't buy it."

I blow out a breath. This is going to be even harder than I thought. "It doesn't matter. I work with you now, so regardless of what you believe about that night, anything other than a strictly professional relationship is completely off the table."

"It was from the beginning anyway. I don't do relationships."

I roll my eyes. "Of course you don't. It's the hallmark of every bad boy football player."

That must press on a nerve because he pushes to a stand, fists resting on the table as he leans forward to try to be intimidating.

It might work on other people, but I grew up with five brothers. It doesn't work on me.

"You don't know the first goddamn thing about me, so don't judge me with your stereotypes," he hisses.

I hold up both hands. "You're right. I'm sorry. Care to explain why you don't do relationships?"

He sits back in his chair and folds his arms across his chest. "Not to you."

"Fair enough." It'll just take a little digging on my part to figure him out. I finally take the seat across from him. "Okay, let's dig into this. I've been hired for the next year, and that means we have time to assess, plan, and execute. Typically when I have a year to rebrand a client, I like to spend the first quarter laying the groundwork for what comes next, and that means we're going to look at your current image and figure out what our new branding is going to look like. In the second quarter, we'll start implementation and use on-field performance. We'll work on your media interactions, including not just what you say, but how you say it. Body language. All of it. And then in the third and fourth quarters, we'll capitalize on what we've built with further community engagement and partnerships that reflect your new image. But you're in a unique situation because your coach and team owner want to start implementation immediately. That means

I'll work out a plan, and we'll hit the ground running. Any questions so far?"

"Yeah, just one."

I raise my brows.

"Why the fuck do I have to do this?"

I blow out a breath. Again. This dude is as frustrating as they come. "Because you're acting like a child, and your big boss man said you have to." I offer a sugary sweet smile at the end.

He remains quiet as I launch into some more details about what I'm here to do, and Lily joins us and gives me all the team information I need so I can join any and all activities that Maverick will be attending—including practice, where I can observe him interacting with other players, access that's fairly rare in this business. But since the Aces hired me, they have the power to allow me in at practices.

Jack may have said I'm not a babysitter, but it's starting to feel like that's exactly what I am.

Before Lily leaves, she turns to Maverick. "Mr. Dalton would like you to stop by Dr. Baker's exam room before you head out for an update. He'd like Ms. Bradley to attend with you."

Maverick grimaces. He must really love this game if he's not just walking out.

He pushes to a stand. "We're done here."

I laugh. "We're not done for the next year, Hotshot."

He raises a brow. "Hotshot?"

I press my lips into a fake smile, and I nod toward the door to indicate that he should go.

And wouldn't you know it? We run smack into my brother on the way down to the exam room. He likely just arrived for practice, and he spots Maverick first since he has a big body that's blocking me from view.

"The fuck you thinking running your mouth about me last night?" Dex demands.

Maverick doesn't say anything, and I peek out from behind him to wave at my brother.

"We're working it out," I say to Dex, and he pulls me into a hug.

"Ev! What are you doing here?"

I'm not really sure how Jack wants me to handle explaining away my role here, so I simply say, "The Aces hired me for some branding work."

"That's amazing! Was that the big, secret client?"

I nod.

"I'm so glad to have you here. Hope you don't have to work with that asshole Jennings," he says, nodding at that asshole's retreating figure.

When he hears the bat signal, he turns around and snarls a little. "Oh, she'll be *working* with me," he says smoothly. He raises a brow, and it's so very clear that he's just trying to get under my brother's skin. "You know she hit on me the other night. I declined, but I would've banged her into next week had I known she was your sister."

My jaw drops, and Dex looks like he's about to punch the guy. His fists are balled up, and I need to do something to stop this trainwreck from taking place right here in the lobby of the Aces' practice facility.

"Come on, Maverick. Let's get you down to the exam room." I say the words tightly, and it's clearly a reminder of why we're here—why Maverick isn't playing. It's Dex's fault, and there's no two ways about that.

Still, Maverick throwing nasty words at my brother won't fix his broken rib. It's just going to give me more work to do.

CHAPTER 7

MAVERICK JENNINGS

On Top of You

"The bottom line is that your recovery is going well, but you're not quite there yet," Dr. Baker says. "I can't clear you for full practice, but I can clear you for position drills and conditioning starting Wednesday. No pads yet. You can begin light cardio at home, and we'll reassess as we go. Just listen to your body and immediately stop if anything feels off."

"Thank you, Doctor." The words are mumbled. It sucks that I'm not clear yet, but at least I can start getting back to work. I guess that's something to be thankful for at a time when it feels like the hits just keep coming.

She's got a lot of nerve trying to get into my head with that line of questioning, but it's none of her goddamn business why I don't do relationships anymore.

It's nobody's business.

I walk out of the exam room, and she's right on my tail.

I don't like it.

I don't want someone following me around for the next year. I didn't ask for this nonsense. "Can you just leave me the fuck alone?" I ask.

She shakes her head, those large brown eyes moving to mine as those full lips settle into a smirk. "No can do. I'm supposed to stay on top of you for the next year."

I raise my brow at her. Staying on top of me and getting revenge on Dex by fucking his sister wouldn't be the worst way to go down in flames.

I smirk back at her. "On top of me, huh?"

Her cheeks flush, and she sputters a little. "Oh, I, uh—that's not what I meant."

"I know what you meant," I say coolly.

"But, hey, good news about getting back to light conditioning, right? Maybe you won't be in such a bad mood once you can exercise again," she suggests.

I shake my head, and I whip over in her direction. "It's not a mood, and a workout isn't going to change who I am at my core. The sooner you come to terms with that, the easier this will be for you." Though I'm sure I'll do my best to make it miserable for her regardless without even trying.

She doesn't respond to that. Instead, she says, "I'll get a schedule together for us that gives us time to touch base each day. Some days will be heavier than oth—"

"Fuck the schedule," I mutter, interrupting her. "Just fix my image so you can move onto your next client."

"It's not that simple, Maverick," she says. "I'm here for the next year whether you like it or not."

"Yeah, well, I don't." I leave those as my parting words, and I storm out toward the navy blue Ford truck with silver stripes I had custom painted to match the colors in Dallas.

What a fucking waste.

All of this is. I don't want to be here, I don't want a babysitter, and I don't want a fucking truck with the wrong goddamn colors.

I peel out of the parking lot, my tires screeching for good measure, and I head toward my condo. I just moved in last month despite having been here in Vegas since May. I was renting a place, and one of the players on my offensive line told me about this building that houses many of the players from the team. They had a couple condos open—likely players who were traded from Vegas considering the timing—so I grabbed the first one that was available.

So far, I guess I like the amenities. There's a doorman, a car that'll take us anywhere at any time, and views that can't be beat. There's also a fitness center and a few restaurants nearby, though I haven't had the chance to try any of that just yet.

I suppose it's home for now, and as much as I wanted to get out last night, today, I just want to get back home, sleep off this hangover, and try to forget everything that happened this morning.

I pull up into the parking garage and into one of the two spaces assigned for my condo, and I head down to the lobby first to get my mail.

When the elevator doors open to the lobby, I see Everleigh standing there, chatting up the doorman.

"I leave the practice facility, and you follow me home?" I demand.

I thought I'd at least get an escape from her here at my home—that our interactions would be limited to practice.

I guess I didn't realize that when she said she'd be on top of me, she literally meant twenty-four seven.

Fuck that.

Her jaw drops. "You *live* here?"

My brows push together in confusion, and the doorman pushes a set of keys across the counter toward her.

"I do."

She picks up the keys, and she lets out a sigh. "I do now, too." She smirks at me again, and I have the sudden image of pushing my cock between her lips to wipe that goddamn smirk off her face.

Fuck that. Fuck her. Fuck all of this.

There's literally no escaping her.

She gets on the elevator while Milton, the doorman, checks for my mail, and once I have it in hand, I take the elevator up as well.

I'm on the seventeenth floor, and all I can do is hope that she's on the second or third—far, far away from where I land. But I have a feeling I'm going to run into her. A lot. She's going to be around. A lot.

And that's why it's even more important that I get that image out of my head of her sucking my cock as those big brown eyes lift to mine, a little bit of fear and innocence in them as my cock fills her mouth and lightly chokes her.

Jesus.

I push that thought out of my head even as my cock swells at the very thought of it, and the doors push open on my floor.

And there she stands, fumbling a bit with her keys as she seems to finally get the door unlocked.

I head toward my door without a word, and she turns with a smile to introduce herself to her new neighbor.

The second she sees me, the smile falls clean off her face.

"Oh, shit," she whispers as she watches me slide the key into my lock to unlock the door that's *right next door* to hers. "We're neighbors?"

I smirk. "It would appear so. Keep to your place, and keep it down. I don't want any interruptions to my daily routine."

50

She rolls her eyes. "I could say the same to you."

"Then do it."

An annoyed snarl escapes her, and she finally opens her door, walks through it, and slams it behind her.

I can't help the tiny lift that plays at the corners of my lips. It's not quite a smile since my mouth seems to have forgotten how to do that, but it's something.

I blow out a breath.

It's something I don't want. It's a distraction I don't need.

And now I won't even be able to escape her at home.

CHAPTER 8

Everleigh Bradley

Ear Up to the Wall

I finally check the group chat messages when I'm inside my new place.

Ford: *Probably a Hemsworth. Is it?*

Liam: *Liam Hemsworth? (The best of the Hemsworth bros, BTW)*

Dex: *She's in Vegas, not Hollywood. My guess is Carrot Top.*

Madden: *Must be someone big for your organization to allow you to give up your entire client roster. I'm guessing some CEO caught in a scandal. Maybe that dude that went viral at that concert on the kiss cam.*

Ivy: *Hmm, someone in Vegas…Wayne Newton?*

Dex: *How do you even know who Wayne Newton is? Aren't you like 16?*

Ivy: *I'm 21, thank you very much, and I was WITH YOU in Vegas when I turned 21. Remember? OH! Backstreet Boys???*

Dex: *I just saw her at the Complex. It's Maverick Jennings.*

I finally reply to the group.

Me: *Dex is right. It's Maverick Jennings.*

Madden: *A football player.*

Me: *A football player. [sobbing face emoji]*

I stare out at the view from this place. I've already done a walk through every room, and maintenance did a fantastic job sprucing it up to look brand new. It wasn't in bad shape before, but it's pristine and move-in ready now, and I'm ready to move in.

The place came furnished, and what's in here is good enough for now. If I decide to stay here long-term, I can replace furniture, and it certainly beats living out of a hotel.

Even if I'm living next to my enemy.

I'm still not quite sure what our schedule is going to be. I don't know how we're going to compromise on much of anything, and since the Aces organization has given me full access to Maverick along with the threat that he'll be benched if he doesn't do whatever I say, I suppose I can just do whatever I want.

Task number one is figuring out what that'll look like.

After I stare out at this view a little while longer.

I can see from the Strat all the way down to Mandalay Bay. It's the same view Dex has several floors above me, and it's likely the same view Maverick has next door.

I could stand here all day staring. Vegas isn't in my blood the way it's in Dex's, but the view is gorgeous, and I imagine it borders magical once it gets dark and the lights turn on.

I force myself to turn away.

I need to get to the hotel and grab my suitcase. I need to stop at a store and buy some linens. I need groceries, too. Maybe a one-stop-shop big box retailer kind of place.

I'm about to head out despite my reservations about running into my neighbor when I hear a strange noise.

Thud…thud…thud…

It's a dull, repetitive sound with a bit of a hum, and I move over toward the wall I share with Maverick.

I would've imagined the walls in this gorgeous building are thicker than they are, but as I get closer and put my ear up to the wall, I finally place the sound.

Thud…thud…thud…

It's the sound of shoes slapping against the belt of a treadmill.

And it's happening right on the other side of my wall.

The doctor cleared Maverick for light cardio, and he's on his treadmill the second he gets home. I mean, good for him. Even though I shouldn't have said it might improve his mood, I meant it.

Knowing he's on his treadmill at least clears me for walking out of the building without perchance running into him, so I head out to take care of my errands.

Three hours later, it's all done…except now I have to figure out some way to carry everything I just bought up into my condo.

I texted Dex when I left the store.

Me: *Are you home and able to help me unload some stuff from my car?*

I have a reply when I put the car in park in the parking garage of the building. I pull into the spot assigned to my condo that's on the left since a rather large truck is taking up half my space on the right. *Someone lives here now, asshole,* I think to myself.

Dex: *No, sorry. Milton can help.*

I head down to the front desk and ask Milton, "Do you have a cart or something I can use to carry a bunch of stuff from my car up to my condo?"

He nods. "I have a cart and these hands." He smiles as he flexes his fingers.

I grin. "Dex told me to ask you. You're the best."

He grabs the cart, and we head to my car, unload everything, and he helps me up to the seventeenth floor with all of it.

"I'll request Mr. Jennings keep his truck within his lines," he says, and of course it's Maverick's truck lazily parked halfway into one of my spaces. I mean, I don't need it, but that doesn't mean he's entitled to it. "Can I help you unload, ma'am?" he asks.

I shake my head. "I can take it from here if you don't mind your cart being returned in an hour or so."

"Of course. Call me when you're finished so I can come get it."

"Thanks, Milton," I say.

As he takes the elevator down, I wonder…am I supposed to tip him? I have no idea how this works. I owned my house in Chicago—which I still do. I didn't sell it because I didn't know how permanent this move was going to be.

At least a year, I suppose.

I throw my new sheets and towels into the washer, put away my groceries, and get my place organized. I put on some music and hum as I work, and I think as I hum.

I think through the plan with Maverick.

I think through the best way to handle him.

I need to do a little research. I don't know much about him at all other than what came up on the headlines when I searched him earlier.

I know I have full rein, but I don't want to piss him off further on day one. I want him to see me as an ally, though I know it's going to take a hell of a lot of work to get there.

His first team meetings start at seven in the morning most days, and he likely has treatment and breakfast ahead of those meetings. I think we'll need to touch base each morning at the very least to go over the strategy for the day. We'll start daily with a quick check-in and any necessary coaching for the day's media coverage, charity events, meetings, that sort of thing.

As I glance through his schedule, it looks like his days are packed pretty full at the practice facility, but there are breaks built in—time to get into gear for practice, a bit of time after lunch. They're short windows but enough to have a quick one-on-one to review headlines, discuss social media, coordinate events, and strategize. We could even meet over lunch, but I think it's more important for him to eat with his teammates since that should be bonding time.

So that leaves me with evenings. It looks like he will generally leave the practice facility between five and six each night provided he doesn't have additional responsibilities, so we can touch base from six until whenever each night.

I need to set boundaries, and I think it's important he does, too.

I jot down a few notes so I don't forget anything I came up with during my humming-slash-work session, and then I grab the cart to return it to Milton.

I don't think twice about exiting my condo. I take the elevator down, thank Milton, and run into my brother, who's just coming in with his wife and son. We get on the elevator together.

"Where are you three coming from?" I ask.

"Not Dad's lounge," Dex quips, and then his eyes widen a little.

"Dad's lounge?" I echo. "Dad has a lounge here in Vegas?"

He clears his throat. "Yeah. It's a VIP place. He tried to rope me into helping him run it, and I did for a while, but I'm out now." He shakes his head. "It's kind of a running joke between Ains and me. I'm not sure why those words slipped out. I wasn't supposed to say anything."

"I want to know more."

The elevator opens and lets me off on my floor, and Dex pushes the button to close the doors before he has to tell me more. I roll my eyes. I guess I'll just ask my father myself.

I'm sliding my keys into my door when Maverick exits his condo.

He stares at me, and it's unnerving.

"Did the workout help?" I ask.

He narrows his eyes at me. "How'd you know I worked out?"

"I could hear your treadmill through the wall." I shrug. Maybe I should be embarrassed, but I'm not.

"Did you hear anything else?" he asks, and for a moment, I wonder if he had a woman in there with him. I'm not sure why that's the particular thought that crosses my mind. It's none of my business what he does in his spare time.

Actually…that's not true. *Everything* he does is my business. Including who he's sleeping with. That's part of his image, too. Right?

I can see why he hates me. But he's been pretty aggressive toward me, too—like telling Jack that I hit on him.

I'm still not over that one. I may never be.

But I have to act like I am, or none of this is ever going to work.

"I wasn't listening. I was getting my own place set up."

He holds up both hands. "Don't let me stop you." He walks toward the elevator to press the button, but before he does, my voice stops him.

"I'm working on drafting a schedule. We'll touch base before, during, and after practice each day, but where would you like to schedule our longest meeting of the day? Before or after practice?"

"Our *longest* meeting?" he repeats. He turns toward me.

"Yes. We'll need several sessions each day—when you're back to practice of course. Until then, we have ample time to assess the current situation and get a strategy together."

"Ample time?" he echoes.

"Yes." I nod resolutely.

"What exactly are your qualifications to be working with me?" he asks, narrowing his eyes at me.

I grit my teeth together as I try to maintain professionalism. "I double majored in behavioral science and media studies, and I have a master's in marketing. I started at Langford right out of college and moved my way through the ranks into brand strategist about five years ago. I've worked with hundreds of clients, and I know what I'm doing."

He turns to press the button. "Keep the meetings short, and we will only discuss what is an absolute necessity as deemed by the team."

"Great," I say brightly. "We'll start tomorrow morning at eight sharp at the practice facility. Same conference room as this morning."

"The fuck we will," he mutters.

"Excuse me?" I ask, pretending like I missed what he said.

The elevator doors open, and he steps on. "I'm not going to the practice facility on game day. We'll meet downstairs in the conference center in this building."

"See you in the morning," I say, and I shoot him a sugary sweet smile as the elevator doors close.

I regret that eight o'clock demand, but I can't change it.

Instead, I guess I'll work my ass off, pull an all-nighter, do my research, and show up ready to impress the unimpressible.

CHAPTER 9

MAVERICK JENNINGS

The Face Facing Forward

When my alarm wakes me at five thirty, I'm less than impressed.

I don't need to get up this early, but I do it because regardless of whether I have practice or not, this is the time I wake up during the season.

But this morning, I'm dreading the task at hand.

I don't want to meet with this woman in a conference room that's too small for the two of us.

I don't want my life dictated to me for the next year.

I don't give a fuck about my image and what legacy I'm leaving behind.

I don't want any of this, but somewhere along the line, the things I want went out the window.

I don't even know what I want. I guess I just want to be left alone so I can focus on what's important: the game.

I suppose that's also *why* it's what's important.

When everything was taken from me, I turned back to football and vowed nothing would ever come between me and the game again.

And then fucking Dex Bradley broke my rib before I even got to start the regular season with a new team. The perfect storm to push into that wound just a little harder. A little deeper.

Today is game day. I should be heading to the stadium.

Instead, I'm sulking at home, dreading a meeting with a woman who's too goddamn hot for her own good.

Never mind the fact that today would've been *his* birthday. Double digits. We should be together. We should be celebrating.

I'm not.

The last time I smiled, the last time I dreamed—the last time I *laughed*—was with his mother.

I get on the treadmill, and I remember that the brand lady heard me in here yesterday. I pull my earbuds out and blast the music as loud as I can, and then I get started on a morning run.

Light cardio, my ass. I take it harder than I should, but my rib's feeling okay today. Each day of rest has helped, and after this workout, I'll take it easy. Or easier, anyway.

I take a shower after my cooldown, and then I grab a protein bar to eat while I meet with her. I head down to the conference room, surprised I didn't run into her on the way.

But of course I didn't. She's already in there, wearing business casual when I'm in trainers and a tee, but just because she wants to be formal doesn't mean I need to be.

"Make this quick. I have film to review," I say, bypassing the usual morning salutations.

"Good morning to you, too," she says sweetly, and her voice has this little tone to it that grates on my last nerve.

She pulls out some paperwork and her tablet, and she nods to one of the chairs next to her. I don't want to slide into the chair beside her. I don't want to work closely with her.

Why am I pushing back so hard on this?

Because I've learned my lesson.

I'm attracted to her, and that's a real problem. Because she's the enemy—not just because she's been put in charge of me for the next year, but because she's Dex Bradley's sister. She's demanding and independent, two major turn-ons, and the last time I gave into chemistry, I ended up…well, like this. What you see today.

My marriage changed me, and I didn't come out better because of it. Instead, I came out of it too skittish to allow anyone in.

I pick a chair across the table. I put physical distance between us so she gets the hint. I'm not sure it works.

"What do you value, Maverick?" she asks. "What's important to you?"

"Football," I answer immediately.

"Aside from your sport." She tilts her head as she studies me.

"Freedom. Control. Money." I meet her gaze.

"Those make you sound cold. Detached. What else?"

I blow out a breath as I try to come up with an answer that doesn't seem to be readily available to me.

"What about the offseason? What do you do then?" she asks after giving me a long enough pause where I don't answer the previous question.

"Travel."

"Where?"

"Wherever the fuck I want. How exactly is this helping my brand?" I ask.

"I need to get to know you a bit more. I can't target a rebrand if I don't understand what the current brand is," she says.

"There is no current brand. What you see is what you get. I don't *brand* myself. I just live my life."

"And fuck the consequences?" she guesses. I don't answer, and she shakes her head with a little chuckle. "You're more like Dex than either of you probably realizes. But that's beside the point. How would you describe what people perceive as your identity?"

"I don't care," I say, enunciating each word for her. "This is stupid."

She glares at me. "I'll thank you up front not to insult my life's work again. Regardless of your opinion of this, you're now the starting quarterback here in Vegas. You know that simply because of the position you chose to play, you're going to be considered the face of the entire franchise this season. The public's perception of your persona will affect every aspect of your life here in Vegas, and it'll also affect the rest of your career and the rest of your life after the game. I have the heavy task here of not just rebuilding your reputation but also training you to be the face of the Aces. And the face you have now is not the face they want facing forward."

"Say face again," I mutter. A childish insult seems better than responding to any of that.

"Tell me about your childhood," she says.

"No. We're done here." I move to stand.

She shakes her head. "Sit," she barks at me as if I'm some sort of dog.

I don't follow the command. I remain standing, and we face off as she slowly rises to a stand, her hands balled into fists that she's now balancing forward on as she snarls at me.

"I get it, Jennings. You hate me. You hate the whole idea of this. And that's fine. Hate it all you want, but we're stuck

64

together for the next year. I *will* teach you to value yourself and your future since clearly that's a training piece you missed somewhere along the way. I *will* be here by your side fighting *for* you while you fight *against* me. I don't really care how you feel about that. So sit your ass down unless you want me to tattle to your boss, and cooperate with me unless you're pleased to spend more time standing on the sidelines watching instead of being the one making the plays." Her eyes glow at me with anger, and I find myself lowering back into the chair.

I'm quite sure no one has ever put me in my place like that before.

It's—dare I say—hot as all fuck.

I wonder what her cunt tastes like.

Shit.

She has me pegged, and I've barely told her one single goddamn thing about myself.

I hate that she has me pegged. Nobody has ever seen through me the way she can. Nobody has ever talked to me like that before, either.

Everyone's careful around me. They're either scared I'll go off on them, or they fall over themselves to get to me. It's pathetic. Men don't have backbones anymore, and the women I seem to interact with don't know how to handle me. They're just warm bodies that give me what I want for a night, and then I'm done.

I don't want anything beyond that. I just want to be left alone, to crawl back into my hole where it's dark and quiet. Where I don't have to have human connection since all I'm left with when I do is pure disappointment.

CHAPTER 10
Everleigh Bradley

The Aces Fam

I can feel it.

I'm starting to crack his resolve.

I've spent the last two weeks meeting him in the mornings and working through some of the rumors swirling about him as I try to get to know the man beneath that tough, sturdy, tall wall he's built around himself.

We have a quick meeting before the game, and we both spot another player on the team as he walks through the lobby. He's probably leaving for today's game. The Aces are playing at home today, and I'll be there up in the stands as I watch Maverick on the sidelines. Call time is nine for players, but since he's not playing, he'll get there around noon.

A short time later, I'm chatting about public perception of his image when the door opens. I freeze, but then I see it's just Dex. I rise and give him a hug. "Knock 'em dead today, bro."

He turns toward Maverick. "Is this media one-oh-one? Train the new guy on what not to say publicly?"

"Eh, your sister's here to keep on top of me for things like that." He shoots me a wink. "And, you know. Whatever else."

I glare at Maverick. "Knock off that bullshit." I turn to my brother. "Good luck today."

He nods and doesn't say another word as he leaves, and I resume where I left off. After our meeting, I head upstairs to get ready for the game as I think through this morning.

If he *truly* didn't care about his reputation, he wouldn't have flirted with me in front of my brother. It's a macho man thing, a pissing contest. But it's also a breakthrough, as much as he won't admit that.

I thought about bringing up what I found in my deep dive into the man sitting across from me, but somehow asking about his marriage felt too personal. I'm supposed to be getting personal, but I'm still treading lightly.

But…yeah. That was pretty shocking, the whole marriage thing. He was in love at some point. Probably. I guess people get married for other reasons. Maybe it was someone else trying to rebrand him, though I can't possibly see him agreeing to marry someone for his image. Maybe he was someone different before. Or maybe the marriage changed him.

He's insanely private about his personal life, and that translates to all the research I did.

Jack gave me access to the owner's suite, and I'll observe from up there. It's far away from the field where Maverick will be standing, but it'll give me the same sort of perspective a fan might have.

Okay, fine—not a normal fan, obviously. Most fans don't get to sit in the owner's suite.

As much as I want to force Maverick to carpool with me to the stadium, I don't. I'm just starting to make a bit of progress, and I don't want to hinder it by coming on too strongly too quickly. He's like a scared little bunny, still to all movement, eyes watching warily, careful not to let anyone get too close, or he'll take off running.

I won't let him run.

I mean, I can't. If I do, I lose my job, so that's certainly a motivating factor.

I arrive in the suite about a half hour before game time, and I'm highly impressed with everything I see here. A buffet is spread out on two sides of the suite, and in the middle are high-top tables we can stand by to watch the game on televisions inside the suite as we eat, or we could opt for the stadium seating stacked below the suite to get the full perspective of the field.

It's not my first time in a suite at an NFL game. I have four brothers who play, and my dad has a suite at Soldier Field for the Bears' home games. But it *is* my first time in a team owner's suite, and it's already packed with people—none of whom I know, so I feel awkward as I walk around.

A woman with dark blonde hair approaches me, and she grins. "First timer?" When I glance over at her, she says, "Hi. I'm Ellie. I can always tell a first timer to the suite—mostly because I'm here every game." She giggles as she sticks out a hand to shake mine.

"Everleigh," I say. "The team hired me to—"

"Babysit Mav? I know. Who's doing his PR, by the way?"

I laugh. Who *is* this woman? She must be someone important if she knows I'm *babysitting* Maverick.

"Terry Dornan out of Dallas. I haven't spoken with him yet, but it's on my list for the week," I say.

"Yes," she says, nodding. "Do you think he'd be amenable to hiring a local publicist? I work with several players on this team. Oh! I'm just realizing you must think I'm a weirdo since you probably have no clue who I am. My husband is Luke Dalton. He used to play for the Aces, and now he does some work with the wide receivers. We work together on agency and publicity. Jack's my brother-in-law."

"And I'm her sister-in-law," a striking woman with chin-length dark hair says, holding out a hand to introduce herself. "Kate Dalton. Jack's wife and former babysitter."

Both Ellie and Kate giggle at their inside joke, but I recall Jack saying he hated the idea of a babysitter when he first arrived in Vegas. And now he's married to his.

Hm.

Could that happen for Maverick and me?

I glance down at him on the field. He's standing by himself on the sidelines. My God, he really hates everybody. He's staring at the field where his teammates are practicing, and it's hard to read his expression from here, but even if I could, I wouldn't know what it said. He's wearing sunglasses, so I can't tell who he's focusing on or where his eyes are looking, but he's definitely studying. At the same time, he's cold. Expressionless. Detached. Arms crossed as if he won't let anyone in.

And it's my job to find something he cares about enough outside of football to attempt to turn his image around.

It's a huge hill to climb, and to be perfectly honest, I'm not sure I have it in me.

So…no. The answer to whether that could happen for Maverick and me, whether he could fall in love with me as I, well, *babysit* him…that's a clear, hard *no*.

"It's nice to meet you both," I say.

"You're Dex's sister, right?" Ellie asks, and I nod. "So you have two reasons to be here. Welcome to the Aces fam. It's a fabulous place to be."

She seems genuinely sweet, as if she cares about the team and the players in her own right, not just because her husband is a former player, brother to the team owner, and quasi-coach. The *welcome to the fam* comment feels sincere, like this truly is one big family. And I think maybe in particular due to the fact that I'm working with the sourest of the bunch, it would bode well for me to have allies here. Ellie and Kate seem like good nominees for that position, and maybe we can even become friends since I'll be here for the next year at a minimum, even though I'm already itching to get back home to Chicago.

"Let me introduce you to everyone," Ellie says, and she takes me around and does exactly that, introducing me to some familiar faces or names that could potentially become friends and allies in this town. I meet Grayson Nash, former defensive back, and his wife, Ava. I meet Desi Nash, whose husband, Asher, is a tight end for the Aces. I meet Jolene Nash, whose husband is the head coach, Lincoln. I meet the wives of players Tristan Higgins, Jaxon Bryant, and Travis Woods: Tessa, Mandy, and Victoria, respectively.

The list goes on, but the suite is filled with wives, some kids, and family members of the Vegas Aces—including my new sister-in-law, Ainsley, as she makes a semi-late entrance just before kickoff.

I sit with her in the stadium seats to watch kickoff since she's someone I know. It's more comfortable than sitting with strangers I've just met, though my instinct tells me that I won't make friends and allies by staying in my comfort zone.

When the Aces score a field goal on their first run of the game, some players run off the field while others run onto it. I keep an eye on Maverick, but when I know it's a pause in the action to accommodate television commercials, I excuse myself from Ainsley and head back up into the suite.

I find Ellie, and I march right up to her. "Tell me more about your PR firm," I begin.

She chuckles. "You know, I never wanted to work with football players. My brother played, and until I met Luke, I didn't know much about the game at all other than the fact that grass stains are impossible to get out of those short white pants."

I laugh.

"That was thanks to my mother. I never did my brother's laundry."

"Who's your brother?" I ask.

"Josh Nolan."

"Oh, right! He played for the Bears for a long time, didn't he?"

She nods. "He finished his career here. I actually met Luke at my brother's wedding. Well, his bachelor party." She rolls her eyes. "Long story. But I came here to start over, and Luke was my first client. I needed a job, he needed a publicist, and voila. Five years later, we have two kids and a thriving public relations firm that he chartered for me, and he added in the agency when he retired so we can tag-team our clients. It's a perfect setup, and I asked about Mav's representation because he should have someone local."

"I didn't want to work with football players, either, but my boss was asked for his best brand strategist, and he offered me up. I agree with you about Maverick needing someone local. My branding background gives me a bit of insight into public relations, but he needs someone like you. I'll float the idea of your company to him and see what he says, though he hasn't been overly amenable to anything I have to say," I admit.

She huffs out a laugh. "Sounds *exactly* like how things started with Jack and Kate. But he came around eventually." My cheeks turn pink at the insinuation, but if she notices, she doesn't say a word. "Listen, if you think it would work better for me to approach him instead of you, I'm totally open to trying."

"It's probably better if you do it," I admit. "Is there anyone here, a coach or teammate or whoever, that you think he might get along with? Because so far, I've seen him rant drunkenly about my brother and, in turn, channel all his negative feelings about my sibling toward *me* since he's being forced into this partnership. So I'm just wondering if there are any allies here that could help me get into his good graces."

She presses her lips together as she thinks about it. "I'll ask Luke. He's around practice a lot and picks up on things like that. Maybe Lincoln, too. He might know."

"Perfect."

We both hear a roar come up from the stadium, and we turn toward that direction to see my brother running across the field with the ball in his hands.

Defensive ends don't typically break away and run for touchdowns, and I totally missed what happened. I'm guessing it was a fumble and Dex recovered it, but either way, the crowd is going absolutely wild as he crosses the white line into the end zone.

Ellie and I both cheer, too, and I glance down at Maverick as the grin spreads across my lips.

He's still standing there, stock-still, arms crossed over his chest, with that cold, detached expression on his face.

I think I might have even more work ahead of me than I thought.

CHAPTER 11

Everleigh Bradley

Why Do You Hate the World

I stayed longer after the game than I needed to.

You know when you meet someone and you just *click* with them? On a friendship level? That's what this felt like. Maybe Ellie makes everyone feel that way, but it seems like we have a lot in common. She owns her own business. I aspire to, and I plan to at the end of my contracted term with Maverick. One year—minus a couple weeks—to go.

She's married, and she has a couple of kids. She's got the full package, from a hot husband she works with to the cute little family they've created together.

I want that, too.

And maybe it's something I can find here in Vegas, but I can't do that if I'm shadowing Maverick Jennings twenty-four seven…which I think is what Jack expects of me.

So maybe hiring Ellie on as his local publicist is a genius idea. Maybe she can be the vessel that occasionally allows me to take a break, so to speak. I suppose I'm setting my own schedule, but I'm nothing if not an overachiever.

I've always been that way.

As soon as I'm presented with a problem, it would seem I immediately conjure twelve different paths toward the solution.

Which is why Maverick is such a goddamn enigma.

I don't see twelve paths toward the solution. I can't even find one.

But I'll keep chipping away until I do, and I really think Ellie might be able to help me with that.

Maverick must've stayed a little bit after the game as well because I find him standing by the elevator, waiting for it to come down to carry him up to the seventeenth floor when I walk into the lobby of our building.

I blow out a breath and consider waiting by the entrance, but Milton blows my cover. "Good evening, Ms. Bradley."

I smile and wave, and at his words, Maverick turns around.

The doors open, and he steps on. So does the couple behind him, and I get on behind them.

The doors seal the four of us in, and the man turns to Maverick. "How much longer until you're in? Because Fletcher is good, but he can't read defense the way you can, and he certainly can't command a field like you."

"Depends what the doctors say. I'm hopeful I'll be cleared for full practice this week," he says. I study him as he answers. He keeps his eyes on the electronic numbers as they flip, and I glance up there, too. Six, seven, eight, nine.

"We need you back, man," the man says.

I wait for Maverick to respond with more than the press of his lips that nobody would mistake for a smile, but he doesn't.

So when we both get off on the seventeenth floor, I smile at the couple and head toward my door.

The elevator doors close, and we're both in front of our doors, sliding our keys into the locks, when I turn toward him.

"What the hell was that?" I demand.

He turns around, his key in the lock and the rest of his key fob dangling the same way mine does. His gaze meets mine, and it lingers before he takes a step toward me. "What the hell was what?"

"That couple. The man was so nice. So complimentary. And you barely acknowledged him."

"I answered his question," he protests. He didn't spare a second of a glance for the couple in the elevator, but his eyes are glued to mine now. He takes another step, and our doors aren't really all that far apart. Two more steps, and he'd be in my orbit. Close enough to smell. Close enough to...

I force it away before I finish that thought.

"Yeah, and then he said 'we need you back,' and you couldn't even be bothered to form a smile." And then, before I know what I'm even saying, I add, "Wonder why everyone hates you? That's why!"

My hands are shaking. He's coming closer. Too close. I lean against my door.

His brows crash together as he closes the gap. "Everyone can hate me all they want. I've told you before, and I'll say it again. I don't give a fuck." He moves until his body aligns with mine, and I can feel the heat rolling off him as my eyes flick up to his. His body is big over mine. He's nearly a foot taller than me, especially when I'm wearing the flat Converse I wore with jeans and an Aces tee to the game today.

His eyes are flashing, and his breathing is labored.

I feel like I can't catch my own breath as the smell of his expensive cologne lingers far too close to me.

"Why do you hate the world, Maverick?" I ask, my voice going from loud to soft between sentences.

He doesn't react to my question. Instead, he angles his head down a little, and my breath hitches somewhere in the back of my throat. I swear to God I can hear my knees knocking together as the rush of my pounding heart throbs in my ears.

My eyes flick to his lips for just half a second, and a fire ignites in my chest as butterflies flutter around my ribs.

He leans down, and his nose brushes against mine. He's going to kiss me, and God, do I want him to kiss me. I close my eyes as I breathe him in, and I wait for his lips to connect with mine.

Somewhere in the back of my mind, I know it's wrong. All wrong. I shouldn't be doing this. I can't do this. He's a client. I can't get involved with him. But what if getting involved is what we need? What if it opens the doors to why he is the way he is? What if it allows him to finally confess everything to me, to let me in, to let me help him? It's a gamble, but it's one I'm willing to take to get the job done. I won't let my heart get involved, that's all.

Aside from the beating of it. The *racing* of it.

The pounding in my ears is so loud, and the desire for him to kiss me is so strong and sure that I don't even hear him as he moves away.

He pulls back, and it takes a second for the air conditioning in the building to sweep down from the air vents, but when it does, that's when I notice his heat is no longer pressed against me.

My eyes fly open as my cheeks burn with embarrassment. I must look like an idiot standing here waiting for him to kiss me when that was probably never his intent at all.

Our eyes meet, and the heat in his has shifted back to icy cold detachment. "I don't make mistakes, sweetheart." His voice drips with sarcasm on the last word.

Tears bite behind my eyes at his cruel words, but I can't let it get to me.

I was mistaken, that's all.

It's embarrassing, but life moves on.

It's time to get back to work and figure out this puzzle that I can't seem to strategize my way out of.

CHAPTER 12

MAVERICK JENNINGS

She's Fucking with Me

She was too close.

Too close in proximity, yes. That too. She smelled like fucking wildflowers and sunshine, and I don't do flowers *or* sunshine. But it wasn't that.

She was too close to getting in.

I don't let anyone in, but being that close to her felt like something woke up inside me.

But giving that side of me life again would only spell the end of everything I've come to know. Working from a place of anger allows me to perform the way I do on the field. Like the man on the elevator said, I command the field. If I'm a less intense version of myself, that might be the trade-off.

In essence, having my life ruined and my heart broken turned me into the valuable player I am today. The brass at Dallas doesn't like my personality? They dealt with it for years when I put up numbers. But then they took the rest of my offense away from me, and it's a team effort. I didn't keep my mouth shut about it, and they didn't like that.

So here I am.

Fighting another day in a new city.

And once I'm cleared to get back on the field, this city will grow to love my numbers, too. My accuracy. My command. Nobody gives a shit about who I am off the field as long as I'm performing on it—or at least they didn't until I came here.

If only fucking Dex hadn't taken that away, forcing me to sit out of the first four games of the season.

I don't give a fuck how I feel next week when I meet with Dr. Baker. I'm playing next Sunday. I'll fake my way through the exam if I have to.

But the rest of it? I think I may be stuck with this woman who literally makes a living out of getting under my skin.

I head to the newest lounge in Vegas, the one Ben Olson took me to the night my rant about Dex went viral. The place is called Legacy, and to be quite honest, I don't give a fuck about the white marble floors with gold veins or the leather chairs.

I like that I won the night I went there with Olson.

I got the membership the night I went with him. It's exclusive and invitation-only, but I'm in now that I've been invited by a member. I opened a credit line that night, and tonight I plan to use that to continue my winning streak.

Only it doesn't quite go that way.

Last time I won, but tonight, I'm losing.

I'm running up a huge tab on blackjack, but I can't seem to stop. I keep thinking my luck will turn around. Then a woman in a tightly fitted French maid outfit brings me more scotch, and every time my glass even comes close to empty, she swings by with another one. In the past, maybe my eyes would have followed her ass each time she walked away, but tonight, I'm focused on the cards. I'm not sure why, and I think that's what's distracting me. That and the fact that this woman keeps bringing me alcohol while I lose more and more and more and drink more and more and more.

I have a limit in my head for how high I'll go, and then I blow past it and set another limit.

It's exactly the behavior this kind of place wants.

I blow out a breath as I lose another hand.

Shit's just not in my favor tonight.

I'm halfway to drunk when I decide to call it, and I head up to the bar to get one more round before I head home. At least that's the plan.

Until I spot *her* sitting at the bar.

Yes, that's right. Everleigh Fucking Bradley is sitting at the bar in this VIP lounge that she has no business whatsoever being at. She's fucking with me. Again. She probably followed me here.

She raises a brow as she raises her glass in my direction. "Seems we had the same idea for escaping each other tonight."

"Yet another failure," I mutter.

She pats the empty stool beside her. "Come on. I'm really not so bad."

"I beg to differ." I don't know why I slide onto the stool as she chuckles at my response, but I do. The scotch, probably. Sober me would know this is a bad idea.

Drunk me knows it, too. He just doesn't give a fuck.

"What are you doing here?" I ask her.

She toys with the cocktail straw in her glass, and I pluck mine out of my glass and start to chew on it.

Her eyes follow my straw, and I glance at her glass. It's filled with some clear liquid over ice. It's bubbling, so I'd guess it's soda, possibly mixed with something since a lime is perched on the edge of the glass.

"Checking the place out," she says.

"How'd you get in?" I ask. I don't say the words, but I thought this was a VIP lounge.

She narrows her eyes at my insinuation. "Through the front door. Probably the same way you did."

I roll my eyes.

"Dex," she murmurs.

"Of course."

She opens her mouth to say something else but seems to think better of it. She shakes her head a little. "What about you? What are you doing here?"

"Blowing through way too much cash and drinking the complimentary Lagavulin 16."

"You're a scotch guy?" she asks.

I glance over at her. "You know scotch?"

"You don't grow up with five brothers and not learn a thing or two about single malts."

"And yet, you're sipping on a vodka soda," I say, venturing a guess.

She holds up her glass. "Casamigos."

"You're a tequila girl?"

"You seem surprised by that." She tips the glass to her lips, and I watch enraptured as the liquid moves from the glass to her mouth.

"I am."

She chuckles. "Why?"

"I guess I associate cheap tequila with college girls and what you've got in your glass with trend chasers." I raise a brow and nod to her glass.

"Trend chasers?" she demands. She shakes her head at the insult. "I drink it because it tastes good, not because I give a fuck about trends."

"Don't you? Isn't part of your entire *life's work* to chase trends?" I point out, using her own words from earlier.

"You're an asshole. Do you know that?"

"I'm aware. And you resort to insults when you've run out of creativity."

"Well, then I guess we've got each other pegged," she says, and I have the sudden urge to kiss her, to taste that tequila on her tongue. To feel those pretty lips as they move against mine.

To take her back to the condo building we share and cut to the right instead of the left once we get off the elevator. To show her a good time just for a few hours, and then return to my own home to sit in regret.

Yeah, it's a bad idea.

But just because I'm aware that it's a bad idea doesn't mean it's going to stop me from doing it anyway.

I order another scotch.

She orders another tequila soda.

The more I drink, the more I want to act on the attraction between us.

I know she wants it. I saw the way her breath hitched when I got close to her. I could feel her heart pounding against my chest when I backed her up against her door.

I wanted to kiss her then, too.

I wasn't drunk then, though. I had enough wits left about me to stop myself.

But tonight, all that shit's out the window.

We're both staring into our drinks, contemplating probably opposite ideas, when some guy walks up on her other side and shouts to the bartender.

"Coors for me and whatever the lady's having," he says, indicating Everleigh. He turns to her. "Nick Crawford," he says, his tone cocky and assuming, as if everyone has heard of him.

Newsflash. I haven't.

"The fuck you think you're doing?" I demand.

He holds up both hands. "Sorry, man. Didn't know you two were together."

"We're not," she assures him. "I'm Everleigh. You can ignore him. We work together."

He glares at me. "You're that football player, aren't you?"

"*That* football player? Which one?" I challenge.

He chuckles. "Definitely a football player with the way you're puffing your chest up right now."

Everleigh presses her lips together, and I think it might be because she's hiding a smile.

Well, she won't be smiling anymore after what I'm about to do. "The fuck you just say to me?" I ask, rising off the stool and barreling around Everleigh and toward this dickwad.

This *might* be the sort of attitude Dallas was done with when they traded me to Vegas.

"I said you're acting like a tough guy. Stand down, soldier."

I can't tell if he's drunk, too, or if I misheard him, but in any event, it's far too condescending. Nobody talks to me that way.

Somewhere in the periphery, I hear Everleigh's voice. "Maverick, stop!"

But it's too late. Nothing can stop this train wreck.

I won't stand for some douchebag insulting me.

I pull my arm back, and my fist collides with his jaw. It's nearly slow motion as he grabs the place of my offense, and I drop my hand as I shake it out at the pain that explodes with the contact of his jaw.

I'm sure I'll get in trouble for that tomorrow.

Maybe I'll even feel bad about it for a change.

I think I'm starting to *want* to feel things again.

And I'm afraid it might be because of the beautiful woman who's determined to ruin my life.

CHAPTER 13

Everleigh Bradley

I Don't Think You're Broken

What a mess.

I'm a brand strategist, not a public relations coordinator, but it seems I'm supposed to be both for Maverick—according to Jack, anyway. I feel like I'm stepping into unknown territory, maybe especially because I've never represented a football player before. Even as I think it, I realize I've never actually represented an *individual* before. It's always been a corporation or an organization.

I'm not quite sure who to hit up. I text my brother first since he's the closest person I have locally, and as an added bonus, he lives in the same building as the two of us.

Me: *Maverick drunkenly punched someone at Dad's lounge. What would you do?*

His reply is pretty quick.

Dex: *Do nothing. Let him sleep it off.*

He's literally no help at all, and I'm not sure I should be sharing details with him considering the animosity between the two men.

I'm lost, but I feel like I met someone who can help.

I have a budget from the Aces. I don't care if Maverick hasn't agreed to my terms. I'm the one running the show here.

Me: *I'm so sorry to bother you, and I know he's not your client, but Maverick's drunk, and he just punched Nick Crawford at a VIP lounge. Can you help?*

Ellie's reply is quick.

Ellie: *Crisis management. Contact his lawyer, contain the issue, and control the narrative. Are you still at the scene?*

Me: *No, we're in a car on our way back home.*

Ellie: *Good. Keep him off socials, sober him up, and we'll work damage control in the morning. Come by my house at nine.*

She sends me her address.

Me: *Are you sure? And thank you. If you don't mind, could you draw up a contract for representation? If he doesn't sign it in the morning, I will on behalf of the Aces.*

Ellie: *I'll have it ready at nine. And I'll have Luke grab some chocolate croissants from Ava Nash's bakery. Best in town!*

It's after midnight on a Sunday night after game day, and she's positive, professional, and readily available. Now *that* is the kind of friend I'm looking for in Vegas.

That's the kind of friend I'm looking for *anywhere*, to be honest.

Except for Penny, I suppose I've let my friendships fall by the wayside in favor of working my way up. But all my life, the majority of my friendships have been fleeting. I've never had a girl gang. I grew up surrounded by boys who played sports, and I was dragged to their games whether or not I wanted to be there.

The way I see it, friendships come and go. My career will last me the rest of my life.

Is that a part of the reason that I'm thirty-two and single? Possibly. Probably.

But the other, much larger part of the reason that I'm thirty-two and single has everything to do with Billy Hawthorne.

I fell in love with Billy when I was twenty-two. God, an entire decade ago.

He didn't fall in love with me until I was twenty-nine.

We were together two years, two days.

He ended it because he was afraid of commitment. We'd gotten to the point where we needed to make a decision on our future together, and he ran.

It's been six months. I've picked up the pieces. I've started moving on.

And it actually sort of helps to be moving on in a place where I don't run the risk of seeing him day after day. We didn't work together or even for the same company, but we worked in the same building. I started at Langford fresh out of college along with Penny, and he was two floors up at a law firm. He was just a mid-level associate, two years older than me at the time I first saw him in the elevator.

Penny was with me. We agreed he was hot as hell, but she was in a relationship at the time with the man she eventually married and now has two boys with.

I saw him again the next day, and the next. My crush grew. We rode the elevator up every morning, and sometimes I'd see him around lunchtime, but I never saw him when I left at five. So I started staying later. I didn't see him at six, either, or seven. But eight seemed to be the magic hour.

Yep, that's right. Independent boss bitch Everleigh Bradley stayed later, worked harder, took on more clients, and built her entire career for the chance to run into the object of her most serious crush to date. Looking back, even *I* am disappointed in my own behavior. I chalk it up to being young and naïve, but on the other hand, it worked. I held onto hope, and eventually it happened.

Something inside me told me he was different, that we were destined to be together.

We both had a strong work ethic. We had a lot in common, actually. We had the same values. We liked the same kinds of movies, music, and television shows, and I always thought that was part of what made our connection so strong and stable.

But when talk of kids came up, he shut down. When the idea of marriage came up, he'd change the subject.

He was happy where we were, and I was ready for more.

So when I pushed too hard for what I wanted, he opted out.

The first month after the breakup was the roughest. I'd given up my personal life when I chose to stay late at the office each night all those years before. Sure, I still got invitations at the beginning, but they dwindled each time I issued the same rejection. *Sorry, staying late at the office tonight.*

I stayed close with Penny since we worked together, but she was busy planning a wedding, so we really only saw each other during the workday.

I had exactly three things in my life aside from Pen: my career, Billy, and, to a lesser extent, my family. And when Billy left me, I clung a little more tightly to the two things I had remaining.

I tried to be closer to my parents, but my father was always asking me to sign oddball documents, and my oldest brother, Madden, would often call and tell me not to do whatever my father was asking.

My mother is a whole other story.

I was always jealous of my friends who would go on shopping dates with their moms, or girls' trips, or even something as silly as a pedicure night. My mom invited me to go get fillers with her once, but it wasn't because she wanted to spend time with me. It was because of the dark circles under my eyes from getting up too early and staying up too late.

I couldn't lean into my family the way I wanted to, but damn if I'm not always trying to fix it anyway. Forcing family dinners when we're in close proximity with each other. Calling my siblings to keep in touch. Creating a group chat for the seven of us when I'm the one who always starts every conversation. Inviting my mom on those shopping trips even if I'm not ready for fillers.

And that left me with one thing: my career. I dove headfirst into it, putting everything else in my life into second place—those family group chats included.

Now it feels like my career is being ripped away, too, because of the drunken idiot who's currently passed out beside me in the car on the way back to the building we both live in.

Milton helps me wake Maverick enough to get him on his feet so he can walk himself upstairs, and I'm forever grateful for Milton's help.

He's subdued on the way up to our floor, and he fumbles with his keys for a few beats. He seems to be moving around just fine, so maybe he's not as drunk as I thought. Maybe he wasn't drunk at all, and he was pretending to be asleep in the car so we didn't need to have a conversation. It's probably for the best. I'm a little tipsy myself.

Before he disappears into his condo, I say, "I booked a meeting with Ellie Dalton at nine tomorrow morning. We can go together. Let's meet in the lobby around eight forty, okay?"

He doesn't reply.

"Hey!" I yell, and he turns to look at me. "Set an alarm for eight. I'll bang on your door to remind you."

He grunts, and he's still messing around with his keys.

"Do you need any help?" I ask.

"No," he mutters, and he gets the door open and slams it after he walks through it. I wait until I hear the slide of the lock, and then I move toward my own door.

Before I even get my own keys out to unlock it, though, Maverick's door flies open again.

I turn to look at him, and there's fire in his eyes as he pins them on me.

My chest tightens under his scrutiny. God, he's hot.

"Why haven't you given up on me yet?" he demands.

"We've only been working together a couple of weeks. Why would I give up on you?"

He lifts a shoulder. "Everyone always does."

I wonder if he'd be so candid if he were sober.

"I won't." I say it simply, but the silence that spans between us after my voice quiets seems to say more. It seems to imply that it doesn't have to do with the job so much as the person.

I'm starting to care.

He's an enigma, and I'm a problem solver.

I always have been.

"Why not?" he challenges. It feels like he's trying to get me to admit that I care.

"Because it's not in my nature to give up. I'm a problem solver, Maverick. I'm a fixer."

He takes a step toward me, and it's menacing. "You think you can fix me?"

I shake my head, my eyes steady on his. "I don't think you're broken."

He scoffs. "You're dead wrong about that."

"What's broken?" I whisper.

He presses his lips together as he does his best to mask the flash of pain I see cross his face. He's hurting. He's hiding something. There's some reason he's chosen to lash out at the world, and I'm going to get to the bottom of what it is. I'm going to find what's broken, and I'm going to figure out how to fix it.

He remains tight-lipped.

"It's okay, Maverick," I say softly. "You can trust me."

A small huff escapes him. I don't mistake it for a chuckle. It's more like a puff of disbelieving air. "You're too pretty to trust."

My brows raise. "Excuse me?"

"You can't trust the pretty ones," he says.

"You're drunk."

"Maybe. But it's still true. And you're as fucking pretty as they come, Ev." It's the first time he's called me Ev. Hell, it might be the first time he's used my name at all.

"Stop flirting with me," I scold softly.

"Is that really what you want?" he asks, and his low rasp causes butterflies to take flight in my belly.

I can't answer that. The truth is no. I don't want him to stop. But we can't take this into a new territory *sober*, never mind when he's been drinking.

"Goodnight, Maverick." I turn toward my door, unlock it, let myself in, and close it without looking back.

Because I know if I look back, I'll see him standing there, and I'm quite sure I won't be able to stop what would inevitably happen next.

CHAPTER 14
Everleigh Bradley

I Love That For Me

I glance at my watch when I feel it vibrating against my wrist.

Billy Hawthorne flashes on the screen, and my stomach turns.

Why would Billy be calling me? I don't answer, obviously. I can't. I'm in a meeting with Ellie and Maverick, and we're drafting a crisis management plan.

"So you were there?" Ellie asks me, and I shake off the distraction of my phone call and send it to voicemail.

I nod.

"Can you describe to me *exactly* what happened?"

"Sure. So we were sitting at the bar, and Nick Crawford came up and offered to buy me a drink. Maverick went off on him since we'd been talking *even though we weren't there together*, we'd only run into each other, and—"

"You don't need to give *that* much detail," Maverick whines.

I lift a shoulder and offer him a glare as I turn back to Ellie. I blow out a breath. "Anyway, Nick made some dumb comment about how Maverick was acting like a tough guy, which Maverick clearly didn't like, and he hauled off and clocked the guy in the jaw."

Ellie closes her eyes for a second and shakes her head. "I'll put in a request for video footage from the lounge, but because it's a VIP place, it may be hard to get."

"My father owns it," I admit.

Maverick's head whips in my direction. "What?"

I glance over at him. "It's why I was there. Dex mentioned it, and I was curious, so I went."

"The pocket I was feeding money into is *your father's?*" Maverick demands, and I laugh.

"Did you lose last night?"

"Twenty K!" he yells.

I can't help my giggle. "Sucks for you, but sounds like it'll pay my future kids' college tuition, so at least you know it's going to a good cause."

He's glaring and sulking at the same time, and I can't help but love the irony of it all. I only showed up because Dex, this dude's mortal enemy, told me about the place.

I love that for me.

I love how angry he is right now, and I'm not sure why.

I want to keep pressing his buttons.

Instead of dreading this job, I'm actually starting to *like* it. Who would've thought?

"Be that as it may, we have an issue to deal with. I need your lawyer's contact info. I'll get in touch with the team, and we'll sell it like you were standing up for Everleigh." She doesn't ask if that's okay, and instead, she turns to her laptop. "Let's issue a statement." She starts tapping on her keyboard. "I'll issue it. Maverick Jennings's publicity team is aware of the incident involving him and another man last night at an exclusive VIP lounge in Vegas. We are gathering details and will release a statement once investigations have been completed. Thank you in advance for privacy as we handle this matter."

"Do we have to issue that?" he asks.

"You need to control the narrative, my friend. This is the way," she tells him. "Next, we'll need you to read a statement. Something apologetic. Hm."

"No," he says, interrupting her before she even gets started. "I'm not issuing an apologetic statement when I'm not sorry."

Ellie glances at me and jerks her thumb at Maverick. "Is he always like this?"

I nod and purse my lips. "Always."

"Maverick, you realize the team could suspend you, right?" she asks.

"The fuck difference does it make when I'm already sitting?" he asks.

I mean…it's a fair point.

"You know what they'll do. They'll have Dr. Baker *clear* me a week early, I'll serve my time, and I'll be back on the field when I was supposed to be." He puts air quotes around the word *clear*.

"Is that how they did things in Dallas?" Her eyes study Maverick carefully. "Because in Vegas, that's not how we operate. You won't be cleared until you're medically healthy to play, and then you'll serve out any sentence deemed appropriate by the team and the league."

He huffs out a sigh. "It's not the first time I slugged an asshole who had it coming, and it won't be the last."

"It'll be the last here in Vegas, Maverick," Ellie warns. "You need to get control of yourself if you want to step foot on that field. I know Jack and Lincoln, and they won't stand for this kind of behavior."

"Can I issue the statement?" I ask Ellie.

She nods. "Of course. It might be better coming from you anyway. It'll explain why you're by his side all the time. Just the intro to the Vegas media circus you were searching for, right?"

I chuckle, and I see her email pop through, so I format it and send it off to the local outlets while she taps around on her computer and Maverick sits there looking uncomfortable.

Ellie looks up. "I was gifted two tickets to the Hope Gala in LA next Monday. You can attend with Everleigh."

I glance over at him. I don't particularly want to attend as his date, but that's not really what this would be. It would be him taking part in a charity event—and a big one, too. She's right. Normally he wouldn't be able to attend an event of this scale, so why not use this time off to our advantage? It'll show him doing some good for once instead of constantly making the *wrong* sorts of headlines.

"No," he says at the same time I say, "Yes."

Ellie purses her lips and turns to me. "Hotels might be tight since the event is sold out, but it'll be the perfect place for him to start showing he cares about more than just himself. The mission is to offer hope and opportunities to underserved youth in the greater Los Angeles area," she says, reading from her screen.

"Thanks, Ellie. It's a great idea." I look up the event, find the location, and book a two-bedroom suite at the hotel where the event is being held, and then I book us two plane tickets, too.

If he won't give me material to work with or ideas for what sorts of ways he can impact the community in a more positive way, Ellie and I will have to work together to create these opportunities for him.

And if he doesn't like it? Too damn bad.

"You should talk to your publicist back in Dallas and let them know we're handling things here in Vegas. Too many cooks in the kitchen, you know?" Ellie suggests.

He gives her a death stare, but he taps something out on his phone anyway.

We leave Ellie's place shortly after that. It felt like a productive morning despite the hell of a time he gave me when I banged on his door at eight o'clock to get him out of bed. I called him first, and when he didn't answer, I sent Lincoln a text to let him know he wasn't answering me.

I hate to be a tattletale, but I'm just doing my job.

"I'm not going to Los Angeles with you," he hisses when we're in the car. I drove despite his protests, but on the way to Ellie's, I explained what we were doing while he sipped black coffee from a tumbler. He was clearly not at one hundred percent this morning, and I couldn't pretend like I wasn't getting the tiniest bit of joy out of putting the music up to a volume that was just a little higher than background noise.

He seems less hungover now than he was when we drove here, but less hungover apparently means more objectionable and louder.

"I'm sorry to say that in fact you are," I say as I merge onto the highway.

"I hate this," he mutters.

"I know. It's not a walk in the park for me, either."

He glances over at me. "How'd you end up stuck with me?"

I keep my eyes on the road as I give him my full, honest answer. "I work for a marketing firm in Chicago. I guess Jack Dalton is friends with my boss, and he asked for my boss's best brand strategist. I gave up thirty-two clients in Chicago for one in Vegas with the hope that I can launch my own branding firm once our term is up."

"Did you know it was going to be me?"

I shake my head. "In fact, I told my boss I didn't want to work with an athlete." My voice is dry as I say it.

"Why not?"

"I have five brothers who are all professional athletes. I'm sure you can piece together why."

"Spell it out," he says.

I can't help my laugh at the irony. "That's why."

"What is?"

"You're all the same. Demanding. Egotistical. Annoying." I shrug. "I wanted to build my own thing separate from their world, and somehow I ended up in it anyway."

He turns and looks out the side window. "So why take the job?"

"Well, for one, I didn't know who I'd be working with when I took it. But my main motivation is that I want to open my own branding firm, and my boss opened that door for me by giving me this."

"Did you want to come to Vegas?" he asks.

I shake my head. "Nope. I love Chicago. I miss it every day. My best friend is back there, my family. I like being close to Dex, Ainsley, and Jack, but I haven't had a ton of free time lately." I sigh. "Did you want to come to Vegas?"

"No. I got a fucking custom silver and navy paint job on a truck that sticks out like a sore thumb in Aces country. A star tattoo on my shoulder. I thought I'd start and end my career in Dallas, but I guess the football gods had other plans."

"I thought I'd start and end my career in Chicago," I admit. "Where did you grow up?"

"Ohio."

"You're a Midwestern boy?" I ask.

"Born and bred." He lifts a shoulder.

"You wouldn't go back?"

"Fuck no. I don't miss the snow and ice in the winters," he says. Those are his words, but his voice gives a subtext that makes me think there's more to the story than snow and ice keeping him from Ohio.

"Do you still have family there?"

"Yeah," he says vaguely.

"Who?"

He clears his throat. "My mom's in Cincinnati. She's not doing well. My dad, who knows. He's a fuckin' deadbeat anyway."

Somehow I'm not shocked he's not close with his family. "Sorry to hear about your mom. Any siblings?"

This is the most I've gotten out of him since the day we met, and it's honestly a little…refreshing. Unexpected, that's for sure.

He shakes his head. "No."

"My dad always talks about the Bradley legacy. How his kids are the family legacy. Something to think about with your own legacy, anyway."

"You've got a litter of siblings, right?"

"Six. Five brothers, one sister, and me. The boys are mostly scattered, but Madden has a place in Chicago, and Liam's still there. My sister's there. I try to keep everyone in a close circle, but it's a lot to wrangle, and it's not always very easy."

"You're a wrangler."

I huff out a chuckle. He's not wrong.

I pull into the parking garage, and that seems to end our conversation. That's the most I've gotten out of him since we started working together, and the pieces are slowly starting to click into place.

Something happened with his parents, perhaps. Something that made relationships even harder for him despite the marriage.

God, I still can't picture him with a woman. He's too gruff. Too grumpy. I can't picture him having fun or taking pleasure.

I bet he's a hell of a good time in bed, though.

I shove the intrusive thought away.

We bid each other goodbye, a rare pleasantry between us versus him slamming his door when I'm mid-sentence. Though I'm sort of open to the idea of him pushing me up against the door and running his nose along mine again, just this time ending with a kiss instead of a harsh remark about how he doesn't make mistakes.

I finally listen to the voicemail from Billy.

"Hey, Ev, it's me. It's been a while, huh? I've been thinking about you. A lot. I heard you moved to Vegas. I'll be in town next week on business and would love to meet for a drink."

He's been thinking about me? A lot? And he wants to meet for a drink?

I blow out a breath.

He was supposed to be my greatest love story, but he turned out to be my greatest heartbreak.

It took me a long time to feel like I'd gotten over him, and I've never really believed in second chances when it comes to love. It didn't work out once. Why would it work out the next time? People don't change. Not really. People are who they are at their core despite the different masks they try to wear to cover it up.

Like Maverick. I think at his core, he's not a bad guy. He's played football his whole life, and I've learned enough about being on a team from my brothers to know that those types of relationships can easily be fleeting. Between injuries, trades, retirements, practice squads, salary caps, and draft picks, players come and go every season. I don't think there's ever been a team that kept all fifty-three men for back-to-back seasons without some movement.

And on top of that, players tend to be absent for big chunks of time during the season, which makes it hard to maintain relationships with people who aren't a part of that lifestyle.

I can see why he has a hard time letting people in.

And I'm working hard to unlock the way in so I can see what's under those masks he's keeping firmly in place.

But Billy? He never wore a mask. He wasn't ready for commitment, and I don't believe that six months later he is.

But…what if he is?

What if he realized life sucks without me and wants me back?

I realized how much it sucked without him the moment he ended things. I went home to an empty house. He'd been staying over nearly every night for two years, and I saw him everywhere.

I missed having him to come home to. I missed commuting to the office building together even though we didn't work together. I missed lunch dates when he could get away. I missed having someone to kiss goodnight. I missed having someone's hand in mine.

I longed for it all for a long time. I craved it.

But we've been apart now long enough for me to have forgotten the minor details that I missed so much when we first broke up.

I've found myself again. Billy didn't like my red lipstick, so I wear it all the time now. He thought bright colors were too overstated and preferred a more monochromatic palette except for the occasional navy or brown.

I've found color in my world again.

I had a one-night stand a couple of months ago.

I can't say I'd do that again, but I got to experience it.

I don't *love* the dating process. I'd love to find someone and for things to just magically fall into place.

And maybe that'll happen here in Vegas. Maybe it won't happen until I return home to Chicago next year.

Or maybe it'll happen if I agree to a drink with someone I thought had already been written out of my story.

CHAPTER 15

MAVERICK JENNINGS

Red Means Danger

My feet slap against the treadmill as I work out a few days later.

My rib's feeling better. I can move with only minor pain now, and I have an appointment with Dr. Baker this morning after a quick meeting with Everleigh.

I wasn't expecting to open up to her on the way back from Ellie's place, and maybe I didn't. But it felt like I did.

I don't talk about my parents to anyone. Ever.

But I told her about my mom. All I said is *she's not doing well.* I didn't give her the bigger picture that some days she doesn't know who I am, other days she thinks I'm a little kid, and still other days she's totally functional. Alzheimer's is a bitch of a disease, that's for sure. Watching her deteriorate has been hell, and I live with the guilt of not being by her side as she navigates this cruel disease.

I keep her note behind a photo of the two of us taken at my wedding. It's the only trace I have left that I was once married, and I only keep it out because it's my mom.

I memorized the note long ago. She wrote it to me right after her diagnosis, long before we knew how bad it would get.

It's short and sweet, much like her.

You come first. Always. Never allow my illness to take away from your own life.

She's at the best memory care facility Ohio offers. I get back to visit a few times a year, usually in the offseason.

I suppose it's why I was protective over my answer when Everleigh asked me where I like to travel.

But she's starting to wear me down, I guess. I'm starting to *want* to confide these things in her, and I'm not sure why yet. Maybe because she refuses to give up on me.

Nobody has ever done that for me...except my mom, who had no clue who I was when I last saw her.

It's heartbreaking. It makes it hard to go, but I do it anyway.

She didn't deserve to be treated like shit by my asshole father. She deserved a better life than the one she got. It's why I did everything I could to take care of her as soon as I could afford to. It's why I pay for the best medical care now.

I can't be there physically and listen to the words in her note at the same time, so I do what I can from a distance.

Even if she never knows it.

She made sacrifices for me my entire life, and I try to return the favor.

I told Everleigh about my dad, too. *He's a fuckin' deadbeat.*

That's all I care to say on that matter. It's still more than I've told most people.

I finish my sprint and slow to a walk for a few minutes before I power down the machine. I make a protein shake and sip it as I study the view out my window.

I take a shower, and as I brush against my cock, I think about jerking off.

But then I realize who is in my head.

The red lipstick.

The red dress.

The black heels with the red bottom.

Red means danger, like when the opposing team is nearing the red zone and we have to stop them. Thinking about her when my cock is hard and in my hand is about the most dangerous sport I can play right now.

I can't seem to stop myself, though. I picture those red-lined lips wrapped around me as I pull short strokes, focusing on the head. Hot water beats down on me, and I lean back against the cold tile of the shower wall as I feel heat starting to pulse through me.

I grunt as I pick up the pace, and I squeeze my eyes shut when I feel the heat ignite as it tears through me. "Fuck," I grunt, and her face flashes through my mind just as my cum erupts out of me. It seems to go on and on as each new pulse spills more cum, and I sag back against the wall for a beat once my release has passed through me. I rinse my cum down the drain, holding both my fist and the head of my cock under the water to wash it away like it never happened.

But it did happen, and twenty minutes later, I'm slightly relaxed and also slightly mortified as I take a seat across from her in the conference room of our building.

She's wearing that goddamn red lipstick again.

I blow out a breath.

"I secured our air travel for the charity event on Monday," she begins.

"What if I'm cleared to play?"

"Shouldn't affect our schedule. We fly in early Monday, and it's back to Vegas Tuesday afternoon. We're getting some positive response to spinning the *fight* at the lounge over the weekend as you defending a woman, namely, me. A teammate's sister. A teammate who you've recently spoken out against. It's actually all coming together nicely," she says, scanning her notes as she talks. "I'll need you to continue to stay off socials while we work behind the scenes on your image. With that said, Ellie has a handful of sponsorship opportunities we'd like you to take a look at."

Well. These women work fast, that's for damn sure.

They have connections that I guess I didn't realize. Having Ellie Dalton on my side is probably a bigger advantage than I first thought. Maybe having Everleigh fighting for me is, too.

I think about my parents again. I don't give a shit about my dad, but the legacy my mother is leaving behind is, well, *me*, and apart from being good at football, I don't think I'm doing justice to the legacy she would wish for me.

When Everleigh mentioned that yesterday, it was the first time I ever thought about how the way I act could reflect negatively on my mother. How what I do could affect *her* legacy.

For the first time, it made me want to *be* better. For her.

"Show me," I say.

She pushes a contract toward me, and the first one is for a sports drink. The next is for a luxury watch brand, and then a tech startup, a meal prep company, and a line of athletic apparel.

They're all fine. Nothing that will change the world. Nothing that will make it a better place…which leads me to wonder something. "What's the purpose of these?"

"I mean, the main goal of sponsorships is to make money outside of your contract, right? But in terms of what we're doing here, we're crafting an image. You get to choose who you want to be. Purely an athlete who's always grinding and working hard? Take the sports drink and apparel. Want to pull off a more polished, elite feel? The watch. Want to seem innovative? The tech startup. And the meal prep, this one in particular, could make you appear like you're just a normal guy who still needs to eat when you get home from work. It gives a *just like us* vibe that could connect you to your fanbase."

"What if I just want to sponsor products I actually like and would use?" I ask.

She lifts a shoulder. "Then that's the image you're portraying. If you'd start being less aggressive with me, we could possibly craft that image together and go from there."

I clench my jaw and grit my teeth a bit at the thought. I *have* been an asshole toward her, but it's nothing new. It's how I am toward everyone.

"The first one. The athlete always grinding. Except when a teammate injures me." I gingerly pat my ribs.

Her lips lift in the smallest smile. "Okay, that's a good start. So yes on the drink and the apparel?"

"I'm not elite or innovative, so those are a no." I push those papers to the side. "This one, though. The meal plan. I could be a normal guy who needs to eat when he gets home."

"And the best part is they're not just paying you, but they'll send you free meals for the next year."

I wrinkle my nose. "I eat pretty clean."

"Then you take in the shipment and pass them over to your neighbor," she says pointedly.

I very nearly laugh. Almost. It's more of a grunt, as if I have to rewire my entire being in order to actually make myself laugh again, but it's the closest I've been in a long time.

"Deal."

"Maybe we can even whip them up together sometime," she says absently.

"Are you asking me on a date?" I ask.

Her eyes widen, and her cheeks turn nearly the same shade as her lips. "No!"

Another grunt that's nearly a chuckle.

She huffs a little as she pulls out a pen so I can sign the contracts I've agreed to. She practically yanks them back after I sign each one, and it's actually quite amusing to see her a little flustered.

"Your appointment with Dr. Baker is in thirty minutes. Jack would like me to attend with you," she says.

I nod. "Let's meet there. I'm going to train a bit afterward, and you don't need to stick around for that."

"If you don't mind, I'd like to. I need to get an idea of what you do, and if we're going with the grinding athlete angle, I'll need to take photos of you in action so we can start building a social media campaign showcasing that."

"Fine."

We head toward the practice facility in our own cars, a welcome separation. Sometimes being in the same room as her gets overwhelming. I guess I'm not used to spending so much time with a single person.

Even when I was married, we didn't spend this much time together. At first, maybe. But things change. Life changes. It's the one constant, I think.

"Everything looks good, Maverick. You're cleared to return to light practice. I want you to sit out of the game one more week, but depending on how things go, you may be able to start as soon as next Sunday," Dr. Baker tells me after the exam.

Even Everleigh looks excited. Maybe we both feel a bit of joy because now we'll have even more separation.

But as soon as I have the thought, I know it's wrong—for two reasons.

One, she's got my schedule and a free pass to every part of my life on the field thanks to Jack.

And two…the thought of more separation from her isn't pulsing the kind of joy inside that I was expecting it to.

CHAPTER 16

Everleigh Bradley

Secret Appointment

I glance through the calendar and see a time slot blocked off tomorrow morning bright and early before Maverick's four-week checkup with Dr. Baker at the Complex. It doesn't say *what* the activity is, but since I'm supposed to shadow him everywhere, it looks like I'll be getting up before the sun tomorrow.

When I meet with him in the evening, I ask him about it. "What's this?" I point to the digital calendar I have pulled up with the five thirty to six thirty time block.

"A weekly appointment," he grunts.

I thought we were getting past the grunting after he punched some guy who dared to look in my direction, but apparently I stand corrected.

"For what?"

He tilts his head and studies me, and he looks away when he answers. "Something I do weekly when I can."

"That doesn't answer my question." I purse my lips. "Is there any chance I'll get to do this myself?"

I shake my head.

"Right, then I guess you'll find out in the morning."

"What time are we leaving?" I ask.

He rolls his eyes. "Five fifteen."

"What should I wear?"

"Whatever you want." He's really giving me nothing here.

"I'll meet you in the lobby at five fifteen." That's what I tell him. In truth, I'll be down there at five so he doesn't escape without me.

Once we go our separate ways, I spend the rest of the evening wondering what the hell a grumpy pro football star does bright and early on Friday mornings before practice.

Does he go get a massage?

Meet with his bookie?

Get in an early workout?

Rehab? Watch film? Meet with someone at the Complex?

A million thoughts run through my mind, but not a single one comes close to being correct. He's only shown me his tough guy side, the side that's all grumpy asshole and attitude.

I dress in my usual business professional attire, line my lips with my badass red lipstick, and click my heels to get down to the lobby by five. He emerges at five ten—a little early, as I suspected, and he's in the clothes he'll wear to practice. Shorts, a tee, and sneakers.

"Are you going to tell me where I'm going so I can drive separately, or am I riding as your passenger?" I ask, bypassing the usual morning greetings since they'll go underappreciated by him anyway.

"Get in the truck," he mutters.

"Okay, I've been through every possible scenario," I say once he pulls out of the parking garage. "And I'm thinking it's either an early appointment with someone at the Complex, a therapist perhaps, or you're going to drive me out to the middle of the desert and leave me there since you see no other way out of this." I glance over at him, and he's not *smiling*, exactly, but I think I spot the tiniest hint of amusement near his eyes as they look out over the road that's just starting to brighten with the light of dawn.

He shakes his head. "Neither."

A huff of irritation rises out of my chest, but I leave it be.

Shortly before the time his appointment starts, we pull into a parking lot, and I read the sign over the old building. *Sunny Acres Animal Shelter.*

An animal shelter?

Maverick's big, secret appointment is at…an animal shelter?

I glance over at him with my brows furrowed. "What are we doing here?"

"I volunteer here once a week. Friday mornings before practice."

"You *volunteer* here?" This big, strong, gruff—and yes, sexy as hell—superstar who refuses to let anyone close enough to get to know him at all volunteers weekly helping animals?

Why does my heart squeeze at that? Why does he suddenly seem less like a total asshole? And why, for the love of all things holy, does he not show anyone this side of him?

All questions I intend to answer…eventually.

But for now, I'm bracing myself for the unexpected.

We head inside, and it's clear I chose the wrong shoes for this morning's activity.

"Good morning, Mav," a woman behind a reception desk says as soon as the door shuts behind us. "You brought a guest today, I see."

"She works for the team," he says thickly.

"We just have a quick application and liability waiver for you to complete," she says to me.

"Of course." She hands me a clipboard, and I scribble out my information while she tells Maverick about what he'll be doing today. I half-listen as I fill out the forms.

"We have two big boys who came in this week, and they need some one-on-one attention. Maybe you could take one, and your associate could handle the other? We'll keep them both leashed if you'd like to walk together. Your favorite girl also needs some love. She misses her favorite paw pal."

Paw pal? Maverick Jennings is a *paw pal?* Friggin' adorable. Hot *and* cute. Lethal. This man is freaking *lethal.*

I blow out a breath and push the clipboard back to the woman, who thanks me profusely for being here, and then the two of us head back to tackle our assignments.

Maverick doesn't say a word as he leads me toward a set of cages, and he starts with the one that says "Bruno" above it, an older German Shepherd. He opens the cage, and Bruno walks tentatively out.

"Do they come in with names?" I ask.

"Some," he grunts as he bends down to his knees and holds out a hand. Bruno walks toward him, his tail wagging but down low, as if he's a little unsure, a little nervous, but at the same time, he knows he likes this guy, and he wants to trust him.

Gracious. I know the feeling, bud.

"Who names them if they don't?" I ask, pushing away that thought.

"I don't know," he mutters. Bruno slowly walks to him, and Maverick doesn't rush the dog. He just waits patiently there on his knees, sitting back on his feet, holding out a gentle hand.

If only he had the sort of patience for people that he seems to have for animals.

Bruno closes the gap, and when he gets close enough, he sniffs Maverick. The tail wagging picks up a bit, and Maverick shifts his hand slowly to scratch the dog under his chin. The wagging picks up even more, and then Bruno moves closer to Maverick, nuzzling his neck. Maverick doesn't crack a smile. I don't think he ever *smiles* or *laughs* or feels any sense of joy whatsoever, but I see something change as the dog snuggles into him.

He seems somehow lighter. The storm cloud that seems to follow above him lifts. The clouds part, if only for a moment. I see a different side to him as he strokes the animal's fur, a softer, sweeter side that he keeps hidden away.

"That's a good girl," he croons.

My thighs clench at his soft words. My stomach clenches, too. I'm pretty sure my vagina even clenches.

I imagine him saying those same words as he slides into me. It's just a flash of an image, one I immediately push out of my head, but my good God, what in the hell is this man doing to me right now?

"Bruno's a girl?" I ask, my voice too loud in the small room as I try to pull myself together, and both the dog and the man jump a little, startled, as if they forgot I was in the room with them.

He lifts a shoulder. "Someone named her Brunhilda, and the staff took to calling her Bruno for short."

So Bruno the girl is apparently a good girl, Maverick Jennings has a soft side, and I'm supposed to try to work with this man and whip him into shape when my usual badass self is suddenly turned all the way on as I see him cuddle a poor animal down on its luck. Great. Right. Okay.

I force the ridiculous thoughts away and pull that badass cape a little tighter.

"How long has Bruno been here?" I ask.

"A few months. She was found walking by the road. No chip, no tags. Nobody knows where she came from or what she went through, but she's quiet and sweet. Everybody wants pups. It's harder to find a forever home for these older dogs."

I kneel down beside them, staying far enough away so as not to disrupt their moment. "How do you not take them all home?"

"It's hard, to be honest. But then I think of my lifestyle, in and out, gone for long stretches, and I know I'm not the right fit. Someday I'll figure out some way to connect these animals with their forever homes, but for now, I'm giving what I can."

"A little bit of time goes a long way, I'm sure," I say softly. "You're doing a good thing here, Maverick."

He grimaces a little. "Yeah, well, don't tell anybody. Wouldn't want to ruin my reputation."

I chuckle a bit at that. He tosses a ball a few times for Bruno, and then we head toward our next assignment with the two big boys brought in this week—two mastiffs that weigh more than I do. I'm a little afraid of mine, to be honest, but Maverick walks in front of me, and I have the gentler of the two on a leash behind.

He mutters to his dog, little phrases I can't quite catch from up here, but one thing is clear.

There's more to Maverick Jennings than I first thought, and I'm ready to figure out how I can use this other side of his to my advantage.

CHAPTER 17

Everleigh Bradley

Freight Train

Nearly a week after our shelter visit, Dr. Baker clears him for full practice, which means he's also cleared to start bonding with his teammates—a fact I point out on the way to the weight room where he plans to start today.

In the last six days, he's been adamantly against me telling *anybody* about his work at the shelter. It's a closely guarded secret, but I can't really figure out *why* he wouldn't want to use it to his advantage. Still, I respect his wishes—even if I keep pressing it.

"Find at least one other guy you can talk to during workouts today," I suggest. "We need to start building bonds for you to become the kind of leader Jack is looking for, and that begins with at least coming off as semi-approachable."

He looks at me like I'm stupid. "Workouts are individualized to each player, and Adrian is meeting with me to amend the personalized plan he created for me coming off an injury."

"Yeah, but don't you, like, I don't know…shoot the shit with the other players while you're in there? You know, invite someone to the shelter?" I ask.

"Do I seem like the kind of guy who shoots the shit with anybody? And the shelter is a hard no. That's mine."

I scowl at him, and he relents.

"Fine. I'll try to shoot some shit."

He meets with Adrian first, who'd been working with him on throwing shorter distances and keeping up his strength with exercises that wouldn't affect his ribs. But now he needs to get back to full game speed and strength, which means he has just a few days to get back to where he was before the injury.

I listen with rapt attention as I try to piece out where I can be helpful, but this is sort of all Maverick from this point. I snap a few pictures as he trains with Adrian, and I send them to Ellie, who's devising his social media plan. He'll need to approve everything first, and I can fully see him telling us not to post any of this, but if he wants his angle to be split somewhere between grinding athlete and everyday dude, we need to get started somewhere.

It's a long day as he starts in the weight room and then joins the rest of the team for drills on the practice field. As a bystander, it appears to me that he never missed a beat. He's at his most natural when he's standing on the line, looking downfield for his receiver as he holds the ball in his hand. He's confident and patient, two words that wouldn't come straight to mind when I think of the little I've gotten to know of Maverick Jennings.

I'm reminded of when he told me he's broken. I'm reminded of when he asked why I haven't left yet. I'm reminded of the way he has exactly zero patience for me.

But this man on the field is someone else entirely. He waits for his moment. He scans the field. He's precise and disciplined.

It's commanding and beyond sexy.

I shake that word straight out of my head.

The only reason it would matter if he's sexy is if I can somehow use it to help his image. My personal feelings on the matter need to be kept in check at all costs.

My phone rings while I'm watching practice, and I see it's my little sister Ivy calling. I send the call to voicemail since I'm working right now.

Practice ends, but Maverick doesn't leave the field with everyone else. In fact, even the coaches leave, and he's still out there on the field. He's running some extra drills, testing things out. He's probably happy to be back here in the place he loves—the one place that gives him respite from whatever it is that seems to plague him. Because something is definitely buried beneath the surface with this guy. You don't just walk through life hating everyone without having some reason why.

I walk over toward him after a good fifteen minutes, and I'm not sure why. It's starting to get dark out here as the sun goes down, and the sky is a brilliant shade of pinks and oranges. Sunsets in Vegas just hit differently than they do in Chicago, especially when there are a few clouds in the sky— a rare occurrence in the desert.

I stand by the goalposts as I watch him run his drills, and I lean against it, watching him. Observing. Thinking.

He's working through some footwork, weaving, dropping back, sprinting. Faking throws. He holds a ball but doesn't let it go, and he repeats the same drills several times before he finally glances over at the sky, and then he walks over toward me.

"You shouldn't be on the field," he grunts. He stops in front of me. He's close enough to touch, close enough to reach out and grab a fistful of his practice jersey. I don't.

Until he moves in closer. "You shouldn't be here at all," he says. His body is flush against mine, and his arm loops around me to haul me into him. That's when I grab a fistful of his jersey.

His eyes are heated as they move down to mine, and I'm honestly a little terrified as I stare up at him. Terrified of the complexity of these feelings that seem to be growing between us. Terrified we'll get caught. Terrified he'll kiss me. Terrified he won't.

His arm is above my head, balancing on the goalpost as he leans into me, and he leans down so his nose brushes mine again, just like the other night. The hate between us seems to cross onto some other plane that's passionate just the same. I think for a second about how getting into bed with him would be absolute *fire*.

The reality is that I'd be *fired* if anyone caught us. If anyone saw us out here like this.

And the other reality is that I can't lose this job. It's my key to the rest of my life. The key to the career I've always dreamed of. I'm here to do a job, not to give in to whatever it is that's burning between my client and me.

His lips are a breath from mine, and I use that fistful of jersey to push him away.

"I can't do this," I mutter, and I run off the field before he can hit me with another line that will only leave me feeling worse.

I'm shaking as I get to my car.

I shouldn't have run out. I should have let him kiss me even though I know I did the right thing.

I need a distraction, so I call Ivy back once I've started my car and pulled out of the parking lot.

"Hi Ev," she answers.

"Hey, babe. What's going on?"

"Mom hurt her arm, and I'm kind of worried," she says.

"She hurt her arm? How?"

"She was at a store and had several dresses draped over her arm, and said she bumped into a clothing rack on accident. Liam took her to the emergency room because she thinks it might be broken, but I don't know, it doesn't seem like the kind of thing that would break an arm. It's just under her shoulder and above her elbow."

"Ouch," I say, wincing at the thought. "Don't worry. She'll be fine. I'm sure it was just a freak accident. Are you there with her?"

"No," she says, and she sounds annoyed that I don't know where she is. "I'm back at school." She's in her senior year of college, and I guess that tracks.

"Hey, keep me updated, okay? Let me know when she's home."

"I will."

We hang up, and I pull into the parking garage and happen to find Maverick waiting for the elevator when I walk into the building. Milton isn't at his usual desk, but two people are waiting at the counter, so I assume he's in back looking for a package delivered for them.

Maverick doesn't acknowledge me, and I feel like I should say something to try to alleviate some of the awkwardness. But I can't seem to come up with anything to say.

We step onto the elevator together, and it's just the two of us. I feel like I'm panting. This space is too small for the two of us, and I'm not sure why there's this sudden magnetism pulling me toward him. I'm quite sure I don't like it.

At all.

But I feel it.

And then this image of being wrapped in those big arms plows into me, and I have this sudden *craving* to know what that would feel like. What was it like to be married to him? What was it like to be *loved* by him…or, hell, even to be *liked* by him? He doesn't seem to like *anybody*.

I feel his gaze smoldering at me, and my eyes edge over to him in the blurry stainless steel of the elevator door. It's too hard to tell if he's looking at me, and I can't help when my head turns toward him.

Our eyes catch, and my breathing stops for a few seconds. He inclines his head a little, and I think he's going to move in toward me.

I *want* him to. The air is charged with sexual energy, and maybe it's been too long since I've had sex, but I just…want it. I want it with him. I want to know what he looks like naked. I want to know what he feels like as he pushes into me. I want to know what his lips feel like against mine, how his tongue would tangle with mine. Would he melt from this vitriolic man full of anger into something kinder and sweeter? Somehow I doubt it, yet I want to see for myself.

I want so badly to not be so attracted to him, but I can't seem to stop it. It's like a goddamn freight train barreling at me, and I'm frozen in place, helpless to jump out of the way of impending danger.

I move back a step so I'm leaning against the elevator wall, and just when I think he might pounce, the car glides to a stop and dings to let us know we've arrived at our floor.

He gets off first. There's no gentlemanly holding out of his hand to allow the lady to step off first, but in doing so, he also blocks my view of the person standing by my door waiting for my arrival.

"Billy?" I say, and I freeze in the elevator doorway. Billy's handsome face with those dark brown eyes and white teeth and bright smile breaks out into a grin as he opens his arms to me as if I should walk forward and step into them.

I don't want to walk into them.

Even less so when he breaks out the "Sweetheart!" and sort of waggles his fingers to beckon me into his arms.

My eyes edge over to Maverick, who isn't pretending to slide his key into his lock like a normal person might do. Instead, he's staring daggers at Billy.

Interesting.

I force one foot in front of the other to meet Billy's outstretched arms. "What are you doing here?" I ask as he wraps his arms around me.

"I told you I was coming into town," he says.

"Right. I didn't realize it was, well, now. How did you know where I live?"

"I checked in with your brother so I could surprise you. Is now a bad time?"

I can't think of what would be a *good* time to have my ex-boyfriend show up on my doorstep, but I guess this is no worse than any other time.

"No, it's fine," I say. I hear a grunt in the periphery, and then I say brightly, "Come on in." I open my front door and disappear inside without so much as a backward glance at Maverick, which I'm sure sets him all the way on edge.

He's a lit fuse. It's dangerous to blow at the flame, and yet…that's basically what I just did.

"So…this is my new place." I hold my arms up to indicate the place.

"Helluva view," he murmurs, beelining for my floor-to-ceiling windows.

"I'll admit, I stand here and stare out at it all the time."

"While you're humming and coming up with your next big plan of action?" he teases.

Well, there's the proof in the pudding. The man knows me. And at one point, he knew me better than anyone else.

God, he's still so devilishly handsome, and I don't exactly have anything else going on at the moment.

But still.

Falling back into old habits would be dangerous.

"Can I get you a drink?" I ask.

"Sure. Casamigos if you've got it. Or we could go out," he suggests.

Like a date? Might actually be safer than having him here in my home.

"How long are you in town?" I ask as I grab the bottle from the cabinet I deemed the *liquor cabinet* when I moved in.

"All week." He's still over by the windows, which gives me a bit of space to breathe. "I have a deposition with one of our high-profile clients, and Andrew asked me to look into a corporate deal for him while I'm here. How's life out here so far?"

"I'm settling in," I say, pouring two glasses because, let's face it, alcohol will help me get through this.

"I heard through the grapevine that you gave up all your Chicago clients to move out here for one. Who is it?"

"Confidential," I murmur, and I pick up both glasses and carry one over to him, my heels clicking on the hardwood floors all the way over.

He holds up his glass without a thanks, and he says, "To reconnecting."

"I'm sorry, Billy, but I can't drink to that. How about to *apologizing* first?"

He looks surprised and a bit miffed, and I wish I would've had the foresight to freshen up my lipstick on the way home. What if Maverick would've actually kissed me on the elevator like I wanted him to, and we both got off the elevator wearing the same shade of red as my ex stood in front of my door?

The thought nearly makes me laugh out loud.

"Well, then. I'm sorry," he says.

"For?"

"For whatever it is I did that offended you."

I huff out a laugh. I can't help but feel like for as much as the breakup hurt, I ended up right where I was supposed to. A lifetime with non-apologies like that one would never work for someone like me. He's going to need to find someone who doesn't mind being held down by the thumb I never realized was quite as oppressive as it was when we were together.

If he wants to hold someone down, I guess. I'm not quite sure he does, given his reason for ending things with me.

"That feels like a real sincere apology," I say.

"I don't understand you," he mutters.

"What's not to get? It's pretty simple. I deserve to be treated with respect rather than you showing up at my door uninvited and waltzing in like you deserve a night in my bed just because we have a history."

His brows dip together, and he sputters a little. "That— that's not…that's not what this is, Ev."

"Then what is it?" I demand. I've dealt with Maverick's surliness all day, and I don't have the energy for mental Olympics with Billy now.

"Two old friends getting together to catch up."

I know him well enough to know when he's bullshitting me. "Right. Okay, then lay it on me. How have you been?" I work incredibly hard to keep the sarcasm out of my tone.

"Truth?" He turns toward me, and I see the man I fell in love with. Only…he looks different. He looks older. Tired. Worn down. "I've been miserable without you. I've tried to justify that I did the right thing, but it turns out I didn't. I was wrong. I never should have ended things. I never should have given up the greatest thing that ever happened to me."

"So you sweep into Vegas a couple months after I move here, expecting me to just drop everything and take you back?" I ask quietly.

He lifts a shoulder, which confirms my suspicions even though his words try to negate them. "No. I don't expect anything from you. But I was hoping maybe you felt it too and would be willing to give this another chance with me."

I press my lips together, and then fuck it all. I chug down the tequila in my glass. "Six months ago, I would've given anything to hear those words. But six months is a long time, and I've changed."

"So let me change with you," he begs.

I shake my head. I feel a little off balance by this entire conversation. "I like wearing red lipstick."

He takes a step toward me. "And it's gorgeous on you."

"I like wearing red dresses. I like my black shoes with the red soles. But you know what I've learned to like most of all, Billy?" I ask, and when I turn, he's mere inches from me. Close enough to kiss if that's the way I wanted this conversation to go. As it turns out, though, it isn't.

"What?" he breathes.

"I like my freedom." I press my lips together and step away from him. I refill my glass of tequila.

He blows out a breath of disappointment or frustration, I'm not sure. But I find that I don't really care.

The only thing I can seem to think about at this moment is what Maverick thought when he saw a handsome man in a suit standing in front of my door.

CHAPTER 18

MAVERICK JENNINGS

I'm Down for a Hate Fuck

I force myself *not* to glance out the peephole into the hallway.

Instead, I put on some music. I select my most aggressive and eclectic playlist with everything from rap to metal by artists such as DMX, Kendrick Lamar, Slipknot, and Skillet. I don't listen to the lyrics. I just like the loud, pumping beats with songs that make me *feel* something as they pound in my chest.

I blast it.

Fuck it. I hope she can hear it. I hope she remembers who her neighbor is. I hope she remembers why she's here.

Who the fuck was that asshole?

He stank of money. More money than he knew what to do with. Has she fucked him? Is he her type?

I push away that hot burn of jealousy that seems to tear up my spine. It's unfamiliar, and I'm not sure where it comes from. It shouldn't come anywhere near me right now, yet there it is.

I have no reason to feel jealous. I stake no claim over her.

But I want to.

I fucking hate her. I hate that she's here. I hate that she's finding a way in. I hate that she's affecting me. I hate that she's Dex's sister. I hate that Jack hired her.

And yet…

I want to fuck her like I want to take my next breath.

Goddamn.

I need to work out this aggression, so I decide to hit the treadmill.

It's getting late.

Day is shifting into night.

I need rest. I know I do. I went hard at practice for my first day fully back at it, and I need to cut myself a break. I should get in the shower and jerk off like a normal person, and instead, I'm sprinting on my treadmill like I'm running away from all of this.

It doesn't help.

I turn up the music.

A good neighbor would use headphones. I never claimed to be a good neighbor.

I run harder. Faster. Uphill to the highest incline.

I'm sweating. I'm panting.

It doesn't erase the image of her lips.

Her ass.

The way she went into his arms like they fit together.

I hated it. I shouldn't hate it when I hate *her*, but I did. I have no reason to be jealous, but I am.

I am.

Who the fuck is he?

Who is he to her? Who is she to him? Why do I care?

My lungs burn as I fight for breath. This is stupid. If I go too hard, I could easily hurt myself before I ever get back onto the field, and that's the last thing I want. I can't let her do this to me. I can't let her take more from me when she already has access to so much.

I force myself to slow down. I can't stop thinking about her. I turn the music up to drown her out of my head, but it's useless.

The song ends, and it's in the dead air between songs that I hear a loud rapping at my front door.

It's louder than rapping. It's pounding. Angry pounding.

I stalk to my door. Let's be honest here, there are very few options as to who it could be. It's not going to be my upstairs neighbor since, according to Milton, they're snowbirds who are currently at their home in Minneapolis. It won't be my downstairs neighbor since nobody lives in the condo beneath me. That leaves us with exactly one option, and I throw the door open to find her standing there.

Her eyes are a little glassy, as if she's had a drink or two. Her face is scrubbed clean of makeup, her hair is piled on top of her head, and she's gorgeous as fuck. She appears to have rolled out of bed to come over here to confront me. She's wearing shorts so short that they could hardly qualify as shorts and a gray tank top that shows off the hard curve of her nipples beneath the fabric.

Fuck.

I can't take my eyes off her tits.

"Turn that down!" she screams at me. She's furious with me, but I don't miss the heat in her eyes as they flick down my abdomen. I'm not wearing a shirt, only a pair of basketball shorts, and I see the way her eyes flick down to my external obliques that create that V-line by my hips that make women forget their own goddamn name.

"Or what?" I snarl as Korn taunts the two of us with "Coming Undone."

"Or I'll call Milton and have him tell you to do it since you clearly have no respect for your neighbors!" She's still screaming despite that heat in her eyes.

I point to my chest, which is still heaving from the exertion of my workout. "*I* have no respect? What about you and your random guests hanging around outside our two doors? For all I know, he's a crazed superfan."

She scoffs. "Right, like he was here to see *you*."

"Who was he?" I hiss.

"None of your goddamn business."

"If you're trying to get inside my head so you can know every last piece of who the fuck I am, then you better think twice about keeping me on the outside." I can't help the growl in my voice at the words.

"You're not letting me in!" she yells.

I throw my door wide open as my eyes flick to her tits for no less than the tenth time since this conversation started. *Conversation*…if you can call it that. "Come the fuck in, then."

Her eyes widen as I walk over to switch off the music.

She doesn't cross over my threshold.

"Too scared to step foot into the lion's den?" I sneer, walking back toward the doorway.

"More like too scared to shake the beehive," she mutters.

I take another step toward her, and another, until I'm standing a foot away. I could reach out and pull her against me, but she takes a step back into the hallway. I follow her step for step, and she backs up until she runs out of space. Her back is against the wall next to the elevator, and I keep that same foot of distance between us.

My eyes flick down to her lips before they move back to her eyes, which are wide with fear.

I close that final gap. My sweaty body presses against her soft, cool frame, and a gasp parts her lips. I lean down and run my nose along hers like I've done twice now, but this time, I don't have it in me to stop.

"Remember when I said I don't make mistakes?" I ask softly.

She thinks I'm setting another trap. Maybe I am.

"Yeah?" she says, her voice tentative like a question and breathless at the same time with me so close.

"I lied." My lips crash down to hers, and she laces one of her hands around my neck, pulling me down with her as I loop one arm around her waist and flatten my other palm against the wall above her head for balance.

Because she knocks me all the way the fuck off balance.

Fucking hell. I hate her, and yet I want to fuck her into tomorrow. I want her to wince every time she sits tomorrow so she can remember who owns her cunt.

I wondered what her lips tasted like since the moment I first saw them.

And now I know.

Magic. Pure motherfucking magic.

Her lips are soft and plush, and at the same time they're confident and sure. They part, letting my tongue in, and we kiss as I pull her body closer to me. Her free hand grips onto my bicep, and my arm automatically flexes with the feel of her hand there. She moans into my mouth, and that's it. The signal that she wants this.

I want it, too. Inexplicably, but I do.

I pull back from our kiss, and a guttural sound of frustration rises from her chest.

"Ugh! God! I hate you!" she says, and she balls her hands into fists that she uses to pound on my chest.

It's cute, really. She's frustrated.

"Feeling's quite mutual," I mutter. I pick her up and toss her over my shoulder, and she's kicking and screaming as I carry her into my place.

She beats on my back, but I'm used to getting plowed into by defensive ends week after week. It feels like a massage coming from her.

"Put me down!" she screams at me.

"Why?" I challenge as I carry her through my family room and attached kitchen, down the hall, and toward my bedroom.

"Because I hate you and I'm capable of walking myself!"

"Yeah, well, if I give you that chance, we might both change our minds, and I can tell by the way I had you moaning during that kiss that it's not what you want."

She doesn't have a response to that other than a small gasp, but she does manage to stop kicking and screaming. We arrive in my bedroom, and I toss her on my bed. I walk around to the drawer where I keep my condoms, grab one, and toss it to her. She sits up and glances at the wrapper where it landed on the bed beside her.

"Your call, babe. I'm down for a hate fuck if you are." I raise a brow and wait.

Her jaw drops and her eyes widen.

I take a few menacing steps toward her until I force her legs apart and I'm standing between them. "Don't pretend like you don't want this. I see the way your lips part when you're studying me. I heard that little moan. I felt the way your hips shifted against mine so you could feel how hard my cock is for you. So tell me, do you want me to fuck you, or do you want to quietly slip out and pretend this never happened?"

A flash of intimidation passes through her eyes as she looks up at me from where she sits on the bed, though her next words contradict the flash I saw. "On the field and in the bedroom," she murmurs.

"What?" I demand.

"The two places where your arrogance takes over." She purses her lips.

"There's a difference between arrogance and confidence."

"Oh? Do tell."

Jesus, she's sexy sitting there on my bed, her eyes gazing up at me with heat and need as her nipples form tight peaks beneath her shirt, begging for my mouth.

I don't invite women to my bed. Ever. This is my home. My sanctuary. I'm not sure why I carried her in here and didn't carry her through her own door, but here we are. Some instinct inside kicked in, and I had to get her into my territory. On my home turf.

"Arrogance overestimates one's abilities," I say, and I lean down. She leans back with me until she's lying on her back and my body is hovering over hers. "There's no misjudgment here. I know exactly what I'm doing on the field, and I know exactly what I'm doing in bed."

"So I'm nothing more to you than a mistake?" she asks, and I'm not sure if she's clarifying or seeking some sort of validation that this would be more to me.

I'm aware of the gravity here.

Regardless of what happens next, we have to spend the next year together. I can't allow her to be a distraction—or at least no more of a distraction than she's already proven to be.

I can't give her the validation she needs, but I also can't call it a mistake until I know the consequences.

"I didn't say that," I mutter. I lean down and press my lips to her neck, and God, she tastes good. I feel her tight nipples through her shirt like they're trying to escape and rub along my chest, and she arches her back into me as she lets a frustrated grunt rip out of her.

"Fuck, you're annoying," she says.

"But you want me anyway."

"Do I?"

"Tell me to stop and I will." I thrust my hips against her, and my legs are positioned in a way that forces my cock right against her cunt.

She groans, and I do it again, harder this time.

"Don't stop," she begs.

I thrust again, and when she moans as her head rolls back and she reaches to grip onto the back of my biceps, I feel the pressure starting up at the base of my spine.

I could come just from thrusting against her like this.

Fuck.

Goddamn, I'm hot for her. Hotter than I realized. I haven't been with a woman in far too long, and it's been even longer since I've been with someone who managed to incite even an ounce of emotion in me.

And hatred is an emotion. A strong one.

She makes me *feel*. For the first time in a fucking decade, I'm *feeling* again. Off the field. It's terrifying, but it's exhilarating at the same time.

I think about kissing her again, but I realize how fucking dangerous putting my mouth on hers is. This isn't about feelings. It's not about falling. It's about getting her out of my fucking head so we can move on like professionals. It's about acting on impulse and fulfilling a need that comes down to basic animalistic nature.

Because sex never complicated anything, right?

I'm making justifications as to why this is a good idea when I know it's not, but I'm powerless to stop it myself. The one with the power here is her. If she said the word, it would immediately end. But she didn't. She told me *not* to stop.

She takes the opportunity to wrap her legs around me, and I continue pumping against her, the frenzy starting to build inside me.

I can hate someone and be fully attracted to them. I can hate someone and fuck them until they can't see straight. I can hate someone and still take pleasure from them.

I pull back enough to reach down for the bottom of her tank top, and I shove it up toward her neck. I'm rough with her tits, those gorgeous tits I can't seem to keep my eyes off of. She arches again, this time to shove her tits closer to my face, and I bury my mouth between them for a few seconds before I move over and roughly grab one of them between my lips. I suck hard, and she whimpers. I do it again. I like the whimper. It goads me on. It tells me that she can feel it, too.

I bare my teeth, giving her nipple a little bite, and I grab her other tit into my hand, massaging it so I can feel the hard peak of her nipple against my palm.

"Oh, God, yes," she groans.

I think about offering some line about how I'll be her sex god, but it feels too unlike me in the moment. I keep quiet instead.

Her legs are still wrapped around me, and her nipple is still in my mouth as I let go of her other tit and allow my hand to move slowly down her torso down toward her hip. I dig my fingers in there before I shift over enough to give myself some space. I reach under those barely-there shorts, discover she's not wearing panties, and slide my finger into her wet cunt.

She shrieks at the feel of my finger as I pump in and out of her. "Yes, Maverick! That feels so good. Give me another finger."

I add a second finger at her command, and the shrieks grow louder. I almost find myself smiling against her tit still in my mouth.

What the fuck?

It's her sounds. The way she's writhing beneath me as I pleasure two different zones at once. I let go of her nipple and replace it with my hand as I grab and pull at her tit roughly, and I glance up at her face.

Her eyes are closed, and her bottom lip is clenched between her teeth. Her neck is arched back as she gives into this pleasure between us, and I can't help myself as my mouth moves back to hers. I need to taste her mouth again. It's a hot, sloppy, frantic kiss as our tongues batter and our teeth clash.

It's quite possibly the hottest kiss of my life.

Who knew a hate fuck could be so goddamn hot?

Her fingertips move to my back, where they scratch the ever-living fuck out of my skin, but all it does is goad me on. I slow my pace where I'm finger fucking her, driving into her with slow, forceful strokes, a total contrast to the way our mouths continue their hasty, rushed kiss.

"Oh fuck!" she cries against my mouth, and her body tightens as she starts to come. Long, undulating waves fall over her as I feel her pussy contracting over and over again around my fingers. I kiss her through it, continuing those hard strokes into her, never letting up, never giving in.

I keep going when her body slows, when she lets out a soft giggle as her body shifts into the sensitive afterglow. Her hips sway with my fingers as if she doesn't want me to stop.

I feel a scratch at my shoulder, and I glance over to see what it is. The condom packet. She must've picked it up, and now she's scratching me with it to let me know it's time for me to stick my cock in her.

I pull back, still fingering her, and her eyes are cloudy with a sly smile playing on her lips as she raises a brow at me. "Are you just going to keep fingering me forever?"

"You didn't tell me to stop."

"I don't want you to stop."

"Then I won't."

It's a battle of who gets the last word, and I shove my fingers in a little harder. She grunts and grits her teeth together.

"Fuck me," she demands.

"If I do, I have to stop fingering you, and you just told me not to."

She glares at me as she contemplates that for a few seconds, and then she shifts her arms so they're wrapped around me. I hear the sound of the condom wrapper as she tears it open, and then her hands move down as she tries to get to my cock.

"Tell me what you want," I mutter.

"I want you, Maverick," she moans.

The words crack something open inside of me, something that's been locked away for a long, long time. She wants *me*.

"Fuck," I grunt, and my mouth covers hers again as I kiss her in that same hasty way where it feels like I'm trying to dominate every centimeter of her mouth at the same time.

She reaches between us for my cock, and I shove it into her palm. She moans when she feels my sheer size, and then she reaches into my shorts and pulls me out. I'm still kissing her, still fingering her, still listening to the sounds of her grunts and moans as she starts to stroke me.

"Fuckkkk," I groan. Fuck. It feels good. It feels so goddamn good as this woman who blew into my life out of fucking nowhere tugs on my cock.

But it was a fuck she asked for, and it's a fuck she'll get.

I pull my hips back suddenly, and she loses her grip around me. I pull my mouth from hers, too, and her eyes fly open.

"No fair," she whines. "You get to finger me, but I don't get to give you a hand job?"

"Flip over and put your ass in the air for me," I demand.

"You'll have to take your fingers out of me first." She's sassy as fuck even when I'm fingering her. Yep, that's pretty much Everleigh Bradley to a T.

I don't want to. I want to keep my fingers right there a while longer. They're doing things to her that are turning me on in ways I haven't experienced in far too long, and it's the anticipation that's making me feel more than I was expecting to feel ever again.

But sex is on the table, and sex with her is the only thing in my field of vision at the moment. I drop my fingers out of her, and I yank the condom from between her fingers.

She's quick as she gets into the position I just asked her for, and as much as I want to look into her eyes as I slide into her, this isn't about making love. It's better this way, better where I don't have to look at her face as I make her fall apart. This is dangerous enough. I don't need to add further emotions into the mix.

I peel her shorts off her body and toss them on the floor. Her ass remains perched in the air, waiting for me, her tank top still pushed up above her tits in the place where I left it.

I roll the condom on and reach around her to feel her tits, heavy in my hand. I let go, and I slap her ass. I'm not sure why I do it other than the fact that this started as a hate fuck, and I'm not ready to admit that something might be changing for me.

She grunts but doesn't otherwise move, and I cup the skin I just slapped, taking my time and being deliberate and slow since what I'm about to do will be neither of those.

I press my fingertips at the top of her crack, and she shivers a little but doesn't otherwise respond. I slide my finger down, giving her a little bit of pressure as I get to her asshole, and she doesn't squirm. Has this woman been fucked in the ass before? Does she like it? Does she want it?

These feel like intimate questions I'm not privy to, yet I want the answers.

I don't deserve them.

It doesn't stop me from craving them anyway.

Again, I think about making some comment about how I'll own her ass next, but it feels too intimate a promise to make when I'm not sure this will go beyond this one time.

I bypass her ass and slip my fingers down to her clit, and she moans as I start to rub her there. "Oh, yes, Maverick. Yes," she hisses, and fuck, my name coming out of her mouth is nearly my undoing. It's as she's reveling in the feeling of me rubbing her clit gently that I get into position. I move my fingers, grip my cock, and slide into her.

And it's fucking glorious.

She lets out a low moan, sending a shot of need straight through me.

She's tight and hot, slick and perfect as I start to move. I pump into her, setting a quick pace with deep strokes, and I watch as she starts to claw the sheets, her nipples rubbing over them as I plow into her, her entire body rippling with my force.

"Holy shit!" she screams, and again, it nearly forces a smile to my lips.

She grips more tightly to the sheets as I pick up the pace, filling my deep drives with all these unfamiliar emotions that seem to claw at me when she's around, and there's nothing sexier than watching what she's doing while I make her come undone.

This woman who is so professional, so in control all the time, so poised and polished and disciplined, is falling apart beneath me, and it's fucking hot as hell.

"Mm, Mav, don't stop. Don't ever stop," she moans, her voice muffled with her face against the comforter.

I don't want to stop, but the tight squeeze of her cunt paired with the soft begging puts me over the edge. I move faster, slam harder, grip more tightly onto her hips as I feel my body start to give way to bliss.

She cries a string of curses as I feel her pussy tighten further over me, and that's when I lose all control. My fingertips dig into those perfect hips of hers as I start to come. A growl bellowing up out of my chest is the only sound I make as my body betrays me, white-hot jets of cum streaming out of me into the condom as her body drains every last drop I have to give.

I'm panting as I pull out of her, but this isn't the time for collapsing and cuddling. Instead, I move off the bed and head straight for the bathroom, where I get rid of the condom and clean off my cock. I hunch over the sink for a moment, afraid to look myself in the eye after giving into the temptation that's been there since before we ever formally met.

Wondering whether I made her forget about that guy who was standing outside her condo earlier this evening.

And when I return to my bedroom, she's just finishing putting her shorts back into place. Her tank top is rolled back down over those luscious tits, and she looks freshly fucked, a soft glow all around her.

She presses her lips together a little awkwardly, and I wait for her next move.

She clears her throat, her eyes edging toward the doorway and away from me. "Well. Let's not let that get in the way of the work we have to do, okay?"

I raise my brows and nod, and she turns to walk out of my bedroom.

I walk her to my front door under exactly zero illusions that this is going to end with any sort of goodnight kiss or sweet sentiment, and I open the door to usher her out and back to her place.

"Goodnight," she says softly. Tenderly. Much more tenderly than I deserve since I'm not inviting her to stay, but it's not like she asked, and it's not like either one of us wants it.

"Goodnight." I watch as she walks to her door, and just before she slips inside, I add, "Next time, I'm not letting you go without tasting your cunt."

I close my door before I catch her reaction to my words, immediately regretting the admission that there might, in fact, be a *next time*.

CHAPTER 19

Everleigh Bradley

All I Want to Do is Talk About It

I lean against the back of my front door as my fingertips come up to touch my lips.

I can't believe his parting words.

Holy shit, for a guy who's so closed off emotionally, he certainly knows how to deliver on the sex front. Just the mere *thought* of his mouth against my pussy has it clenching in need for him as if he didn't just deliver not one, but *two* of the most intense orgasms of my life.

I thought Billy was a good lover.

Holy hell on a hot dog, he had *nothing* on Maverick Jennings.

The man can use his body. And his hands.

I wonder how many other women he's entertained there. I wonder if he allowed them to stay the night. I wonder if he hated them, too, or if it's something that makes me special.

I also wonder what sort of fuckery he performed on my brain that's making me think these thoughts in particular. His hatred of me makes me special? I need to get a fucking grip.

But no. Instead, I continue to lean against my front door with my hand on my mouth as I float on a cloud of bliss.

Yeah, I'm fucked all right.

I was angry about Billy showing up unannounced. I was a little tipsy from the amount of tequila I had to get through the conversation I had with my ex. I was tired and ready to go to bed but couldn't sleep over the blaring music coming from my asshole next-door neighbor.

When I went over there banging on his door, I didn't expect the outcome to be him banging me. A hate fuck, he called it.

It felt like more.

I'm still not sure why I agreed to it. I'm not sure why I thought it was a good idea. I'm not sure what it'll mean for us working together going forward.

But I am sure that it was a night I'll never forget.

I freshen up and slip beneath my covers. I was under no illusion that he'd invite me to stay, and so I left before it got even more awkward than it already was. On my part, anyway. I don't know that Maverick would ever feel awkward about a damn thing in his life because I'm pretty sure he doesn't feel anything at all.

I think he's figured out some way to shut off his emotions, and it's sort of become my job to tap back into those.

That's not why I had sex with him, though it could be a benefit.

I had sex with him because I couldn't seem to stop myself. I walked over there ready to rip his head off, and instead we took our aggressions and our feelings out on each other in this unexpected but beautiful chaos.

I clawed at his back. His bed. He slammed into me with those punishing, decadent drives. Our mouths fused together in the sort of brutal devouring that left me breathless.

And now I'm back home alone with only the memory of what we just shared and the sweet satisfaction aching between my thighs.

I don't let the fears about what this could mean creep in. He's the one who labeled it a hate fuck, but it felt like something else to me. I refuse to identify what it could possibly be, though. If it was only a hate fuck for him, allowing myself to walk down any other path will only lead to disappointment. And I've had enough of that out of men.

Sex doesn't have to mean anything. It can be two bodies simply taking pleasure from each other. But even though I have the thought, I know it's just me trying to justify what we did.

If Jack found out, would I be fired?

He didn't seem to care when Maverick told him I'd hit on him *even though I hadn't*. Besides, didn't Jack marry the woman put into the same position I'm in with Maverick? I doubt he'd have grounds for firing me considering his own personal life.

I wonder if I should tell Ellie.

I shouldn't tell anyone.

It's nobody's business.

Even though all I want to do is talk about it.

I glance at the clock. It's after two in Chicago, so calling Penny is out. She usually doesn't answer late-night texts, but I shoot her one on the off-chance she's up.

Me: *I miss you. You awake?*

My phone rings ten seconds later. "Hey."

"What's wrong?" Penny asks.

"I just had hate sex with Maverick Jennings."

Silence greets me on the other end of the line.

"Pen?" I say tentatively.

"No, I heard you. I just...what?"

"I know. I went over to his place to yell at him since he was blaring music, and instead, he invited me in for a hate fuck," I admit.

"And…"

"It was more spectacular than you could even imagine," I say quietly.

"Oh, Ev. What are you going to do?"

"I'm not sure. I guess that's why I called you." I glance at the clock, and I realize *it's after two in Chicago*. I know I thought it before I sent that text, but it didn't really register. "What are you doing awake?" She has two little boys and a husband, and they're on a pretty traditional schedule, what with school and work routines.

"Oh, you know. The usual. Fighting with my husband, couldn't sleep. I was playing a game on my phone when your text came in."

"You two are fighting again?" I ask softly, abandoning my own reason for calling since this feels bigger.

"I feel like he's not the man I married. He only cares about power and money. He didn't get home until after the boys went to bed tonight, and he didn't even bother to tell me he was going to be so late. I feel like a single mom, honestly, and I'm wondering if I just should be."

"Do you still love him?" I ask.

She's quiet, and then I hear a sniffle. "I don't think I do, Ev. But the kids…"

"I know, babe. The kids. But you can't stay unhappy for the kids. They'll be happier if you are happier. And then you'll have set times where he *has* to step up for them. He won't have any other choice."

"You mean divorce," she says flatly, her voice low.

"If you're unhappy."

"I just…" She sighs heavily. "It never felt like an option for me, but I don't know how much longer I can hold on like this."

"I'm right here, babe. For whatever you need. A week in Vegas? Consider it done. I know people who know nannies who can take care of the kids while we go hit the town and forget all about Brent Calloway."

She offers a small chuckle despite the situation. "What would I do without you?"

"We'll never have to find out."

"Tell me about Mav's cock."

I burst out into laughter. She's nothing if not direct. "I didn't get a really good look at it since he had me on all fours."

"Tell me he touched your ass. Let me at least live vicariously through you."

"He threatened to, but he didn't put it there. Yet."

"Yet?" she repeats.

I sigh. "It can't happen again, Pen. I think it has the potential to really mess up my head. He's cleared for full practice, which means I need to be at the practice facility by seven tomorrow so I can spend the day with him and pretend like just looking at him isn't enough to give me an electric shock."

"Oh, babe. It'll be okay."

"Will it?" I ask.

We're both quiet for a beat, and then she says, "I can't guarantee it'll be okay for either one of us, to be honest. But we have to believe it will be. What's the alternative?"

"Yeah," I mutter. "Tell me how much Stuart is suffering with me gone," I say, changing the subject from that depressing thought.

She giggles. "He hired a couple interns and divided your clients between the rest of your team. It sounds like everyone is overwhelmed and wondering how you serviced thirty-two clients all on your own."

"Twelve-hour workdays, usually seven days a week, for starters," I say. Even as I say it, I realize how much easier it was than the job I'm doing now.

Of course, emotions weren't involved in my previous role. They certainly are now, both positive and negative—but it doesn't matter. A single ounce of emotion can be exhausting either way, and I have far more than an ounce around Maverick.

"What's your schedule like out there?" she asks.

"It's about to change since Maverick was just cleared to return to practice. We'll go in early and meet up to chat about our action plan for the day, and I'll try to coach him on how to interact with teammates and the media. I just left his place, so I imagine he'll be cranky in the morning, but he's pretty much always cranky and hates everyone and everything except football."

"And you," she chimes in.

"He's the one who called it a hate fuck, though I will admit it felt less like hate and more like…" I trail off as I try to figure out the right word.

"Like he was worshiping your vagina?" she supplies.

I scoff, though the more I think about it, the more I think…yeah. Maybe exactly that.

If that's how he hate fucks, how does he do it with someone he *likes*?

I crave the answer to that. I *need* the answer to that.

But I don't think it's an answer I'll ever actually get.

"Yeah," I say sarcastically. "I don't think I want to talk about him anymore." I'm not sure why I say it. I called her to talk about him, after all. But what we did felt private, and I don't particularly feel like I want to share any more details than I already have.

Even that feels like too much. Like what we did should have remained between us.

I don't sleep.

I'm too keyed up after sex late at night, especially sex like that. I try, but I toss and turn, hot under the covers as I remember what it felt like when his mouth was on my breast or when his finger was in my pussy or when his tongue was battling mine for some unclear victory.

I'm up too early, and I take my time getting ready. I put in the sort of extra effort I used to put in when I was trying to catch Billy's eye on the elevator all those years ago.

What the hell am I doing?

I'm not sure, but I wear my red slip dress with my black blazer and black shoes, knowing full well how dangerous it is to go into a locker room filled with horny men looking like this.

There's only one horny man whose eye I want to catch, and he happens to be walking out of his own condo at the same time I exit mine.

"Good morning," I say brightly, as if I got my full eight hours and I'm wide awake.

He grunts a *morning* at me as he locks his door, and we wait for the elevator together. "You know, if we carpool to the practice complex, we could chat in the car on the way and knock some of our meetings out of the way."

He spares a glance at me as the elevator arrives at our floor. "I'd like to stick to my usual routine."

I nod, trying not to feel any certain way about that. Would it be nice if he wanted to spend a few extra minutes with me? Certainly. I shouldn't feel offended that he doesn't. After all, this is his livelihood. His entire life.

He clears his throat as we ride down to the first floor. We're alone on the elevator, and the tension is thick. I half expect him to say something about last night, and I half expect something foolish to come out of my own mouth about last night, but none of that happens. Instead, we walk together wordlessly toward the parking garage. I grapple with what to say. Something. Anything.

I come up short.

Just before we get into our separate vehicles, I ask, "Would you rather have our morning meeting over breakfast in the cafeteria or in the conference room Lily took us to?"

"Conference room if we have to do this at all," he grunts, and it shouldn't surprise me that he'd choose the less public route. I tell myself it's because I look damn good today and he wants to keep me to himself, but a likelier explanation is that he doesn't want to be followed around by his babysitter in front of his teammates.

But outside of the cafeteria means fewer opportunities for him to bond with his teammates. I guess I'll have to figure out some solution, but for today, I'll take what I can get.

He grabs breakfast for himself and brings it into the conference room to eat while I start my spiel. I go over the signed contracts and what he needs to accomplish with his new sponsorships. I coach him on how to interact with the media today. We discuss what to say regarding his return to practice. I tell him to be nice to his teammates and to try to talk to at least two new people today. He thinks it's a stupid idea and doesn't spare my feelings in letting me know that.

"One more thing," I say, glancing at my calendar.

He raises his brows expectantly.

"I see your birthday is at the end of the month. You're a Halloween baby?"

"My birthday is on Halloween, yes," he says dryly.

"Great. And you'll be…"

"Thirty-three," he supplies.

"Right. Anything you'd like to do to mark the occasion?"

He shakes his head.

"Okay. Well, that's all I have for this morning. I'll be on the practice field observing and continuing to build out our plans."

Before either of us moves to stand, Lily pokes her head into the conference room. "Sorry to interrupt, but Mr. Dalton would like a word with you both in his office before Mr. Jennings heads to practice."

We both stand.

"We're done here," I tell Lily, and we follow her to Jack's office, where we each slide into a chair opposite his desk.

My phone starts to ring, but I send it to voicemail without checking who it is. Whoever it is will have to wait because Jack Dalton will not.

"Good morning," he says, looking up at us both. His brows crinkle together for a beat, and I swear to God, he can see on the two of us that we slept together last night.

I know it's a ridiculous thought the second I have it. You can't *tell* just by looking at us.

Still. It feels like he can see right through us.

He clears his throat, and then he says, "Maverick, Lincoln and I would like you to travel with the team this weekend to Cincinnati. Stand on the sidelines with a headset, get your head back in the game. Call plays. That sort of thing." He turns to me. "We'd like you to travel as well as part of the team staff."

Maverick scoffs at that. "I can't even get away from her on the plane?"

I *hate* that his words cut me. I hate that I physically flinch at them. It's just more proof for Jack that there are feelings involved, and I try to convince myself that his words are spoken as a way to continue the farce in front of Jack.

Jack turns to Maverick. "She'll sit with staff. You'll sit with players. She'll have her own room at the team hotel. If you have further questions, keep them to yourself."

"Yes, sir."

I don't know if I've ever seen Maverick stand down before. He must have a hell of a lot of respect for Jack—he's maybe the *one* person in the world that Maverick has a single ounce of respect for. Is there anyone else? I don't have the answer to that since despite what happened between us last night, he still hasn't let me in.

And the more time I spend around him, the more I'm convinced that he will *never* let me in.

CHAPTER 20

Everleigh Bradley

Finding Dad

I don't listen to my voicemail until Maverick is out on the field and I'm up in the bleachers. "Hey Ev, it's Liam. Ivy told me to call you when I had an update, and, well, I have an update. I'm at practice now, but call me back when you can."

I'm not sure why my blood runs cold, but it does. I just get a bad feeling from the tone of his voice.

I can't call him back now when I'm at practice. What if it's bad news? It's going to have to wait until lunchtime, and I'll spend the rest of the morning absolutely dreading this phone call I have to make.

I try to bury myself in work. With Ellie as my partner, we're off to a good start on refurbishing Maverick's image, and I go over Ellie's suggestions for his newest sponsorships. She booked him a few appearances over the upcoming weeks, mostly at bars or clubs, as a way to get his foot in the door to start meeting people in Vegas.

Before I know it, it's lunchtime, and I slip into the conference room to call my brother back while the team goes to the cafeteria to make their food selections. I brought a measly salad for lunch, though Lily told me I'm welcome to take my pick of food from the cafeteria. Regardless, I don't feel very hungry as I pull up my brother's contact.

I dial it, and I think it's going to hit voicemail when he actually answers.

"Hey, Ev," he answers.

"What's going on with Mom?"

"She, uh…" He stutters a little, and he sighs. "The doctors did an X-ray. They felt the break shouldn't have happened to a healthy bone." It feels like he's sort of dodging around what he wants to say.

"What does that mean?" I ask.

"They said the way the bone broke looks like it sort of exploded from the inside and is typically indicative of cancer."

"Cancer?" I murmur softly as the word plows into me with the force of a thousand bricks.

"She scheduled further imaging and a biopsy to confirm, so right now it's speculation. Have you talked to Dad recently?"

"No. Why? Is he okay?"

"He's in Vegas," he says. "You didn't know?"

"No. I had no idea." I've been too busy banging my neighbor.

"Well, he's not answering his phone, so we haven't been able to tell him what's going on. Can you try to get in touch with him?" he asks.

I wonder if he's here at his lounge. I wonder if Liam knows about the lounge.

I try calling my father, too. He doesn't answer my call, either. I guess I have plans for tonight after practice and in between packing for my trip tomorrow.

I meet with Maverick again after practice, this time in the conference room at our building. "Ellie devised this social media schedule. Let me know when you get your first shipment from the meal plan so I can take photos of you eating. The sports drink company sent a tracking number showing your shipment will arrive tomorrow, and I've already been in touch with Milton to put it in your fridge so it's ready when you get back from Cincinnati. And the apparel should be at the front desk now, but we don't want to bombard socials with three different posts, so we'll multitask some of this."

"Are you okay?" he asks.

I glance up at him, surprised by his question. I think it's the first time he's acknowledged my feelings in any way, shape, or form.

I clear my throat as I recall him telling me once that his mom isn't doing well. Maybe this is something he could understand.

"I'm distracted. Sorry." I sigh as I wonder how much to tell him. I'm not sure it's real to me quite yet, so I keep it simple. "My mom broke her arm."

"Oh," he says softly. "I'm sorry. I hope everything's okay."

My eyes lift and meet his. "Thank you."

He doesn't say anything more on the subject, and neither do I.

"That's all I've got. I'll see you in the morning at the Complex." We'll meet there and take the team bus to the airport.

He nods, and he stops at the front desk while I take the elevator up by myself. I haven't heard from Liam, and I know Dex is getting ready to travel in the morning as well, so I decide to keep the news to myself until we know more.

I throw some clothes into my small suitcase and pack up my toiletries.

And then it's time to try to find my dad.

I drive over toward the lounge, and when I walk in, a hostess greets me. I don't remember her being here last time, but maybe she only works when the big boss is in town.

"I'm Everleigh Bradley. Is my father in tonight?" I ask her.

"I know who you are," she says, and she leans in a little conspiratorially. "And yes. He's downstairs."

"Downstairs?" I echo, and she nods toward a door in the far back of the lounge that I assume leads to some sort of break room or office. I offer her a smile. "Thanks."

I head back in that direction, and I try the handle, but the door is locked.

"Ma'am, you can't go in there." A man dressed in all black who I didn't notice was standing there stops me.

"I'm looking for my father, Thomas Bradley."

"Of course. Mr. Bradley is here tonight. Give me a moment." The man flashes his face at a camera I didn't even see, and the door opens.

It's not a break room back there as I assumed. It's a hallway with another door. I don't allow the door to close, instead following closely behind the man in black. He turns when he sees me. "I said you can't come in here."

"And this is my father's lounge," I repeat. "I need to see him."

Before he can make a move to kick me out, a side pocket door opens, and two men walk in from outside. My eyes zero in on a man behind another man in a black suit, and my breath catches in my throat as my brain registers that he's here.

Maverick Jennings.

What the hell?

He hasn't looked up yet to see me as the man with him taps in a code on a pad and flashes his face to open another door.

That door opens just as Maverick's eyes lift to meet mine. Before I can react, I turn toward the open door. I see a set of stairs leading down into what must be the basement. I can't see anything beyond the stairs, but my father is walking up them, Maverick is about to start walking down them, and I'm confused as hell.

My father's eyes meet mine, and his widen. What the *fuck* is happening?

"What is this?" I demand.

"You can't go down there!" the man in the suit behind me yells, but I push past my father to piece together what's going on.

When I get to the bottom of the stairs, it all becomes clear.

It's dark down here, with round poker tables sitting under bad lighting. It's nothing like the crowded, luxurious lounge above us that's clearly a front for whatever's going on down here. It almost could pass for a storage space, but it's clearly not. Instead, there are maybe twenty or so people sitting at tables playing various games.

About ten million questions immediately zip across my brain.

Does Dex know about this underground casino? Do any of my siblings?

How long has this been going on?

Is this where my family's money comes from? I always thought it was the real estate development firm my dad has run since before I was even born. But what if it was this all along?

What if the Bradley money is *dirty* money?

"What is this?" I demand a second time, trailing back up the stairs to confront my father. The man in black doesn't respond as my father walks through the door, and I follow behind him.

Maverick is gone. He either went into the lounge or disappeared out the back door into thin air.

"Everleigh," my father says, and he moves to take me into a hug. He yanks me off the steps and back into the hallway, and he turns to the man in black as he slams the door closed. "I said nobody comes down here without credentials. You're fired."

"Dad, stop. I forced him to let me in. Besides, if this is your place, why don't I get credentials?" And what the ever-loving *fuck* was Maverick Jennings doing here? How does *he* know about this room owned by *my own father,* and I don't?

"This is a restricted-access area," he says rather than addressing my question. "Why are you here?"

"Liam's been trying to call you. Mom broke her arm." I can't force myself to form the *C* word. Liam said it's speculation, so until we have proof that's what it is, I'll continue to hope for the best.

"Shit," he mutters. He doesn't move to pull his phone out of his pocket, which tells me he might not even have it on him. "I've been dealing with some things here and haven't even checked my phone. I'll call her right away."

"Quick question first." I narrow my eyes.

"What?" he murmurs as he glances behind me at the closed door.

"Why was Maverick Jennings here?"

He pauses, and then he says, "He's a whale."

"A whale?" I repeat.

"A high roller. He spends a lot of money here, so he gets privileges other clients don't."

I don't think he knows about my position working with Maverick, but I can't imagine spending wads of cash at what looks to be an illegal backroom would in any way reflect positively on his image.

I don't particularly want to have this conversation with him, but I know I'm going to have to since we saw each other here tonight.

Add it to the list of conversations I don't particularly want to be having at all.

CHAPTER 21

MAVERICK JENNINGS

An Errand

What the fuck is she doing here?

Anger courses through my veins, but that's nothing new.

Did she follow me here?

The really fucked-up thing is that I have to keep reminding myself about how much I hate her. The problem?

After last night, I *can't* hate her.

Instead, I can't stop fucking thinking about her. One night and it's already a fucking obsession.

It's why I came here to gamble. I thought a game might take my mind off her, but I wound up here in her father's casino. My plan was to play in the secret underground room. Instead, I'm in the main lounge at the bar sipping Lagavulin 16 as if I wasn't just trying to get downstairs.

I try to tell myself that the only reason I keep coming back here is because of the underground room. If I win big, I don't have to pay taxes on my winnings. And if I lose big, the casino doesn't have to, either.

I knew it belonged to the Bradley family since Everleigh told me it did, and I suspected the man in the suit who walks around schmoozing players was the Bradley patriarch. I can see a little of Dex in him, a little of Madden. I don't know the others as well, but I've either played with or against all four of the Bradley football brothers at some point in my career.

Maybe it was the fact that Everleigh told me the money I'm depositing here will go to her future kids' college tuition. It was a sassy way for her to tease me, but the idea of the money going to her felt more right than it going to some other establishment here in town.

I wish that weren't true, but I can't change it.

Just like I wish I could stop thinking of the way her face twisted as she came. Just like I wish I could stop thinking about what the fuck her cunt tastes like. It was a slip of phrase that I should've kept inside, but the truth is that I need to know just as much as she wants me to know.

It's getting late, and I need to travel with the team tomorrow even if I'm not suiting up to take the field.

That's what I tell myself, anyway. I certainly don't stand at the bar instead of going to a table because I'm hoping to catch her before she stalks off—so I can confront her to ask her why the fuck she followed me here.

I spot Everleigh stalking through the lounge, so I chug what's left in my glass and take off toward her. I catch up to her just as she exits the lounge and walks over toward the valet to bring her car around.

I walk over and stand beside her. "What are the odds I'd run into you here for a second time?"

"Pretty good considering my father owns it. What are you up to, Jennings?" she demands.

"Just paying toward your future kids' college tuition funds."

She purses her lips, and maybe the sex didn't have the same effect on her that it had on me. "Illegally?"

I hold up both hands. "I was invited to a private poker game. That's all it is."

"And it's ammo for you. Something for you to hold over me," she says flatly.

I wish I could say I won't, but I'm not sure that's true. Knowing something about her family gives me an advantage, and if push comes to shove, I'll do what I have to in order to come out on top.

I suppose *that* is the legacy I'll leave behind. The grinding athlete who stops at nothing to win against every opponent. Jack didn't bring me over to the Aces so I'd be compliant. He brought me over to win.

I don't respond to her words, instead asking, "Can I bum a ride home?"

She offers a small glare as she folds her arms over her chest, and with a purse of her lips, she finally nods. "Fine."

Once we're in the car and on our way, I break the silence by asking, "Why do you keep following me?"

"I didn't!" she yells at me, slamming her open palm against the steering wheel. "I went there to look for my dad. I had no idea you'd be there. I had no idea I'd find him in some basement doing God knows what sort of illegal activities." She's still yelling, and clearly she's angry.

I reach over and slide my hand on her leg in some effort to calm her down. "Okay. Sorry for asking."

She bats my hand away. "Stop it."

"Stop what?"

"Being a totally different person. You've made it clear we aren't friends, and your hand on my leg is crossing into territory neither of us wants."

I think about her words. Yeah, I *am* a totally different person after what happened last night.

She unlocked pieces of me that I stored away. She opened up doors that had been closed for years. She awakened feelings I didn't think I was allowed to feel anymore after all I've been through. It's confusing as fuck, and I tried to play it off like it didn't happen, like everything was business as usual this morning.

It's not.

It took one goddamn night for me to feel something I didn't think I deserved, and now that I've felt it, I'm afraid I won't be able to let it go. It's an addiction. Something I crave. Something I need. Something I'm terrified of.

Something that has the power to change me.

"What if I'm starting to want it?" I ask quietly.

Her head whips in my direction, and I see brake lights in front of us, so I gesture toward the cars. She slams on the brakes.

I blow out a breath.

"What the hell are you saying?" she asks.

I don't know what I'm saying. "Never mind," I grunt.

We sit in silence the rest of the way back to our building. We take the elevator up together with no further words exchanged, and we disappear into our separate condos without so much as a goodnight.

Morning dawns, and her car is still in the parking garage when I take off for the Complex, and I feel conflicted as to whether I actually wanted to run into her this morning or not.

Once we board, she sits with the team staff up front, and I can't see her from where I am toward the middle of the plane. I sit beside Brandon Fletcher, who will be starting the game tomorrow, and he makes small talk as I grunt replies and try to get a view of the gorgeous woman sitting up front.

When we land, we're taken by bus to the team hotel, and it's after we've gotten our room assignments and most of my teammates have started to disperse toward their rooms that I ask Coach Nash for a special favor.

"I know this is a bit unorthodox, but since I'm not taking the field, I wanted to ask if I could take the time between practice and dinner to run an errand."

His brows dip together. "What sort of errand?"

I clear my throat. "My mother lives about five miles from here, and I'd like to pay her a visit."

His eyes soften a little. He knows nothing of my situation with my mother, but what I know of him is that he's a family man and he's very close with his own mother. "Of course, Mav. Take all the time you need."

"Thank you."

Everleigh is waiting for me near the elevators after I finish my conversation with Coach. "What was that about?" she asks as she pushes the button for the elevator to head up.

"Nothing," I mutter.

She narrows her eyes at me, but she lets it go. "I'd like to touch base with you after practice."

"I can't."

"Why not?" she asks, indignant.

"I have things to take care of. I'll be back for dinner. We can talk then."

"I want you to eat with the team. We'll meet after dinner," she says.

"Fine." I sigh as we step onto the elevator together, and she pushes the button for the eighth floor. "What floor?" she asks.

I glance at the envelope holding my key that has *814* scrawled on it. "Eight."

She glances at my envelope. "I'm 816. Looks like we're neighbors."

Can't escape her at home. Why would on the road be any different?

I don't make that comment aloud, but the truth is that tonight I'll be going to bed thinking about how her headboard is against the same wall mine is. I'll be thinking about how she's just on the other side of the wall in that tight gray tank top that I shoved up to her neck and those tiny black shorts I pushed to the side as I sank my fingers into her hot, wet cunt.

Great. Just exactly what I want to be thinking about when my only option is to push away what I'm feeling and bury it down good and deep, never to feel or speak of it again.

We enter our separate rooms right beside one another, and I call my mother's facility to let them know I'll be visiting in a few hours.

I attend practice in my street clothes and watch from the sidelines as I stand beside Coach Richards, the quarterbacks coach. We confer on a few of the plays, and he seems to admire my play-calling abilities. I guess that's something, anyway, to hold onto for the future.

Could I work with quarterbacks when my playing days are over?

Not like this. Not when I won't let anybody in. Not when everyone is afraid of me.

It's the first time I'm making that realization, and I glance over at the bench where Everleigh is sitting. She's staring straight at me. Observing. Studying. Making these realizations long before I do. As if she knows me even though I've been careful to keep her at a distance.

I don't know if I need to put an immediate stop to that or let things happen as they may. Is it because nobody's ever taken the time to understand me? Is it because everyone else gives up on me so easily?

I'm not sure.

But what I am sure of is that it's throwing me off balance. It's making me unsteady, and the last thing this team needs is an unsteady quarterback.

I have one week to pull my shit together.

I'm nervous in the back of an Uber on my way to visit my mother. The only time I feel any sense of nerves is when I do this.

It's been three months since I last saw her, and I have no idea what to expect. Last time was hard. She had no idea who I was, and it took me a few days to bounce back after that.

I check in at the desk, and the woman wearing a nametag that says "Marie" on it asks, "Would you like to meet in a common area or in her room?"

"Wherever she's most comfortable."

She nods and offers a smile. "Susan's on duty today with her, and she'll be up in a moment to escort you back."

A secure door opens, and there's Susan. "Maverick to see Marilyn Jennings," Susan says, and I walk over to greet her.

"How's she doing?" I ask.

"She's had a hard day, but seeing someone familiar might help," she says with a smile.

I walk back with her, and my mom is in her bed when we walk into the room. "Marilyn, your son Maverick is here to see you."

My mom's head jerks over to us, and she studies me for a few beats before she purses her lips and looks away. "I told you I didn't want to see Raymond again after what he did to me."

Raymond. My father.

I blow out a breath.

It's hard enough coming here, but to be mistaken for that asshole is a punch to the gut I wasn't expecting.

I know we look alike. I know we share features. You know what else he shared with me? The secrets he forced me to keep when I'd catch him cheating on the poor woman in the bed mistaking me for the very man I hate.

"I'm not Raymond," I say softly. "It's me, Mom. Your son Maverick."

She turns back to me and squints like she can't piece together who I am. She shakes her head. "Did you tell that woman you won't see her again? Because I won't sleep in the same bed as you until it's over with her."

I glance at Susan for help. "Marilyn, this is Maverick. Not Raymond. Your son is here to visit with you."

"I don't have a son," she says to Susan. She ignores me. "Although we're trying. Or we *were* before I found out he's been sleeping with his secretary. Raymond and I just got married a year ago, and he's already cheating on me. Can you believe it?"

I knew he had a history of cheating on her. Those were the secrets he pressured me to keep. But I didn't know it spanned back before I was even conceived.

What an asshole. Even now, every single piece of information I learn about him only confirms that.

But she stayed with him. She stayed married to him for over twenty years before she finally kicked him out just after I left for college.

And now she's mentally in a time warp that happened over thirty years ago.

It's heartbreaking. It puts this pressure on my chest that feels tight and unbearable. I suck in a breath, but it feels like I can't take a deep enough one.

I knew things were declining with her memory, but it felt easier when she didn't know who I was at all than this.

I glance around her room. The whiteboard says, "Today is Saturday, October 10." The same photo I have from my wedding of her dancing with me is on her dresser, and there's a new label that says "your son Maverick" beneath where I'm standing in the photo.

Susan walks over to the dresser and picks up the frame. She hands it to my mother. "See, Marilyn? This is Maverick, not Raymond."

"Maverick? What a strange name. Sounds like something Ray would've come up with."

I went through a phase where I hated my name. I think every kid does, though Maverick was more unusual than most back then. But I looked up my name when I was in junior high, and I learned that my name means an independent, unconventional, nonconformist.

That might've been the moment I decided to live up to what my name meant. That was the moment I learned to respect it rather than to hate it.

I know what she said isn't personal. She wouldn't have agreed to name me Maverick if she didn't like the name. But it feels like it's the first time she's ever heard the name, and while it isn't about me, it still stings.

"May I sit with you for a while?" I ask her.

She wrinkles her nose a bit, and then she seems to relent, nodding to the chair in the corner. Susan stays nearby in the doorway, watching our interactions since my mother doesn't even know who the fuck I am.

"So you're my son?" she asks, and she seems confused.

I nod as I walk over to her bedside rather than to the chair. I take her hand in mine. "I'm sorry you're having a hard time, Mom. I love you very much."

She squeezes my hand, and she starts to cry. Seeing her like this makes *me* want to cry, too. But I don't. Not now. Not ever. Now is the time to keep my appearance strong for her.

"Tell me about you," she says with a sniffle. I hand her a tissue and sit in that chair.

"I'm thirty-two. I play football professionally, and I'm here in town because my team is playing the Bengals tomorrow."

"You should be with your team, honey," she says.

"I'm just recovering from an injury."

"Oh!" she cries. "No! What happened?"

"I broke a rib, but I'll be back in the game next weekend. Promise me you'll watch?"

"She watches every game you've ever played in," Susan says from the doorway with a wide smile. "She's very proud of you."

Emotion pulses behind my eyes again, but I force it away. It's unfamiliar, and it wasn't there last time. I was able to get in and out, and while the visit was difficult and hurt, I didn't leave the place crying. I can't understand why I'm feeling so much more of the visit *this* time compared to last. "Thanks, Mom."

"Are you married?" she asks, nodding toward the photo of us. "Do I have grandchildren?"

I shake my head. "I'm not married anymore. And no. No grandchildren." Having to tell her that sparks my own painful memories.

She *should* have one. She should have a daughter-in-law, too. She *did* have one.

But then it was all ripped away, and the aftermath is what broke me. It's what turned me into the monster I am today.

That's when it dawns on me.

Someone else is changing that.

I didn't cry the last time I visited my mother even though the visit was painful as fuck. I didn't allow myself to feel. But someone else unlocked those feelings, and now I'm a goddamn mess as I sit here fighting back the waves of emotion plowing at me from every angle as I have to explain to my own mother who I am.

When it's time to go, I tell my mom, "See ya later."

She says it back, and it gives me some hope that not all is lost. It's how we always say goodbye.

Before I leave, I talk with Susan, who gives me all the latest information, and I let her know I'll come visit again as soon as I'm able.

And then I head back to the hotel feeling incredibly drained from the single hour of time I spent away from my teammates, knowing I need to face Everleigh after dinner.

CHAPTER 22

Everleigh Bradley

I Need to Forget

Something's off with Maverick, but I can't put my finger on what.

I've studied him enough to know that he's not himself right now. It's in the way he's sort of hunched over where he usually stands straight. Maybe his rib is bothering him.

He's sitting with a group of teammates at dinner, yet it seems like he's sitting alone. He stares at his plate, barely picking at his food. He doesn't interact with anyone. I'm not even sure why he bothered to show up.

I need to know where he went. Or maybe I'm just curious to know. Curious as to why he left by himself to take care of something. What was he taking care of?

I'm supposed to be shadowing his every move, but this felt…confidential. And I'm not sure why.

Once dinner ends, players are dismissed for the evening. They can't really go anywhere since they have a curfew, and most players congregate to watch film together or head up to their rooms to get into their game mindset for tomorrow.

Maverick stays at the table picking at his plate until the tables have been mostly cleared. I've been getting to know two of the females on staff—Stephanie, who manages the team's social media accounts, and Allie, who's part of the public relations staff—and they both just headed up to their rooms for the night.

I walk over to Maverick, who finally glances up at me. His eyes are positively *tormented*. What the hell happened?

"Is now a good time for our meeting?" I ask tentatively.

He clenches his jaw for a beat, and then he grinds his teeth. "Fine."

I sit across from him despite the waitstaff in here furiously picking up the room from the team who just gathered in here.

"Just a quick debrief. The day seemed to go well. I saw you talking with Brandon on the plane. I'd venture to guess he'd be on the bitter side that you'll be starting over him since he's been waiting for his moment for the last decade, but any bonds are worthwhile. See what you can do with your O-line. Did you see the quarterback from San Francisco got his offensive linemen trucks? Others have done gift cards, YETI coolers, Rolexes, you name it."

He looks at me like I've lost my mind, and I purse my lips.

"Look, I'm not saying you have to win them over with gifts. But theoretically, these guys will be saving your life each week when you're out there, and it wouldn't hurt to at least befriend them. Hell, share some of the sports drinks or apparel with them for all I care."

He raises his brows and returns his eyes to the table.

"Anyway, one day at a time. We have the game tomorrow and the Hope Gala Monday. That's as far as I'm taking your agenda for now, but keep those sponsorships on your short-term radar." I open my phone and go over the stats on today's socials, and he barely grunts in reply to anything I say.

I stop talking and openly stare at him for a full ten seconds, and he doesn't remove his eyes from his staring contest with the table. "Dude, what's going on with you?" I ask.

His eyes lift to mine. "Did you just call me *dude*?" Those six words are the most he's strung together during this conversation.

"I did. Sidestep it. What's up with you?"

He blows out a breath. "Nothing. It's been a long day. I need to head up to my room."

"You're not playing tomorrow," I remind him.

He glares at me.

"Fine. I'll walk up with you."

He presses his lips together, but it buys me a little more time. We wait together for the elevator, and we step on with a few other people. We get off together on the eighth floor, just the two of us, and as we walk down the floor to our rooms, I finally get up the nerve to ask. "Where'd you go earlier?"

He doesn't answer as he pulls his room key out of his pocket. He taps it to his door, which we arrive at first. I move to stand in front of my door, digging through my crossbody for my own key.

He opens his door. "I went to see my mom," he finally says softly. He doesn't look at me.

I freeze as I recall his words that she wasn't doing well. My head whips over toward him. "How is she?"

He sighs as he steps into his room and turns back so his door is resting against his backside. He avoids eye contact with me, but even from here, I can see how affected he is by this. "Worse than the last time I saw her."

"I'm sorry," I say softly. "Do you want to talk about it?"

He presses his lips together, and his face seems to flush a little as if he's fighting back emotion. I've never seen him like this. Eventually he shakes his head, and then he heads into his room without another word.

For the very first time, I realize that Maverick Jennings actually has a heart somewhere in there.

And right now, I think it might be broken. But I need to make him see that just because his heart is broken doesn't mean *he* is broken.

I just have no clue how to do that.

Sleep evades me mostly because I can't stop thinking about Maverick and the haunted, hollow look in his eyes as he told me where he went. I can't help but wonder what's going on with his mom, and I can't help but want to confess to him about my fears when it comes to whatever might be going on with my mom.

A little after one in the morning, my phone buzzes on the nightstand. I pick it up, and a soft breath escapes me when I see who it's from.

Maverick: *Are you awake?*

I realize I'm wearing the same outfit I wore when he hate fucked me the other night, and I have no idea what I'm walking into. If he's ready to talk, I'm ready to listen. If he wants more naked time, well, let's be honest. I think I'm up for the promise he made about tasting my cunt next time.

I'm up for being whatever he needs me to be, and that's a really scary thought as I grab my room key and my flip-flops and quietly make my way next door. I knock lightly, and he opens the door a moment later.

His hair is mussed like he was trying to sleep but was just tossing and turning, and he's just wearing a pair of basketball shorts. No shirt. God, he's hot, from the ink on his skin to the abdomen he clearly works hard to maintain.

I try not to drool as I think about what a fright I must look like—no makeup, hair piled on top of my head, teeny-tiny shorts that keep me cool while I sleep barely covering my ass.

But the way he's looking at me makes me think I'm not frightening at all.

In fact, the way he's looking at me makes me feel like the sexiest creature who ever walked the planet.

He hooks an arm around my waist to pull me into his room, and the door closes behind us as I set my palms on his warm chest to balance myself. His mouth doesn't slam to mine the way I expect it to, but he's full of intensity as his eyes bore down into mine. He's panting just slightly as he moves us further into his room. The lamp by the window is on, casting a glow around what amounts to a standard hotel room, a carbon mirror copy of the room next door.

"Are you okay?" I whisper.

He shakes his head, still no words coming from him. He shudders a little, and I move my hands from his chest to hook them around his waist. I lean into him, resting my head where my hands just were, and I simply hug him. I hold him, and my God, I have no clue what this man is going through, but it's clearly something.

"You don't have to suffer alone," I say quietly. I run my hands up and down his back. "I'm right here."

He doesn't say a word, but I feel him cling onto me as he exhales shakily. It makes me wonder if he's ever had someone say those words to him. *I'm right here.* Maybe his mom, and maybe she's in a position where she *can't* say that to him anymore, so now he feels well and truly alone.

I still wonder about his wife. What happened to her?

I could've dug more into it. I haven't. Maybe out of respect for him. Maybe because I want to find out from him.

A choked sound slips out, and I think he might be crying.

I don't dare move a muscle.

He's finally letting me in—but on his terms. For whatever reason, whatever he's going through…he didn't want to be alone.

He trusted me enough to text me at one in the morning, and I showed up seconds later.

Maybe that's all this man has needed all along. To feel like there's someone on his side fighting alongside him rather than against him. To be on his personal team instead of someone who might come or go at any time—like his teammates who retire or are traded or who walk away from the game at the end of a season.

It's only now I realize he doesn't have a constant, and suddenly…I want to be that for him. Maybe I *am* that for him. I've become that in the five short weeks we've been working together. Somehow. Through the negative energy, through the hatred, through the feelings of wanting to be anywhere else, we've transitioned into this place where we only want to be with each other.

I don't know how. I'm still quite sure I hate him.

But intense feelings are intense feelings, and maybe they're starting to give way to something else as I learn more about him.

He shudders again, and I tighten my hold on him. We stand embracing like that for several minutes before I pull back. I walk him over to the bed, and I make him sit first. Then I sit beside him, spacing us so I can pull him down and allow his head to rest on my lap while I rub soothing circles on his back.

"You don't have to say a word, Maverick," I croon softly. "But if you want to, I'm right here to listen."

He doesn't talk, but he does draw in a deep breath as he seems to pull himself together, as if he's drawing strength from being here with me in this way.

He does some more deep breathing before he lifts his hand and sets it on my thigh next to his head. It's warm. Hot. It pulses tingles that seem to radiate from the place he's touching and skip right up toward my pussy.

My hand that's rubbing circles on his back moves so my fingertips dive into his hair. He flips onto his back so his head is still in my lap, but now his eyes meet mine. I lightly run my fingertips from his temple down to the sexy jawline peppered with stubble, and he sighs softly as his eyes turn intense on mine.

"I need to forget," he whispers.

I lean forward and press my mouth to his, and he reaches around the back of my head to hold me in place as he deepens the kiss to urgency nearly immediately, his tongue dancing with mine in what's already become a familiar, beautiful tempo. I pull back, no easy feat with the way he's holding my head. "I can help with that," I murmur.

He lets go of my head and sits up, and he guides me so I'm lying on my back. He moves over me, covering my body with his, and his eyes connect with mine. He searches there and seems to find what he's looking for, and then his hips slam to mine.

"Ah!" I cry out, and he covers my mouth with his hand.

"Quiet," he demands, and he's right. We're surrounded by teammates and coaches and staff, and nobody can know that I'm in here, that we're doing what we're doing right now.

I nod, and he lets go of his hold over my mouth.

He drags his lips along my neck, and then his mouth moves toward my ear. "I love hearing the sounds you make when I'm fucking you, but you have to be quiet tonight."

I shiver at his words, snagging my lip between my teeth as his mouth continues to drag along my skin. He *loves* the sounds I make.

"I made you a promise last time, and right now, I'm going to make good on it," he says.

I tremble beneath him, and he wastes no time in moving down my body, peeling my shorts and underwear off me, tossing them to the ground, and diving in.

His tongue goes immediately to my clit, and then he slides it down, tracing my entire slit as he pushes his tongue inside me. He moans as if he's tasting the best meal he's ever had in his life, and his mouth moves up to my clit again as he pushes a finger into me.

"Oh fuck," he hums against me, and a rocket of pleasure explodes through me at the feel of his hot breath on my trembling flesh. "You're so fucking perfect."

Oh. My. God. How the fuck am I supposed to stay quiet?

My fingers dive back into his hair, pressing him harder into my pussy as I ride his face and let go to revel in the pleasure he's delivering.

It's good. So good. *Too* good. Without warning, my body almost immediately betrays me, as if just merely spending time around this man is enough to keep me on the verge of a constant orgasm, and it barely takes a few flicks of his tongue to set me over the edge. I dig my fingers into that luscious hair of his as my body bucks off the bed, but he stays with me, sucking my clit as I make my way through the foggy haze of complete and total bliss.

I do my best not to scream my way through it, but I think I black out for a few seconds from the onslaught of pleasure, so I can't be sure what the hell I say or do.

He pulls back and rocks onto his knees as his eyes meet mine, and he does that classic *wipe the mouth with the back of his hand* move that nearly sends me spiraling into a second climax. "Now I know, and I'm already addicted," he mutters.

Addicted.

He's already *addicted* to the way I taste.

It's like he's two different people. Maybe three. But this is the one I want to spend time with. The guy who knows how to use his tongue and gives me compliments like he's already addicted to me.

I'm still lying in bliss, his words swirling around me with that sweet afterglow of his heavenly tongue, when his grunt pulls me back to earth.

"I didn't bring any condoms."

My eyes open lazily. "Neither did I."

His eyes shift to my pussy, still wet and glistening from what he just did. "I want to fuck you."

"I want you to fuck me, too," I say.

"Can I?"

I nod. "I'm on the pill."

His eyes seem to narrow at that into nearly a glare, as if he's considering *why* I might be on the pill, remembering the man who was standing outside my door the other day. We never talked about it. I never told him that he was my ex stopping by to try to rekindle things. I never told him that I basically made Billy leave before I went over to scream at Maverick to turn his music down a couple hours later, only to end up in his bed.

"And I'm not sleeping with anyone else right now," I add softly. His glare eases at that, and he moves so he's hovering over me. "Are you?" I ask as our eyes connect.

He shakes his head slowly without a word as he reaches down between us to pull himself out of his shorts and grasp his cock in his fist. He strokes it a few times before he guides it into me, nothing between us, and a low moan rolls out of me in sync with his growls of pleasure.

"Fuck, Ev," he murmurs, shortening my name. He hardly ever addresses me by name at all, and hearing him murmur it in the heat of the moment feels more intimate than I was expecting.

His mouth drops to my neck, and he peppers kisses there as he starts to move. I close my eyes as I wrap my arms and my legs around his body while he takes me for a ride.

"Open your eyes," he demands, and my eyes fly open to meet his.

His are stormy and dark, the blue irises nearly black like this as intensity seems to pour out of him and into me as he slams into my body. He's taking no prisoners, giving no mercy as his hips drive against mine in a slow, punishing rhythm. It's hot. It's hard. It's powerful. It's filling a need I didn't realize I had.

As our eyes connect, my tightly coiled body seems to spring free, and a soul-shattering orgasm plows headfirst into me. I cling to him with my entire body as I ride out the wave. His mouth covers mine as he swallows my need to cry out, and as my body finishes contracting over his, he lets go of me, pulls out of me, rocks back onto his knees, and grips his cock in his fist, pumping up and down his shaft.

He aims at my lower stomach as his own orgasm takes over, and hot white streams land on my skin, branding me, scalding me, marking me as his.

I watch his face as he gives into the pleasure, and his eyes are focused on my stomach where his cum lands as grunts drop from his lips in time with each new pulse. When the pulsing stops, he jerks himself off a few more times, then rolls the head of his cock through his own cum.

"Jesus, you're pretty like that, all marked up with my cum."

My jaw might drop open. I'm not really sure.

But I bask in the glow of his words. It feels like approval, and that means something coming from this man who seems to hate everything and everyone.

If nothing else, this was a success.

I helped him forget whatever happened tonight, and that was what he wanted.

He walks to the bathroom and returns a moment later with a washcloth. I'm damn near shocked as he wipes off my stomach, taking sweet care of me, a heady contrast to the intense sex we just had. He gets rid of the washcloth and returns to me only to find that I've stood up and put my clothes back on.

"Stay," he commands softly.

"We both know I can't."

"Yes, you can. We'll just tell anyone who might happen to catch us that we had an early meeting in my room."

"With me dressed like this?" I ask, holding a hand in the air to indicate my body.

He tilts his head, relenting. "Fine. Can I just…I don't know." He's muttering, and he wants to ask for something, but I'm pretty sure he doesn't know how to ask. He's the kind of guy who never asks anyone for anything. "It's fine. You should go."

I want to stay the whole night just like he asked. And maybe if I wasn't in the post-sex haze of the two orgasms he just pleasured my body with, I'd be thinking clearly enough to come up with a plan. I could go grab my bags and just stay in here with him. We could shower together, stay together, *be* together.

There's too much at stake. I'm just starting to get through to him. I can't let Jack or Lincoln catch us. If I were to lose this job now, just when we're making breakthroughs, just when we're getting closer…I feel like it would do irreversible damage to this poor man who's clearly going through some shit that he's not ready to talk about yet.

But we have a trip to Los Angeles planned for Monday. We're sharing a hotel suite—with too many beds, but maybe we'll share one anyway. Apart from attending the actual event, it'll be twenty-four hours where it's just the two of us.

I finally nod and press a soft kiss to his lips before I reluctantly make my way back to my own room next door.

CHAPTER 23

MAVERICK JENNINGS

Standing on the Sidelines

I hate standing on the sidelines when I should be out on the field, but Coach is letting me communicate with Brandon and call plays, and at least I feel like I'm a part of the game. Even if it isn't the part I want to be involved in. I'm listening to the plays being called upstairs through a headset, and I give Coach my opinion when I'm asked.

And I rip the headset off my head and throw it on the ground in anger when I'm ignored and it leads to a turnover.

Fuck.

She was gone when I woke up this morning, as expected, but I was hoping she'd fall asleep too and be there anyway. Maybe that's why I'm in a pissy mood.

Or, probably more likely, a pissy mood is just my general demeanor.

The repercussions didn't matter to me as much as being with her did.

I don't know what's happening.

Instead of hating her very existence and the people who brought her here, I find myself glancing over at her during the game.

I've never glanced at a woman during a game.

Not even back when I was married.

I've always been hyper focused on gameplay. Warming up. Intentionally stretching. I couldn't let a woman interfere with that.

And now I can't stop thinking about what happens when her year is up. When I'm all fixed and no longer need a brand strategist. When I have my future mapped out, when I have all the sponsorships I can handle, when my legacy is secured.

My legacy.

What a goddamn joke.

The only motivator I had before to work on my *legacy* was for my mother's reputation. But my mother doesn't even know who the hell I am. What difference does my legacy make?

Zero. None. Zilch.

And yet, as I glance over at the woman who's been trying to help me with it anyway, I can't help but think that maybe it *does* matter. Maybe I want to change for her. Maybe I want to be someone worthy of someone like her.

I don't know how to do that. How to be that. How to open up to her. How to tell her what happened in my past that made me the man I am today, the one who has no fucks left to give because they were all buried with my past.

She's awakening them. She's making me want to care again. And it's confusing as hell.

I never wanted to care again. It's easier not to.

Or maybe I want to continue being the fuck-up I am so she'll have to stick around longer than a year.

Our eyes catch, and she looks surprised that I've taken my focus off the field. I return it where it should be as expected, not sure why I'm suddenly more interested in watching her survey the field and look over at me every so often than I am in watching my teammates on offense.

It's not what I was expecting.

It's not something I'm ready for.

I want to put the shield back up, but I'm afraid if I do, I'll lose access to the first thing that I've wanted since it all went down over ten years ago.

The Aces win. Handily. We head back to Vegas after the game. She sits with the staff even though I want her next to me. We don't say goodbye. Her car is already in the parking garage when I get home, and she must already be upstairs because she's not in the lobby.

I stare at her door a few extra seconds, willing it to open, before I head into my own condo.

I'm being stupid.

But when things got too hard to handle on my own, she was there for me. When the demons held sleep hostage, she stepped in and battled them for me without even knowing how important it was that she showed up for me.

Nobody shows up for me. I'm alone, and I have been for a long time.

She once told me I wasn't broken and that it was okay to tell her why I think I am. I didn't take her up on that, but it might be time to confess. It might be time to get it out of the place where I've let it sit, rotting and festering for ten long years. It might be time to let her in. It might be time to reclaim my life rather than continuing to live in the shadows, battling the demons alone.

I never wanted to. I was better off this way for over an entire decade. Ten fucking years.

And then she stepped into my life, all red lipstick and danger, and made me see that maybe, just maybe, there could be something else in this life to bring me some semblance of joy again.

I've been standing on the sidelines of my own goddamn life for too long. It's time to take it back, and she's the one who's making me see that.

I walk over to the mantle where I keep the photo of my mother and me from my wedding.

I allow the memories that I've worked so hard to push away to rise to the surface. I think back to this exact moment. I'd just married the love of my life. We were young, only twenty-two, college graduates getting married the week after graduation—before my first season as a pro football player got underway. It was quick, but we dated all through college, and when you know, you know. Right?

I knew.

I don't know if *she* knew.

Distance helps define things, and it's easier to see now that she loved the idea of being a football wife more than she loved actually being one. She loved being a football girlfriend, too. Of course she did. She was a cheerleader. I was the captain of our college team. We went together like peanut butter and jelly.

Or so I thought.

I was wrong, and I didn't find out until it was far too late, creating scars in the already broken heart that would never, ever fully heal. I'd never, ever fully trust again. Little did the man in this photo, the one dancing with his mother at his wedding reception, know. There's so much joy in this photo.

It was before my mom's diagnosis.

It was before I found out the truth about my wife.

It was before I knew exactly how much I lost.

It was before my first season ever started as a pro football player.

So little joy has followed the events that took place a mere month after this photo was taken. We were still newlyweds. We were still celebrating. I had to leave a few weeks later for my first training camp, and football was the only reprieve from the harrowing loss that was eating me alive.

The harrowing loss I've constantly lived with for a decade.

I deserve the chance to move on. I never thought I did until someone pointed out to me that maybe I'm not broken.

Maybe the one who created this mess was the one who was broken, and I was just the debris in the aftermath. One of many pieces of debris, really.

I pack for my one night out of town tomorrow.

I think about texting Everleigh. I think about asking her if she can come over.

I don't.

I also don't get much sleep.

When morning dawns, I get up and run on the treadmill. Since we won, we don't have practice today or tomorrow, but Coach has sent some film for me to review. I can do it on the plane later, but I decide to do it now so I can focus on other things while I travel.

I study, analyze, and make mental notes to prepare for our home game against the Eagles this weekend—my first regular season game as the starting quarterback of the Vegas Aces.

And then it's time to meet Everleigh.

Unfamiliar nerves dart through me. I run my sweaty palms down the front of my shorts to dry them off as I sling my overnight bag over my shoulder and my garment bag over my arm. I head out into the hallway, and I find my neighbor locking up her door, a small suitcase that'll fit in the overhead by her feet.

"You ready for LA?" she asks.

I nod, and I find myself without words.

I hope they come because I want to tell her everything. I need to tell her like I need to breathe.

We take a car toward the airport, and before I lose my nerve, I reach over and take her hand in mine in the backseat. I lower my voice so it's just for her, and I say, "I hated the idea of this when Ellie first mentioned it, but now I'm glad to have some time with you."

She squeezes my hand, and she looks a little confused, like she's not quite sure what to say.

I'm confused, too.

"Me too," she says.

I blow out a breath, and I don't want to tell her everything here in the back of a car where someone else could overhear it, so I don't say anything at all.

We arrive at the airport. We grab lunch. We board our flight. She pulls out her laptop and immediately gets to work, so I review the film again since this doesn't feel like the time to bring up my past.

We land, and we're ushered to the hotel where the event is taking place. We head toward check-in. "Checking in. Last name is Bradley," she says, and she pulls out her license and a credit card.

"I see you've requested a two-bedroom suite," the hotel clerk says, tapping a few keys. "With tonight's event, unfortunately all our two-beds are taken, but I can get you into a one-bedroom suite."

She glances at me and snags her lip between her teeth. "Does that have more than one bed?"

The clerk shakes her head. "There's a couch in the living area, but it doesn't convert to a bed. I can send up extra sheets if you'd like."

"That's not necessary," I say.

Everleigh glances over at me, still worrying her lip between her teeth.

"It's fine." I incline my head a little meaningfully, and she looks nervous as she turns back to the clerk.

"It's fine." She lets out a little breath, and then the clerk hands over our room keys and sends us on our way.

We call the elevator, and the suite is fine. It has a king in the bedroom along with the couch as described, and if Everleigh is uncomfortable with the situation, I'll just take the couch.

"I need to get dressed since the event starts in an hour," she says, and she ducks into the bathroom.

I sit on the couch, a little perturbed we haven't had a chance to talk at all yet, and she takes her time in there. So much time, in fact, that forty-five minutes later, I decide to get into my suit.

She emerges as I'm buttoning the jacket, already uncomfortable and hot as fuck as I yank at the collar that feels like it's choking my thick neck, and she freezes in the doorway of the bathroom.

My breath catches in the back of my throat.

She's an angel. Or a devil. I'm not really sure.

She's in red again. Angels don't wear red.

Plump lips colored red. Black pointy heels with red bottoms. Her hair falling in loose waves around her shoulders. Whatever she did in there, however much time it took…it was worth it.

And she'll be on my arm tonight.

Granted, she'll be on my arm as a publicist might be, not as my date. But we're far removed enough from our world in Vegas that I can pretend, if only for a moment.

"Damn," I murmur.

Her eyes heat as they move along my suit. "Back at you."

I clear my throat and don't hide the fact that I need to shift my hard cock, and she chuckles as she rolls her eyes. "Men."

I roll my eyes back. "You."

She presses her lips together as she crosses the room and picks up the purse she dropped on the table when we walked in. She grabs a few items out of it and transfers them into a smaller clutch that matches her dress. "You ready?"

I shake my head. "I'd rather fuck you first so I'm not walking around with a hard-on the entire night."

"Sorry, but we'll be late if we don't get down there now." She walks over to me and fiddles with my tie, which I'm sure is already meticulously straight. It's a reason for her to touch me, and I loop an arm around her waist and haul her into me so she can feel how hard I already am for her. She lets out a soft moan, and I want to kiss her. My eyes flick to her lips. "Don't you dare," she warns. "You'll smudge my lipstick, and you'll have red all over your face."

"Worth it," I say, and I lean down and press a soft kiss to her neck. She grabs hold of my biceps, and I bare my teeth against her neck for a second. She moans before she pushes me back, and I very nearly chuckle at it.

Jesus, she's even pulsing a near *smile* in me.

This woman.

"We need to get down there. I signed you up for a red carpet walk with one of the children benefitting from the funds raised from last year's Hope Gala, and the red carpet walks start in five minutes."

My chest squeezes that I'll be walking with a kid.

I don't really mix with kids.

I thought I could, but when that was ripped away from me, my dreams died with it.

She turns and slides her arm through mine, and together we head down to the gala. She has no clue of the turbulence racing through me.

She has no idea that this is dredging up memories I thought I'd left in the past.

The Hope Gala raises funds for children facing illness, trauma, and hardships. I had no idea kids would even be here, let alone that I have to escort one of them in, but it's too late for me to protest.

I draw in a breath as I see the line of kids near the lobby.

Everleigh walks up to a man with a headset and a clipboard. "Maverick Jennings is here," she announces, and she pushes me in front of the clipboard guy. He wears a nametag that says Carl.

"Jennings, Jennings," he says, scanning the list. "Right. You're with Bella Brown." He glances up at the kids. "Bella Brown?"

A little girl who can't be older than five or six raises her hand shyly, and Carl waves me over to walk with him toward Bella. Everleigh follows behind me, and Carl stops in front of Bella, who looks like she's going to pass out. I wonder what happened to her—to any of the long line of kids we passed to get to her. I wonder if it's trauma, illness, or hardship—which category she falls into and how she benefitted from this gala.

She's got dark brown eyes and nearly black hair, and her eyes won't quite meet mine. My chest aches for this little girl and whatever it is she's been through. Did her dad cheat on her mom and ask her not to tell the one parent she trusted…like I had to do? Something tells me whatever she's been through was far worse than that, and my own experiences still haunt me to this day. I can't imagine what this girl has been through.

I kneel down so we're at eye level. "Hi, Bella. I'm Maverick. How old are you?"

Her big doe eyes move to meet mine, and she whispers, "Five."

"Five! Wow. Are you in kindergarten?"

She nods.

"Do you like school?"

She shakes her head, and I can't help a small laugh at that.

An actual laugh.

Holy shit.

"Why not?" I ask.

"I'm absent a lot."

I wrinkle my nose for her benefit as I wonder why. Is she neglected? Is she sick? Is someone in her family ill? Does she even have a family? And if she misses a lot of days, does she have friends? Or is it impossible to make friends when you don't consistently attend? "That's hard. I'm sorry. I didn't like school much either."

"Why not?"

"It was hard."

"It's hard for me, too. Especially math," she says.

"What are you learning in math?"

"Adding numbers."

I make a face like that's just the worst, and a soft giggle escapes her. The joy that lights my heart at the sound of a little girl giggling because of a face I made when she seems like she must have a pretty tough life is unlike anything I've ever felt.

"You ready to walk me into the gala?" I ask her.

Her eyes widen, but she gives me the slightest little nod. I straighten, and she slips her hand into mine. The little cold hand takes me by surprise. It's tiny in my big hands, and I find myself wanting to protect her from whatever it is she's been going through, whatever trauma or illness she faces. I want to make it go away for her. I have no clue how to help her when I don't even know what her situation is, but I have resources. I have means.

We walk the red carpet together, and we stop at the step and repeat to smile for photos. I glance at her, and her smile is about as nonexistent as mine is. I pick her up into my arms to let her know it's okay, and I force my mouth into the shape imitating a smile. It feels unfamiliar and foreign to me, but when I look at her with all my teeth showing, her lips move into a similar shape. We look together at the cameras, and I press my cheek to hers as the bulbs flash in our faces.

I carry her into the ballroom, and Carl's associate, Beverly, walks over to me. "We'll take Bella from here, Mr. Jennings. Thank you so much for escorting her in."

I just met little Bella, but I'm not quite ready to leave her just yet. I set her down, then kneel down to her level. "Thanks for walking me in. Those cameras are so annoying, but being with you made me smile."

"Me too," she says quietly, and she throws her arms around my neck. I have no idea how I bonded with a five-year-old girl in the last five minutes, but I did. It feels like we shared something important, like we're more alike than we realized.

I give her a hug, and she lets go and scampers off toward a woman who looks a lot like her. I'm about to head in that direction to talk to her mom or her aunt or whoever she is when they walk through the doors and back into the lobby.

"How do I get in touch with Bella's family?" I ask Beverly. "I'd like to help if I can."

"Information for all recipients is confidential," she says with a smile. "Your monetary donations tonight will go to help children just like Bella."

It's just as important to help other children. I know that. But I also want to help Bella.

I rush away from Beverly and into the lobby, but she's gone. Vanished. Like it was all some sort of dream.

I blow out a breath as I return to the ballroom to find Everleigh, my heart sinking that I can't do more for that poor girl.

I don't see Everleigh's red dress when I scan the room, and I head back to the lobby in the direction I came from, where I see her talking to Carl.

He hands her a piece of paper, and she thanks him as I saunter over to her.

My brows pinch together. "What's that?"

"Bella's guardian's name, home address, and phone number." She smiles triumphantly, and I can't help myself.

I take her into my arms and press my lips to hers as joy fills my chest in a completely unexpected way.

CHAPTER 24

Everleigh Bradley

Can We Talk

"Whoa there, Hotshot," I say, pulling back. Just because we're not at home doesn't mean we can make out in a hotel lobby. It's a particularly bad idea with so many cameras around, but I guess this is his way of thanking me.

And also…

Holy shit.

Holy shit.

Am I the only one who saw him with that little girl? Because *swoon*. Swoon City. I feel like I'm that GIF of Blanche from *The Golden Girls* where she's spraying herself with a water bottle because it's so hot.

I'm equally hot. For Maverick.

There's no denying it.

I was already in the general vicinity of Swoon City just from seeing him in a suit. But then seeing him with a kid? Lord help us all.

It's like he turned into someone else entirely around that little girl. He melted from this grumpy asshole into a caring, kind man with a heart of gold. I've never seen him like that before.

He smiled. Smiled! I've never seen it before. To be honest, I wasn't fully sure he had teeth in there until he grazed them against my nipple, but he does, and they're pearly white and straight, and his entire face lights up when he bares them. Swoon again.

I had to do something. When I saw his face fall after Bella ran out and Bev gave him the standard answer about confidentiality, I had to find some way to help. So I went to Carl, used my charming personality, and conjured up her info only to get the soul kissed out of me when I handed it over.

Yes. My soul left my body. I believe it may have moved over to attach to his, which is potentially a very, very big problem.

But I'm plowing forward—soulless, I guess. I have no other choice. We have a gala to attend.

He rests his forehead to mine for just a beat. "Thank you," he says softly. He pulls back, and I see the emotion in his eyes.

"I could tell it was important to you."

He presses his lips together and nods, and then we head into the ballroom.

It's a nice event. Maverick writes a fat check to the organization, we eat our dinner, and we listen to the keynote speech. When dinner ends and dancing begins, he glances over at me. "Can we go now?"

I chuckle, and I nod as I pat his arm. "You did good, Jennings." We head toward the elevator. "I didn't know you were so good with kids," I say after he pushes the button and we wait.

"I'm a man of many talents."

Ain't that the truth?

Others join us on the elevator, so we're quiet as we wait to get to our floor. Once we're in our room, he immediately strips out of his suit jacket, undoes his tie, and unbuttons his shirt, stripping it all off until he's standing in front of me wearing just his pants.

It took all of ten seconds for him to get undressed, and I couldn't help but freeze and stare. My eyes fall to the tattoos on his arms, and I finally ask about them. "Why did you get a pirate ship?"

He lifts a shoulder. "It all goes together. The whole scene is a reminder to stay above water even when times get tough. The sharks circling remind me of all the threats in life, the anchor is for the stability I feel like I'm constantly chasing, and the pirate ship is a symbol of rebellion and nonconformity. I liked the symbolism since that's what my name means."

"And the star?"

He purses his lips. "Apparently a bad mistake when I thought I was going to play for Dallas for my entire career."

"What if the star is your light in the dark?" I walk over and trace the blank space where the star is outlined. "Fill this in, and it's got new meaning. It's hopeful instead of regretful. A star guiding your ship at night."

It's clear he never thought of it that way by the way he tilts his head at me.

I raise both brows as I kick off the heels that are killing my feet. "I can rebrand anything. It's my secret superpower."

He reaches for me and hooks his arm around my waist. "Interesting."

"What?" I ask, a little breathless this close to him when he's not wearing a shirt.

"I'd say your secret superpower is the way you fuck, but if you want to go with the rebrand thing, that's cool too."

I chuckle at his words. "You're just saying that to get me into bed."

"Did I need to say anything to get you into bed?"

I giggle as I swat at his star with new meaning.

"I mean, there *is* only one bed here, and you're welcome to it if you want it. I can sleep on the cou—"

I interrupt him when I move to my tiptoes. "Shut up," I say, and I press my lips to his. We're alone now, and I don't need to pull away because we're in public. His palm slides to my jaw, and his big hand holds me half on my jawline and half around my neck. His hand is warm against my skin, and it pulses this needy ache in me that only he can satisfy.

He takes his time. He's slow and luxurious in this kiss. He's not rushing me toward the bed, or to the couch, or even up against the windows, instead taking the time to allow our tongues to dance as my arms wrap passionately around him and he hauls me in closer to him with one arm around my waist.

It's perfection here in this cocoon. The outside world can't touch us in here as we grow closer, me in his arms as he clings to me, holds me, worships me.

He pulls back first, and I think it's because he's going to take me into the bedroom, but instead, he surprises me by saying, "Can we talk?"

Okay, *surprise* is too mild a word for the shock that courses through me—that this man of so few words would stop one of the steamiest kisses of my life in order to *talk*.

"Of course," I say, stepping back out of his orbit as I force that needy pain between my legs to take a backseat while I listen to whatever it is he wants to say.

He draws in a deep breath, and he wanders over to the window. He keeps his gaze out there as he talks, as if it's easier for him to say what he has to say without having to face my eyes. The whole idea of it sends a shudder down my back.

"I know we've only slept together twice, but before we make it three, I need to say some things. I've been through some shit that shut me off to ever wanting to get involved with someone again. And then you swept into my life like a fucking tsunami with your rebrand and red lipstick, and something woke up inside me that died a decade ago."

He turns to face me, and I realize I'm holding my breath as I wait as patiently as I possibly can for his words.

"My dad spent my entire childhood cheating on my mom. Usually in front of me, and always with a line about how I needed to cover for him, like we were buddies instead of father and son. It hurt my mother, it hurt me, and that's why I think he's a bag of shit to this day. I never wanted to be anything like him. I took a different course and got married young, right out of college. She was my high school sweetheart. We'd been together six years by the time we got married—through most of high school and all of college. A month after our wedding, she died in a car accident, and I found out that night that the baby I didn't know she was carrying had also been killed."

"Oh my God, Maverick," I whisper as tears heat in my eyes. "I'm so sorry."

He presses his lips together. "If only that were the end. If only that were the worst part of it."

My brows crash together as I have no clue what he means.

"I found out at the funeral that she'd been cheating on me. The man she'd been cheating with, a friend of mine, showed his face and admitted the baby was his." His voice breaks on the last line, and tears start to tumble down my cheeks at the incredible pain this man has endured.

No wonder why he hates the world. No wonder why he prefers to be by himself. No wonder why he hasn't let anyone in.

It's been nothing but betrayal after betrayal for him his entire life.

But somehow, some way…he's letting me in. He trusts me. And I hold that sacredly. I won't let him down. I can't.

"My entire childhood tumbled back as I was in the midst of grieving my wife. I lost her to this horrible accident, not knowing I'd already lost her long before that. I thought my life would be different, but she was no better than my goddamn father was. We were supposed to have this child, a boy or maybe a girl who would have turned ten this year. Ten. Double digits. And he wasn't even mine. And instead, I'm alone because I've been too fucking scared to let anyone in. The only person I have left is my mom, but she's long gone." His voice breaks again, and he doesn't hide his own show of emotion as he starts to break down.

My voice is soft as I ask, "What happened to your mom?"

"Her memory. She has Alzheimer's, and it's advancing. Fast. She thought I was my father when I visited her on Saturday."

"Oh, Maverick," I murmur. I swipe at the tears still tracking down my cheeks as I think about how hard that must have been for her to mistake him for someone he holds so many negative feelings for. "You're not alone anymore. I'm right here." My voice is a whisper, and he moves away from the window and back over to me.

He takes me in his arms and buries his face in my neck. "I know."

He clings to me, and I wrap my arms around him to hug him and hold him in a way he hasn't had in far too long, in a way that lets him know that someone is right here on his side.

"Why did you tell me?" I ask softly as I hold him.

"Because I trust you."

My heart both shatters and swells at the same time—that he hasn't had anybody to turn to in an entire decade and that I have the privilege of being that person for him.

His lips move from my neck to my mouth, and if our time on Saturday night was filled with intensity, this time is filled with emotion.

His tears mingle with mine as this connection we share is helping him let go of the pain and revel in something better. He deserves happiness. Love. We all do. And suddenly, I want with all my heart to be the one to give it to him.

He walks us toward the bedroom while we kiss, and he drops his pants and boxers and kicks them off along with his shoes. He lets go of me just for long enough to reach under my dress and slide my panties down my legs, and then he sits on the bed and pulls me down on top of him so my legs fall onto either side of his.

He gazes at me, and I see the longing there, the need. The want. The intensity. The heat. All of it, but also this time, there's something else, something big. Maybe it's love, or maybe it's just feelings that could be the start of something like love, but either way, I want to drink in the way he's looking at me for the rest of time. I want to be the only woman he looks at with these eyes, and as he pushes himself into me and I start to slowly ride him while our eyes continue to hold that gaze, I feel a searing sense of the same thing as it races through me.

I'm not sure where it comes from, but it's there, deep, intense, and raw, and it's something I never expected to feel with this man who hated the very idea of me before he even met me.

I'm getting through to him, and maybe this was always meant to happen. Maybe we were destined to cross paths so I could rebrand his legacy.

But what I never expected was the thought that maybe I'd end up being a part of that legacy with him.

CHAPTER 25

MAVERICK JENNINGS

Bingo Card

I pull her mouth down to mine as she rides on top of me. Emotions I never thought I'd experience again are raging through me as I finally allow myself to *feel* again.

Because of her.

She's unlocked something in me, and maybe this is all we'll ever have—these three times. Maybe we're drawn more closely together because we're away from the spotlight in Vegas.

But if this is all I get, it was worth it.

In the back of my mind, I know it's wrong to give into this temptation. She's been hired to help me, and if things go south between us, we could both find ourselves in a lot of trouble. But trouble has never stopped me before, and it won't now, either.

I kiss her like my life depends on it as she holds onto my shoulders for balance and moves over me. Hell, if this is trouble, I want to get into a lot of it.

I grunt as the edges of release start to claw at me. I wrap my arms more tightly around her, and I start to shove up into her, taking control from the bottom. She cries out as I hammer into her, and this is much better than having to be quiet in a hotel room when we're surrounded by people I work with. *We* work with.

She throws her head back, breaking our kiss, and she pushes her chest toward me. I suck one of her nipples into my mouth as she starts to come, and she claws at my shoulders as she lets the pleasure take over.

It hits me at the same time. I've never been so in sync with a woman before the way I am with her, as if our bodies were made to pleasure the other. I let go as my cock swells inside her just as her pussy grips tightly onto me, the pulses racing through us both as each throb of my body fires another hot shot of cum inside her.

As the throbbing finishes and the pulsing slows, she falls into me, her head buried in my neck as I still inside her. I don't want to pull out. I don't want to leave this space. It feels safe here, and safety is something that's been missing in my soul for far too long.

The problem is that once I'm on the outside again, I'm not sure we'll have that safe space. At some point, she's going to realize that we shouldn't be doing this. Or worse, she's going to realize that she can do better than me. She's going to leave like everyone else has. It's some broken piece of me that drives everyone I love away without even knowing that I'm doing it.

She breaks the connection first. She lifts up so I drop out of her, and she walks over to the bathroom to clean up while

I think about how I want it to stay in her, owning her, marking her, and branding her as mine.

I grab my boxers and pull them on, and I lie back on the bed, falling onto the pillows. She grabs underwear and her tank top. It's too many clothes, but it also gives us the space to have a conversation.

"So after attending tonight's event, have you considered what sort of impact you could make with your own charitable foundation?" she asks.

"No post-sex talk about how great it was?" I tease, and she seems surprised that I'm teasing her. I guess I'm a bit surprised by it myself.

"It was more than great, Maverick," she says softly. She climbs onto the bed and rests her head over my heart, and I wrap my arms around her. "I just sometimes don't know what to say to you, and I figured I'd gloss over the awkward stuff by getting back to business."

"I don't ever want you to feel awkward around me," I say. "I know I can be hard to read, but you can always compliment my talents."

She presses a soft kiss to my chest.

"And to answer your other question, yes. I've done some research on therapeutic sports. I turned to football as soon as I learned that I had a little talent, and I threw myself into it. It was my therapy when I was dealing with the shit my father put me through. I've donated to different nonprofits that use sports for confidence building and healing after trauma, but I think I'd like to start my own foundation."

She shifts up onto her elbow, and her eyes light up brightly as they fall onto me. "For real?" She sounds excited about the prospect.

I lift a shoulder. "Yeah."

"That's amazing, Mav! This is exactly what we've needed to show the other side of you, the side you don't let anyone see. Wait," she says, and she jumps out of bed and runs over to her purse as I process her words. I stare at her sweet little ass as I realize she's right. I don't let anyone see, mostly because I don't allow myself to feel. But maybe we've turned a corner on that.

She pulls her phone out, and she taps on the screen as she walks back to me.

"Look at this," she says, and I stare at the photo she's showing to me.

It's Bella and me walking into the gala, a shot Everleigh took from behind. The two of us are hand-in-hand, two completely different people from completely different worlds who somehow bonded over shared trauma even though I know nothing of hers and she knows nothing of mine.

I feel an unfamiliar heat pinch behind my eyes as I stare at the picture.

I draw in a breath as I hand her phone back to her, and she sets it on the nightstand and moves back into position with her head on my chest. I wrap my arm around her so my fingertips are resting lightly on her bicep.

"So you channeled your pain into athletics, and you want to help kids do the same?" she asks.

"Something like that."

"I can have Ellie do some research. She has connections with the charity division at the Aces, and they'll help you set it all up and get it off the ground. We could start with this idea of therapeutic sports and even add in other aspects to it later. I'll look more into it. And you can be as hands-on or hands-off as you want to be," she says.

"I'd like to be involved," I say as I think about Bella and other kids I could help with this program. Football gave me a reprieve from what I was going through, and I want to provide that for other kids. Maybe *that* is the legacy I want to leave behind. Making life a little easier for someone who's been dealt a shit hand.

"Are there any other charities you'd like to get involved with?" she asks.

I clear my throat. "Alzheimer's research."

She's quiet for a beat, and then she asks, "When was your mom diagnosed?"

"Six years ago. She was on the younger side, but life expectancy is usually only four to eight years."

She makes little circles on my chest with her finger. "Are you close with her?"

"She was all I had when I lost Christina. I leaned on my mother a lot that first month after the accident, and then I threw myself into workouts. It was my first season with the Cowboys, so football became my life. Training. Studying. Analyzing. Anything not to have to think about her."

"And it turned you into the player you are today," she murmurs.

"I suppose it did. But it also turned me into the asshole I am today."

"You're not an asshole," she says softly.

"Oh really? Didn't you once call me a divisive asshole?"

She giggles as she taps on my chest. "Yeah, I did say that, didn't I? No wonder why you hated me."

"I didn't hate you," I say softly.

"Yes, you did."

"Okay, I did," I admit. "But the feeling was mutual."

"It was."

"And it had more to do with you being forced on me and then finding out you were Dex's sister," I say without thinking. The truth is that maybe I've come to accept that she was forced on me, but the fact that she's Dex's sister won't ever change. If push came to shove, would she choose me or her family?

For a split second, her father's casino comes to mind. I'm not sure why it chooses that moment, but it does, like it's some sort of foreboding omen that we started with her family coming between us, and there's a danger that it could possibly spell our end as well.

That's just the way my mind works. I'm always looking for how everything has the potential to fall down around me.

"I can't change who my brother is," she says quietly.

"I know. And it doesn't matter." I press my fingers into the flesh of her arm.

"Doesn't it? Or will he break another rib someday, and you'll take it out on me?"

Before I get the chance to answer that, her phone starts to ring. She shifts to glance over at it, and her brows dip down. "It's my best friend. She usually texts—"

I hold up a hand. "It's fine. Answer it."

"Penny?" she answers. She listens, and then she says, "Oh, God. Take a deep breath, babe." She listens some more. "Shit. Are you okay?" She paces in front of the windows. "I'm so, so sorry. What can I do?" She pauses in her pacing and glances over at me. "Of course you can. I'm here for whatever you need. I'm in LA but returning tomorrow." She resumes pacing. "I love you, Pen. You're going to be okay. Promise."

She says goodbye and hangs up, and my brows crinkle together as I study her. "Is everything okay?"

She shakes her head a little, and she stares out the window. "My friend was at home with her boys, and her husband is out of town on a work trip. She got a message from a friend with a video in it from an hour ago that's already going viral, and the message was like, 'Isn't that Brent?' She watched the video, and sure enough, her husband was making out with some other woman at a Bulls game. He's not even out of town. He's cheating on her."

A text dings on her phone, and she opens it. Penny shared the video.

She sits on the bed, and together we watch as the first few seconds of the clip show the basketball game, and then the cameras cut to a couple passionately making out in a suite. The announcer says something about how there's more action in that suite than on the court. The clip switches to what's clearly a little later in the game, and the cameras pan back to the same suite to see the man and woman drinking margaritas.

"That asshole!" Everleigh mutters.

"Jesus. Is she okay?"

"No! It's a viral video that her friend shared with her, which means it's making the rounds already. Brent is this high-powered realtor in Chicago. One of those slimeballs whose face is on every other billboard and the side of buses and has a stupid commercial on the radio that gets stuck in your head. Everybody knows who he is, and now poor Pen is sitting at home while he's out there *cheating* on her *publicly*." She punches a fist into her other open palm. "Ugh! I want to punch him!"

"What can we do?" I ask.

"She needs to get out of town with the boys until this blows over. You know how the media today is. They'll take it and run with it, and her face will be all over by morning. But she's in marketing, so she knows what to do. She asked if she could come stay with me for a few days, and I said of course."

I think about offering to let Everleigh stay with me while her friend stays with her, but I'm not sure we're at that place yet. I let it go as she continues telling me about her friend.

"She was talking about the *D* word last time we spoke," she says quietly. "She said she didn't love him anymore, but she wanted to do it on her terms. Not like this. It's so messy, and her family is going to be all over the internet by morning."

"Those poor kids," I lament, feeling for them even though I don't know them. "How old are they?"

"Sammy is seven, and Benji is five. Two little boys about to have their world completely changed because of their stupid dad. And now there will be a divorce, and Brent will make it hell on them, and it's just awful."

"Divorce is like death," I agree. "It's the death of a marriage, and the effects are rippling and tough on kids at any age. My mom finally kicked my dad out shortly after I went to college, and I felt like I had to be there for grief support even though there wasn't an actual death."

"How long were they married?"

"Twenty years."

"That's a long time to be with someone and for them suddenly not to be a part of your life," she says softly, and it's true. It was a strange sort of divide that came when my mother had to learn how to do the things he did while dealing with another kind of grief as her son went off to college. It's why I tried so damn hard to call her every day, to stay in touch, to let her know someone was always thinking about her. But as time went on, I got busier, and it got harder to fit in the calls until they became weekly, and then monthly, and now…

I visit when I can, but I haven't called her in years. I wonder if it would help to hear my voice more often.

"What are you thinking?" she asks softly.

"How I used to call her every day, and now I can't remember the last time I spoke to her on the phone."

"But you just visited her," she points out. "She knows you love her."

"Does she?"

"Of course she does." A beat of silence passes between us, and then she says, "I'm worried about my mom, too."

"Why?"

"She broke her arm, and the X-ray indicated cancer. She's getting a biopsy and scan this week, but we won't know the extent of what's happening until we get the results."

I pull her in a little closer, a little more tightly. "You've been quietly battling this?" I ask.

"Yeah."

"Are you close with her?"

"Not as close as I've always wished we were," she admits against my chest.

"Why not?"

"Life gets in the way. She's always more worried about appearances than reality. I always wanted the type of relationship where we could go on girls' trips or get manicures together, and instead she invited me to get fillers with her once because of the dark circles under my eyes." She sits up a little, and her voice is full of bitterness when she continues. "Which would perhaps explain how she might be dealing with a serious illness but hid it. She didn't want anyone to know she was tired, or that she was having pain, or whatever else was going on beneath the surface. Instead, she kept up appearances and continued to run in her high society circles as if everything was fine and dandy. God!"

She's swiping furiously at the tears leaking from her eyes by the end of her tirade, and I sit up and wrap my arms around her. I hold her tightly against me, simply holding her so she knows that I'm right here for her the same way she keeps showing up for me.

"Bonding over non-death grief and our mothers' illnesses wasn't on my Bingo card for this weekend," she says into my chest, her voice muffled.

I offer a grunt of a chuckle. "It wasn't on mine, either."

Neither was realizing that I'm in love with Everleigh Bradley, yet here we are.

CHAPTER 26
Everleigh Bradley

Stuck

I feel so much closer to Maverick after our night in Los Angeles, but as the plane touches down back in Vegas, reality starts to set back in.

First of all, the viral video of Penny's cheating asshole husband is *everywhere*. I can't escape it on any social media site, and I hope and pray she deleted all of hers so she doesn't have to see it.

She texted me her flight information, and she'll be here with the boys in a few hours.

But aside from that, I can't help but feel the punch back to reality with where I'm at with Maverick.

We can't hold hands in public. For all intents and purposes, I'm parading around as his publicist. I'm issuing statements on his behalf, arranging interviews as he gets back to practice this week, and curating his persona to be a little less prickly. We can't *be* together, which makes these intense, strong feelings all the more confusing.

We ride together back to our building, and it's as the elevator carries just the two of us up to our floor that I say, "When we're at the Complex or stadium, you should probably still act like you hate me."

He turns toward me, and he cages me in. He's so fast that I'm breathless as he grinds up against the front of my body. "But I don't hate you. I want to fuck you."

"Same," I manage to squeak out. "But we need to keep it professional in front of anyone associated with the Aces. My brother included."

He clenches his jaw with disapproval as his eyes sear down into mine, and the elevator doors open on our floor, forcing us off. This time he kisses me outside my door.

It's one of those kinds of kisses that makes my toes curl, but I know Penny and her boys will be here any minute. Sammy and Benji don't know it yet, but their lives are about to be flipped upside down.

I head inside and make sure my place is ready for guests. I have one guest room that really isn't big enough for a woman and two boys, so I unpack my suitcase in the guest room instead of the master bedroom. This will work fine for a few days.

I get a call from Milton that I have guests, and I tell him to send her up. I wait by my door for her, and I'm surprised when Maverick comes out of his condo, too.

"Pen's on her way up," I say.

"I figured when I heard your door open. Can I meet her and her boys?" he asks.

I nod. "Of course. I'm sure they'd love that."

The elevator doors slide open, and I rush to pull Pen into my arms. She starts to cry, and Maverick correctly assesses the situation.

"I bet you're Sam, and you're Ben," Maverick says, pointing to the two boys.

Sammy narrows his eyes. "Are you a football player?"

Maverick narrows his eyes back. "How'd you know that?"

"My mom said you're Auntie Ev's boyfriend," Sammy says, and Pen pulls back and mouths *sorry*.

Maverick's eyes catch mine, and mine are wide with horror. We're *so* not there yet, but it's also the easiest explanation for a child to say he's my boyfriend since we can't exactly say he's the dude I'm currently screwing even though we haven't defined anything yet.

"No, Sammy, honey. I said he's the man Auntie Ev is *working* with," Penny says, correcting her son.

I laugh. "We work together, and yes, he plays football."

"Prove it," Sammy says.

Maverick grunts a little bit of a chuckle. "Come on." He heads into his condo, and the boys look at their mom, who looks at me.

I nod. "Maverick is great with kids."

He turns around, and his eyes dart to mine, and they seem to soften just a little. He takes them into his condo, giving Penny and me a minute alone.

"How are you doing?" I ask.

"He didn't come home last night, so at least there's that. He did call to check in this morning like he always does on business trips before the boys go to school, but I didn't answer. The boys don't know anything, but my God, it's everywhere. *Everywhere*. I had to turn my phone *off* completely because of the number of messages I've seen. I had to redirect our path at the airport when their *father* was on a television screen making out with some other woman. I don't know how to protect them from this. I don't know how to protect *myself* from this. I just knew I couldn't be there at home when he got home."

"You can stay here as long as you need to," I say.

"The boys will need to go back to school. I can't keep them out forever."

"Then move here," I say with a shrug.

"Like it's that easy? Just—" She snaps her fingers. "—move?"

"I did it."

"And how's that working out for you?"

I nod toward Maverick's place. "Not too shabby."

She cracks a small smile. "I'll think about it, but I don't want to make any rash decisions. And besides, enough is going to change for those boys. I don't need to rip them away from their friends and everything they know, too."

"Good point. But I'd love to have you here."

"Aren't you coming home at the end of your contract?" she asks.

I lift a shoulder. "To be determined."

Maverick's door opens, and the boys exit to the hallway.

"He wasn't lying," Benji confirms.

"Yeah, we had to believe him when he had like seventy billion Aces shirts," Sammy concurs.

"I'll see if I can get you two some Aces swag while I'm at practice tomorrow. Do you want to come watch?" he asks.

They both look at Penny, who looks at me again.

I shrug. "I have an all-access pass. It doesn't say I can bring guests, but it doesn't say I *can't*."

"Can we, can we, can we, Mom? Puh-lease?" Sammy begs.

"I got nothing else on the agenda," she admits. "Let's do it."

The next morning, we all head to the Complex, and Maverick participates fully in practice. He's already game ready, and I can't help but watch his powerful legs, his concentration, his accuracy as he looks down the field and makes a play.

God, he's hot.

I've banged that dude three times. Lucky me.

The boys are really well-behaved, and there's a family area inside where they climb for hours on the play structure, and Penny gets some much-needed quiet time of her own.

Thursday and Friday are much the same. I coach Maverick on what to say to the media. I get in touch with Ellie to get started on Maverick's foundation idea. We go over some of the ideas he wants included in the foundation. We visit the shelter again.

I have long talks with Penny, who needs to get home for the weekend since the boys both have soccer games and they've already missed enough. Some of the excitement around the viral video has died down, though I'm not sure it'll ever really go away. Either way, Pen is ready to face it head-on. While she had her quiet time, she spoke with a lawyer, and she's headed home armed with divorce papers.

Maverick and I are basically forced to keep things as professional as possible until Friday evening hits. I'm standing in the lobby with Maverick waiting for the elevator, and I'm pretty sure he's going to pounce as soon as we get upstairs.

And then my phone starts to ring.

I check the screen. It's Ivy calling.

That sick feeling is back in the pit of my stomach, and I get the distinct feeling I shouldn't answer, that it's going to change the course of this evening. But I have to. I need to know what's going on.

"Ivy?" I answer.

Her voice trembles as she says, "It's cancer. And it's worse than we thought."

I close my eyes as if that'll end this nightmare.

We always think we have this unlimited amount of time. I'll get closer with my mom when I move back to Chicago next year. I'll go with her to her weekly facials. Maybe I'll get her to do a mani-pedi appointment with me once in a while.

We don't realize it's too late until it's too late.

"How bad?" I whisper, and Maverick's eyes whip to mine. The elevator doors open, and he ushers me on.

"The PET scan showed all these mets on her bones and—"

"Mets?" I ask. I feel Maverick's eyes on me.

"Metastases. The biopsy confirmed it started in her breast and has metastasized to her bones."

"Oh my God," I murmur, my eyes filling with tears. "So what's the treatment plan?"

"It's stage four, and for what she has…there's not really a cure. It's just about keeping her comfortable at this point. Maybe giving her some more time," she says, her voice breaking.

I have a million questions. How's she doing? How did it get so bad so fast? But I ask the one that seems to press hardest into me. "How long does she have?"

"They don't know. The doctor said it's likely a year. Maybe less."

I feel myself starting to break down at that. How my little sister can hold it together while she tells me this…well, maybe she's stronger than me.

I'm going to lose my mom in a year or less, and I'm stuck here in Vegas for the next year, stuck with a man I hardly know yet I'm falling for, stuck in a job that will open all sorts of doors for my future.

Just stuck.

"Thanks for letting me know. If there's anything I can do…" I trail off.

"Yeah. We're all sort of at a loss. I'm here if you need me," she says, the little sister taking care of her big sister.

"Thanks, Ivy. Love you." We don't say that enough.

"I love you, too."

We hang up, and as much as I don't want to break down in front of Maverick, I just worked my ass off to keep it together over the phone with my sister. The second I end the call, the dam bursts.

He pulls me into his chest and holds me, and somehow, it's exactly what I need. He doesn't ask questions, doesn't press. I'm sure he could hear Ivy's voice telling me the bad news anyway.

We get off the elevator, and he ushers me toward my condo. I unlock the door, and he follows me in. I realize it's the first time he's actually been in here.

He doesn't take the time to look around or see what he can learn about me from my décor. Instead, he sweeps me into his arms and carries me to the couch as if I'm a child, and he sits with me on his lap while I cry into his chest.

This isn't something I ever wanted to bond with someone over, but I guess we're both losing our moms, and the sad reality of that feels like a knife through my chest.

And maybe I'm stuck here as we live this new reality, but being stuck here in Maverick's arms feels a lot better than I ever imagined it would.

CHAPTER 27
Everleigh Bradley

Back to Square One

"**C**ome with me," he says, and he holds his hand out to me.

"Where are we going?"

"You'll see." He leads me toward the elevator, but rather than pressing the button to go down, he presses it to go up.

My brother lives on the top floor, so I assume that's where he's taking me—maybe to tell Dex about my mom, to hold my hand while I do it.

Which is why I'm surprised when he cuts to the stairwell instead of my brother's door.

I follow him up the stairs to a door marked *Rooftop Access.*

I didn't know there *was* rooftop access in this building, but apparently there is.

He props the door open so we don't get locked up here like some scene straight out of a comedy, and we walk over toward the side that looks out over Las Vegas Boulevard. He hasn't let go of my hand yet. I haven't let go of his, either.

We stare at the famed skyline for a few quiet moments.

"Have you ever heard of finger breathing?" he asks.

I glance over at him with furrowed brows and shake my head.

He lets go of the hold he has on my hand, and instead, he turns in toward me and holds my hand up in the air between us. "Breathe in," he says as he slowly traces the outside of my pinky finger and stops at the top. "Hold here," he says, and he pauses for a beat before he traces the path down the other side of my finger. "And let it out." He pauses again between my pinky and my ring finger, and then he does it again. "In," he instructs. "Hold." He pauses at the top. "Out," he says, tracing back down. He goes through all of my fingers, and he breathes with me on the last two rather than instructing me aloud. "Sometimes when I get overwhelmed, I come up here. It's quiet, somehow more peaceful than my place even when I'm alone. I look out over that skyline at a place that's anything but quiet or peaceful with its flashing lights and tourists and dancers and money being lost and won, and I do my finger breathing, and it recenters me. It calms me."

He's still holding my hand in the air between us, and I wrap that hand around his. I use my other to trace his jawline, my fingertips light on his skin, and I stare up into his eyes. Something shifts between us, some new understanding, or a new bond, or something. I'm not sure what, but I feel it, and it feels somehow like it's us against the world. Like together, we can do anything. Like we can stand up here staring out at that skyline, breathe deeply together, and everything will turn out okay.

When I wake in the morning, it's with Maverick's arms around me. It's only the second time we've spent the night together, but this time was different.

We stayed up on that rooftop a long time just talking. We talked about my fears, about my complicated relationship with my mother, about everything. He listened, and he told me more about his own complicated relationship with his mother, too, as he held my hand.

It felt like I was giving him pieces of myself that I won't get back. Like I took pieces of him for myself, too. Like our souls were entwining.

Would I have felt that way if it had been Billy there to comfort me? Unlikely.

I was together with Billy longer, but what I'm starting with Maverick feels different. Deeper. More passionate. More important.

It's a Saturday morning, and the Aces have a home game this weekend, which means light practice today. I get up and take a quick shower, and Maverick is awake in my bed when I emerge dressed for the day.

"Feeling okay?" he asks.

I nod. "Thanks for last night. I needed that."

He gets up and wraps his arms around me. "So did I." He presses a kiss to the top of my head, and it makes me wonder what an actual relationship with him would be like. Would it be tender nights and sweet mornings?

Something tells me that with a guy like Maverick, the answer is no. He let out his tender side for a night because I needed it, but even with me, he doesn't always show that side.

And with anyone else? He *never* shows that side.

Before we leave for practice this morning, he has an interview with two popular former players who started a podcast, and I help get him set up. He has a home office in his condo where he can record things like this. A jersey from his college days hangs in a frame behind his desk, but no traces of the Cowboys are here in his office—or the Aces, come to think of it. His office has a recliner chair in the corner with a small table beside it on which sits the latest Patterson thriller. I can't help but wonder if he gets a thrill from reading them. I wonder what gives him a thrill at all.

I sit in the chair to give him a few coaching tips before the podcast begins. "Stick to what we're trying to do here. If you want to mention the foundation or the Hope Gala, great. Keep it positive. You didn't get screwed by the Cowboys; you've learned a lot from the Aces. Can you tell me your top three talking points?"

"Grinding athlete, everyday kind of guy, football-focused?" he guesses.

I chuckle. "Works for me. Don't let them trap you. Pivot whenever you need to. Questions?"

He grimaces as he keeps his gaze focused on me, and then he shakes his head and connects to the call.

"Hey, Mav. I'm Reggie Bishop," Reggie says.

"And I'm Darren Vickers," Darren says.

Reggie takes over. "Thanks for joining us. We'll give you a quick intro and then launch into our questions. Anything off-limits?"

"I don't discuss my personal life," he says.

"We won't ask. We'll keep it focused on gameplay. Ready?" Reggie asks.

Maverick nods.

"Okay, going live in three…two…one. Hey athletic supporters, it's your boy Reggie Bishop—"

"And Darren Vickers!" Darren interrupts.

Reggie picks up from there. "Coming at you from Detroit. Today we have Maverick Jennings with us, star quarterback formerly of the Cowboys and ready to start his first game coming off an injury with the Vegas Aces. Welcome, Maverick."

"Thanks," he grunts. I make eyes at him and wave my arm in a *give them more* kind of motion, and he grimaces a little as he adds, "Good to be here."

I almost laugh out loud. It's like pulling teeth around here just to have a normal conversation.

How is this the same guy who held me in his arms all night and told me about how hard it is to watch his mother's memory deteriorate?

"Let's get into this injury first," Darren says. "What happened?"

I give him warning eyes that he seems to take to heart.

"Accident during practice that ended up fracturing a rib." He pats his side. "Good as new, though, and I'm ready to take the field tomorrow."

"Can you describe the accident?" Reggie presses.

"A teammate was overcompensating."

"Which one?" Reggie asks.

Maverick sighs, and I get nervous for a second as I repeat the word in my head over and over. *Pivot! Pivot!* I feel like Ross on *Friends* for just a second. And then, miraculously, he pivots. "It's not something I want to focus on."

It's clear he's already struggling, though.

"Right," Reggie says. "You've made a lot of headlines lately. Can we expect more, or would you care to comment on that?"

"I'm working on some new things and hope to make positive headlines going forward." He glances up at me, and I nod with a bright smile and a thumbs-up.

"Tell us about it," Darren says.

"I'm working with the Aces on a new foundation to benefit kids who have experienced trauma, for one. I've recently taken on some new sponsorship opportunities, including a partnership with Athlenergy, a new energy drink on the market that promotes hydration and muscle function."

"Oh, send some of that shit my way," Darren says, and he and Reggie laugh.

Maverick doesn't crack a smile.

"Let's talk about the headset incident in Cincinnati last weekend," Reggie says.

I suck in a breath. Man, they're not making this easy on him.

"What about it?" Maverick asks.

"Rumor has it Dallas shipped you off because of an attitude problem. Was that the kind of thing they were referring to?"

Oh God, oh God, oh God. What is he going to say?

"Dallas shipped me off because *they* had an attitude problem," Maverick says.

I close my eyes as I wince.

"How's that?" Darren asks.

"I put up the numbers with almost no support, and they blamed me anyway. Vegas snapped me up because they want to win. End of story," Maverick says.

"Who'd you clash with most in Dallas?" Reggie asks.

I stand up and try to get his attention to *pivot*, but he's focused on the screen now and purposely ignoring me.

"Who *didn't* I clash with? After week eight, nobody cared anymore. Every goddamn player in that locker room was just collecting a paycheck at that point. And half the coaching staff didn't have a clue what they were doing. I'm better off here in Vegas."

I press my lips together and close my eyes.

I can't interrupt him, and I can't legally cut his microphone despite the temptation plowing into me. We're live, so I can't even request edits.

Dammit, Maverick.

It gets worse from there.

He starts naming *specific* coaches who did him dirty. *Specific* teammates he didn't get along with—and why they didn't get along.

Where in my fucking notes did it ever say he should do *that?*

I'm standing there shaking my head, waving my hand in front of my throat to indicate he should *cut*, all the things…and he's ignoring me in favor of trash talking his former team.

Just when I thought he was turning a corner, we're back to square one with yet another mess I'm going to have to clean up for him.

When the call ends, I glare at him. "What the fuck was that?" I scream.

"It was me being honest." He shrugs, and his total lack of accountability does nothing but piss me the fuck off.

"You trash talked your former team! How is that spinning anything into positivity? And what about pivoting? You didn't pivot! You made a mess for me to clean up. I thought we were turning a corner!" I'm yelling, and I'm angry.

"We did turn a corner. But that doesn't mean just because I turned a corner with you that I forgive my former team for what they did to me."

"You wouldn't be here turning corners at all with me if they hadn't let you go," I hiss.

"That doesn't change the fact that I never wanted to be here."

"God, you just don't get it! You can't just say *one* nice thing about being here—like that you're getting me out of the deal."

"Am I getting you, though?" he asks. "We're hiding, Ev. We're pretending it's nothing in public."

My brows pinch together. Is he already jumping ship, scared of how big and important this could be, fucking things up to back out of it before it even gets started?

"It's not like you're innocent," he mutters.

"Excuse me?" I ask, my hand flying to my chest as rage pulses through me.

"The big Bradley secrets. The illegal casinos. What if that got out? What would that do to your future brand strategy company?" he asks.

The question feels like a punch to the gut, and at the same time it feels like a threat. "Those don't belong to me. You knew about it before I did."

"Doesn't change the fact that your last name is on it."

"Are you threatening me?" I ask softly.

He stares carefully at me, and he doesn't answer.

I thought after the talk we had last night, he'd leave my family out of this. My mother is dying, for Christ's sake. Exposing my dad's illegal gambling ring is the last thing my family needs right now as we all gear up to fight for her life—to fight against losing her too soon.

It just makes me realize that I need to hold even more tightly to my family's secrets…and if push comes to shove, I need to hold more tightly to my family, too.

CHAPTER 28

MAVERICK JENNINGS

Burning Too Hard, Too Fast, Too Soon

What I said about her last name was out of line. There's no denying that.

She rushed out of here and slammed the door behind her, and that's fine. Everything inevitably ends anyway. It's just a fact of life. I'm saving myself worse pain later by letting this come to a screeching halt now.

I could've kept my mouth shut, but like I told her, I was just being honest. It didn't *feel* out of line in the moment. I was simply sharing my experience.

I get why she's mad, though. She's not wrong. She'll have a mess to clean up. She'll have to issue a statement about it. She'll have to talk to my sponsors and talk them down to keep my paychecks coming. But that's her job. Well, hers and Ellie's, I guess. If it weren't for idiots like me, they wouldn't continue to be gainfully employed. Right?

Probably wrong, but I can spin just about anything into a justification if I try hard enough.

I manage to avoid her all day at practice, during which she spends the majority of the day on the phone—presumably fixing the mistakes I made earlier.

I decide to head out for an early evening run outside after I get home. The weather is starting to cool, and even though I pushed hard at practice, my legs feel the need to move.

When I walk out of my condo, she's heading toward the elevator, too—but with a stroller holding a kid.

"Who's that?" I ask.

She glares at me. "Jack. My nephew."

Oh, right. Dex's kid. I press my lips together and nod.

We're both quiet on the elevator, and I think of how many times we've ridden this same elevator together and the varying amounts of tension we experience together on it. Sometimes sexual tension. Other times it's hatred. This time, she's angry. And rightfully so.

"I'm sorry." My voice is quiet.

She looks surprised as she turns in my direction, but the surprise shifts into a bit of annoyance as she presses her lips together. "You should be. I spent all damn day cleaning up your mess, and I still have more work to do."

"But your nephew interrupted it?" I guess.

"Ainsley had to run some errands and asked if I'd watch Jack for a few hours, so I'm taking a break to get some fresh air with him." She purses her lips at the end.

"Mind if I join you?" I ask. It's a huge step for me. I don't ask people for things—most especially their company. But something tells me that I need to right this ship with Everleigh. She can help me or hurt me, and I would much rather stay in her good graces than continue to offend her.

I blow out a breath. Goddammit. None of this was ever supposed to be in the cards. I was supposed to come to

Vegas, quietly play my ass off, win some games, and eventually get them to pay me what I'm worth.

Instead, I'm all fucked up over some chick.

She glares at me again, but eventually she relents. "Fine."

"Where are you heading?" I ask.

"There's a park a few blocks away. I figured I'd take Jack there, maybe push him in the baby swing or let him crawl around in the grass. Come to think of it, it wouldn't hurt you to touch grass once in a while."

I shoot her a smirk, and she shoots one right back.

We step off the elevator, and she waves to Milton as we exit the building. She immediately takes off. Like sprinting takes off. I wasn't expecting it, and I find myself chasing after her.

I've never chased a woman in my entire existence. Ever.

Even Christina chased me before we finally got together.

But I am physically chasing Everleigh right now, and it feels like a big, flashing, neon symbol of what's happening between us right now.

She doesn't need to play hard to get, and I want her to know that.

And by the same token, I don't need to play games, either. I don't need to give my brutal honesty on a podcast just because it means she'll have to spend a few more hours thinking of me. I don't know whether that was my true motivation during that call, but I'm also not sure I can honestly say it wasn't.

Fuck. This is all so goddamn confusing.

I miss the days before she was sitting in Jack Dalton's office waiting to take my ruined life—I mean my *reputation*—over.

But I've learned the hard way that it's easier to live in the present than to be wistful over the past.

And so we push on.

I catch up to her fairly easily. "Trying to lose me?"

"If only that were an option," she says, panting.

"You could quit," I suggest.

"So could you."

"Fair enough. I won't," I say, my breathing still even.

"Neither will I." She pants a little and slows to a jog before she asks, "What are you, some superhuman? Why aren't you out of breath after chasing me?"

"I run harder and faster than that on a daily basis," I point out. "I was just letting you think you were getting away from me."

"Said every stalker ever."

"I'm not a stalker. You said I could come with."

"Out of common courtesy. Not because I wanted you here." She slows to an even slower jog, and I have to wonder why she spent all that energy sprinting at the start. Some people never learn, I guess.

So I ask. "Why'd you really take off?"

"I don't know. I'm angry."

"I know you are. But just so you know, burning your energy too hard too fast will just wear you out too soon, and then there won't be anything left in the tank when you need it."

She frowns a little as she glances at me. "Interesting metaphor, don't you think?"

My brows draw down as I try to get her meaning.

She clears her throat. "Like us. Are we burning too hard and fast too soon?"

"I don't know," I mutter. Something to think about, anyway.

We get to the park, and we leave those thoughts behind us even though they don't stray too far. She unbuckles Jack from his stroller, and she sets him in the baby swing. I stand in the back and push the swing to her, and she pushes it from the front so she can watch the baby and take pictures of him while he flies through the air with his baby giggles.

It's sweet, really—and I don't do sweet. But he's happy, and she seems happy, so I'm trying to push away the cloud that has hung over me for a decade.

"Any word on your mom?" I ask quietly.

She presses her lips together. "Nothing new. It's so weird, like they expect us to be patient with this stuff when we don't know how long we have. I don't want to be so patient that I run out of time, you know?"

"Yeah. I do know. My mom has gone downhill faster than we were expecting, and half of me feels like I should be by her side, while the other half of me knows she wouldn't want me to be."

"How do you know that?" she asks softly—almost fearfully. Like she's been considering leaving here to be with her mother.

I don't want her to leave. At the same time, I'd understand if she did.

"She told me."

She's wearing sunglasses, but I still feel her eyes as they whip toward me. "She did?"

"When she was first diagnosed, she wrote me a note. I keep it behind the photo I have of her and me on my wedding day."

"What did it say?" she whispers.

I recite it from memory. "You come first. Always. Never allow my illness to take away from your own life."

"She sounds like she's a good mom."

"The best," I agree.

"Have you spoken to her since the visit?"

I shake my head.

"Have you called her?"

I shake my head again. "Have you thought about calling your mom?"

She shakes her head, too.

"What if we call them right now?" I suggest.

"Like…together?"

"Sure. Why not? We don't have to be involved with the other's call. Just to be here for each other. For moral support or whatever."

"Moral support," she repeats, murmuring. She nods. "Okay. Let's do it. You first."

I blow out a breath. We're both dreading these calls for our own reasons, but I'll go first if it means she'll go eventually. She needs to talk to her mother. That much I know. Whether they get along or not, or however close they are, I can tell that she needs this. But she also needs someone to push her into actually making the call.

Maybe I'm getting to know her better than I realized.

I dial the number to the nurse's station at my mom's care facility.

"Floor unit, this is Susan," the nurse who cares for my mother answers.

"Hi Susan. This is Maverick Jennings. How's my mother today?"

"She's in good spirits today. Would you like to talk to her?" she asks.

"Yes."

"I'll put you through. One minute." She puts the call on hold, and a minute later, I hear my mom's voice.

"Hello?"

"Hey, Mom. It's Maverick."

"Maverick! Hi! How are you?"

"I'm good, Mom," I say, and I feel myself getting choked up at how *normal* she sounds today. She's not accusing me of being someone else, not angry with me, not confrontational. "How are you?"

"Oh, you know. Busy watching my shows, that's all. When are you going to come visit me?"

I can't exactly tell her that I was there just a few days ago, so I don't. "As soon as I can, Mom. What shows are you watching?"

"I'm really into these *Real Housewives*. Have you seen them?"

I can't help a small chuckle at that. "No, I haven't."

She launches into the latest scandal—something of which she recites every detail. It gives me hope that maybe she's turning a corner, that maybe I can have her back, that maybe she'll get better. But the hard truth is that she won't. That's just what this illness does.

If I can get moments like this, though…well, that has to be enough. And so I cling to every word she speaks as she recounts her show.

"Susan is telling me it's nearly dinner time, so I better go," she says.

"I love you, Mom. And just so you know, you're the very best mother I ever could've asked for."

"Oh, Mav. That's such a sweet thing to say. I love you, too, honey."

We end the call, and I feel good about the words I just said to her.

I just had no idea as I said them that they would be the last I ever spoke to her.

CHAPTER 29
Everleigh Bradley

The Best Mother

I feel myself tearing up at his words to his mother. I'm glad I convinced him to call her. I'm not sure he would've thought to do it if I hadn't brought it up, and by the same token, despite the shudders bolting through my chest, I'm not sure I would've had the nerve to call my own mother without him beside me.

"Everleigh?" my mother answers when it's my turn.

"Hi, Mom." I start to cry. Ah, fuck. I'm supposed to be holding it together for my mom—supposed to be holding it together in front of Maverick, too—and I'm failing on both accounts. "How are you feeling?" I ask, my voice trembling as I try my best to ward off the emotion. I focus on continuing to push Jack in his swing.

"I'm…well, to be perfectly honest, I've been better. I assume you've heard the news?"

"I have, and I'm sorry."

"We're not telling anyone, okay? I just…I don't want the looks the ladies will give me. I don't want the sympathy. We're just plowing forward. I have a life to live, and everything's okay."

Isn't that what got us here? Plowing forward, pretending everything is okay…

I can't imagine she didn't feel *some* sort of change in her health. No pain in her breasts, no fatigue, not anything at all. It doesn't add up, but knowing how vain she is and hearing her words about plowing forward tells me that she probably knew but didn't care to do anything about it.

She had no interest in knowing the truth—or at least in finding out sooner so that this could've been identified and treated earlier. And who knows what path she might've had if it had been? Maybe I wouldn't feel scared that this is the last conversation I'll ever have with her as we all sit by waiting for her time to run out.

But knowing her the way I do, she never would've voluntarily taken treatment. She's avoided any sort of medical doctor for years and years. She only goes to cosmetic doctors these days.

"Is there anything I can do?" I ask.

"No," she says. She doesn't sound sad or scared, but on the other hand, she also doesn't sound like she's in good spirits or joking.

She's always been hard to read. Why would this be any different?

"I have the Unity Gala tonight and appointments to get to, dear," she says. "You know how it goes. Spa, salon, stylists. The three most important S words."

Right. Not strength, self-respect, or self-awareness. Not support, service, or selflessness. Not success or security. But spa, salon, and stylists.

It's actually sort of incredible that my siblings and I turned out to be success stories given our roots. Maybe we all have done our best to navigate away from them. Maybe this position here in Vegas was always meant to get me out of Chicago. It feels like I'm stumbling through it in a lot of ways, but it also feels like I'm holding my own and starting to build the base of my own company. It feels like I'm working hard to achieve my dreams. Success, strength, and support. Those are my three S words.

"Of course." I clear my throat. Is this where I tell her I love her and don't want her to leave me too soon? Is this where I say she's the best mom I could ever dream of having, the way Maverick said it to his mother?

Is that even true?

No. The truth is that I dreamed of having someone raise me who also valued success, strength, and support. I dreamed of those mani-pedis with someone I could share my dreams with. I dreamed of mother-daughter bonding activities, the sorts I ended up doing with Ivy when she was younger—from arts and crafts to going with her to try on prom dresses.

For the first time, I wonder if I should invite my little sister out to Vegas to stay with me for a few days. We could get mani-pedis together and go shopping and fill our days with the sorts of activities we both missed out on with our mother.

It's not so much that it's too late to change any of that now with my mother. It's more the fact that she doesn't want to change anything. And not knowing how much time she has left leaves me feeling like I should give her what she wants.

I blow out a breath.

"Well, have fun tonight," I finally say.

"Thank you." She ends the call, and that's that.

I called. I tried to express myself to her. I failed.

But let's be honest here. I failed because she made me fail. She didn't open herself up to any sort of commentary at all.

She wants to pretend it doesn't exist, and who am I to mess that up if those are what could amount to her final wishes?

It's her life to live. She's the one who never wanted to be close.

I don't even realize I'm crying until Maverick thumbs away a tear from my cheek. I glance up at him. "Your call went better than mine."

He offers a sad sort of smile, and he walks around the swing and pulls me into a hug. He holds me tightly for a few beats, and it feels good here in his arms. Better than I was expecting it to feel.

Necessary, even.

I pull it together. After all, I'm the caretaker, and right now, I have a baby in my charge along with a man who's suffering in much the same way I am.

Maybe my mother is rejecting my need to feel like I'm doing *something* to help, but since she never was the caretaker in the family the way moms tend to be, I took that role upon myself. And I'll continue to do that.

To that end, I text Archer once Maverick lets me go and moves back around the swing.

Me: *Thinking about you, little bro.*

I text Ford next.

Me: *You doing okay with the news about Mom?*

I text Madden, Liam, and Ivy just to check in. It feels more personal than our group chat. I'll see Dex tonight when I drop off Jack.

That's it. I touched base with all six of my siblings. If Mom won't let me take care of her, I'll do my best to take care of her children.

And as my eyes meet Maverick's over the swing, I can't help but think maybe I've finally met someone who can take care of me, too.

MAVERICK JENNINGS

Emotions

I bounce on the balls of my feet as I pull my arm back and throw a football five yards to my first target.

I get another ball and repeat the drill to my second target.

My aim is on point today, and I'm ready for this. The stands are starting to fill with fans as we finish our warm-ups. Some have been outside for hours drinking and grilling in the parking lot, while others just arrived and grabbed their first beer.

I don't care about any of them. I only care about the woman watching from the owner's suite wearing a red Aces jersey with *Jennings 1* on the back.

It's a surprise when I see that, and I can't seem to take my eyes off of her. Goddamn, she looks *good* with my name on her back.

I haven't seen her all day. Game days aren't like practice days. She isn't allowed on the field, and I stayed at the team hotel last night. I left the hotel earlier than the rest of my teammates so I could get into the locker room and do some deep breathing. I needed to get into the right headspace.

We run a few team drills, and then we head into the locker room.

And here I am with less than an hour until game time.

Coach Nash gives us a pregame pep talk. I meet with Coach Richards and my O-line.

We line up in the tunnel.

We run out onto the field to the loud cheers of a stadium ready for their starting quarterback to finally take the field.

The National Anthem is played. We win the coin toss and defer to the second half.

Adrenaline courses through me as I watch kickoff.

I glance up at the owner's box, and I see her. Even from here. Even from this distance. It's like a light is shining down on her, and I realize it is. She's sitting in a seat in the sun, probably not on purpose, as it angles over her through a window on the opposite side of the stadium. It'll move in a few minutes, and she won't be in that beam of light, but somehow it feels perfect for the moment. She raises her hand in a little wave, and I take my right hand to brush off my left shoulder. I watch as her face seems to light up even more at the inside joke, and then I return my gaze to the field.

I keep it there for the remainder of the game. She's here, and I know that. I acknowledged that. But I need to keep my focus where it belongs during the game, and that's on the field.

The Eagles are forced to punt, and we take over at the twenty-three. I draw in a breath in my first regular season play at my new home stadium. I hear the chants.

Mav-er-ick! Mav-er-ick!

I'm fucking ready.

Jeff Tyler, the Aces' center, snaps the ball to me, and I fall right back into my old rhythm. I drop back, scan the field, and execute the play Coach Nash just called. The ball sails into the arms of Asher Nash, who runs down the field to catch a few more yards before he's taken down.

The crowd goes wild at our gain, and we line up again.

This is it. This is what's in my blood. This is what I live for.

I feel more myself than I've felt in a long time—longer than the last time I was on the field. And I suspect it's because a part of me that I'd written off forever has started to heal.

When my wife died, a part of me died along with her. But when I found out she'd been cheating on me…well, that was a cruel sort of pain I wouldn't wish on my worst enemy. To be mourning someone, full of grief, and to learn she wasn't at all who I thought she was made me feel like I lost her twice. I was mourning her death, and then I was also forced to mourn the fact that she didn't love me enough to be honest with me. On top of that, I had to mourn an unborn child I thought was mine for a few days until I found out it wasn't.

It made me feel like I was unlovable. That does things to a person. I didn't even have her here to have it out with her. To yell at her that I hated her. That I felt broken and betrayed because of her. I yelled at her ghost. I hated her memory. It's when I was forced to shut off my emotions.

But Everleigh is tapping back into them. It's still new, but I feel it on the field.

I soak every single emotion in as deeply as I can.

I feel the rush of adrenaline that I was missing for far too long. I feel the excited respect of my teammates as they slap my helmet to tell me my throw to Asher was perfect. I feel the nerves twisting through me as I play my first home game with the Aces. I feel the pressure to get this win, but I also feel the pride in my teammates, in our preparation, in our shared vision to win this game.

We pull out the win. Easily. Handily. Maybe *because* of those feelings.

I feel that unfamiliar tug on my mouth as my lips turn up into a bit of a smile when I walk into the press room after the game and the first question is fired at me. "How'd it feel to be back on the field?"

"It felt like I was right where I'm supposed to be."

They ask more questions, and I think Everleigh will be proud of my answers.

I want her to be waiting for me outside the locker room when I exit, but she isn't.

She shouldn't. It's not like I can rush up to her and take her in my arms and kiss her the way Dex is doing with his wife, or the way Asher is doing with his.

She's not my wife. I'm not exactly sure what she is. My brand strategist. The woman I've slept with a few times. The woman I can't stop thinking about. The woman some kid said I was the boyfriend of. The woman who made me call my mom.

I should call her again.

I'm riding a high after winning the game despite having nobody to greet me afterward, and I jump into my stupid silver and blue truck, pull up the number to my mom's facility, and make the call as I back out of my space in the parking lot.

"Floor unit, this is Susan," Susan answers.

"Hi Susan. This is Maverick Jennings. How's my mother today?"

She clears her throat, and my chest tightens with a bit of anxiety. "She's having a bit of a tough day. The doctors diagnosed her with pneumonia, and she's been more confused and agitated than usual. We just got her comfortable enough for sleep."

"Oh, I see. Okay. Can you let her know I called and have her call me when she's awake?" I ask.

"Of course. Great win, by the way. We had the game on for her, and we all cheered you on."

"Thanks," I say softly. It's nice to hear, but it doesn't mean as much if it isn't coming from my own mother's mouth.

We hang up, and I head home with a bit of the wind knocked out of my sails.

I figure I'll just call it a night, but when the elevator doors open on my floor, I'm surprised to see Everleigh Bradley standing next to her door, leaning on the wall as she scrolls her phone. When the elevator doors slide open and she spots me, she slips her phone into her pocket.

I stare at her for a beat. Jesus, she's pretty. That long, dark hair tumbles in waves past her shoulders, curling down by her tits. Her lips are cherry red to match her nails—maybe in homage to the colors of the team she cheered for today. My team. While she wore my number, and she's still wearing it. And her eyes, those dark brown eyes with the long lashes and a bit of mystery or mischief or *something* behind them, they pin me to my place.

"Good game," she says quietly.

"How long have you been standing out here waiting for me?" I ask.

"I asked Milton to text me when you got in," she admits.

"Why?" I grunt, narrowing my eyes at her.

"Because I haven't seen you all day. Because I...I—"

I raise both brows. "You?" I prompt. There are a million and one ways she could end that sentence, but the one she chooses sort of stuns me.

"I missed you."

My jaw slackens a little. I can't remember the last time someone told me they missed me.

I don't get close enough for anyone to even think those words, let alone say them aloud. And after they register and swirl around in my head for a beat, I realize something. I take a step toward her. "I missed you, too."

Hope seems to blossom in her eyes as they meet mine. "You did? You just seemed so…"

"Focused? I was. When I was on the field, I was focused on the game, but make no mistake, Ev. I was feeling every emotion that I've pushed out for a decade. I was in the moment. The adrenaline rushed like it used to. The celebration after scoring was genuine. I've been slaughtered by my coaches for returning to the sidelines without giving credit where it was due and instead discussing what we could've done differently, but not today. Today was…I don't know. It was filled with something I lost a long time ago."

Her voice is small and tentative when she makes her suggestion. "Joy?"

I stare at her as I let the word register. Joy. Is that what Everleigh is bringing back to me?

I remember smiling with that little girl at the Hope Gala. Wanting to spend time with Everleigh. Feeling everything on the field today.

I think she might be right.

I can't bring myself to repeat the word in fear that it'll slip away again, but I do know one thing that'll bring it to me— or will bring me satisfaction, anyway.

I move toward her and wrap my arm around her waist to haul her into me, and my mouth crashes down to hers. She doesn't hesitate a single beat as she lifts herself up and wraps her legs around my torso. Her hands are on my jaw as she kisses me back with all this pent-up energy that we've both had to put on the back burner all day. For the last couple days, really.

But now? The game's over. I don't have practice tomorrow. We'll spend the day together either way—and I'd much rather spend it naked than working on my *brand*.

My brand will work itself out with her by my side. This is more important.

This hallway is ours, but that doesn't mean those elevator doors won't open. People could see, and that's not something either one of us is ready to risk. With that in mind, I walk her over toward my door. I manage to fish my key out of my pocket and unlock my door, my mouth never leaving hers.

She grunts into me as I walk her into my condo, slamming the door behind us. I can't make it to the bedroom. I need her here, now. I need to be inside her. I need to continue this high of *feeling*.

I turn and push her back up against the front door. She's still straddling my waist, and I start to thrust my hips up. I'm humping her right against my door, and I wish we were naked so I could be fucking her instead. She's tender as her fingertips move from my jawline to thrust into my hair, and I'm the opposite of tender as my animal instincts kick in. I push her down off me so she's standing against my door. I make quick work to yank her jeans and panties off, leave the jersey on, and reach into the shorts I changed into after my post-game shower. I pull my cock out, stroke it a few times, and lift her back up into my arms so she's leaning against my front door again with her legs straddled around my waist.

I reach down under her leg to position myself, and then I line up with her body and thrust into her.

I still for just a beat, and her eyes open mere inches from mine. A hot, intimate moment passes between us as our bodies still, our eyes still, everything seems to still except for the beating of our hearts.

It's a connection unlike any I've felt before, and when I start to move, that connection only seems to intensify. My mouth slams back to hers, and somehow I'm also perfectly content just fucking her right here up against my front door.

I focus on the feel of her hot cunt as it surrounds my cock, of the slip and slide in and out of her as I pump away. I focus on the feel of her legs as they tighten around me, as her kiss starts to get more frantic, more chaotic, more urgent.

And then her mouth breaks from mine, and she whispers in a plea, "Oh, God, Mav. I'm coming. I'm coming so fucking hard. God, this is what you do to me." She claws at my back, leaving scratch marks with her red nails over my shirt, and I fucking love it.

Just hearing those sweet words drop from her lips pushes me into my own climax. My release is long and hard as I pump into her, my face buried in her neck while I growl out some curses. And once my body starts to come down from the high, once I start to move back from that sweet edge of pleasure, I carry her over to the couch. I'm still inside her when I lay her down and hover over her. I'm not ready to go again quite yet, but I'm still hard enough that I don't fall out. I pump in and out of her, enjoying the sensation of extra sensitivity after just coming inside her.

I pull back, and our eyes meet again. Her eyes search mine, those big brown eyes moving back and forth between my blue ones, and I wonder what she's thinking. I wonder what she's feeling.

When I see the way her eyes are so pure on mine in this moment, I have to believe she's in this for far more than just her career.

She feels it, too. Something is growing between us, and it's not something I'm going to be able to just set aside.

Because I opened myself up to feeling again, and that means I'm opening myself up to heartbreak again, too.

CHAPTER 31

MAVERICK JENNINGS

Incoming Call

The sun is already up when I wake, and Everleigh is asleep in my arms.

The last time I felt this content, it was all ripped away, and that's why I wake with a feeling of dread rather than of contentment like I should feel.

I didn't find out about Christina's accident from some phone call. I always thought it would've been easier if I had.

No…I found out when I drove by. She drove a black SUV, and when I saw a black SUV upside down in the ditch, my first thought wasn't that it was hers. In retrospect, I often wondered if I should've felt it when she passed. It was immediate. On impact, they said. I should've known. Should've felt the light shutting off.

I didn't.

She was coming home from the grocery store. They always say the worst accidents happen close to home. You have that level of comfort that you're almost there. We were in Ohio, and it was summer. Someone who witnessed the accident said a deer ran in front of her, and she swerved to miss it.

The last thing she saw was a deer in headlights.

The image haunted me every day until the funeral. And then I found out what she'd been doing behind my back, and the image of the deer was replaced with images of her underneath another man.

Those images have haunted me for a decade, and they didn't really start to fade until my brain started to fixate on red lips and red heels.

I rustle a little as a feeling of uneasiness pulses through me. This woman has thrown me all out of sorts, but the truth is probably that I've been out of sorts most of my life. Maybe for the first time, I'm...*in sorts*. Or whatever the opposite of *out of sorts* is.

My phone buzzes on my nightstand with a call, and when I see *Montgomery Memory Care* flash on the screen, a shudder runs through me.

That sickening feeling of dread rises up in my throat.

I suddenly *feel* it. I feel the thing I *didn't* feel when Christina died.

I know what the words are going to be before I even answer the call.

If it were my mother calling me when she was awake, as I asked Susan to have her do, the incoming call wouldn't say *Montgomery Memory Care*. It would say *Mom*.

"Hello?" I murmur so as not to wake Everleigh, but she starts to stir anyway.

"Hi Maverick. This is Susan from Montgomery Memory Care."

"Is everything okay?" I ask before she can give her reason for calling me. Traditionally she has called me every other week with an update. Tuesday evenings after my mother is asleep. This isn't our regularly scheduled time.

"That's why I'm calling." She pauses, and then she plows forward with her reason for the call. "I'm so sorry, Maverick. Your mother passed away in her sleep early this morning from the pneumonia. If it's any consolation, she went peacefully."

"Oh." It's all I can manage to say.

"She was a lovely woman. It was my honor to work with her for as long as I did," she says. She rambles on about how my mother had already made all her own arrangements, so there's not much to do but get to Ohio to say my final goodbyes. "She knew your schedule, so her wishes were to have her funeral on a Tuesday since she knew it was your day off."

For some reason, the thought pricks a heat behind my eyes.

She arranged her own funeral to happen on a Tuesday so I could attend.

She always put me first, and now in her death, I wish I would've put her first more often.

I wish I could've been there with her in her final moments. I wish I could've had the chance to say goodbye.

"Thanks," I mumble to Susan, and eventually she runs out of details to share, and we end the call.

By the time I set my phone back on my nightstand, Everleigh is sitting up in bed, her large brown eyes pinning me with concern. "What's going on?"

"My mother died." The words sound somehow wrong coming out of my mouth, as if they're not real. It hasn't hit me yet. I wonder when it will.

"Oh, Maverick," she murmurs, and she throws her arms around me to hold me. I let her. I lean into her, my head on her chest as I try to fight off the emotions threatening to swallow me whole. I shouldn't have opened the door to them, but I did, and now I have to feel the full and treacherous weight of losing the only person in the world I could ever truly count on.

She's the one who helped me pick up the pieces when I lost my wife.

She's the one who brushed me off when I found out the baby I thought I lost wasn't mine to lose.

She's the one who helped me with my chemistry homework when I just didn't understand, who made sure my practice uniform was always clean, who held the seat of my bike when I demanded to take off the training wheels.

Who's going to help me pick up the pieces now that I've lost the most important person in my life?

Another shudder runs through me, and I fight off that heat behind my eyes. Except for the last time I visited my mother and called on Everleigh to be with me, I haven't cried since I saw that black SUV turned over in a ditch. I'm not going to start now.

But as Everleigh holds me in her arms while I tremble and fight away these emotions, I feel like maybe I have an answer to who could help me pick up the pieces.

"I'm so sorry," she whispers. "What can I do?"

"Come with me to Ohio."

"Of course." She doesn't hesitate. She doesn't ask questions. She doesn't care about when I need to go. She'll just *be there*.

That's all I need.

"If it weren't for you, I wouldn't have gotten to say goodbye," I say quietly into her chest.

She hugs me tighter, and I hear her sniffle.

She's crying. She's letting her emotion out. She's not hiding them from me.

And in doing so, she lets me know that I don't have to hide from her, either.

CHAPTER 32

Everleigh Bradley

That Complicated Head

I quietly hold him as he finally unleashes his emotions. His mom just died. I don't expect him to hold himself together. I don't expect him to be the gruff, unfeeling man he was when I met him.

He feels this—as he should. And I'll be right here to let him feel it all by his side.

"Sorry," he eventually says.

"For what?" I honestly can't imagine a scenario where he feels like he needs to apologize for anything.

"Just…it's intense. I'm intense. I know I am. And this is heavy."

I shift us so I can take his jaw between my fingertips, and my eyes meet his. "You don't need to apologize for anything. Yeah, it's heavy. But you know what? Life's fucking heavy, and sometimes we need to lean on someone else to help us bear the weight."

He blinks as if this is news to him. It's something he's never considered—going through something *with* someone else instead of against the entire world.

"I've never felt like this before, Ev," he whispers.

I press my lips to his. "Neither have I."

"I'm your client," he says—as if I need the reminder.

"I know." I drop my fingers from his jaw.

"We shouldn't be doing this."

I shake my head. "We shouldn't. But we are. And I don't want to stop."

"I don't, either," he admits. "But we can't get caught."

"Jack would fire me if he knew I was sleeping with you. It would ruin my entire future."

His eyes move back and forth between mine when he says, "He'd fire you if I told him I've fallen in love with you."

My breath hitches as my chest tightens. "Why would you tell him that?" I ask carefully.

"Because it's the truth. I love you."

Tears pinch behind my eyes. "I love you, too."

His mouth covers mine, and there's no more talking as he pushes me back onto the bed, gets rid of our clothes, and spends the morning showing me that his words are true.

For the next week, we continue being professional in public, and we spend our private time largely naked. The following Sunday finds us winning against the Texans at their own home stadium, and we head back to Vegas with the team Sunday night only to turn around Monday afternoon and hop on a plane to Cincinnati.

I've managed to touch base with all six of my siblings, and everyone is handling the news of our mother's illness in the way I'd expect. Madden has helped her with final arrangements. Dex is sending her photos of her grandchild more often. Ford is helping Madden. Archer responded to my text to let me know he's aware of the situation and that he's out of town since his season is over. Liam and Ivy are spending as much time as they can with her since they live closest to her.

And then there's me. The caretaker, making sure my siblings are okay since my mom won't admit something's really, really wrong. I guess I have to step up into the shoes she never wanted to wear.

It's so strange to be going to a funeral to say goodbye to someone else's mother knowing that I might be going to my own mother's funeral in the not-so-distant future.

It's depressing, actually.

Maverick is quiet as we board the plane, and it feels a bit like he's starting to shut down—or shut me out.

I call him out on it when we're in our first-class seats just before takeoff.

"Talk to me, Jennings."

"About?" he asks, flicking his eyes toward the window.

"What's going through that complicated head of yours?"

He turns back to me, no emotion in his eyes as he mutters, "Nothing."

I narrow my eyes at him. "You think I'm going to let you get away with that? Think again, pal."

"Pal?"

I shrug.

"Better than *hotshot*, I guess."

I can't help a small laugh at that. "You can't be so open with me one day and shut down the next. It doesn't work like that. I'm right here, and I'm not going to let you shut me out. I'm not going to let you push me away. Not when you invited me to be here with you."

He snags his bottom lip between his teeth, and then he presses his lips together. He reaches over and grabs my hand in his. "Thank you," he whispers.

My brows dip together. "For what?"

"For not letting me slip back into old habits. I'm not used to having someone around who cares."

"Well, get used to it. Pal."

He gives me a huff of a chuckle at that.

"What are you really thinking?" I ask.

He sighs, and he looks up at the ceiling as the plane starts to taxi down the runway. The flight attendants are talking about safety, but all I can listen to is his voice.

"I'm nervous," he admits.

"You?" I ask, shocked that those are his words. He seems like the least nervous person I've ever met. "About what?"

"I'm nervous my father is going to show up to the funeral, and I'd prefer to keep you away from him," he says through a clenched jaw.

I'm not sure why he wants to keep me away. It's not like I'm going to run off with his dad. But then it dawns on me that he *hates* his dad, and maybe he just wants to protect me from that.

"There are actually quite a few people I'd prefer not to see who might show up. I've been dreading this day more and more, and I'm sorry I didn't admit that to you sooner," he says quietly.

I squeeze his hand in mine.

"I don't really care who shows up and who doesn't," I say. "Regardless of who's there, my hand will be firmly in yours. And that is something you can count on."

He squeezes my hand back. "Thank you," he whispers.

The flight is fairly lengthy, and a sense of nervousness seems to fall over both of us the closer we get to our destination. We're quiet as we each do our own thing, me working—as usual—on some different opportunities Ellie has shared with me as he studies film ahead of next week's game.

When we finally land, we take a car to our hotel. We check in, call for room service, and take some time to just relax before the funeral tomorrow. It's just a normal, everyday sort of activity with what feels more and more like the man who has become my boyfriend.

We don't have sex. We're not climbing all over each other as we have been for the last few weeks, but instead it's this lovely sort of quiet time that we really haven't had the chance to experience yet.

He chooses a movie from the on-demand options, and we snuggle on the bed after we eat as we simply enjoy each other's company in a way we never have.

We fall asleep like that, tangled together, relaxed and comfortable with one another as we both separately start to dread what we know is coming tomorrow.

When morning dawns, things look virtually the same as they did yesterday, but the big difference is today is the day Maverick will have to say goodbye to his mother.

It's a day he's surely thought of and has probably dreaded but knew would eventually come. It brings to mind my own fears, as I know my own mother's time is coming as well.

The difference is that he's close with his mom. He had the kind of relationship once upon a time with her that I had always dreamed of having with my mom but never got to experience.

It's not too late, a tiny voice in my head whispers. I think back to the last conversation I had with her and realize that just because it's not too late doesn't mean it was ever meant to be.

I force those thoughts away. Today's about Maverick.

I slip into the black dress I brought for the occasion as Maverick slips into his suit. Despite the heat I definitely feel climbing up my spine as I see him emerge all dressed up, I'm well aware that this isn't the time to act on those feelings.

"Wow," he breathes. "You look incredible."

"I was actually just thinking the same thing about you," I say, and he pulls me into his arms.

He holds me for a few quiet beats, breathing me in as he seems to pull strength from our connection. I hold him to me as well as I try to be what he needs, hoping it's enough. Hoping *I* am enough as we face this difficult day together.

Eventually he lets go and takes my hand in his. We head down to the front of the hotel, where a car is already waiting to take us to the funeral home.

The day will start with a service at a church, the burial, and finally a luncheon where we'll greet other people who cared about his mother.

As the car travels on toward our destination, I sense his nerves pick up. I grab his hand as I promised I would, and he looks gratefully over at me. My heart skips a beat when I see the appreciation in his eyes that I am here with him, that he doesn't have to go through any of this alone.

It makes me wonder whether I'll have his hand to hold in mine when the time comes when I have to do this with my own family.

Before me, I think he *was* alone except for his mother. Maverick has no brothers or sisters to face this with, no one to stand between him and the father who betrayed his family so often should the man decide to show up today.

I feel a sense of nervousness for him that he may be forced to face the man he carries so many negative feelings for. I find myself in a strange position as I wonder whether I'll meet his father today. We're not at a *meet the family* stage yet, though I feel a dart of sadness rush through me that I never got to meet the mother who gave so many of the characteristics that I love about him, that the first time I'll ever interact with her is at this funeral today as I stand by his side to help him say goodbye.

We pull up in front of a church, and he pauses for a beat in the backseat before he gets out of the car. He draws in a deep breath and finally opens the door. He walks around the car and helps me out, taking my hand in his and not letting go.

When we walk into the atrium, a few people are gathered, but it's not a huge affair. It makes me wonder a little bit about her final years and whether she had anybody aside from Maverick who would come visit her and spend time with her. Maverick lets out a soft breath beside me as a man who I immediately identify as his father walks toward us.

My chest tightens as a shudder runs through me at the obvious similarities between these two men.

His dad is tall like he is, maybe an inch or two shorter, coming in a little over six feet. He's lean and handsome, and it's easy to see where Maverick gets his devilish good looks from.

It's also pretty easy to see how his father could take whatever he wants. He has an immediate charm about him that puts me a bit on edge. It's a little wonder how he was able to score however many women Maverick claims he was able to, even though we both know his loyalty should have been to his wife.

He stops short of his son and gives me a once-over before his eyes focus on Maverick. "It's been a long time," he says.

"Wish it could have been longer," Maverick replies.

His father sighs. "This isn't the time."

"You shouldn't even fucking be here," Maverick hisses. "All you did was hurt her for her entire adult life, and you have the fucking nerve to show your face here."

I'm not quite sure what to do. On the one hand, his father is right that this isn't the time for airing dirty laundry.

But on the other hand, Maverick deserves to grieve in whatever way he needs to. And if that's attacking a man who, by all accounts, did more harm than good to the woman we're here to say goodbye to, then maybe that's his right.

Instead of doing anything at all, I just keep my hand planted firmly in Maverick's and let him handle this the way he needs to. The way his mom would have wanted him to.

"When the divorce was finalized, she told you she never wanted to see your face again. I would imagine that includes in the afterlife," Maverick says.

"I just came to pay my final respects," his dad says a little wearily. His eyes edge over to me. "Aren't you going to introduce me to your girl?"

My heart wavers in my chest as I wait with bated breath to hear what his response is going to be. The truth is that I *am* his girl, but only in secret. We still have to play that I'm simply his brand strategist, here out of an obligation to my client rather than because he needs me here.

Even if we weren't together, it's logical that I would've needed to travel here with him today.

"Not that it's any of your business, she's my publicist," Maverick says thickly.

I shouldn't feel upset that those are the words he uses to describe our relationship that's so much more than that, yet I do.

His dad's eyes moved down to where our hands are joined. "Awfully cozy for a publicist," he grunts, and it's yet another example of seeing the son in the father's reaction.

He would hate that I even have that thought, but I can't help it. There are just so many similarities between them. And I know beyond the shadow of a doubt that Maverick hates that fact.

I try to ease the tension by sticking my hand out toward him. "Everleigh Bradley," I say.

"Bradley," he repeats. "As in the Chicago Bradleys?"

I nod. "One and the same."

"What are you doing as a publicist when you shouldn't have to work a day in your life?"

I force myself to school in my reaction to his question, though honestly, I'm quite affronted by it. "I suppose it's just my overly ambitious nature."

He raises both brows as if he's rather unimpressed by that, but I have little care regarding whether or not the man is impressed with my life choices. The only thing I care about is helping Maverick get through this day unscathed, and so far, it feels an awful lot like I'm failing.

"Excuse us," Maverick says, and he yanks me away from his father and through the atrium toward the doors that open to the church.

He nods his hellos at some of the others already seated for the service, and we take a seat in the front row.

We listen as the minister talks about life, trying to give some comfort to those here suffering at the loss. I wonder if his words are helping anybody. I wonder if Maverick feels any sense of comfort. I wonder if he'll ever talk about it or if it's something he'll just keep locked up inside like so much of the suffering he does in silence.

When the service is over, the minister invites guests to come up to the altar to say their final goodbyes. We walk up to the front toward the altar where her casket lies, and she's surrounded by gorgeous bouquets of white flowers. A photo of her smiling sits on a small table beside the casket, and I stop to study her there for a beat. I see the similarities he has with her as well. The kindness behind her eyes is evident in the photo that was chosen, and it's the same kindness I saw emerge from Maverick at a charity event as he spoke with a little girl who experienced trauma at some point in her life.

He draws in a deep breath as he clearly does his best to put that altercation with his father behind him, and I stand to the side to give him a moment of privacy. My eyes flick to one of the largest bouquets, and I see a little card attached to it.

Our deepest condolences. -Jack Dalton and family

Tears pinch behind my eyes as I think about how he's really not so alone. He's with a team now who cares about him as a person rather than just his successes on the field. Hiring me was never supposed to be a punishment. It was meant to help him, and if I do say so myself, I think it has.

He reaches for my hand to pull me up next to him, clearly indicating that even if this is a private moment, he still wants me to be a part of it.

"Mom," he whispers softly. "I'm so sorry. I wasn't there for you in your final hours, and I'm so sorry you never got to meet the woman who's done so much for me. Who has given me so much. Who has made me believe in love again."

Tears pinch behind my eyes as I listen to his sweet words.

"I'm sorry he's here today. I wish I could have done my part to keep him away because I know how much he hurt you and how much you hate him, but despite all that, everyone deserves the chance to say goodbye to the people they love. Even though I know he didn't treat you the way you deserved, he still loved you in his own way. I'll be forever grateful to you for all you did for me. I know this isn't goodbye, it's just another see ya later."

His voice breaks at the end, and the way he says the words leads me to think that that's the way they must have always ended their conversations. It's sweet and touching.

He avoids his dad at the burial, but a few people walk up to him and offer their condolences. At the luncheon, he sticks by my side as more people offer condolences. People seem to respect that he's a man of few words, and very few people try to make conversation with him. The longest conversation I witness is between him and Susan, the nurse who cared most often for his mother at the memory care facility where she lived for the last several years of her life.

And just like that, it's all over. We head out without a goodbye to his father, and we get on a plane to return to life in Vegas as if everything is normal.

It's not. There's a hole in Maverick's life with his mother gone. He just confronted his father. We grew closer, as nothing quite bonds you to another person the way being there for them at a close family member's funeral does.

And now we have to resume living in secrecy as we continue growing closer and falling harder.

CHAPTER 33

Everleigh Bradley

Close the Door

I t's back to business on Wednesday. It's so weird how life just goes on.

One minute his mom was here on this earth, breathing and laughing and *living*, and the next, she was gone. But the world keeps turning. He has a game to play, and he's called bright and early on Wednesday into the quarterbacks coach's office—along with me, whom the coach requested to see as well.

We arrive together, and Maverick knocks lightly on the doorframe.

"Come on in," Coach Richards says. "And close the door."

Maverick's eyes meet mine, and his brow is a little furrowed as he closes the door. We each take a seat in the chairs opposite the coach's desk.

"I'm sorry to be so blunt, in particular after the funeral you attended together yesterday. My condolences, by the way."

He pauses, and then he says, "I got a message this morning telling me that the relationship between the two of you may have crossed over a line. Is there something I should be concerned about?" he asks.

We exchange a glance, and in doing so, it's basically an admission.

My chest tightens as I feel the pressure caving down on me.

"That's what I thought. The message indicated that the two of you have been together behind closed doors. As you both know, this is completely unacceptable," the coach tells us.

"Is it, though?" Maverick asks quietly. "She *is* turning my image around. The latest headlines have cast me in a positive light. My follower counts are climbing. Comments have skewed away from the negative and focused on how I'm back, how I'm making an impact, how my reputation is changing despite my slip-ups."

I'm frankly shocked that he's been listening during our morning meetings lately. I thought he was mostly just staring at my boobs.

It seems like he actually *wants* this change. That he's working for it.

That he wants me to be impressed with the turnaround.

I am.

Heartily.

I'm proud of the work we've done. I'm proud of *him*, and the pride beams from my eyes at his words.

But Coach Richards, on the other hand, is not. "Look, I don't want to go to Nash with this, so I came to you first. Just deny it, take the warning, and stop whatever it is that's going on so we can focus on the game. All right?"

Maverick is apparently choosing this moment to slip back into old habits. "No. It's not *all right*. It's bullshit. I can live my life however I please, and if I choose to fuck my brand strategist or a teammate's sister or whether she's one and the same, that's nobody's business but my own." He glances at me, clearly expecting solidarity. "And hers."

My cheeks turn as red as my lips as my eyes widen at his choice of words. *Way to sugarcoat things, jackass.*

I close my eyes and blow out a breath. "Yes, we've, uh…*been* together. We're seeing each other," I admit. "It's been nothing but positive, Coach. He's opening up to me, and it truly is having a positive effect on his reputation." I rattle off a few statistics off the top of my head.

Coach Richards stares dumbly at me. "It doesn't matter. You're employed by the team, which means the two of you cannot be together. End of story. Now fix it, or Jack Dalton finds out, and he'll be the one to fix it for you."

"With all due respect, he ended up marrying the person sent in to fix him. What if that's our path, too?" Maverick asks quietly.

Oh my God.

Holy shit.

Marriage?

Is he serious right now?

I figured he never wanted to get married again after his first marriage. He just doesn't seem like the type.

But he's right. He's turning around. Little changes here and there could equate to bigger changes.

Still. Marriage?

I mean…yeah, I'm falling in love with him. Or rather, yes, I love him. But I haven't thought quite that far ahead. I haven't put future meaning to those words.

But he's talking *marriage*. That's a serious commitment. Lifelong. I know I want to be married *someday*. I know I want to have kids *someday*. But…fuck. I didn't even want to *work* with an NFL star a few months ago, never mind *marry* one.

It's just not how I ever envisioned my life. I never wanted to be a football wife.

But I want to be with Maverick.

It's not like I can take or leave the parts I want and don't. I get the whole man, and he's a work in progress. I guess I am, too. Aren't we all? I thought by the time I turned thirty, I'd have it all figured out. I blew past that two years ago and still don't have a clue what I want out of life.

But I know what I don't want, and that's sitting in someone's office having my career threatened because I got involved with a client.

What would Mr. Langford say?

He'd fire me, too. Would it matter? Financially, no. I have my trust fund to fall back on. I can use that to start my own business. But reputationally? Yes, it would matter. Very much so. I'd never be taken seriously in this business. I'd forever be labeled the woman who slept with a client. The world of publicity really isn't all that big, and reputations stick with us forever. Nobody would take me seriously, and people would always wonder if any male clients I acquire were only on my roster because we were sleeping together. Or worse—I'd only attract male clients because of my reputation as a client-fucker.

My mind is running away with this.

Coach Richards stares at Maverick a long time after his use of the M-word. Eventually, he says, "Whatever it is you're doing, make sure you're not doing it here. Be careful. Both your reputations are on the line here."

He's not wrong.

I'm fuming when we leave his office. I whisper-yell in the hallway, "Did you have to be so blunt?"

He glances at me, his brows furrowed in confusion.

"You said you're fucking your teammate's sister," I say.

He holds both hands up wildly in my direction as if to say, *well, I am.*

"Ugh!" I cry out in frustration.

He links an arm around my waist and hauls me toward him.

"Not here," I whisper-yell, setting my hands on his chest and pushing him away. He looks offended that I'm pushing him away, but I can't stand here in this hallway with him holding me in his arms when the other coaches' offices are just down the hall, when Jack's office is just up the stairs, after the warning we just got.

He storms off toward the locker room, and I head into a conference room to get a little work done before I head out onto the field to watch practice.

He's a little on the grumpy side today, but when isn't he? And who would blame him? He came from his mother's funeral. Most people would take some bereavement time, but not Maverick Jennings. I think the field is where he best works out his emotions, anyway.

Practice has ended, but Maverick stays on the field a little longer to run extra drills. It's during that time that Coach Nash approaches me where I'm sitting on some bleachers.

"You're doing a good job with him," he says quietly, nodding toward the field.

"I'm doing my best to turn things around."

"So Coach Richards mentioned," he muses, both of us still looking at Maverick.

I sigh, not committing to a response other than that.

He turns toward me, and my eyes dart to him. "Look, what you do in your spare time is your own business. Just be careful with someone who's so volatile, okay? I can't have him losing whatever progress he's made because of some emotional journey you've taken him on."

I want to defend myself. I want to tell him it's not like that. I'm not out to break his heart or hurt him. I'm here to support him, and we've fallen for each other along the way.

Somehow, though, it feels like my admission would only make things worse.

"I won't mention it to Jack, but consider this your fair warning. If Richards and I know, it won't be long before word gets out. You know Dex isn't going to take kindly to it. Just be careful, okay?"

I look away from him and back at Maverick as a wave of emotion plows into me. I nod a little. "Okay."

And then I slip out of the training facility and head toward home.

CHAPTER 34

MAVERICK JENNINGS

Don't Move

I don't want to go home after practice.

I'm not sure why I do it, but my car leads me straight for her father's lounge. I don't have a game tomorrow, and I need to blow off some steam, I guess. I have practice in the morning, but I can show up for practice tired. I'm not planning to stay very long anyway.

It's stupid to show up here. I'm in season, and the league has rules about this sort of thing—not gambling in a casino, but definitely the underground part. But it hasn't stopped me before. Maybe I'll just stay in the legal area for a few minutes before I head home.

I walk in the front doors and grab myself a drink at the bar. I play a few rounds at the tables upstairs, and I lose every hand.

I need to change my luck.

I head toward the host who always escorts me around the side of the building toward the underground portion, and we make our way through the coded doors to the basement.

It's loud down here tonight, with music playing over the din of dice as they're thrown on tables, cards that are dealt to cheers or disappointment, and general chatter.

I'm immediately greeted by another host downstairs, and we discuss how much I want on my credit line tonight.

I should've been smart enough to cash out my winnings the last time I was here, but I made a quick exit. This place still has twenty-five grand of my money, so I tell her to put it all on my line. My hope is to double it tonight and walk away with a boatload of money.

If I can give to the Bradley pockets in this manner, I can take it away, too. And maybe tonight, I just want to take a little away from the Bradleys. I'm still hurt that she pushed me away even if deep down I know it was probably the right thing to do.

I'm hurt over a lot of shit, I guess, and tonight I just want to lose myself in some mindless fun.

I sit at one of the few blackjack tables down here, and the dealer issues me my chips as the waitress brings me my usual scotch without even asking.

Ben Olson is at the table, too. "Jennings!" he greets me. He chugs what's left in his glass. "I need to get home. Good to see you, man, but shouldn't you be home resting up for practice tomorrow?"

I nod. "I'm not planning to stay long."

He gets up and nods at me. "I'll see you around."

After he leaves, I win the first hand.

I win the second hand.

I've got a ten showing, and the dealer has a four. I double down. I have five grand on the table, and I've only been here for about ten minutes. I'm actually winning as I try to turn this shitty day around, and that's when I hear the shouting voice that breaks into the din down here.

"Hands where we can see them!"

The room goes absolutely silent as the music is cut and some overhead lights are flipped on, casting the entire large room in the harsh glow of fluorescent lights.

My head whips over to the sound of the voice, and my heart sinks into the pit of my stomach as I spot the SWAT team here to raid this place. To make matters even worse, it's not just the Vegas police. I spot the FBI, too.

Fuck.

I am *so* fucked.

My chest tightens as I raise my hands in the air. The cards still sit on the table in front of me, five grand worth of money on a hand I'll never know whether I won or lost.

I lost.

That much is clear.

The dealer raises his hands, too—as do the other players at this table where we were all winning.

As far as I know, the police care more about the operators in these underground casinos than the players…which means Everleigh's father is pretty well fucked.

As his wife deals with the cancer diagnosis she just received. As the entire *family* deals with that news. Now the patriarch is going to prison?

Jesus.

The family is falling apart at the seams. I need to get to Everleigh. I need to tell her what's going on. I need to warn her, at the very least.

The thought of what happened today between us is the furthest thing from my mind as protective mode kicks in. I reach for my phone, sure the officers raiding this joint won't see me, but they do.

"Don't move!" one screeches at me, and I innocently move my hand back into the air. *Fuck.*

Of all the goddamn nights to choose to come to this place, it had to be tonight. I should never have stepped foot through the doors.

"Secure the exit!" someone yells.

"Exit secure!"

"We'll be holding you all for questioning," the one who seems to be in charge says. "We're here in a joint operation with the Nevada Gaming Commission to investigate an illegal gambling operation, and you're all detained until further notice. Do not touch your phone until instructed."

Shit. Fuck!

I suck in a breath and try to calm my racing heart. This is bad. Really bad. Not only am I caught in this illegal place, but I'll at the very least be issued a citation, which is public. I could even be arrested. I think it's just a misdemeanor, but an arrest coming off the issues with my reputation would mean I'd lose sponsorships, and my team would likely both fine and suspend me. I'll lose the respect of everyone around me, and who knows what'll happen to Everleigh?

The Aces might fire her because she couldn't control me. Ellie could take a hit from this, too.

Either way, I'm not seeing the twenty-five grand I had on the line again. It's an illegal operation. The feds will seize all of the assets in this place, and that means I didn't just lose a hand or two.

Twenty-five grand is swirling down the drain, and I wave goodbye to it as I wait my turn for questioning and wonder how quickly I can get to Everleigh to let her know what's going on.

CHAPTER 35

Everleigh Bradley

Choose

I jolt awake as I hear the knocking on my door.

I don't remember falling asleep, but I must have.

I told Milton to text me when Maverick got in, and I waited and waited until my eyes drifted closed.

I glance at the clock, and it's four in the morning.

Why would someone be pounding on my door at four in the morning?

I jump out of bed, my heart pounding in my chest as I make my way over to answer it. I find Maverick standing there. He looks…disheveled. Tired. Angry.

"I have to tell you something," he blurts.

"Where have you been?" I ask.

"The Legacy Lounge." He clears his throat as his eyes dart away from me. "Can I come in?"

I open the door a little wider, and he walks through it. He's pacing, and I've never seen him like this.

"What's going on?" I demand.

"Sit," he says.

"I'm not a dog." I roll my eyes and cross my arms over my chest.

"Fine, then. Stand. I don't care. Listen, I was at your father's underground casino tonight when it was raided. SWAT, the FBI, and the Nevada Gaming Commission all busted in."

I gasp at his words. "What does that mean?"

He's still pacing. "We couldn't move, couldn't use our phones, couldn't do anything until they talked to each of us."

"You're just getting in?" I ask.

He nods. "I was issued a citation, but they want information. They want me to give up the name of the owner. Nobody would do it, but Ev, if I give the name before the team finds out, they could drop the citation, and all this would go away. If I don't cooperate, I could be charged with a misdemeanor. Even the citation will get me a suspension from the team, but a misdemeanor means the league will open an investigation, and I could be sidelined until it all goes away. The feds mean business, and they're not going to let me off easily. They want to make examples out of all of us. But I came to you first. I need you to tell me it's okay to give his name." He's begging me, pleading with me, his eyes searching mine as he waits for me to give him the green light to name my own father.

Tears pinch behind my eyes that he would even ask me that, and at the same time, I realize that he *did* ask me. He could've just given the name and gotten out of trouble. He hates my brother. He hated me until not so long ago. He probably hates my dad, too—if not before, then certainly now. Yet he didn't. He's here, asking me for permission, and I'm stuck as my stomach rolls and my legs feel like they're going to give out at any second.

What do I do? Choose the man who I barely know, or choose the man who gave me life?

As if the universe can hear my question, my phone starts to ring.

It's my father.

Of course it is. News must've gotten back to him that his casino was busted, and he may not have much time before the authorities show up on his doorstep. He's probably making the rounds and calling all of his children right now despite the fact that it's four in the morning here in Vegas.

Shit. Shit!

I know it's about this same situation. It has to be.

But what if it isn't?

What if something happened to my mom? What if she's declining or even worse and he's calling to let me know? I can't *not* pick up.

"Dad?" I answer.

"Everleigh, I need your silence. I need you to promise you'll put our family first. Our legacy. Promise me, darling." He's begging me. I've never heard his voice like this before. Never. "Listen, if you tell anyone that I'm tied to that place, I'll go to jail. It stays between us. Promise me."

I don't know what to do. I can't put him through whatever it is he'll have to go through if his secret comes out, not when we're all worried about my mom.

"I promise," I say softly, my eyes on Maverick as I watch his shoulders physically deflate at my words to my father.

"Is Mom okay?" I ask quietly, turning away from Maverick.

"She's the same. But I suspect seeing her family in ruins wouldn't help the situation," he says. "I know it's early there. I'm sorry. I'll talk to you later."

He cuts the call, clearly satisfied with my response, but Maverick clearly is not.

"What do you want me to say?" I ask quietly. "You're asking me to choose between my family and—"

"And my reputation," he finishes flatly. "The very thing you moved across the country to fix."

"I can do both," I protest.

"Can you? Because it would save me a hell of a lot of trouble if I could give the police your father's name." He shakes his head and clenches his jaw as he walks toward my door. He opens it, and he turns back toward me before he walks through it. "How are you going to clean it up when my citation becomes a misdemeanor and it's on my record because you're protecting a man who never showed you any loyalty?" He slams the door closed, and I stare at it as tears start to tumble down my cheeks.

He's right. I did move across the country to fix his reputation, and we were on the right track. Things were getting better. He was starting to earn back the respect of his teammates, his coaches, his colleagues around the league. He fell for me, and I fell for him. We were in this together. We were ready to take on the world as we did our finger breathing on the roof the other night.

But now he has a citation, and things could get worse once the DA reviews the case. They'll try to make an example out of him—especially when he won't talk. And he won't…because he's protecting *me*. He's protecting *my family*.

And I can't do the same goddamn thing for him.

Two hours later, I'm showered and ready for the day as I sip my second cup of strong coffee. I'm getting ready to head to the practice facility when I hear more pounding on my door.

Thank God. I was worried Maverick was going to head to practice without seeing me first, and we definitely need to talk.

I whip the door open without bothering to peek through the peephole, and I say, "Thank God."

"For what?" my brother asks.

"Dex," I say with surprise in my voice. "What are you doing here?"

His brows dip. "Who did you think would be knocking on your door at six in the morning?" His eyes edge to the front door on the other side of the hall, and he narrows his eyes at me.

I realize then that Dex doesn't know everything that's gone down between Maverick and me.

"What are you doing here?" I repeat instead of answering his question. I open the door to let him in and turn away from him.

"Did Dad get to you?" he asks.

I nod. "He called earlier begging me to promise I wouldn't associate his name with that place. But Maverick was there, and if he names him, he'll get off easier."

"He was strategic in how he set things up so he'd never take the fall," Dex says. "I'm not sure how much it would matter if he *did* name him. Speaking of thanking God, I'm pretty damn grateful this morning I got my name out of that place months ago."

"I can't believe Dad tried to set *you* up to take the fall," I say.

"I don't think that's what it was. I genuinely think he just wanted my connections, and he was willing to pay me for them."

"Why do we always defend him?" I ask.

He gives me a wry smile as he shrugs. "Because he's our father, and he raised us to do that."

I set my hand on my forehead. "This is such a mess. I'm supposed to be cleaning things up, and instead it feels like I'm in an even bigger mess protecting a man who has never shown any loyalty to me when it might not even matter." I realize I'm using Maverick's words, but it's true.

"What's going on between you and Jennings?" he asks.

My eyes dart away from him, which is a dead giveaway.

"Yeah, that's what I thought," he mutters.

"I didn't mean to fall for him," I say softly.

He wrinkles his nose. "Fall for him?"

I lift a shoulder. "But in the moment, I still chose Dad. Over Maverick. Over my job. I told Maverick I could protect both, but I don't know if I can."

"Yeah. If the only way to clear Maverick's name is to name Dad as the brains behind the operation, you're pretty well fucked."

"Thanks," I say dryly. "I need to make a call before I head to the Complex."

He nods as he walks toward my door. "I'll see you around."

I dial Ellie's number as soon as the door clicks shut behind my brother. It's early, but I figure I'll just leave a voicemail—until she answers.

"Everleigh, hi. I saw the news about Maverick," she answers.

"Do you ever sleep?" I ask.

She chuckles. "No. My youngest came in with a nightmare at five, and I was up so I checked headlines. I guess that was a mistake. What do you know?"

I debate exactly how honest to be here. On the one hand, she's become a friend. I could confide in her that Maverick and I have a relationship that's more than just brand strategist and client. But I don't necessarily want her to know my own connection to that casino. The fewer people who know, the better. Loose lips sink ships and all that.

I clear my throat. "The DA will work with him if he gives up information about the operators, but he's staying quiet."

"Then we make him talk," she suggests.

I'm quiet a beat as I consider that, but I'm still stuck here. I can't let him turn my own father in. It'll be a far worse punishment for a felony operating illegal casinos versus a misdemeanor for getting caught at one. "I don't think we can make him do much of anything."

"True. Okay, so we either make him look like an innocent bystander who didn't know this was an illegal operation, or we own it and sell the redemption story hard," she says.

"I don't think it's plausible he didn't know. He was in the basement of a casino with a coded door," I point out.

"How do you know?"

I can't exactly say it was because I once saw him there and was thwarted by my own father, so I make up an excuse. "He told me."

"Right. Then he owns it, and we bury it. We release a controlled statement, flood the media with something else, control the narrative, and cross our fingers that his sponsors don't start dropping him."

"What would you flood the media with?" I ask, scared to hear the answer but already knowing what it is.

"I wouldn't use his mother, if that's what you're asking," she says quietly. "It's insensitive even though it would help solve a lot of this."

"It's off the table. If you want to talk about the big donation he just made to Alzheimer's research, that's one thing. But using his mother's funeral as a defense would be gross."

"I agree, and I won't. I can't speak for how the media will twist things, though, and it would garner plenty of sympathy." She changes the subject before I can further comment. "I know Jack will want this cleaned up quickly, so keep him off socials, and I'll do what I can to mitigate."

"Does the team know?" I ask quietly.

"If I know, you can bet your ass Jack will be calling Mav in first thing this morning," she says.

"What should I do?"

"Don't leave his side, but if you can, find out who else was there," she suggests. "Maybe we can use that to spin attention away from Mav. Or if we could figure out who's behind this place, we could use that somehow. I don't know. I'm just brainstorming here."

Don't leave his side. That's going to be a tough one considering he has every right to feel hurt and betrayed by me after promising my father I wouldn't name him. But it's what I'm being paid to do, so I'm out of options. I guess it's better than her other option of figuring out who's behind this place since I already know the answer to that.

"Okay."

We end the call, and I walk over to Maverick's place, crossing my fingers that this won't be as bad as I think it will be while my heart thunders in my chest.

CHAPTER 36

Everleigh Bradley

Back to Enemies

He throws open the door and glares at me. He doesn't invite me in. Instead, he leans on the doorframe, and I stand in the hallway as he waits for me to go first.

"So we're back to being enemies, I see," I say dryly.

"We're not enemies." He sighs, and it's a deep, aching sort of sigh. "Everybody always leaves, and I'm really goddamn sick of it."

"I'm not leaving you," I protest, but it's weak.

He sidesteps my words. "What's the plan?" When my brows furrow, he adds, "I assume you've spoken with Ellie."

"We're going to do our best to bury it," I say. I don't admit that Ellie hinted how talking about his mother's funeral would be one way to cast the story in a different light. He doesn't need to hear it when he already feels betrayed by me. "Can you name anyone else who was there so we can throw attention off of you?"

"If I'm not naming your father, I'm not naming anyone else who was there," he says flatly.

I nod. "Understandable. Ellie's going to issue a statement so we don't invite too much speculation. It'll be brief and essentially say it's a non-story and you're not in any trouble, you're cooperating fully, blah blah blah."

"I'm *not* cooperating fully," he points out. "I didn't give them the name they wanted."

"Did you tell them you knew the name?"

He lifts a shoulder. "I was noncommittal about it."

"Ellie told me to keep you off socials and stay by your side today."

He shakes his head.

I roll my eyes. "Come on, Maverick. I don't want to go back to hating each other." I move in toward him a little, but he doesn't move. He's a wall of man in his doorway. A hot wall of man who's clearly upset with me. "Please don't hate me," I whisper. I want to reach around him to wrap my arms around his torso, but I stay put.

He's quiet a long beat. Eventually, his eyes flick to mine, and he says darkly, "You know I don't." He reaches for me and hauls me into him. "But I can't be with someone who refuses to choose me."

"They're my family, Maverick," I say softly. "If you name him, he'll go to jail. How could we ever have a future together if it's you putting him there?"

"Sometimes we choose, and right now, you're choosing to put my reputation and my career in danger." His voice is soft.

"You're putting me in an impossible position."

"There's always a choice. I need to get to practice." He practically walks into me, so I move out of his way as he reaches into his pocket and grabs his keys. He locks his door. I could get in the elevator with him to give us more time...but I don't even have shoes on, let alone my car keys, my tablet, my phone, my purse—all the things I need to take with me to watch him at practice all day so I can work to try to find some way out of this disaster.

I'm not sure there *is* a way out. I might've sealed my fate when I chose to put my father over the man I've fallen for.

* * *

I head to the Complex and sit in the bleachers as I work. I should be watching Maverick. I should be taking notes on how he's interacting with his teammates and coming up with media talking points, but instead I'm knee-deep in research about my own damn father's illegal casino to try to piece together anyone else that might've been there. There has to be *someone* who can take the heat off Maverick, some celebrity with a bigger name that people would find interesting enough.

There's not. Not that I've found yet, anyway.

And so I make a phone call that I know is going to sink my ship, but I have no other choice.

"Everleigh, what is it?" my father answers.

I sigh. "What can you tell me about this lounge?"

"I can't talk about it. I'm in town. Can you meet me?"

I glance at Maverick. He's fine. He'll be fine if I slip out. This is in the name of protecting his image, anyway. "When and where?"

"I'm staying at the Fontainebleau. Meet me there in thirty minutes."

"Fine," I mutter, and I head to my car.

Thirty minutes later, I'm standing in the lobby of the hotel when I see my father rushing toward me. He ushers me without a word toward the elevators, and we head up to his room.

"Why are you being weird?" I ask.

He glances at the camera in the corner of the elevator, and he doesn't answer my question. He remains silent until we're in his room behind a closed door.

"You are not to bring up the lounge over a phone call. Ever. Do you understand?" he says.

"Why not?" I narrow my eyes at him.

"People are listening," he hisses as he paces in front of the windows. "I've been very careful, and I'll not have one of my own children blow this up for me."

"Then you probably shouldn't be doing illegal things, Dad," I point out.

"Be that as it may, I could be in a lot of trouble if I left a loose thread out there. What do you want to know?" he asks.

"Who was there the night it was raided?"

His brows furrow. "Why do you need to know?"

"Maverick Jennings is my client. I'm trying to clear his name, and throwing attention to someone else is one strategy."

"To bury the story?" he guesses.

"What would you have me do?" I ask.

"Ignore it. No need to make a statement." He shrugs as if it's not a big deal.

"Clearly we work in different industries. I realize you've kept a lot of secrets, but I'm working with a celebrity figure whose fans deserve a statement." I shrug back at him, though mine is a bit more sarcastic than his was.

"I can't give you that information." He stares out the window instead of at me.

"What if you're arrested?" I ask quietly.

"Then your mother goes through this whole thing alone." His phone rings, and he glances at it. "Look, I don't have a lot of time to chitchat right now. I'm waiting for a secure call from the Caymans, and—"

"A secure call from the Caymans? Isn't that where people hide off-the-books money?" I ask.

He gives me a look that very plainly says *duh*, and I can't help but wonder exactly how bad my father is. How many illegal activities is he a part of? How much time *should* he be doing in prison?

And who has he set up to take the fall for all of this?

I don't know the answer to any of it, and he's not in the mood to share. In fact, I'm not sure why he invited me over here at all.

"Do you know how the feds found out?" I ask.

"They've been after me a while, but I always covered my tracks. It sounds like they've been tracking a number of my clients, not the least of which was your boyfriend."

So he's saying it was at least partly Maverick's fault his place was busted.

Great.

Add it to the list of reasons why Maverick and I were just never meant to be.

"I guess that's what happens when you lure in celebrities," I say, not bothering to mask my irritation. "So who else was there?"

He shakes his head. He's not going to give me a single piece of information.

"Why'd you tell me to come here if you weren't planning to give me anything to work with?" I finally ask.

He turns from the window and toward me. "I invited you here to ensure your silence, Everleigh."

"You asked me to promise you over the phone, and I did. It was enough to break what might be the most important relationship of my life, but that wasn't good enough for you?" I ask softly.

His eyes don't soften as they should at my words. If anything, they harden. "Toughen up. You're a Bradley, and Bradleys always come first."

I stare at him for a beat, and then the question blurts out of my mouth before I can stop it. "Who's going to take the fall for your crimes?"

His mouth twitches for just a second before he schools his features and turns back toward the windows. A phone starts to ring with a shrill, loud ring, and that must be the call he was waiting on. "I need you to excuse me. This is a private call." He nods toward the door as he picks up the call, and he leaves me wondering why in the hell I possibly chose his side over Maverick's.

I try Madden's number as I pull away from the hotel to head back to the Complex. He may be at practice, or I may have caught him at just the right time.

"Ev?" he answers.

I burst into tears.

"Ev, what is it? Is it Mom?" he asks.

Every conversation with any of my siblings will start that way, I fear. From now until it happens.

I force myself to pull it together since I'm driving. "No, it's not Mom. It's Dad." My voice trembles. "I just saw him, and we had this weird meeting where he was being all sketchy and talking about accounts in the Caymans. He's up to something, Madden."

"Of course he is. He's *always* up to something, and it's high time we all learned that."

"He just told me to toughen up because I'm a Bradley, and Bradleys come first," I say. "And then I asked him who's going to take the fall for his crimes, and he didn't answer."

He sighs. "One of the seven of us, no doubt. How many times has he asked us to sign shit when we had no idea what it was? He's hiding stuff, Ev. He's working hard to keep his assets away from anyone who might try to seize them, but it might be too late."

"So what do we do?" I ask. I *beg*. There has to be something that can be done here. I just let go of possibly the best thing that ever happened to me because of our father. I need to do *something* to justify that. To prove I made the right choice.

"Sit back and watch the fireworks, I guess. And trust me, there *will* be fireworks."

I blow out a breath as I sink back into the driver's seat and hope that when they detonate, the seven Bradley siblings are able to escape without getting burned.

Or the rest of them, anyway, since I'm already a little too close to the sparks.

CHAPTER 37

MAVERICK JENNINGS

Slam

I slam the medicine ball as hard as I can at the ground. I pick up the twenty-pound ball, lift it over my head, and slam it at the ground again. And again. And again. It's great for working out frustration, and I'll be recovered enough by Sunday to throw the football with the accuracy I'm known for.

She made her fucking choice.

I slam the ball at the ground again.

But we still have to work together.

I slam the ball once more.

Day in and day out.

Slam.

I have to live next door to her.

Slam.

Ride the elevator with her.

Slam.

See her in the bleachers. *Slam.* The owner's suite. *Slam.* My dreams. *Slam.*

Fuck her. Fuck her for choosing her criminal father in this mess. We had something, something big. Something important. Something worth fighting for. And she still chose him.

Fuck that goddamn statement they released today, too. It's clearly a statement meant to control damage to make it seem like there's no story to investigate, but to me it just feels like lies.

Mr. Jennings was in attendance last night at a private event that was interrupted by law enforcement. He was not charged with a crime and has been fully cooperative. We have no further comment at this time.

I still haven't been formally charged, though I didn't escape unscathed. A citation is still an accusation that I was doing something wrong.

I was. I shouldn't have been there, and I fully take the blame for that. I knew it was wrong, but I went anyway. I wanted to blow off steam. I wanted a night of mindless fun. I've been there plenty of times, so I thought I'd be safe to do it again.

There are a lot of perks to these underground places. The taxes, yes. But also the fact that there are only people like me there. Everleigh wanted me to give her names, and I could have. Ben Olson got out just in the nick of time, but as for the others?

Lots of executives in suits, plenty of actors and musicians, a local news anchor, a bunch of tech guys. There was even a judge there. A *judge.* The police have all their names, and that judge is certainly more fucked than an NFL star with a questionable reputation to begin with.

But I won't give those names up. It's not my gossip to share.

I thought Ellie told her not to let me out of her sight, but I haven't seen her since before lunch. I wonder where she went. I wish I didn't care.

"Jennings, Mr. Dalton wants to see you in his office. Now," Coach Nash tells me as I slam the ball at the ground again.

I nod, pick up the ball and stick it on the rack, and I follow him up to Jack's office.

Everleigh is sitting in it when I arrive.

Everyone looks serious, and a tingle of nervousness dances up my spine.

"Have a seat," Jack says. He looks between Everleigh and me. "We have a problem."

Just one? I want to ask it, but I know better than to be sarcastic to the team owner.

"Tell me what happened last night," Jack says to me.

I press my lips together, and then I give a fairly bland recount of my night. "I went to a casino I've frequented before after practice. I headed down to a private basement section, and the police raided it about ten minutes after I walked in. I was detained and questioned. I was issued a citation, and I was told the DA would be easier on me if I gave up the name of the person who owned the place."

"Did you?" Jack asks.

I glance at Everleigh, and then I look back at Jack. I shake my head.

"Ellie and I are working hard to bury the story," Everleigh says.

Jack nods at her. "When a player is issued a citation by law enforcement, we have to report it to the league."

"What if I got the citation dropped?" I ask quietly.

"It would have to be pretty quick in order for me not to report it."

I glance over at Everleigh, and she's staring straight ahead at Jack.

She's not budging.

"The league may hand down their own punishment, or they may not. But you've violated a team rule, and that means suspension, Maverick."

The word sends a shot of anger straight through me, but before I can protest, he continues as my stomach churns.

"I thought you'd be trying a little harder to keep your ass on the field considering you missed the first four games this season with your rib injury. I'm disappointed in your behavior. We knew bringing you here was a risk, and I still fully believe in Ms. Bradley's capability to help you turn this around. But be aware that sponsors don't want to take a risk on players like you. Your opportunities are going to dry up, they're going to drop you, and if you can't straighten yourself out, *we* will drop you, too. We can't continue taking the hits to our team reputation because of you. Little kids look up to you, man. Is this what you want them to see?" He pulls up a photo of me, one from not so long ago when I drunkenly ranted about Dex.

It's a little embarrassing, sure. But I didn't bother to *feel* embarrassment until Everleigh opened those doors to my emotions again. I didn't give a single fuck what anyone thought about me.

I glance over at her again.

She could make whatever might come next much easier on me if she would just let me name her goddamn father.

But she won't.

"Mr. Dalton, if I may," she says. "I think a suspension will only draw more attention to Maverick's behavior, and it's just going to make it harder to bury the story."

He lifts his shoulders. "Rules are rules. There's nothing I can do."

"Don't you own the team?" I ask. I shouldn't. I should keep my goddamn mouth shut, but I can't. "You could bend the rules."

He narrows his eyes at me. "If I bent the rules for every player that came in here and asked me to, what good would a set of rules be?" He shakes his head. "No. I can't. You'll serve your time. It's a one-game suspension, and that means I'll need your credentials through Sunday evening. You can return to the Complex on Monday morning if you so choose to practice." He holds out his hand, and I hand over the little plastic card that lets me in and out of the building.

Fuck.

I blow out a breath, and then I storm out of the office without being dismissed.

I wonder if this means I won't have to see *her* until Monday morning, either.

It doesn't.

The media finds out I'm suspended, and for as hard as Everleigh tried to bury the story, they run with it. They tear the fuck into me, and a public fallout means more time with my brand strategist, of course.

Everleigh looks flustered as I open the door after hearing her bang on it later that same evening.

"What?" I hiss.

"May I remind you that you brought this on yourself, Mr. Jennings?" She storms into my place. She sits at my kitchen table—uninvited, mind you—and pulls out her laptop.

"And yet you hold the solution in your very hands," I muse. I lean my backside against my kitchen counter and fold my arms over my chest rather than joining her at the table.

"This isn't the time for jokes."

"What is it the time for, then?" I ask.

"The media is tearing into you, Maverick. Don't you care?" She scrolls some headlines. "They love nothing more than to stir the pot with patterns. Look at this! Locker room rumors, previous suspensions, tantrums, interviews with your former teammates, many of whom have nothing good to say. Even gossip about your personal life." She gestures wildly to the screen as if I have a single ounce of fucks left to give.

"No, I don't care." I shrug and shake my head. "Let them."

"Let them?" she screeches. "I can't! I'm being paid to *not* let them, and I can't keep up with scandal after scandal with you!" She's yelling at me, clearly overworked and stressed.

"I can't help it that the media wants to dig up old dirt. You and I both know that things were turning around until the bust, and we both know that there's one key that could unlock a way to make all of this much easier. You chose not to turn that key, and here we are."

"You're blaming *me* for this mess?" She slams her laptop lid shut as some throaty noise erupts from her.

I lift a shoulder. Blame is a strong word, but I'm also not *not* saying that.

"I never should have slept with you," she hisses. "Hell, I never should have even moved to Vegas. I *knew* in my gut it was going to be a goddamn football player, and here we are. My career is about to go down the drain, and all you can do is sit there and blame *me* for *your* poor decisions."

"Yeah," I mutter. "You're right. We shouldn't have slept together. I should never have given in to the feelings I had for you. It was easier when we just hated each other."

She presses her lips together and glances up at the ceiling as she clearly tries to ward off tears. I wish I could regret the words as they fall from my mouth, but the truth is that I'm trying hard to turn those emotions off again.

It was easier back when I didn't feel anything at all than feeling like this.

CHAPTER 38
Everleigh Bradley

Spin Old News

Mr. Jennings acknowledges that he has made mistakes and will do better in the future. He has no further comment at this time.

Mr. Jennings is working hard to learn from his past mistakes and change his behavior. We have no further comment at this time.

Mr. Jennings takes full responsibility for his actions and is committed to earning back the trust of his team and his fans.

It's on repeat. Put a fire out here with a bland, nondescript statement. Put another fire out there with another bland, nondescript statement.

Mr. Jennings isn't, in fact, trying to do better or change his behavior.

But that's not what I tell the media.

No, I spin old news, put out the same statements over and over, and try to highlight the good he's done.

It's hard.

He broke my heart with his words. I fired the shots first, sure. Absolutely, I did. But he didn't have to come back and say that it was easier when we hated each other.

Even if he was right.

And so that's where I find myself. Hating him again, but this time it's paired with a side of worry. What the hell is he going to do next?

He's back to his old self again, especially this weekend since he's suspended. Rather than keep a low profile—which is what *most* professionals in a situation where he was suspended for his behavior would do—he's doubling down. He was photographed drinking at a club last night after our conversation. He was photographed later in the evening—or the early hours of this morning, I guess—at a strip club.

The asshole *went to a strip club*. To drink, to touch boobs, to stick dollar bills into thongs, who knows? All I know is that he wasn't with me, and he's not making himself look any better.

His birthday is tomorrow. He's turning thirty-three on Halloween. I asked him once if there was anything he wanted to do to mark the occasion, and he said no. I wonder what he'll do now that he's on his own.

I think about going through with my plan. I was going to take him to dinner, and then I was going to give him his gift. Instead of doing that, I call the place where I bought his gift and ask them to send it directly to his place rather than to mine.

He can still have it. It's already paid for anyway. This way I won't have to interact with him.

I work my ass off burying the nonsense he participated in last night. I highlight the same stories—a handful of charity events, his little moment with that girl at the Hope Gala…and that's about all I can find. There's so much more out there that's *negative* that I'm having a hard time covering it all up. I think about bringing up the shelter, but that's just for him. He's been adamant about that since I first mentioned it, so I leave it be.

No sense in creating even more bad blood between us.

Even Ellie is out of statements to make up. We've circled the same verbiage a hundred different ways. She has other clients, but I don't. This is wholly on me, and I hired Ellie to help me. I've turned to her a million times in the last twenty-four hours, but not being able to give her the full picture makes it harder to ask her for help.

Still, she's working on some things in the background. Appearances at youth camps, more charity events, things of that nature, while she also reaches out to his sponsors with our plans of what he's doing to turn himself back around.

It's just hard to sell that when he's being photographed at places he shouldn't be. I lost what little control I tricked myself into believing I had when I said those nasty words to him—when I chose against him instead of with him.

My phone rings just before I'm going to take a lunch break on Friday, and I see it's Penny calling.

My chest tightens as I realize what a horrible friend I've been.

"Hey," I answer brightly. *Too* brightly. *Fake* brightly.

She sees right through me. "You can fool the media, but you can't fool your best friend."

"I should be the one calling to check up on you, not the other way around," I say.

"Yeah, probably, but honestly, I've had a little time for it all to sink in, and despite everything, I'm happier than I've been in years. So what's going on with you? I keep seeing these headlines about Maverick Jennings, and Stuart has been running around here muttering things under his breath all morning."

"Stuart has?" I ask, my voice trembling a little. If Stuart is upset over what's going on with Maverick, well…that can't be good for me. It likely means Jack has been in touch with him.

And that could mean the end of this job for me.

"Yeah," she says quietly.

"Shit," I mutter.

"Yeah," she repeats. "I wanted to give you the heads-up, that's all."

"Great. Just fucking great. I'm going to be fired because Maverick Jennings is an asshole."

"You're not going to be fired. Maybe just taken off his project," she says, trying to be comforting.

"Same difference. It won't matter. It'll be a hit to my reputation, and I won't be able to open my own firm because nobody will want to work with the girl who couldn't fix Maverick."

"Some people just don't want to be helped," she points out.

Isn't that the truth? I blow out a breath.

"Nobody has to know he was your client," she adds.

"I knew I didn't want to work with an athlete. This right here. This is why." I hang my head as I try to come to terms with all of this. My career and my personal life are coming to a screeching halt at the same time, and there's not a damn thing I can do to save either one of them.

The prospect of opening up my own firm is slipping further and further from my reach.

I lost the man I loved.

I'm in a city that's not my home.

I feel alone and lost. I feel like everything has been ripped out from under me in one fell swoop.

And it feels like it has an awful lot to do with my very own father.

"I know, Ev. What can I do?" Penny asks.

"Nothing," I mutter. "I have to let this play out and see what Stuart decides."

"You know I'm right here if you need to talk."

"Well, if I get fired, I'll be back in Chicago ASAP, so let's plan on a girls' staycation weekend somewhere fancy. Okay?"

"Definitely. But you're not going to get fired," she says.

That remains to be seen. She fills me in on the latest office gossip at Langford, and then she adds, "I forgot to tell you that I talked to Billy the other day."

"Oh? What did he have to say?" It's not curiosity so much as I can hear in her voice that she wants to tell me. Talk about *old news.*

"He wants you back, Ev. He told me that. He said he was disappointed with how things went when he was in Vegas, and he was hitting me up for how he can win you back. Maybe if you're back in Chicago…"

She trails off, but the insinuation is clear.

"Nah. That ship has sailed."

"Are you sure?"

I think about the night he came by here and what I felt for him versus what I felt for Maverick after he left. "Yeah. Totally sure. I fell for Maverick, Pen. It was different than how I fell for Billy."

"Was?" she asks.

"I'm afraid that ship might've sailed, too."

"Oh no. Why?"

"It's complicated."

And then I proceed to tell her everything.

Is Maverick right? Would letting him name my dad as the operator of that underground casino solve all these issues? I have no idea. He was issued the citation either way. But we don't know what comes next. The DA could decide to go hard on him, and he could end up far worse off than being suspended for one game.

It's all speculation until the DA has time to review the evidence. If the raid occurred, they already have evidence, and they probably already have my father's name, too. I don't know much about this stuff, though—I guess that's not all that surprising considering the extent my father went to hide it all.

I suppose now we play the waiting game. Wait to hear from the DA. Wait for my phone to ring to see if Stuart is going to fire me. Wait to see if Jack is going to call me in again even though he claimed he doesn't blame me for Maverick's missteps.

Wait for Maverick to continue making my job harder.

Wait for a miracle that will somehow turn this entire thing around and put me back in his arms. What I said about wishing we'd never slept together was purely out of anger, and I miss him.

I don't regret our time together, but I also know that at this point, I can't go backward. I made my choice—even if it was the wrong one.

Now I have to live with it.

CHAPTER 39

MAVERICK JENNINGS

Birthday Gift

It's my birthday. It's Halloween.

My mom always called me on my birthday. Maybe it was Susan who reminded her to call me these last few years, but I don't even have her to wish me a happy birthday this year.

Nobody from my team calls me. The *brothers* I was supposed to *bond* with. Not a single one of my coaches. Not even anybody from the practice squad.

I put myself here. I'm in trouble. I never should've gone to that goddamn casino. I never should've gone to the club, either, or the strip joint. I didn't even watch the dancers. I just sat at the bar drinking scotch.

I should be getting ready to go out tonight—or at the very least, entertaining my girl for a while.

Instead, I'm sitting by my windows overlooking the Strip as I nurse a hangover.

Actually, if anything, I should be getting ready to play football tomorrow. Staying at the team hotel, eating right, going to bed early.

Not considering opening a new bottle of scotch alone at noon.

My phone dings with a text from Milton.

Milton: *You have a package at the desk.*

I wonder for a beat if he messaged the wrong person, but this is Milton. He doesn't make mistakes.

I set the bottle of scotch down on the counter. This isn't me. Turning to alcohol—I didn't even do that a decade ago. I'm not sure what's so different this time around. Maybe because my emotions just shut off last time as a means of self-preservation, and this time I'm actively trying to avoid them.

I'm not sure, but everything is falling apart, and I don't know what the fuck I'm supposed to do to get my life back on track again.

I had a glimpse of the good life. I was so close. Almost there.

And then it slipped away. Just like everything always does.

Could I forgive her for choosing her family over me? The answer to that should be clear. Of course I can. But it's not. Not when she knew my history. She's one of the few I've ever shared my story with, one of the few people here to help my reputation, and she *still* chose the other side.

It's a running theme in my life. Everyone always chooses someone else. My father chose those other women over bonding with his son. Christina chose my friend to get pregnant with. Dallas chose to get rid of me.

I thought things would be different here in Vegas. It should have been a fresh start, and instead, I'm back to where I started.

I head downstairs, and Milton hands me a large manila envelope.

"Happy birthday, sir," he says to me.

I glance up at him, surprised he knew. "Thanks," I murmur. He's likely taking in my disheveled appearance. I didn't even put shoes on to come down here—bare feet, a sloppy T-shirt and mesh shorts, my hair matted down, my beard growing in.

I head back to the elevator and take it up without opening the envelope. I'll do it when I'm alone since I have no clue what could possibly be inside.

When I get to my floor, of course Everleigh is just locking hers up.

She glances at me, takes in my appearance, and purses her lips.

I take in her appearance, too. She looks tired. She probably is. She's been cleaning up after me for two days. If she's even half as emotionally drained as I feel, I guess I have to admit that she's going through some shit, too.

But that doesn't motivate me to be any more understanding.

"What?" I demand.

"Happy birthday," she says quietly.

She rushes onto the elevator before the doors close and takes it down.

My stomach clenches that this is where we're at. Me yelling at her again. Her judging me.

I head inside and tear open the envelope, and I read the words scrawled at the top of the page, likely by whoever took down the order for whatever this is.

Happy Birthday, Maverick. Love, Everleigh

My eyes skip down the page to the name of the company and then, below it, the actual gift.

Vegas Custom Autos

Custom auto paint finish for Ford Raptor. Suggested colors: black and Vegas Aces red. Client's choice.

My chest tightens.

I haven't had the time or energy to hunt down a place to repaint the truck I just had done in Dallas colors, and she did it for me. I said it once aloud to her. A one-time complaint about my regret.

Fuck. She fucking did it for me.

She takes care of me. She listens. She remembers.

How could she choose *anyone* else over what we were starting?

Maybe it's harder for me to understand because of my own complicated relationship with my father. I suppose I chose football over my mother, but that was at my own mother's urging. She didn't want me to change my life to accommodate her. In fact, it was an explicit request.

But Everleigh is changing *her* life to accommodate her father. He asked, and she felt pressed. I know she's loyal to her family. Fuck, her loyalty is one of the things I love about her.

But this meaningful little gift is another thing, and it just serves as a reminder of everything I've lost.

I toss the paper on the counter. I can't bear to look at it.

A knock at my door lifts my spirits a bit. People don't typically drop by unannounced in a building with a doorman, which means it's her. It *has* to be her.

It's not.

To my utter shock, it's her brother.

"Can I talk to you?" Dex asks.

"Talk," I grunt.

He stares at me for a beat, and I stare back. I finally back down and open the door a little wider, walking away to let him in without saying the words to actually invite him in. I don't invite people in—not physically, and not metaphorically.

I wander over to my windows, and Dex falls into place beside me. I'm silent while I wait for him to make the first move, and predictably, he does.

"You doing okay?" he asks.

"Not really."

"Did you know my dad had me bringing in whales when he first opened the lounge?" he muses.

We're both still staring out the window, and I make some grunting sounds.

"I got out when it put my relationship in jeopardy," he says, as if that's opening the door for me to tell him about my relationships that are or are not in jeopardy because of the very same lounge he's referencing.

When I don't answer, he asks, "What's going on with you and my sister?"

"Nothing," I say, which feels like a truth and a lie at the same time. "Not anymore, anyway," I amend.

"Then what *was* going on with you?"

I blow out a breath. "Look, I don't know you."

"No, but if something's going down between you and Ev, then maybe we get to know one another. You know what I'm saying?"

"We were together. It was good." As if that's not the understatement of the century. "But when your underground place was raided and I was caught there, I had a choice. I could give up the operator's name, or I could protect your sister. I let her decide, and she chose family loyalty. So whatever it was…it's over now."

"It doesn't have to be," he says softly.

I glance over at him, surprised by his words.

"But let's get one thing straight," he adds. "It's not my fucking lounge. I got out when I could."

"Okay," I say. I don't really care what his role is in the place. It belongs to the family, so it's tied to him.

"Look, a few months ago, I would've said *fuck you*. We don't get along, Jennings, and maybe we never will. But if you make my sister happy, I'm willing to try."

I huff out a mirthless chuckle. "That's the thing. I *don't* make her happy. She chose to let me take a potentially worse fall than I have to because she doesn't want me to name your father. I can't be with someone who won't put me first."

"That's what my girl said, too. But it's a two-way street, Mav. Just remember that."

Of course I remember that. I feel like I've done my part. Haven't I?

Maybe Dex is right. Maybe I need to do something about it. But what?

"I need to get back to the Complex," he says. "I just came home to kiss my wife and my kid at lunchtime, and I thought I'd stop by and see if you needed anything on my way out."

I probably do. But I have no idea what—or how to ask Dex Fucking Bradley for it. My teammate. My enemy. The brother of the woman I love.

Fuck, this is complicated.

CHAPTER 40
Everleigh Bradley

Where to Work

I twist my hands nervously in my lap. I have a feeling I know why I'm here, and I don't like it.

And when Ellie shows up, sits in the chair beside me, and takes my hand in hers, my fears are confirmed.

I draw in a deep breath, and Lily says to both of us, "You can head into Mr. Dalton's office."

I've never been fired before, but I'm bracing myself. I don't think I'll still be able to say that once I leave here today.

I slip into the chair opposite Jack Dalton.

"Make this quick, Jack," Ellie says to her brother-in-law. "I need to return about ten calls regarding your suspended quarterback." Ellie may be one of the few people on this planet who could get away with talking to her brother-in-law like that.

"I'll be very quick. What are you two doing to mitigate what's going on with my star quarterback?"

I glance at Ellie, sure she's going to take the reins, but instead, she nods at me.

"I've been playing the boring statement, *nothing to see here* game while highlighting the few good deeds I could find in his track record." I nod to Ellie. "If you have more charity work, we need to jump at it." I make plans in front of Jack. Maybe he won't fire me if he knows I'm still working behind the scenes.

"I've been trying, but few organizations want to work with someone with his reputation. They're concerned they'll get him to sign on only for him to pull a stunt that gets him benched." She shrugs.

"I don't blame them," Jack says. He glances out the window. "I wanted to leave these types of things up to the GM and the coaching staff, but I see a lot of myself in Maverick. It's why I decided to take a more hands-on approach with him, but I think maybe I've still been too hands-off with him. I've decided to go in a different direction with how we're handling his behavior. Instead of having you as his brand strategist, I'm going to personally step in to mentor him. I've set aside the few tasks I held onto at Dalton Developments until further notice so I can put my full attention here. I'm grateful to you both for all the work you've done. Ms. Bradley, you're free to return to Chicago, and Ellie, I'll see you at dinner on Tuesday. I may still have some things for you to do with Jennings since you're familiar with his background, but I'll be taking him under my wing for the foreseeable future."

I want to ask what that means, but I realize it's not my business anymore.

It could have been, but I chose a different path.

"Thank you for the opportunity to work with one of your players, Mr. Dalton," I say, not fully sure I mean it considering it was never what I wanted out of this career. "It's been a pleasure."

"It certainly has," he murmurs, and he pins me with those navy blue eyes of his. "You know, Ms. Bradley, our marketing department may be able to use someone with your skillset. I know it didn't work out with Jennings, but that's more on him than on you. Would you be interested?"

I give him a tight smile. "It's a wonderful offer, really, but I should probably return home to Langford. Mr. Langford would be furious with me if I let you poach me."

Jack chuckles. "I can understand that. But if you're looking for something more permanent in Vegas—"

"Then she'll come work for PCPR," Ellie finishes, giving Jack a glare.

He holds up both hands, and I can't help a tiny smile as it plays at my lips that these two are fighting over me. But what I told him is true. If I'm leaving Langford, it's going to be because I'm starting my own business, not because I'm going to work for someone else. And it won't be here.

Maybe I can still plow ahead with my original plan, but Stuart's condition for the out he was going to give me was contingent on lasting a year here on this contract. I didn't. And while Jack is framing it as going in another direction, the truth is that he's firing me.

It's going to make it harder to start my own company.

"In any event," Jack says, "you'll get a good report from me to Stuart. You've been a great asset to us, Everleigh, and I don't want you to mistake my intentions here."

"It feels a lot like I'm getting fired," I say in a small voice. I think about begging him to keep me here, but I don't want to come off looking desperate, and I also don't want to give away the fact that I want to stay close to Maverick since I've fallen for him. Maybe this is my sign that he isn't mine to fight for. He's already made it pretty clear he doesn't want that fight anyway.

"I'm certain it does, but rest assured, that's not what this is. If you'd prefer to stay here and finish out the year on the contract, I can reassign you. If you'd prefer to transfer back to Chicago, I'm sure Stuart is suffering without your talents close to home."

I don't have to put a lot of thought into this, to be honest. "That's nice of you to say. I guess if I'm being let go from my current responsibilities, I'd just as soon head home." I'd rather not stick around and be face-to-face with someone who doesn't want to be around me—someone who broke my heart after I broke his first.

I guess we're both responsible for the wreckage we've left.

I say my goodbyes to Jack and Ellie, and I head home. It's hard walking out of the Complex for what is likely going to be the last time, so of course I bump into my brother just to make things a smidge harder.

"Ev, where you headed?" Dex asks as he walks in through the front doors just as I'm about to walk out of them.

"Home," I say quietly. I glance around, and then I realize I don't really care who hears me. "Jack fired me."

"What?" he breathes. "What the fuck? Because of Jennings? It's *his* fault, not yours. Fuck that dude. I'm going to rip him a new—"

I hold up a hand. "Dex, stop. Please. It wasn't a good fit. You and I both know I wasn't cut out to work with athletes, least of all one like him."

"Like him?" he repeats.

I lift a shoulder and twist my lips as I look away. "Someone who really doesn't *want* to change."

"Yeah," he murmurs. "I need to get to practice. I'm sorry this is how things went. Can I take you to dinner on Monday?"

I shake my head. "I'm going home. I think Vegas just isn't for me. I'll let what happened here stay here and all that jazz. I'm going to get my feet back under me in Chicago."

Except what happened here won't stay here. It's Vegas, sure, but the way my chest feels heavy and my head hurts and my legs feel like jelly—I'm pretty sure all that's going to follow me home.

And the way I feel about Maverick Jennings will definitely follow me home, too.

CHAPTER 41

MAVERICK JENNINGS

Corporate Brand Strategies

When your team owner's assistant calls and beckons you into the office, you don't have much choice but to go. Especially when you're stuck at home rather than at practice since you're suspended.

I mean, it's not all a waste of time. I made the appointment with the auto paint place, and I worked out.

But that's about all I've done on this, my thirty-third birthday.

It's not likely that Jack is calling me in to wish me a happy birthday, though.

I arrive and head straight for his office, and Lily nods me in.

"Mr. Jennings, take a seat," he says, and I do as I'm told. "You seemed…*objectionable* to the idea of a babysitter shadowing your every move to help you straighten out your image, and so I've decided to give you what you wanted. I let her go."

I draw in a sharp breath, and my chest feels as if its caving in on itself. "You what?"

He lifts a shoulder. "If you're not going to take these brand strategies seriously and instead you're going to fuck around with the woman I've hired to help you, you leave me no other choice but to take matters into my own hands."

My stomach churns at his words.

Now by *fuck around with*…does he mean literally or in a more figurative sense? Does he know Everleigh and I have been sleeping together? Is that why he did this? Did Coach Richards tell him?

I keep silent as I wait for him to detail exactly what taking matters into his own hands means.

"To that end, I've let Ms. Bradley go, and I'll be working with you directly. I may bring my wife, Kate, on board as well to help as needed since she's the one who whipped me into shape. Well, and my son, but you don't have children. Do you?"

I shake my head as I do my best to hide my utter annoyance at the direction of this conversation. I knew he wasn't calling me in because it's my birthday. If anything, this is about the worst present I could possibly think of.

I'm silent as he starts to drone on about his plans to fix me. All his brand strategies that he thinks are going to solve this problem.

"You're a multi-million-dollar asset to this team, and it's time you start acting like it. I don't want to threaten bench time, but I want to remind you of your bonus structure. You've already lost the million-dollar bonus for staying out of trouble this season, but I have a call into your agent to discuss a possible restructure of your contract. My offer is that for every week this season, if you meet certain criteria, you'll get a bonus."

"What criteria?" I ask.

"You attend all press obligations and any additional events I put on your calendar, you stay out of trouble, no fines, no citations, no legal trouble, and you actually play the game."

"And what bonus?"

"Five hundred thousand each week."

It's a good offer. A great one, actually. There are still ten weeks left this season, minus a bye week. That gives me the potential to earn four and a half million extra dollars if I do what he says—which is helpful at this point since my meal prep people pulled our agreement after the citation was made public.

But he's not doing what Everleigh did. He's not trying to get me to open up. He's not trying to get inside my head to understand why I am the way I am. He's throwing money at the problem.

He's taking the corporate approach. She took the human one.

Which makes sense. To him, I'm nothing more than an asset. His goal as a team owner is to maximize profits and win games, and I'm nothing more than a tool that can help make that happen.

"Once we get the restructure in place, we'll work on your events. We'll avoid podcasts for a while and stick with statements and talking points drafted for you. We'll work on some youth outreach stuff, philanthropy, team promo. Polish you up a bit. No more bars and clubs. You stay home, and you focus on the game. I'll put you on a tight leash if I have to."

More treating me like a commodity instead of a person. He's not asking the questions. He's not getting to know me. He doesn't care that I once was married, that my wife died in a horrible accident over a decade ago, that I found out she was pregnant at the time. He doesn't ask about any of that. He still doesn't know that I found out at her funeral that the kid wasn't mine and that I've been carrying this around with me for ten years.

He doesn't know that I didn't talk about it. Ever. With anyone. Until Everleigh. She got me to open up. She's the only one who's ever been able to reach me.

Do I still make mistakes? Fuck yeah, I do. I'm only human, and like all her statements said, I'm working on myself. I'm learning.

He doesn't know that if he takes her away from me, he's also taking away the progress only she was able to make.

And I certainly can't tell him that I'm in love with her.

"We have a lot of opportunity to right this ship, so let's get to work," he finishes. He studies me for a few seconds, and then he adds, "I want to make clear that I'm doing this because my goal is to make you the leader I know you are."

"Feels corporate," I grunt.

He chuckles. "Thanks for the honesty. And maybe some of it is. My decisions have to be driven by business because that's what this is. You know that as well as I do. But I can't run my business properly when my players are running around getting into trouble. I have to draw the line somewhere, and if my first attempt at passing this off to someone else didn't work, then I guess I have to do it myself."

"It *did* work," I argue. "Or it was starting to, anyway." I keep my gaze focused out the window.

"Did it?" he prompts.

I finally return my eyes to his. "It's complicated, but yes. Everleigh was the first person to get me to open up since I lost my wife in a car accident ten years ago."

His eyes widen as he sinks back into his chair. "Jesus, Mav. I'm so sorry."

My eyes go back out the window. "Nobody takes the time to get underneath why I am the way I am. Until Ev. But that's why. There's more to it. My wife…she was pregnant at the time. It wasn't mine, something I found out at her funeral. Sometimes I imagine what it would've been like. I always thought he would've been a boy that should've been mine." I clench my jaw. "In the end, everybody leaves. Including Everleigh now."

Jack is quiet for a long time. So long that I almost glance over at him, but I don't. I can't. I've left too much of myself out there to be judged now, and it feels open and raw and vulnerable.

"I'm sorry, Mav. It's a shit hand you were dealt, and you deserved better."

I glance up at him, and he presses his lips together and shakes his head.

"Don't you see, though? This is it. Your legacy. You can show people that they can survive trauma. They can rise from the ashes. You did. You went through hell, and you made it through to the other side. You've been a pro football player for an entire decade despite the darkness trying to weigh you down. I saw those images of you with that little girl from the Hope Gala. *That* is the Maverick Jennings I brought over to the Vegas Aces. *That* is the man I know is somewhere inside of you, the one that you choose to suppress. And *that* is the angle we're spinning here."

I shake my head. "It's not about angles. I don't want to publicize my history. I'm telling you this to help you understand me. I never told anyone about it, and Everleigh managed to pull it out of me. She made me fall in love with her. She made me choose her. But she didn't choose me back. So everyone leaves, and I'm back in the ashes where I was a decade ago, only under different circumstances this time."

He presses his lips together and tilts his head with sympathy as he narrows his eyes at me. "Yeah. Different because you've got me on your side this time. And together, we're going to make a difference."

I'm not sure what he means by that just yet, but I have a feeling he's not the type of man who's going to let it go.

CHAPTER 42

Everleigh Bradley

Where to Work

I'm crying as I walk around my condo, haphazardly tossing items into a suitcase as if I care what I bring back to Chicago with me and what stays here.

It's better this way. I'll get to go home, spend Mom's last few months with her. Or year. However much time she has.

I really just need my toiletries, maybe a few clothing items. My red lipstick. My favorite heels. Everything else is back in Chicago anyway.

I never should've taken this job in the first place. I am terrified to tell Stuart that Jack fired me, but honestly, he probably already knows. Still, it's a call I know I need to make.

Before I get the chance to make the call, though, my phone rings. I glance at my screen and see my brother Ford calling.

I draw in a deep breath and say a few practice *hey*s aloud so I don't sound like I've been crying before I answer. "Hey."

"What's wrong?" he immediately asks, clearly catching me.

"I was fired," I wail.

"Because of Dad," he says flatly.

I mean…I guess in a way, it does all lead directly back to him, doesn't it?

More wailing is my response. And some babbling. "And I fell in love with Maverick Jennings but it's over now because he was caught there at Dad's lounge and the police said if he named the operator the DA might let him off but he didn't and he came to me and I said he couldn't and now he feels like I didn't choose him."

"Well, you didn't," he points out, ever the man of logic. As if I need that right now.

"Whatever," I mutter.

"This whole thing gets even messier. Did you know about Dex?"

"That Dad wanted him to run it when it opened?" I ask, supplying what information I know.

"Yeah. I guess he was bringing in whales. But Dad had listed his name as the operator originally. If it hadn't been for Ainsley…" He trails off as I think that one through, finally filling in the ending.

"The FBI would be on his ass right now."

"Yeah. And instead, they're on someone else's," he murmurs.

"Who's?" I demand, a little nervous to know the answer.

"Archer."

"What?" I breathe. "How do you know? And how did Dad get him involved? And how? Just…*how?*"

"I'm trying to find out more. Tatum called me. She and Archer are done," he says quietly.

Holy shit. "They're *done?* And she called you?"

"She always calls me when they're fighting. It used to be the way I kept tabs on him," he admits.

"But then you went and fell for your younger brother's girlfriend," I say. It's a clear accusation, but it's also common knowledge between Ford and me.

"Shut up," he mutters petulantly.

"Did Archer know Dad put his name down? Is that why they broke up?"

"I'm not sure, but right now it's all very hush-hush. I wouldn't be surprised if authorities came to talk to you, too, though. To all of us," he says.

"Are they listening right now? Do we need to get our stories straight?" I don't know if I'm joking or not.

"I don't know," he murmurs. "But what is this telling us about our father? Why should we be loyal to a father who would turn his back on his own kids and turn one of us in to save himself?"

"Is that what happened?" I ask.

He's quiet a long time, and I'm not sure if or when we'll get the answer to that. Eventually, he says, "I need to get back to practice."

"Are you okay?" I ask.

"Are you?" he counters.

"No," we both say at the same time.

I blow out a breath. "Love you, little bro."

"Love you, big sis." He ends the call, and I'm left reeling.

Archer?

Really?

He avoids the family for years and years, plays baseball when the rest of the boys play football, only to reappear to take the fall for our father's crimes?

Something is going on, and I intend to find out what.

You know…right after I nurse this broken heart.

I pull my suitcase toward the door and glance around my condo one more time. It's been fun living here, and I actually have the contract on this place signed for another ten months, so maybe I'll come visit once my heart has mended a little. Once I have my feet under me again. Once I think I can face him without feeling the sting of what could have been.

Okay, fine. On second note, maybe I won't be back for a while.

I walk out the door, and I lock up. I briefly debate knocking on Maverick's door to say goodbye. I stare at the door, and I glance at the spot where he pinned me up against the wall to almost kiss me—the same place he pinned me up against the wall to actually kiss me.

I blow out a breath, and then I press the button to call the elevator.

I stop by the desk since Milton's there, and I say, "Can you let Dex know I went back to Chicago?"

He nods once. "Any messages for Mr. Jennings?"

I press my lips together and shake my head as tears brim in my eyes.

"Oh, Ms. Bradley," he says gently, and there's a kind of apology in his tone without him having to say it. "Can I offer you a ride to the airport?"

"I'd appreciate that."

"For what it's worth, you really did turn that man around," he says quietly.

"Thank you. I hope so, but Mr. Dalton didn't seem to think so."

"Will you be back?" he asks.

"I'm not sure." I walk over to him and give him a hug. "Thanks for everything, Milton. You've been a lifesaver more than once."

"That's why they pay me the big bucks, ma'am." He winks at me.

I head to the car waiting out front, and twenty minutes later, I'm getting out at the airport. I check in for my flight, check my bag, and head toward the gate.

I call Penny on the way.

"Evs!" she answers, and she sounds happy. On the other hand, I'm crying again. "Oh, no," she says. "What happened?"

"Jack fired me, and I'm catching a flight home right now."

"Oh, Ev. I'm so, so sorry. What can I do?"

"I know it's Halloween and you'll be busy with the kids, but maybe I can see you tomorrow or something?" I beg.

"I'll do you one better," she says. "I'm trick-or-treating with the kids tonight and then dropping them at their dad's apartment afterward. I'll come over to your place, and we'll veg out and have a sleepover like the good ole days before I got married and you got Billy-ed and we both got fucked over."

"Deal. I'll pick up ice cream on my way home. And vodka."

"And I'll raid the candy bags for all of the M&Ms," she offers.

I feel like she was probably going to do that anyway. "If you see any Snickers bars…"

"You got it. I'll call you when I'm on my way."

I feel a little better as we hang up, and a short while later, I'm boarding my flight and leaving behind this place that has caused so many issues and so much pain.

CHAPTER 43

MAVERICK JENNINGS

Sending Minions

I'm watching the games from home on the day after my thirty-third birthday.

This isn't the way to start a brand-new year.

It feels like my life has done a complete one-eighty over the last week.

It took ten years to make the first turn and one week to turn all the way back.

Except it feels somehow worse this time. Losing Christina sucked. It changed my very DNA. Losing my mom was harder. And losing Everleigh…

I don't know.

It feels like something I can never recover from. Like I can't go on. There's no motivation to push forward.

I know there is. Obviously. But right now, everything just feels so…pointless.

It feels almost painful enough to just let go of the reasons why I had to end it in the first place, but if she's not choosing me now for the big things, what kind of future could there possibly be for us?

I blow out a breath as I stare at the screen. Brandon Fletcher was just sacked. Could've been me laid out on my back as the commentators make their stupid comments about what the offensive line should've done to protect him.

But it wasn't me in that position because I'm fucking sitting here, suspended because of my own stupid decision.

And who knows where it'll lead? The DA could call me up tonight with questions, and if I don't give them the answers they're looking for, I could be in an even worse situation.

That is why I feel alone. That's why I'm staring listlessly at a television with a bottle of Lagavulin by my side as I work on numbing out these stupid fucking emotions just so I can get through the day.

I'm allowed back into the Complex on Monday, and I'm there burying myself in my workouts for the entire day. One day turns into another, and another, and yet another, until a week has gone by without her. I work my ass off in the weight room, on the treadmill, in the pool. I spend time finger breathing up on the roof, contemplating what I can do to get her back, wondering what would happen if I just went against her wishes and named her father anyway. It would save me a hell of a lot of trouble, and it's clear she's done with me anyway.

I won't do it despite the temptation. She might not be protecting me, but I'll still protect her. It's what you do when you love somebody.

I put in more volunteer hours at the animal shelter than my usual one a week. In fact, I go every morning before practice. When our bye week hits, I stay longer.

Bruno is still there. I think about taking her home.

I don't, but I spend a lot of time with her.

Since it's our bye week, I don't even get to play in a game. If we did, though, I'd have already turned back into the cold quarterback who doesn't celebrate well-executed plays but instead returns to the sidelines with a vicious comment about how we could have done it better.

Even if we win by a good margin, it's still not a reason to celebrate. We always make mistakes, and you know what I'm really fucking tired of?

Mistakes.

Stupid or otherwise.

Jack hasn't been my shadow the way Everleigh was, but he *is* making sure *someone* is checking on me every day.

Apparently because we live in the same building, today is Dex Bradley's turn.

Just the person I *don't* want to see.

I've been avoiding him this week, a fairly easy thing to do on our bye week, but today, I can't avoid him. He knocks on my door, and the last time I opened it to him, he blabbered on about how relationships are two-way streets and I should do something to get Ev back.

"Jack sent you today?" I guess when I open the door.

Yesterday it was a defensive lineman who lives in my building. The day before, it was Lily. Must be nice running your own empire and sending your minions to do your dirty work.

"Yeah," he admits. He stands in my doorway and shuffles on his feet a little. "You okay?" he asks.

I turn away from the door and walk into my condo without inviting him in nor declining his entry. "I'm not going to any underground casinos, if that's what you're asking. Are you supposed to check to make sure I'm home, or is this more of a welfare check?"

He pulls out his phone and pretends to snap a photo of me. "Proof of life."

I roll my eyes as I plop back onto my couch. I stretch my legs out and cross them at the ankles, and Dex sinks down into the recliner.

"It almost felt like you were starting to warm up to being here, and now it seems like you hate everyone again. What happened? Is it Ev? Because I can call her and fix this."

I hold up a hand. "Stop. It's not Ev," I lie.

He shoots me a *yeah, okay* look that's absolutely brimming with sarcasm.

I blow out a breath. "Fine. It's Ev."

"Knew it," he says, pumping a fist into the air.

"She took off, man. She's done with Vegas, done with me, done with all of it."

"Yeah, because Jack *fired* her because she couldn't get you under control," he says.

My jaw slackens before I clench it tight again, my teeth grinding at his words. "That's not what happened," I hiss.

"You don't think so?" he bites out. "Everybody knows it, Maverick. Everybody. So don't sit here whining like a little bitch when we both know why she's gone."

"Ah, so you're going the route of tough love. Let's see, we've had sympathy, humor, and logic." I tick each one off on my fingers as I name the approaches that have been taken with me thus far. "Seems like the right time for tough love, and it's on brand for you."

He huffs out a sigh. "Yeah, maybe. I've got more skin in the game than the others, though. She's my sister, and I know that's why you're acting out."

"I'm not acting out," I say with a bit more defensiveness than I should. "I'm sitting right fucking here in front of you. I'm not even drinking tonight since we have a game in two days. I'm not at a club. In fact, I'm being so good that I'm not even watching porn. You can report that back to Jack."

Dex stands and wanders over to my windows. "I spend a lot of time in my own place looking out over the view as I contemplate my decisions. My life. But honestly, since my kid came into my life and I got married, I haven't done it as much. Less to contemplate when you're happy, I guess."

"Rub it in a little more."

"Why is that rubbing it in? Not everything is a personal attack, you know," he says. "I can be happy, and you can *not* be, and we can still coexist."

I don't have anything to say to that, and he turns around to face me.

"What happened with my sister?"

I stare at him carefully for a few beats, and ultimately I decide…why the fuck not just go for honesty here? "We fell for each other. She got me to open up about things I never told anyone. She came to my mom's funeral with me." I shrug. "And then, well, you know the rest. We've been over it."

"Spell it out for me," he says.

"I was at the Legacy underground casino the night it was busted. I was told the DA would go easier on me if I named the operator, that they might even drop the citation before I took flak for it from the team. I asked Everleigh for her permission to name your father, and she declined. End of story. Why are you making me relive this shit again?"

"I'm looking for a loophole." He shakes his head. "I'm not finding one. Ains ended it with me, you know. She felt I was putting her and my son in danger because of the lounge. I had to make a choice, too."

"But you chose her," I point out.

He shakes his head. "I didn't at first."

"So you're saying there's hope that your sister will change her mind?"

"I don't know what I'm saying. Our family history…it's complicated. And now with Mom sick, surely you could understand the situation Ev was in. She's a protector, Mav. Always has been. Hell, she tried to protect you, too, with her brand shit. But you asked her to choose between the family she's known her entire life and a man she's known all of a couple months. What would you have picked?"

"Anyone over my own father, that's for damn sure," I mutter.

"Okay, but she didn't. She couldn't. There are seven of us Bradley kids that she's looking out for. There's one of you. Can't you understand that?"

"Why are you talking to me about this?" I ask, my voice gaining in volume. "She walked away. She chose your goddamn family over what we had built. All this bullshit…it's a big part of why I never wanted to get involved with someone again."

"Again?" he asks.

I nod. "Again," I murmur. "I was married once. It's complicated, but I found out too late that she'd been cheating on me."

"Jesus, Mav. I had no idea."

"Nobody does. I'm notoriously private because I don't show weakness to anybody."

"Getting cheated on isn't a weakness," he points out.

"Sure as fuck felt like it weakened me. I found out at her funeral after I found out she'd been pregnant when she died in a car accident. Imagine trying to move on from that ordeal."

His brows are raised, and there's sympathy in his eyes. "Fuck, dude."

I nod toward him. "That look. That right there. The sympathy." I make a face of disgust as I shake my head. "That's the shit I don't want." My voice is venomous as I say the words. "That's why I don't tell anyone. It's why I shut everyone out. It's why I let everyone think they're my enemy. It's easier to go through life like that than to feel what I've felt the last week we ended things." I press my lips together and shrug like it doesn't affect me even more than the accident that ended my first marriage.

"My sister cares deeply, and you forced her into an impossible position. I'm sorry you didn't like it when you got your answer, but sometimes loving someone means understanding what they're faced with and fighting with them rather than against them."

I blow out a heavy breath as I get up and walk toward the door to indicate that it's time for him to go. He did his welfare check, and we're done here.

"You're right," I finally say. "And sometimes it means letting them go when they walk away."

CHAPTER 44

Everleigh Bradley

Wallowing

"Another scoop?" Penny asks the following Saturday night.

I nod, and she gets me a big one filled with goodies before plopping it into my bowl. She pushes it across the counter to me with a spoon before she makes her own bowl.

She made me come over after she got the boys to bed. I'd rather be at home wallowing under a blanket in front of my television as I watch some sappy rom-com, but instead I'm at Penny's place for a girls' night eating Snicker's ice cream and drinking a tequila sunrise.

Mr. Langford fired me.

Not only did I lose Maverick in this whole mess, I also lost my job.

I thought I'd have something to return to here. I guess I'd already been replaced in the Chicago office, and he didn't have a space for me—or losing the position in Vegas told him everything he needed to know about me.

So it's one more thing to wallow over. One more thing I've lost. One more reason I should have listened to my initial gut instinct when Langford first told me about the job in Vegas.

When I say she *made me* come over, I mean it. It wasn't at gunpoint or anything dramatic like that, but she told me I wasn't allowed to sit at home by myself on a Saturday night, and she'd either pack up the boys and bring them to my place—which she *really* didn't want to do—or I could come there. Those were the two options she gave me, and as much as I want to sit at home cursing my life, she's right. It's not healthy to wallow alone.

The ice cream and tequila don't really go together. At all. Both options are working hard to heal what's broken…but it's not working.

A night with my best friend—wallowing under a blanket in front of *her* television rather than my own as we watch a sappy rom-com together—is helping a little. I'll spend the night in her guest room, and we'll spend the day together tomorrow entertaining the kids. I want to help give her a little break since her deadbeat nearly ex-husband currently only sees them every other weekend, and I have a plan to steal them away to take them to the movies tomorrow so we can gorge ourselves on popcorn and slushies while we watch the latest and greatest animated movie. I can be cool Auntie Ev and fill them with sugar and carbs before I send them back home.

And then I can return to my lonely existence and wallow on my own some more.

I blow out a breath as I feel myself not looking forward to that at all.

"How are you doing?" I ask Penny, if nothing else to get my mind off of my own problems, as she slips onto the stool at her counter beside me.

"I'm hanging in there. I just want this thing finalized so I can move on with my life, but Brent's making things incredibly difficult."

"What's he doing?" I ask.

"He's dragging everything out. Arguing every point. He wants to see his kids every other weekend, but he also wants authority on making decisions. He's disputing every single thing my lawyer comes up with. Child support, division of assets, you name it." She sighs heavily. "I'm afraid I'm going to give in on things I shouldn't just to be done with his bullshit."

I dig around in my bowl for some chocolate. "I'm sorry. What about the viral video? Can't you push things forward with that evidence?"

"Not really. It doesn't show him endangering our children or anything. It just shows him being a stupid cheating son of a bitch, and apparently there's nothing illegal about that."

I wrinkle my nose. "That sucks. But the good news is he's out of this place, and you don't have to deal with him every day."

"Yeah. But the bad news is that he wants to sell it and force me and the kids to relocate." She purses her lips, and she looks like she's going to start crying.

"Can you buy him out?"

She shakes her head. "I make decent money at Langford, but not enough to buy him out. Not when our finances have been combined for the last ten years."

"Can I buy him out?" I ask.

Her brows twitch, and her head whips over to me. "What?"

I shrug. "I have a trust fund, and I want to help. I've heard real estate is a good investment." I say it for her benefit. I don't want her to feel like it's charity, but my best friend deserves a fresh start, and if I can be the one to give it to her, I will.

She shakes her head. "I couldn't possibly ask you to do that."

"You didn't ask," I point out. "Look, I wouldn't have offered if I didn't want to do it. If you don't like the idea, then you can come stay at my place for a while until you can get on your feet. But I don't want you to have to uproot the kids when they're already going through a lot of changes."

"Can I think about it?" she asks, snagging her lip between her teeth.

I nod. "Of course. The offer isn't going anywhere, Penguin." I try to be creative with my nicknames for her. Since her full name is Penelope, I go with anything that starts with *Pen.* You know, like Pencil, Pensive, Penchant, Penalty, Penicillin, Peninsula, or Pennylicious. But Penguin is probably my favorite.

She giggles. "Whateverleigh, Everleigh."

I wrinkle my nose. I've heard *Evie-boo, Neverleigh, Beverly,* and *Foreverleigh* from this girl, but *Whateverleigh* is a new one.

"It's a no?" she asks.

"Sorry my name doesn't lend itself well to nicknames."

She giggles, and I laugh too. Despite the heaviness in here, I can always count on my best friend for a good laugh.

My phone dings with a new text, and she shoots me a sharp look.

"What?" I ask innocently.

"Phones on silent after children are asleep," she reminds me.

I make a face and turn off my volume. "Sorry. I guess if I ever have kids someday, I'll understand why."

"You will—both understand and have kids, I mean," she says.

I shrug. "The window on that feels as if it's getting smaller. I'm thirty-two, got dumped by the guy I thought I'd have kids with someday, and then got into something new only for that to end as well." I make a face, not really sure how to define what happened between Maverick and me. Can we really call it a breakup when we were never actually together? How do we define what we had, and how do we define the end of it when we never really defined it to each other?

I'm not sure it matters. We're apart now, and that seems to be the thing that matters in all this.

And I hate it.

If I could turn back time…would I? Would I handle things differently? I'm not sure.

"So who just texted you? Tell me it was Manly Mav."

I shoot her a look. "Manly Mav?"

"What?" she asks. "Do you prefer Mountable Mav? Monstercock Mav?"

"He did have a monster cock," I mutter. I grab my phone and take a peek. "Nope, it wasn't Monstercock after all." I flash the screen at her to read the text.

Billy: *Heard you're back in town. When can I see you again?*

She raises her brows as if to ask…*well?*

"Should I reply with half past never o'clock?" I ask as I consider my response.

"It's really over?"

I nod. "I think it's that whole hindsight thing. He didn't like my red lipstick."

She shoots me a look. "So?"

"It's part of who I am. You know? It's those little things. And honestly, after being with Maverick and comparing them side-by-side, which I know is wrong as fuck, the things I felt for Billy were perhaps nothing more than a crush."

"But what you felt for Mav?"

I press my lips together as tears heat behind my eyes. My stomach churns, and it's not from the ice cream-tequila mix. "More than a crush," I finally say.

"Then go get him, Ev. What's stopping you?"

"It's just so complicated," I say. "He wants to feel like I chose him, but when it came down to it, I couldn't pick someone I've only known a couple months no matter how much I think I've fallen for him. I knew Billy for *years*, and he turned out to be someone other than what I thought he was. But my family…they're the ones who've been there to pick me back up my entire life, you know?"

"Do you feel like you've said that a hundred times in the last few days?" she asks.

My brows quirk. "Why?"

"Because it sounded canned, babe. I suspect even *you* know it's nothing more than an excuse."

I lift a shoulder. "So what if it is? It doesn't change anything. He doesn't want to be with me if I can't put him first."

"Then…put him first. Duh." She smacks her forehead as if the answer is so obvious.

It's not.

Not to me, anyway.

"So…what, then? Turn my own father in?"

She presses her lips together. "Yeah, I guess you've got yourself a conundrum there. Would you consider giving him the permission he needs to tell the DA who he thinks is behind the operations?"

I twist my lips. "I'm not sure," I murmur. I feel like I've already made my decision on that.

Still…maybe talking to my father about it will give me the closure I feel like I'm so desperately looking for.

"One more question," Penny says. I raise my brows as I wait, and when the question comes, it's one I'm not sure how to answer. "You said your family has always been there to pick you up your entire life. Can you honestly say that specifically about your father?"

I don't have an answer for that.

I finally text Billy back. I'm all out of fucks for today, so I don't play games as if I have some left to give.

Me: *You broke me when you ended things, but I'm whole again. I'm sorry, but I won't travel back down that road again.*

I send it off, and when he doesn't reply, I'm pretty sure my message went through loud and clear.

I may not be with Maverick anymore, but that doesn't mean I'd even consider for a second settling for anything less than everything I deserve.

CHAPTER 45

Everleigh Bradley

Think about Your Family

Movie day with the boys is a success, and it's after I drop them off that I decide to drive to my parents' place instead of back to my own. Before I take off, I text my sibling group chat.

Me: *I'm in Chicago heading to Mom and Dad's. Anybody need anything or have a message for me to deliver?*

Ivy: *Just left there. Sorry I missed you.*

She's the only one who responds. The four football players remain silent, not surprising since it's a Sunday evening—game day. Archer doesn't reply, either, even though it's not game day—which is also not surprising.

Unless my parents are attending some event, they should be home. I haven't seen my mother yet since I've been back in town, and I had this idea to talk to my dad one more time about everything that happened with Maverick and me to see if we can reach some sort of agreement.

On my way to my parents' house, my phone rings, and I see it's Jack Dalton's assistant, Lily, calling me.

"Hello?" I answer.

"Ms. Bradley, hi. Is this a good time for a quick conversation with Mr. Dalton?" she asks.

"Sure," I say. Is there ever a time to reject a call from Jack Dalton?

"Great, I'll patch you through."

The line cuts before I can even say *thanks*, and I hear Jack's voice through the line a moment later. "Hello, Ms. Bradley."

"Hi," I say a little tentatively, and I'm met with a chuckle.

"I know this is out of the blue, but I had an idea, and it's something I need your help with. Do you have time to swing by my office tomorrow?" he asks.

"I, uh…I actually moved back to Chicago, Mr. Dalton. I'm not in Vegas."

"Oh," he says, sounding a bit surprised. "Okay, well. Would you be willing to move back here?"

I can't help a little laugh at that. "I guess it depends on your offer. As you may know, I'm currently out of a job."

"I heard. Stuart also told me that you had planned to start your own brand consultation company. Is that still happening?" he asks.

I sit up a little straighter in my seat as I try to figure out how to reply to that since I've spent most of my time here in Chicago so far wallowing.

"If it is," he continues before I get a chance to say anything, "I think I may have a job for you if you're open to consultation. I know I offered you a position here with our marketing department, and it wasn't the right fit for you, but if you're done with Langford and you're a free agent, I'm shopping around for the best and brightest. And I've already gotten Stuart on board with my plan."

"But you let me go," I protest.

He laughs. "Not because you were ineffective. Because Maverick is impossible."

"It took you a whole week to figure that out?"

He sighs. "Nah, I knew before. But I learned this week that you're the only person in the world who can get through to him."

"So you…want me back to be his brand strategist again?" I ask.

"Not exactly." He fills me in on what he's learned about Maverick over the last week and what he intends to do to help Maverick make a difference and leave a lasting legacy. And then he tells me what he needs me to do.

"Can I think about it?" I ask. I pulled into my parents' driveway in the middle of his offer, and now I'm just sitting here with the engine running.

"Of course. I'll be here tomorrow waiting to hear from you."

"Thank you for thinking of me, Mr. Dalton," I say softly.

"I had no other option, Ms. Bradley. You're it." His voice is low, too.

We hang up, and I blow out a breath as I stare straight ahead at my parents' mansion.

It's a big ask. I'm back home now, close to my mother, close to my family. My roots.

At this point, it feels like it's too hard to turn back and put my heart on the line again.

I told Jack I'd think about it, but mostly it was so I could end the call—not because I'm seriously considering it. Still, I'll think it over. I'll weigh it. Maybe I'll even talk to Penny about it. And then tomorrow, I'll call Jack back and tell him thanks but no thanks. I never wanted to work with football players, and I stand by that. My first attempt to work with one was an absolute fucking disaster.

I finally cut the engine and head to the front door. I ring the bell, and a moment later, my mother answers it.

"Everleigh, darling. What are you doing home?" she asks, and I walk in and give her a hug.

She seems shorter. Is that weird? It's been a few months since I've seen her, and in the meantime she was diagnosed. She couldn't possibly be shorter, could she?

She's smaller, too. Weaker. But she's still my mother.

"I'm back in town for a bit," I say. It's nonchalant, as if I didn't get fired and I'm not totally flailing as I reel from what Jack just said to me.

I hear my father's voice from down the hall. "Who was at the door, Vivienne?"

He appears in the foyer, and he looks surprised to see me. "Everleigh." He walks over and gives me a quick hug that feels more out of obligation than love. Or maybe it's just my imagination.

And that's when I spill my guts. "I was fired because I couldn't get Maverick Jennings under control, and he's about to get in a boatload of trouble because he won't name the operator behind the Legacy underground lounge. You know why he won't name that operator? Because of me." My voice trembles as the waterworks begin. "Because I told him not to. And we were involved. I fell in love with him. But he can't be with someone who doesn't choose him, and I didn't choose him. I chose *you*. So give me a good reason why I shouldn't fly back to Vegas and *beg* him to take me back."

My father is quiet for a few beats before he finally says in a quiet voice that's both menacing and scary, "You want a good reason? The legacy, Everleigh. Think about your brothers and sisters. Think about your mother."

I glance at said mother, who's rolling her eyes at my father's words. He misses it completely as he focuses on talking in circles instead.

"Think about your family," he continues. "You were right to choose us. We're the ones who will be here for you always. Not some guy you've known for a few weeks."

I realize for the first time as he talks…he really has nothing to say. He's telling me to think about the family, but what he really means is to think about *him*. He's putting himself first. None of us have *ever* come first. Ever. Not a single one of us.

My father may be in for a boatload of trouble if his name is associated with that place, and maybe it's time he pays for that. Maybe it's time he realizes what it really means to put family first…especially the family we make with the people we choose instead of the ones we were given by blood.

"I *am* thinking about family," I hiss at him. "Are you?"

"What the hell is that supposed to mean? You kids, your mom…you're *all* I think of. What do you think all of this is for?" He holds his hands out wide as if to indicate the mansion, the fortune, all of it, and my mother rolls her eyes again.

"Is it for Archer?" I hiss.

When he freezes at the mention of my brother's name, that's the moment I know that *I chose wrong*.

He doesn't answer.

"I heard through the family grapevine that his name was on the underground casino. Is that true?" I press.

"It's complicated, Everleigh." He sounds like he's scolding a child, and I feel like I'm just about done here.

"No, Dad. It's a pretty straightforward question. Was Archer's name associated with your illegal casino?" I ask, spelling it out for him.

He sighs and presses his lips together. "Yes," he finally admits.

"Oh, Tom." When my mother shakes her head and rolls her eyes for a third time, I realize that even *she* is fed up with his lies, condemned to living the rest of her days with a man who thinks of no one but himself.

"Then change it. Get his name off," I hiss at my father. "Take the fall for your son if you care so goddamn much about the family legacy."

If I'm supposed to be the protector of my siblings, maybe this is my moment. My mother has never taken on that role, and my father keeps pushing all of us into danger. But I'll do whatever it takes not to let Archer go down for this—including telling Maverick to name my father.

Maybe *especially* that.

It's what I should have done from the start. The feds won't care that it was Archer's name on the paperwork if my father is the one behind it, and I'd imagine two of his own children testifying against him—Dex and me—would be enough to take him down.

"It's not that simple," he says.

"Then figure it out." I walk out with those as my last words, and I scramble to figure out what to do next.

Yes, I chose wrong. I just hope it's not too late to fix it.

CHAPTER 46

MAVERICK JENNINGS

Mr. Dalton's Office

I guess Jack was too busy to send his minions today, so I'm waiting outside his office after practice on Wednesday evening.

It's been a long day.

I'm tired since I've been getting up early every morning to visit the shelter.

It's the only thing that helps ease the ache. Petting dogs. Who would've thought?

Wednesday is the day I push the hardest in practice. It may be midweek, but it's the furthest practice day away from gameday, so it gives my body a few days of recovery to push the hardest and be ready to go on Sunday. Each day after today gets the littlest bit easier until we hit Sunday and it's time to take the field.

Coming off our bye week, today was harder than usual. I didn't exactly rest last week, but I didn't have daily practice and drills to keep me on my toes. I'm ready to go home and rest up so I can get here and get back at it in the morning.

My focus is here now. Again. Right where it should be. It's on the game. I'm not running around doing stupid things because of the constant threat that my job could be at stake with Jack overseeing my progress. I still haven't heard from the DA, and I could be in legal trouble. I'm doing everything I can to stay under the radar.

And truth be told, I don't *want* to do anything. I just want to be alone. I just want to sit in the dark and stare out the window at the blinking lights of the Strip as I imagine people having fun and living life and not feeling like everything's been ripped out from under them.

But instead, I'm here at Jack's office, waiting for some unknown fate that's more than likely going to put me in an even worse mood.

"Mr. Dalton will see you now," Lily says, and she nods to the closed door.

I glance up at her, and she nods.

"You can go in." She offers a small smile, and it's a little weird that I'm opening the door on my own to his office—something I've never done before.

And when I open the door, I'm floored at what's behind it.

A red slip dress. A black jacket. Black heels. Red lipstick. The gorgeous, smart, capable, strong woman who makes my heart beat harder, faster, stronger. The woman who makes my spine race and my cock harden.

The woman I'm so goddamn in love with that it physically feels like a blow to my guts just seeing her standing in front of me and knowing I can't go to her and take her in my arms.

The woman who owns me.

I press my lips together and nod a polite greeting at Everleigh without words, and I turn my attention to Jack. He nods at Everleigh, so I turn back to her, a little confused as to why she'd be here.

She draws in a breath. "I chose wrong," she says simply. She wrings her hands a little nervously, and I have the sudden urge to walk over and take her hands in mine.

I don't. I stay still as she continues talking.

"I'm here to make it right, Maverick. I've decided to launch my own brand consultation company and have applied for a business license here in Vegas, and I'm here to offer you my services if you'll give me another chance. This is just you and me, not your boss hiring a babysitter for you, but me wanting to finish the job I started with the man I love with my whole heart."

My jaw slackens as I'm not quite sure what to say.

Jack pipes in then. "And I've hired Ever-Brand to help with a community project that I'd like to start here within the team. I want to create a peer mentorship program for athletes dealing with loss or other struggles, and my goal is to create a mirror of the program within the community, perhaps connected to the new foundation you're building." Jack walks over to me and claps a hand on my shoulder. "You don't owe anyone your story, but you can leave a big impact on this team if you allow your brothers to see your struggles and how they too can rise from the ashes. And if we can reach young athletes in this community who are struggling, imagine the legacy you can leave behind." He pauses, and I'm about to say something…but I'm not sure what. "Excuse me a moment, I need a word with Lily." He walks through it and closes it behind him, sealing Everleigh and me into privacy.

I turn to look at her, and her eyes are hopeful as she looks at me. "I'm sorry, Maverick," she whispers. Tears shine in her eyes. "I should've chosen you from the start. If you need to give my father's name, do it. If it'll save you an ounce of trouble, do it. Even if it won't…call the DA and do it. You have my full, unequivocal support, and you should have had it all along. I know that now. I've been so miserable without you, and I'm here to fight for you. To fight for us. I need you to know that you will always come first for me."

"But I didn't," I say quietly.

"You did. You always did. I just felt pushed into an impossible corner, and I went with my brain instead of my heart. But my heart? She chose you. She will always choose you, and it took me a little time to get my brain to understand that, but we're all in alignment now."

"Those sound like a bunch of fancy brand strategist words," I say.

She laughs a little nervously, but her face is serious. "Please tell me you'll give me a chance."

"As my brand strategist?" I ask.

"Ideally both as your brand strategist and as your girlfriend, but I'll take what I can get."

My brows might just fly off my forehead. "Girlfriend? We never used that word before."

"We never defined what we were before, Maverick," she points out. "But we were definitely something. We never defined when it was over, either, but the way I've felt sick over losing you for the last two weeks has told me how very much I need you in my life."

"Maybe we don't need a definition."

"Is that a yes?" she asks, the hope in her voice killing what little defense I have left in me.

I don't want to give her a hard time, but something in me can't quite help it. Maybe it's the fact that we started out as enemies, and somehow she was able to get through to me enough to thaw me out. She warmed me up and made me feel things I hadn't felt in years—maybe ever.

"I don't think I'm boyfriend material."

"You're not," she says, shaking her head. She takes a step toward me, narrowing the wide gap between us. "You're intolerable, and you're grouchy almost all the time. You push everyone away, I've seen you smile maybe once the entire time I've known you, and sometimes you can be kind of mean."

My jaw slackens. This isn't exactly what I was expecting from her big Hail Mary to win me back.

She narrows the gap more with another step. She's a few feet away now, within my reach.

"But you've also somehow captured my heart. It beats for you, Maverick, and I'm not sure why. I know inside of you is a kind soul who's been beat down by situations out of his control. I know deep down that you care more than you possibly can show, that you have so much love to give, that you're great with kids and dogs, that you're deeply passionate about the things that mean the most to you, and that you're not only hot as fuck, you really, really know what you're doing in bed."

She takes that final step, and she tentatively rests her hands on my biceps.

"So you don't think you're *boyfriend* material? It's okay. We don't have to use that word. But whatever label we give or don't give it, you own me, Maverick Jennings, and I will choose you every single day if you'll let me."

The truth is that I've been miserable without her, too. I missed her, and just being in the same room with her again is warming me from the inside in a way my cold heart has been missing since she left. It's falling over me, that wave of emotion that I've been pushing out with her gone.

I want to be with her. I don't want to play games. I want a life with her. I want to feel things. I want to feel *joy* again.

I never thought I wanted to be a husband again after the horrific way my first marriage went, but with Everleigh, it feels like anything is possible.

I twist my lips, quiet a few beats before I say, "You think I'm mean?"

Her lips quirk up into a smile. "I said *sometimes* you can be kind of mean. Just…aggressive, I guess."

I frown a little, and then I reach around her waist and haul her to me. "I'll show you just how aggressive I can be when I get you naked."

Her breath hitches, and her eyes are on mine. She looks almost nervous. "You mean…right here in Mr. Dalton's office? Now?"

I can't help it. I smile. I *grin*. It's wide, and it's just for her. Only for her. "I don't think my boss's office is the ideal place for makeup sex, do you?"

She narrows her eyes at me. "Who said anything about makeup sex?" she asks, her voice sassy. "I was just offering you my services."

A little chuckle erupts out of me, and I realize this is happiness. True happiness. Joy. It's that concept I was missing, and it's back with her here. "Services? Is that what we're calling it now?"

Her eyes search mine as she cracks a smile. "Oh, shut up and kiss me already, would you?"

I'm hit with her beauty as she stands here in my arms, her hands resting on my biceps, her eyes crinkled at the corners as she smiles at me.

Who am I to deny her what she wants?

My mouth crashes down to hers, and her hands move to tangle in my hair as our tongues dance together to make up for lost time.

I missed this woman. *God,* did I miss her, and holding her here as we kiss reminds me just how much I need her in my life.

My first love story didn't have a happy ending. But I think this is the one that's going to last the rest of our lives.

CHAPTER 47

Everleigh Bradley

She Offered Me Her Services

He's kissing me, and I'm falling apart from his touch, about to get naked as suggested here in his boss's office, when he pulls back, leans his forehead to mine, and says, "Your place or mine?"

We hear a knock at the office door and jump apart just as it opens. "Everything okay in here?" Jack asks.

We both nod, and I know we're caught just from glancing at how red and swollen Maverick's lips are. But I don't really care. A man who looks like Jack Dalton has certainly been there before.

"Did we come to an agreement?" he asks.

"Yeah, she offered me her services, and I decided to take her up on them," Maverick says, and there's a hint of teasing in his tone. "On one condition."

I think my heart stops for a minute.

We didn't talk conditions.

"What?" I ask, curiosity getting the best of me.

"I'd like to connect players in need of companionship with an animal shelter where I volunteer."

Tears spring to my eyes at the notion of it.

He's found his path, and he figured out in a split second how to connect his secret passion project with his new legacy.

Jack clears his throat as he nods. "I think that's an incredible idea. Lily and I are working out logistics, but there's an office on the first floor not far from the conference room that the two of you could share." He nods at Maverick. "You can do your mentoring in there, as it's a quiet, safe space, and if you bring a pup around here every once in a while, I don't think anyone would complain." He looks at me. "And when Maverick is practicing or in the weight room, you're welcome to use the space for whatever work you need to get done. Do you think you can share?"

I giggle again. What is wrong with me?

"Yes, of course," Maverick says, and he sounds so…un-Maverick-like. Agreeable. Amenable.

"Who are you?" I ask, turning to look at him.

"Your client," he says.

I raise both brows. "Yes, I think we can share."

Jack laughs. "Well, Everleigh, I have to say…love does wild things to a man, and it looks pretty damn good on Jennings."

My cheeks burn at his words since I know it's me he's referring to, but I can't help but agree with the sentiment.

We work out a few logistics with Jack, and then we head home.

Separately, of course, since we arrived separately, but I follow behind his *black and red* truck, tears brimming in my eyes as I stare at the familiar Vegas Aces logo on the tailgate.

He's not a Cowboy anymore. He's an Ace now, and somehow having that logo on his truck makes it seem official.

I follow him all the way into our parking garage, and I pull into the assigned spot that's right next to his. I get out of my car as he hops down from his truck.

"The black and red look good," I say softly.

He nods, and he walks toward me, stopping just short of me. "Someone very special to me helped me with that."

"How special?" I ask, closing the gap between us and moving into his arms.

He wraps himself around me. "So special that I'm about to take her to my place and worship her pussy until morning."

I shiver at his words. "I really hope you're talking about me."

He chuckles, and that's twice now in one day when I'm not sure I've ever really heard that sound out of him before.

I like it. A lot.

"I am," he says, and he drops his lips to mine for a kiss that's far too short. "Now get your ass upstairs so I can get you naked."

I laugh as I pull out of his arms, and he swats my ass playfully. Then we race toward the lobby. Once Milton has greeted us with a warm smile and a "happy to see you two together again," we head up in the elevator.

And can I just say that it's far and away the steamiest, sexiest elevator ride of my life.

It's just the two of us—obviously, given my previous statement—and the second the doors shut, he's on me. Everywhere. His body surrounds me as he pins me to the elevator wall, and he thrusts his hips against mine. His voice is low, and his breath is hot when his mouth moves near my ear.

"The whole way home, I pictured all the different ways I'm going to fuck you," he murmurs.

I shiver.

I'm not cold, but goddamn, that was hot.

"Starting with?" I prompt, the cool, confident vibe I'm going for completely obliterated by the tremble in my voice.

"It's been far too long since we've been together, so I'm going to start with something hard and fast. Then I'm going to take my time. By the time the sun rises, my goal is for you to have…" He trails off, and then he says, "No less than four orgasms."

"That's a deal I can get on board with."

His mouth crashes to mine, and he kisses me like a man starved until the soft ding tells us we've arrived at our floor. Nobody's in our hallway, so he continues to kiss me as he guides me backwards out of the elevator and toward his condo. He fumbles in his pocket for his keys, his mouth still on mine, our tongues still tangling. I hold his jaw between my hands to keep my mouth on his and to feel the stubble there, a reminder that this is really happening and it isn't just some wild dream.

It would be faster for us to just stop kissing for a second so we could get inside his place, but we can't seem to stop. We can't seem to disconnect our mouths, to stop touching each other. We're both desperate to get as close as we possibly can and to stay that way.

He drops his keys, and rather than pull apart and bend down to pick them up, he pushes me against the wall, where he thrusts his hips against mine again and continues to kiss me. His hands move down to my ass, and he pulls me toward him to force our bodies still closer, eliminating any possible space between us that might've been there before.

My body aches for him everywhere, but the epicenter of need is squarely between my legs. I moan into his mouth, and he pulls his mouth from mine.

I think he's bending down to grab his keys, so imagine my shock when instead I feel his hand move under my dress and tug at the edge of my panties. He yanks them over and thrusts a finger into me, and I tip my head back, hitting it against the wall as I moan at the feel of his finger inside me again. He gets down on his knees, tosses one of my legs over his shoulders, keeps my panties to the side, and swipes his tongue through my pussy.

Right. There. In. The. Hallway.

I set my hands on his head with the intention of finding a place to rest them, but suddenly I find myself pulling his head harder toward my pussy as I shamelessly grind on his face. He grunts, and the deep sound reverberates through my entire core, the hum sending a shockwave of pleasure straight through me.

He yanks at the lace of my panties, and they snap clean away from my body.

God, that was hot.

I cry out as I continue grinding on his face, his finger moving in and out of my pussy as he sucks on my clit. He's so good with his mouth that it's literally mere seconds before I'm falling apart over him, my legs quaking and my body shaking as I come hard, flooding his mouth with my own wetness.

He stays with me until I finish, until I sink back into the wall and my body relaxes, and then he says, "Jesus, fuck, woman. I was just bending down to grab my keys when your sweet cunt got in my way."

I can't help a laugh at that.

And I also can't seem to move as he rises and unlocks his door. He must sense that I'm utter jelly at the moment because he picks me up and carries me over the threshold like a bride.

He sets me down on his couch, and he heads toward his refrigerator. He brings me back a bottle of water. "Here. You just lost a lot of fluid, so I'm going to need you to hydrate."

I giggle as I smack his arm, but I hydrate as the man requested.

He wanted to do me fast and hard the first time, and he's already chalked up one orgasm on his way to his goal of four.

"Let me know when you're ready," he murmurs.

I set the bottle of water on his end table after I chug half of it, and I nod. "Ready."

He looks surprised, but he doesn't question it. Instead, he holds out a hand and helps me up. He walks me over toward his windows, and he stops in front of a recliner chair that didn't used to be there.

"Your new thinking chair?" I guess.

He shakes his head as a salacious smile forms on his lips, his eyes hot on mine. "My new fucking chair."

"I hope it's just for me," I half-heartedly tease.

"It's just for *us*."

He pulls his cock out from the shorts he's wearing, and he strokes himself a few times. "But that's for later. The slow version. Maybe orgasm number three." He's so composed as he continues stroking himself while he talks to me. "Right now, though, number two? I want you naked and leaning up against the windows. I want handprints there that will make my house cleaner question what the fuck I was doing up against the window. Take off your clothes."

I scramble to follow his instructions, dropping my jacket, red dress, and bra on the floor. He licks his lips as if his mouth is watering, and his eyes flick along my body, branding me everywhere with his hot gaze.

"God, I missed you," he murmurs. I'm about to reply when he issues his demand. "Bend over and put your hands on the window."

I'm about to get sassy with a *yessir* or something similar, but I refrain, instead doing exactly as he asks. I feel his hand as it moves along my skin, cupping the curve of my ass before it moves up and around to my hip, and still upwards as he grabs onto my breast. He tugs at my nipple, sending a shock of need through my system, and then he lines up behind me. He thrusts toward me a few times before he enters me, his cock warming in my ass as I think about the day he'll claim that as his, too. The thought sends a shiver through me. I've had anal sex before, but somehow I feel like it would be less about the act itself as a goal and more about pleasure for both parties with Maverick.

He bends over me and takes both my breasts in his hands, massaging them and tweaking my nipples as we both stare out at the view beneath us. Anyone could look up here and see a woman getting fucked by her man on the seventeenth floor of a building, and there's something intrinsically hot and powerful about the exhibitionism of it all.

He lets go of one of my breasts in order to fist his cock, and a second later, he's sliding into me. I'm still so wet from what he just did to me in the hallway, and now we're fucking against his windows. I'll never be able to look out these windows upon this view again without thinking about this moment—how good it feels, how *right* it feels. How we're together again, and how we overcame the obstacles that nearly severed our ties for good, but we didn't. We got through it, past it, and now we can leave it behind as we move toward a future that's just for the two of us.

The thought has me clawing at the window, trying to find something to grip onto as my body hurtles toward its second climax in only a few minutes.

"Jesus, Ev, yes. Your cunt's so fucking tight," he murmurs, his voice raspy and deep as he picks up the speed of our rhythm. "I want to fuck you all night, but I'm almost there."

"Give it to me," I scream at him, clawing more at the window as I start to fall apart.

"Come for me, baby." His command is loud and clear in the quiet space, and I do.

I fall completely apart, drowning in the vast ocean of pleasure that he and he alone can give to me. I cry out his name as I come undone, and I grab onto his hand over my breast, squeezing onto it as I hold onto the window with my other hand for support.

A loud roar rips from his chest as he groans my name, and he starts to come, too. He unleashes his cum inside me, and I'm still crashing through the wall of bliss as we find our bliss together, our bodies in unity as we each bask in the pleasure of the other's body.

As both our bodies start to slow together, a heavy fog of warmth falls over me. I feel sated and happy, content and fulfilled. He pulls out, and I grunt a protest, but I'm so exhausted after the intensity of the last few minutes that I can barely make myself move.

"Now those are the kinds of services I'd rate top-notch," he deadpans, and I can't help a laugh.

He must sense my inability to move because he picks me up and carries me over to his bathroom, where he turns on the shower and sets me on the bench inside. He removes the rest of his clothes, and he joins me, steam billowing around us as he uses the handheld shower sprayer to get me wet. He washes me down with the body wash that smells like him, and he shampoos my hair. I barely lift a finger to help, which is wonderful since I'm not sure I could if I wanted to.

He takes care of me, cleaning me and then drying me when he's done, and once we're both dry, he asks, "Do you need to rest?"

I should say yes, but I can't get enough of him. We're halfway to four.

I mean, it would be a shame for him not to reach his goal when we're halfway there.

I bite my bottom lip and shake my head.

He smiles, and he carries me through the condo back toward the chair overlooking the Strip. He sets me down so my feet hit the floor, and he sits. "Come here," he says softly.

I climb over him, settling my legs on either side of him. I move to hover over him, and he slides into me.

I wrap my arms around his neck, and his hands move to my ass, where he moves us up and down, giving us a slow rhythm. His eyes are on mine, and I see it all there.

I see love and lust. I see adoration and need. I see the future, and it's full of him. Of us. Of moments like these.

I see four in one night—as he'll do to me shortly after midnight tonight once again with his tongue.

I see a future that's whatever we want it to be. I see us fighting every single day for each other—*choosing* each other because this is the most important relationship of our lives.

I see red lipstick and black and red trucks and shoes.

I see mutual love and support.

I see snarky banter and driving each other up the wall as I know he'll do to me just as much as I'll do to him.

But mostly I see forever.

EPILOGUE

Everleigh Bradley

The Legacy

I glance around the conference room, and my chest feels a little tight as I think back to the first time I sat in this very room with the very same man sitting across the table.

It wasn't all that long ago, really. A little over three months.

I remember thinking how freaking gorgeous he was, and that sure hasn't changed. If anything, he's getting hotter with time, if that's even possible. From the ink on his skin to the smirk on his lips, I'm head over freaking heels for him.

I remember thinking he was going to be impossible to work with. Some days that's still true.

But I never could've imagined that *this* is where we'd end up.

I never imagined a female German Shepherd named Bruno would be lying in the corner of the room on her brand-new doggie bed. She's *our* Bruno now. One of the first things we did after we made up was adopt her. I'll no longer be traveling with the team, and my place is awfully quiet when it's just me there all alone. So I'm not anymore.

I never would have thought that we'd be giving birth to a whole new legacy, one where I help organize his schedule from this conference room while he mentors players in an office that belongs to us now—one that we share, one that he let me put up a Christmas tree in since the holiday is just a few weeks away.

When Mr. Langford asked me if I'd take a job in Vegas, I really never could have imagined it would end with me finding the love of my life—a freaking football player, naturally. The exact type I spent my entire life fighting against.

But here we are.

And honestly? I couldn't be happier. I guess sometimes when we just let life happen rather than fighting against it, we end up exactly where we're supposed to be…even when it's not where we *thought* we'd be.

I thought my future would plant me in Chicago with a lawyer.

Instead, I'm in Vegas with the football superstar who just walked into the conference room where I'm working. He walks to me first and presses a soft kiss to my lips, and then he walks over to Bruno to scratch her under her chin.

"The DA called while I was at practice," he says softly.

My breath catches in my throat. "Oh. And?"

"I couldn't pick up, but I need to call back tonight. What do you want me to do?" he asks.

"I want you to name my father. It might help protect my brother."

"Archer?" he asks, and I nod. I filled him in on what I know, which isn't much. But I have a feeling with an investigation underway, we'll find out more sooner than later. "Should I call now?"

"Sure."

He draws in a breath and dials the number. "You sure?" he asks me before anyone picks up, and I nod.

"Protect yourself," I say softly. I reach over and take his hand in mine. "Protect *us.*"

He nods, and I hear the district attorney's assistant pick up the call. Maverick is transferred, and the DA starts with a few basic questions about what was happening the night of the raid. And then he asks the question we've been waiting for. "Do you have any information regarding who was operating the casinos?"

Maverick clears his throat, and his eyes are on me when he says, "I believe it's Thomas Bradley."

I let out a breath of what feels like relief. I'm angry with my father for putting Maverick and my brother in this position, and I want him to pay for what he's done. It might be hard on my family, but he shouldn't have been committing crimes if that was what he was truly worried about.

"Do you have proof?" the DA asks.

Maverick looks a little helpless. "No. I don't. I interacted with him several times at the lounge, and I saw him in the backroom. All I have is my word."

"Thank you for your time. We'll be in touch if we have additional questions, and you'll likely be subpoenaed if this case goes to court."

"That's it?" Maverick asks, surprised.

"That's it." The DA cuts the call, and he stares at his phone in disbelief for a few beats.

He glances up at me. "That's it, I guess. For now."

"Good. I hope it is." That might be it for him, but that likely *won't* be it for my father and also possibly my brother.

He clears his throat, and then he goes for a total change of subject. "How many teammates am I seeing tonight?"

"We have three on the agenda," I say.

Coach Nash talked up this peer mentorship program, and players were absolutely *scrambling* at the chance for one-on-one time with their very own quarterback. This isn't just an opportunity for Maverick to empathize with other players. It's a chance for real, actual team bonding. He's giving some of himself to the men he plays with, and they're giving part of themselves back to him. It's an even exchange, and I've seen more than one of these big, macho football player dudes walk out of his office fraught with emotion.

It's an absolutely beautiful thing to witness.

"Who's up first?" he asks as he slides into the chair across from me when he's done with practice before his peer meetings begin for the evening.

I scrunch up my nose. "Dex Bradley."

He raises his brows in surprise, and good God, what I wouldn't give to be a fly on the wall in that room.

Maverick's pretty damn good at keeping secrets, though, and I think he's gaining strength in allowing himself to be a sounding board for some of his teammates. He doesn't tell me a word about what goes on in that office, and it's not my business, anyway.

Even if it's my brother.

This is sacred to Maverick.

"Who else?" he asks, otherwise unfazed by who his first peer is.

"Evan Wilkinson and Austin Graham."

He presses his lips together and nods. "You look hot today," he says quietly.

I laugh. "So do you."

"I bet that red dress would look nice on the floor of my bedroom." He quirks an eyebrow.

"Even better with your pants on top of it," I shoot back.

"And your panties—"

"Jesus, you two," Dex whines, interrupting us as he walks into the room. "Can you save it for after hours?"

My cheeks turn pink, but Maverick is as cool as always.

"You ready?" Maverick asks my brother, and Dex glances at me.

He opens his mouth like he wants to say something, but then he closes it, turns back to Maverick, and says, "Ready."

They head toward his office, and I bury myself back in my work. Maverick has definitely turned himself around—especially in the most recent few weeks—but that doesn't mean my work is done. It's just transitioned a bit. Now instead of hopping onto the defensive, I'm working on building his lasting legacy.

He doesn't want to share the details of his story publicly, but he might be open to it in the future. He's enjoying the one-on-one time with his teammates, but he's open to doing public speaking engagements with local high school teams interested in launching his program that's part of his new foundation as Jack suggested.

His goal is to create a program in high schools that will build leadership and help student athletes work through trauma. In his own experience, he had the coaches to help build his talent but nobody to guide him through the pressures and expectations that were put on high school kids who were good enough to go pro. He wants to give seniors tools that they can pass down to freshmen, tools they can use for the rest of their high school careers and into whatever path they take in their future.

It's a beautiful sentiment, one I fully support and stand behind. And it has sort of become my job to brand that program. We're calling it MAV, short for Mentorship, Accountability, Victory—also short for Maverick—and we're launching it locally first. I've gotten Desert Lights High School on board, and we'll be launching the program over the summer when football student athletes participate in their annual summer camp. I'm deep in the planning process, and I've already booked several podcasts for Maverick where he can talk about this program as he begins to build the legacy that was always waiting there inside him for someone to unlock.

As it turns out, it was Jack Dalton and I who each held one end of the key. We both knew there was potential in Maverick despite the fact that I was forced into working with him. Jack saw it first, and he knew how much the Aces needed a guy like him. Not the brooding, grumpy asshole, but the guy underneath that façade—the one who's been through some things and can use his own experiences to positively help those around him who are also suffering in silence.

They don't have to be silent anymore knowing they have someone like Maverick on their side.

And as my brother emerges from Maverick's office thirty minutes later, I can't help but narrow my eyes.

I get the feeling they weren't in there talking about trauma at all—at least not from the smile on my brother's face and the twinkle in Maverick's eyes.

I study the two of them as I wonder what's going on.

"Bye, Ev," Dex says, and he waves as he walks by the conference room.

"What was that all about?" I ask carefully since I know what goes on in the office is confidential.

He chuckles a little, and he gives me the smile he so rarely graces anyone with. He may have melted a little with this peer mentorship thing, but in general, he's still mostly a fairly grumpy asshole—I mean *perfectionist*—who smiles once in a while now since he's got a girl like me.

"Oh, you know, just your brother warning me not to hurt you. Issued a few threats as if he could really kick my ass." He rolls his eyes.

I narrow my eyes and purse my lips for a beat. "As I recall, my job here working with you back at the beginning of the season was delayed because my brother laid you out on your ass and broke a rib." It's probably not the *best* idea to bring up the past, but I can't seem to help myself.

"That wasn't kicking my ass. That was hitting a player in a vulnerable position."

"Po-tay-to, po-tah-to," I say, as if to say it's the same thing said a different way.

He lowers his head so his gaze falls a little darkly upon me. "I'd like to get you into a vulnerable position. Say…each limb tied to the four corners of my bed?"

I giggle even as I heat up at the thought. "How does every conversation turn back to sex?"

He shrugs. "It's my superpower."

"What's your superpower?" Evan Wilkinson asks, sidling up to the office doorway.

"Nothing," Maverick mutters, and my laugh follows him out as he walks to his office—grumpily—to chat with the next teammate.

As I watch him walk away, I marvel at where we were and where we are now.

We escaped the red zone and ended up together, giving us the happy ending we both deserve but never thought we'd find in each other.

Want more Mav & Ev?
Scan this QR code to download a bonus epilogue!

Scan this code to join Lisa on Facebook
at Team LS: Lisa Suzanne's Reader Group!

Acknowledgments

Big thanks first as always to my family. Thank you to Matt for the love and support and to our kids who all this is for.

Thank you to Valentine PR for your incredible work on the launch of this book.

Thank you to Valentine Grinstead, Christine Yates, Billie DeSchalit, Serena Cracchiolo, and Patricia Rohrs for beta and proofreading. I value your insight and comments so much.

Big thanks to my ride or die bestie, Julie Saman. We'll always push each other to hit those deadlines no matter how impossible they may seem!

Thank you to my ARC Team for loving this sports world that is so real to us. Thank you to the members of the Vegas Aces Spoiler Room and Team LS, and all the influencers and bloggers for reading, reviewing, posting, and sharing.

Thank you to my ARC Team for loving this sports world that is so real to us. Thank you to the members of the Vegas Aces and Vegas Heat Recovery Room and Team LS, and all the influencers and bloggers for reading, reviewing, posting, and sharing.

And finally, thank YOU for reading. I can't wait to bring you more sports romances where swoony superstar heroes ride emotional roller coasters to their happily ever afters.

Cheers until next season! We're heading back to Vegas with Everleigh Bradley's story, RED ZONE! What happens when she's hired as a brand strategist for the Vegas Aces' newest bad boy quarterback? .

xoxo,

Lisa Suzanne

About the Author

Lisa Suzanne is an Amazon Top Ten Bestselling author of swoon-worthy superstar heroes, emotional roller coasters, and all the angst. She resides in Arizona with her husband and two kids. When she's not chasing her kids, she can be found working on her latest romance book or watching reruns of *Friends*.

Also by Lisa Suzanne

Grayson & Ava

Spencer & Grace

Asher & Desi

Tanner & Cassie

Miller & Sophie

FIND MORE AT
AUTHORLISASUZANNE.COM/BOOKS

www.ingramcontent.com/pod-product-compliance
Lightning Source LLC
Chambersburg PA
CBHW030107310726
48970CB00004B/1183